For a better quality c

...ADE

...aid. Or at least that's what she
...elt like a lump of meat in her mouth
...d swollen and heavy. What she actually
...an," but sweet, faithful Rowles understood her.
...n army," he said, by way of explanation as he
...ne door behind him, grabbed a metal-framed canvas
... and shoved it under the door handle. Then he ran to
...r bedside, leaned over and kissed her on the cheek.

"They may not check too carefully," he whispered.

The door handle rattled immediately. She'd thought he
was being optimistic.

The boy she trusted more than anyone else alive crouched
down beside her bed with a machine gun aimed at the door.
It was cocked and ready to fire. He was defending her with
his life, and she felt an overwhelming flood of affection for
him. It took a huge effort but she managed to lift her right
arm out from under the covers and reach across to stroke his
light brown hair. He glanced up at her and she smiled at him.
His wide eyes and small freckled nose gave him the face of
an angel, but stare deeper into those eyes and there was only
pitiless darkness. Hard to believe he was only eleven.

An Abaddon Books™ Publication
www.abaddonbooks.com
abaddon@rebellion.co.uk

First published in 2010 by Abaddon Books™, Rebellion Intellectual Property
Limited, Riverside House, Osney Mead, Oxford, OX2 0ES, UK

10 9 8 7 6 5 4 3 2 1

Editors: Jenni Hill & Jonathan Oliver
Cover: Mark Harrison
Design: Simon Parr & Luke Preece
Marketing and PR: Keith Richardson
Creative Director and CEO: Jason Kingsley
Chief Technical Officer: Chris Kingsley
The Afterblight Chronicles™ created by Simon Spurrier & Andy Boot

ISBN: 978-1-906735-53-1

Printed in Denmark by Norhaven A/S

THE AFTERBLIGHT CHRONICLES

CHILDREN'S CRUSADE

SCOTT ANDREWS

Abaddon
Books

WWW.ABADDONBOOKS.COM

ACKNOWLEDGEMENTS

Justin and Simon for criticism and advice, Paul, for letting me play with his marvellous toys, Ben, for escorting me through the corridors of power and letting me see the bits that aren't on the guided tour, Jon, for commissioning me in the first place and trusting me to complete the trilogy, and Emma, without whose patience and support none of these books could ever have been written.

PROLOGUE

Caroline opened her good eye and winced. It was hard to divorce the pounding in her head from the shockwaves of the explosion that still reverberated around the small room. The walls were painted white but they glowed orange as the fireball billowed up the street outside.

Even with her head swathed in bandages, her hearing muffled, and her vision clouded by the lingering anaesthetic – not to mention the fact that one of her eyes was healing underneath a thick gauze dressing – Caroline knew instantly what was occurring.

Someone was attacking the base.

The night was warm and the window was open. It rattled in its frame and a wave of hot air pushed the curtains towards the ceiling.

She was lying flat on her back with her hands on her belly and was wearing what felt like a cotton nightdress. The crisp white sheets felt luxurious on her bare calves. It had been so long since she'd felt clean sheets.

She remembered her mother ironing the bed linen in front of the telly, watching *Eastenders* from within a cloud of steam.

The curtains fell back into place and the orange glow faded and began to flicker as fires took hold. Caroline heard the crack of small arms fire; sporadic at first, then constant and concentrated. Fire and a firefight. She wondered how long it would take for the conflict to reach her room, and what would happen when it did.

She sniffed the air, expecting cordite and smoke, but instead smelled lilies, strong and pungent. She focused on the chest of drawers that sat against the wall directly in front of her. The sense that she was one step sideways from reality was reinforced by the uneasy feeling that the world was somehow flatter. If she never recovered the use of her other eye then things would always be this way; the depth of the world reduced to one smooth surface, like a painting or a television image.

On top of the chest of drawers stood a large green vase which held about ten flowering lilies, their petals white with streaks of purple and yellow. They were exquisite.

Caroline wondered where Rowles had found them, and smiled at the thought of her best friend.

Then she frowned. Where was he?

Engines now, outside. Deep, throaty roars and the rumble of caterpillar tracks coming closer. Tanks, then. She could not imagine who would have the resources to attack this place, the most heavily defended position in the country, the base of operations for the entire British Army.

She licked her lips. Her mouth felt musty and she had a sharp, bitter taste at the back of her throat, like bile or grapefruit. Wondering what the time was, she gently turned her head until she could see the clock on her bedside table. 10:15. Not so late, but it was already dark outside.

She stroked her belly through her nightshirt, feeling the flat planes of her abdomen and the hollow empty ache inside, a reminder that she had not eaten for at least 24 hours. Then she thought: it may be more than that. How long had she been unconscious? It could be days.

She felt no disquiet at the prospect of having lost time in this nice, clean, envelope-smooth bed. What a nice place to lose time, she thought.

A distant whine grew into a piercing shriek that swept across the outside sky like a banshee. Fighter jet. No, two fighter jets. As they screamed overhead there was a whoosh and a hiss then a series of loud explosions as the planes launched missiles into the most entrenched positions, or eliminated British tanks or buildings.

Her nice warm bed didn't seem a safe place to be, but Caroline did not panic. She was too weak from surgery to lift herself into a sitting position, let alone leave the bed and search for shelter. The knowledge of her helplessness freed her from fear. There is no point, she told herself, being afraid of something you can't change; you will survive or you won't and there's nothing you can do to influence the outcome either way.

A tank ground to a halt beneath her window. She heard a whirr of engines as the turret rotated and the gun was manoeuvred into firing position. Then a moment's pause before her bed shook as the shell was fired.

Now she could smell gunpowder and the tang of hot, oiled metal, but the smell of the lilies was not entirely swamped. She imagined the flowers fighting back against machinery, and winning.

Since the explosion had woken her, Caroline had heard no noises from inside the building where she lay, tucked up safe on the second floor in her convalescent room. Now she heard the unmistakeable clatter of boots on the stairs at the end of the corridor. It was one person, running. Looking for somewhere to hide, perhaps? Or coming for her?

The footsteps got closer, then she heard many more pairs of boots coming up the stairs in pursuit.

Caroline scrunched her toes against the soft, smooth bed sheets in a tactile farewell just as the door to her room burst open.

"Caroline?" It was Rowles. He was breathing hard, on the verge of panic, which was unlike him.

"What's happening?" she said. Or at least that's what she tried to say. Her tongue felt like a lump of meat in her mouth and her lips seemed swollen and heavy. What she actually said was "Wa han," but sweet, faithful Rowles understood her.

"American army," he said, by way of explanation as he closed the door behind him, grabbed a metal-framed canvas chair and shoved it under the door handle. Then he ran to her bedside, leaned over and kissed her on the cheek.

"They may not check too carefully," he whispered.

The door handle rattled immediately. She'd thought he was being optimistic.

The boy she trusted more than anyone else alive crouched down beside her bed with a machine gun aimed at the door. It was cocked and ready to fire. He was defending her with his life, and she felt an overwhelming flood of affection for him. It took a huge effort but she managed to lift her right arm out from under the covers and reach across to stroke his light brown hair. He glanced up at her and she smiled at him. His wide eyes and small freckled nose gave him the face of an angel, but stare deeper into those eyes and there was only pitiless darkness. Hard to believe he was only eleven.

He smiled back and just for a moment his eyes lightened. There was still some feeling in there, after all. She hoped one day she'd hear him laugh. But she didn't think it likely.

She remembered her father laughing at an old repeat of *Morecambe and Wise*, his eyes creased to slits as he literally held his sides and rocked back and forth on the sofa like a laughing policeman at a fairground.

If Rowles was going to die here, she was glad she could die with him. She'd heard Matron refer to them once as Bonnie and Clyde, so it was fitting.

The door ceased rattling and the footsteps clattered away.

A moment later she heard boots descending the stairs.

Rowles stood up and walked around the bed, then pulled the curtain aside a fraction and looked out at the battlefield.

"I don't know why they're attacking, but I think they're winning." There was a huge explosion nearby and he pulled back from the window, shielding his eyes. "It's not safe to stay here. We have to go."

Caroline wanted nothing more than to run away with him, but she would need to be carried, manhandled, pushed in a wheelchair. She was twelve years old and would have described herself as solid, even stocky. Rowles was eleven and thin as a rake. There was no chance. She wanted to tell him to go without her, to save himself and leave her be. But her treacherous mouth wouldn't form the words and, she realised with some surprise, she was too selfish for that. She wanted to be with him, no matter what.

"Wel air," she grunted.

"Good idea. I'll go look for one. Back in a mo."

He pulled the chair away from the handle and cracked open the door. Once he'd assured himself that the corridor was clear he slipped out, pulling the door closed behind him.

Caroline was alone again.

The noises of fighting were moving away now. The building in which she lay was quite near the main gates and she presumed it was their destruction which had signalled the start of the assault and woken her up. Now the fight was moving into the centre of the base. But below her window there was a steady rumble of incoming trucks, tanks and other vehicles as the Americans flooded in to join the fight.

She wondered where Matron was. It was unlike her to leave them alone; she should have been with Rowles, giving orders, taking decisions, making the children feel safe, protected, even loved, with a sly glance or a flash of a smile in the direst of circumstances. Rowles' presence made Caroline feel safe, Matron's made her feel she belonged.

She remembered her older sister's arm around her shoulder at their Grandad's funeral, reaching up and taking her hand, feeling her sister squeeze it for comfort.

Footsteps and voices in the corridor. Rowles was no longer alone.

The door opened and a tall man with thick black hair and heavy features entered. He was wearing jeans and a t-shirt, but had an SLR machine gun slung across his chest. She recognised him – he was the doctor who had been there when she regained consciousness after the operation. Jones? Johns? She couldn't recall his name.

Rowles came in behind the man, pushing a wheelchair, then closed the door.

The doctor leaned over her.

"Can you hear me Caroline?" he asked.

"Yuh."

"Can you move at all?"

She lifted her arm feebly and wiggled her fingers until the effort became too much and the limb flopped back down, useless.

The doctor smiled. It was obviously meant to be reassuring but there was something calculating in his eyes, something which made her withhold trust.

"We're going to lift you into the wheelchair," he said. "It may hurt, but I haven't got any anaesthetic on me, I'm afraid. Then we're going to take the lift down to the rear doors where I've got a jeep waiting. If we move quickly, I think we'll be able to get ourselves away from here before they secure the perimeter." He turned and nodded to Rowles, who wheeled the chair alongside the bed then took Caroline's hand.

She was sad to leave her clean, white cocoon, but the pain in her head as the doctor and Rowles pulled her into a sitting position made it hard to concentrate on anything but staying conscious.

"One, two, three," said the doctor, grunting on "three" as they lifted Caroline out of the bed and into the chair. Once she was sitting again, the pain in her head receded.

Outside, there was a whoosh and then a tremendous explosion directly beneath the window. Bazooka, perhaps? The window finally came off its latch and smashed against the interior wall, showering the now empty bed with shards of glass.

The doctor went to take the handles of the wheelchair, but Rowles stepped behind her. The doctor, looking over her head at Rowles' determined, territorial look – which Caroline could picture clearly, even though she was facing the other way – nodded. He turned and opened the door, then waved for Rowles to follow him.

They moved quickly out of the room and into the corridor, turning left and heading for the grey lift doors twenty metres away. Caroline observed the flat details of the corridor as she rolled past door after door, all closed. They reached the lift and the doctor reached out to press the call button, but before he could make contact the lift pinged, the doors slid open, and an American soldier stood before them, gun levelled straight at the doctor's chest.

The soldier and the doctor stood there for a second, frozen in surprise. But the soldier's reflexes were tuned for combat, and when the moment passed he was quickest. Deciding that he didn't need to waste ammunition, he brought his gun around and smashed the butt across the doctor's face, sending him crashing to the floor, stunned.

Caroline was intrigued by the soldier's uniform. It was a camouflage pattern of light and dark browns. Desert clothes, hardly suitable for warfare on the rolling green plains of England.

The soldier stepped over the prone doctor and relieved him of his weapon. Caroline could tell by the tiny vibrations in her chair that Rowles was still gripping the handles tightly, resisting the temptation to go for the gun that was slung across his back, waiting for the right moment. Perhaps the soldier hadn't even noticed the strap that ran diagonally across the boy's chest. Or perhaps he'd made the same mistake that so many had made before him, ignoring the tiny boy, failing to consider him a threat. If that were the case, Caroline knew he'd soon regret that judgment.

The soldier stood upright and looked down at the two children. He didn't say a word, just held out his arm, lowered his index finger, and rotated it to indicate that they should turn around and go back the way they'd come.

Caroline felt her chair move to the left, beginning to describe a circle, then the chair stopped at about 45 degrees and Rowles stepped back from the handles, grabbed the strap, brought his gun to bear, and fired at the soldier's chest.

There was a dry click as the gun jammed and then another of those moments of stunned surprise as boy and man stood facing each other.

Caroline saw the doctor begin to stir on the floor behind the soldier.

The look of astonishment on the soldier's face faded into amusement and he laughed at Rowles.

Oh dear, thought Caroline, allowing herself a tiny smile. *That's not wise.*

Rowles launched himself at the soldier with a cry, using his gun as a club, beating the man's chest and arms. The soldier lifted one big hand and swatted the gun aside, then lifted the boy off the ground in a bear hug, pinning his arms to his sides.

The doctor was up on all fours now, shaking his head to clear it. There was a loud scream of engines above as the jets made another pass, and a clatter of boots on the stairs at the far end of the corridor, as the soldiers returned.

"Little boy," said the soldier in a thick Brooklyn accent. "You're feisty, aintcha?"

Grasped tight, his feet off the ground, his arms useless, with no weapon to defend himself, Rowles looked puny and weak compared to the man who held him fast.

But Rowles was not beaten yet. With a feral snarl he bared his teeth, leaned forward, and bit hard into the man's throat.

The soldier staggered back and released his hold on the boy. But Rowles did not fall to the floor. Instead, he wrapped his arms around the soldier's neck and his legs around his waist, and continued biting, gnawing, crunching and savaging the man's throat. He growled as he did so, like a wolf ripping out the throat of a helpless lamb.

Great fists raised and smashed the boy's head again and again and Caroline winced at the soldier's scream of pure agony and terror, but Rowles was limpet tight to the man, impossible to dislodge. The soldier took another step back and lost his footing, tumbling down and smashing his helmet against the floor. Rowles leaped up, pulled the knife from the soldier's leather sheath, grasped it tightly in both hands and brought it down in a mighty arc, straight into his heart. The soldier's legs kicked furiously, but his death throes gave the boy no pause.

Rowles pulled out the knife, cut the gun's strap with one swift slice, freeing the M-16 from the soldier's chest, then turned to the doctor, who had by now regained his feet.

"Quickly," he said. The doctor reached forward, grabbed the handles of Caroline's chair and spun her around, pulling her behind him as he backed into the lift.

The clatter of boots was deafening now. Helmets appeared, rising up the stairs at the far end of the corridor. Rowles, his back to Caroline, fired a short burst at the stairwell, which caused the helmets to vanish from view.

Then the boy turned to look at her. His eyes were pitch black, blood dripped from his face and chin, and when he spoke she could see strands of flesh stuck between his teeth.

She realised in that moment that she loved him more than she had ever loved anyone in her life.

"Run," he said softly, his voice full of regret.

The doctor pressed the button and the doors of the lift began to slide closed. Caroline lifted her arm, reaching out her helpless fingers towards Rowles. Their eyes met and she knew, with absolute certainty, that she would never see him alive again.

Through the tiny crack as the doors closed she caught a glimpse of him turning away from her and running down the corridor. Then there was gunfire and screaming, and the soft buzz of the lift's engine as the metal cage lowered her gently to the ground.

As her eyes filled with tears, she caught a faint hint of lilies on the air.

PART ONE

CHAPTER ONE

"When is it acceptable to kill another human being?"

The question hangs there as Green waits for an answer. It takes a moment but eventually a girl three seats back raises her hand.

"Caitlin?"

"When they're trying to kill you, Sir?"

We make them say Sir and Ma'am at St Mark's. Old skool.

Green writes this on the whiteboard. I make a mental note to add whiteboard pens to our scavenging list; we're running short.

"Anyone else?"

More hands go up now that someone else has taken the plunge. Green indicates them one by one, writing their contributions up.

"When someone's trying to kill a friend of yours."

"Or a family member."

"When someone is a murderer."

"Or a rapist."

Green doesn't react any differently to this suggestion, but I shift in my seat, uncomfortable both for him and for myself.

"Or a paedo."

"In a battle, like a war or something."

"As part of an initiation."

Okay, we'd better keep an eye on that one.

"When they're stealing your food or water."

"If they try to take over your home."

"For revenge."

Green turns quickly back to the class. "Who said that? Was that you Stone?"

The boy nods, unsure if he's about to cop a bollocking.

"Revenge for what, though?" asks Green intently. No-one answers. The class seems confused. "You see, Stone has hit the heart of the matter. A lot of your suggestions – murderer, rapist, paedophile, thief – wouldn't killing them just be an act of revenge? I mean, the crime's already been committed. You're not going to bring back the murder victim, un-rape someone, un-abuse a child. So why kill the criminal other than for revenge? And if it is revenge, is it a justifiable thing? Is killing for vengeance a crime, or a right?"

Another long pause, then a boy at the back, quite close to me, says: "But in those cases it isn't just revenge, is it, Sir? Coz they might kill again, or rape or abuse or steal. So by killing them you're protecting everybody."

Green claps his hands, pleased. "Yes!" he says forcefully. "But what about prison? If you could lock the person away and thereby protect everyone? Remove the danger, and what purpose does killing the criminal achieve then, other than vengeance? So again, is vengeance okay?"

"But there aren't any prisons any more, Sir," responds the boy, warming to the discussion. "And food and water and stuff are hard to get. So it's a question of practicality and resources, isn't it?"

I can tell Green is pleased. This boy is lively and engaged.

"So are we allowed to do things now, after The Cull, that we would have considered immoral beforehand?" demands Green.

"Yes," says the boy firmly. "The world has changed. The morals they had before The Cull are a luxury we just can't afford any more."

"You don't think morality is absolute?" responds Green, who once fired a clip's worth of bullets into an unarmed man and has never displayed a hint of remorse. "That some things are just wrong, no matter what?"

"Do you, Sir?"

Jesus, this boy's, what, fourteen? And before I can help myself I tut inwardly and think 'kids these days'. I smile ruefully at my own reaction. Am I getting old? I notice, as well, that he said 'they'. He was born ten years before The Cull, but already the people who ran the world then are another breed, as ancient and unknowable as the Romans. How quickly we forget.

Green beckons the boy forward. "Come to the front, Stone."

The boy rises and walks down the aisle to the front of the classroom, the other children gently laughing at his discomfort. Green hands the boy a book.

"Turn to page thirteen and read Vindici's speech." The boy begins to read, stumbling over the archaic language at first, but gradually gets the hang of it. I sit, transfixed, until he cries: "'Whoe'er knew murder unpaid? Faith, give revenge her due!'" and I notice a momentary grimace that flashes across Green's face as the knowledge of his act of vengeance twists in his guts.

I quietly rise from my seat, nod encouragingly at Green, and sneak out of the classroom.

When I was at school, plays like *The Revenger's Tragedy* seemed ancient and irrelevant, hard to understand and full of abstract moral question that meant nothing to us. But these kids? This generation of children who saw everyone they've ever known and loved die slow, painful deaths and then had to survive in a world without law, authority or consequence get that play on a level I never could, and Green – twenty-one now and no longer the uncomfortable, persecuted teenager I first met – has turned into a fine drama teacher; impassioned, encouraging, good with kids. He's also a pacifist now, and refuses to touch a gun under any circumstances.

I'm oddly proud of him. Which, given our personal history, is quite something.

I stand in the hallway and listen to the babble of voices drifting out of the four classrooms that stand adjacent to it. It's a good sound, a hopeful, productive noise. It's learning and debate, friendship and community. And it's rare these days. So very rare.

I glance up at the clock on the wall. 10:36. Of course GMT no longer exists, so the world has reverted to local time – the clocks at St Mark's take their time from the sundial in the garden. I wonder if time, like morality, is absolute. Does GMT still exist somewhere, like those echoes of the big bang that astronomers and physicists were always trying to catch hint of, waiting to be rediscovered and re-established? And if the clock that set GMT is lost, and we someday recreate standard time, what if we're a millisecond out? How would we ever know? I linger in the hallway, surrounded by the murmur of learning, and daydream of a world in which everyone is always a millisecond late.

That's what the security and community of St Mark's allows me, allows all of us – the chance to daydream about the future. I can't imagine that any of the survivors who are stuck out in the cold, scavenging off the scraps of a dead civilization, ever daydream about anything but the past.

Morning break's at quarter-to, so I decide to swing by the kitchen and grab a cuppa before the place is overrun.

I head deeper into the old house, following the smell of baking to Mrs Jenkins' domain. Sourcing ingredients to feed seventy-three children and sixteen adults would have been a pain even before Sainsbury's was looted to extinction, but now it's a full time job for Justin, ample Mrs Jenkins' very own Jack Spratt.

He finds it, grows it or barters for it; she cooks it. We've got a thriving market garden that the kids help him maintain, plus a field each of cows, sheep and pigs, not to mention the herds of deer that roam the area. We don't have any vegetarians here. This year we're experimenting with grain crops and corn, but it's early days yet. There's a working windmill in a nearby village but demand is high so we only get a sack every now and then, which makes biscuits and bread a special treat. Our carpentry teacher, Eddie, is working on designs for a windmill of our own, but it's still on the drawing board.

Jamie Oliver would approve of our kitchens – everything's fresh and seasonal, and there isn't a turkey twizzler in sight. But there is a pan of fresh biscuits lying cooling on the sideboard as I walk in, so I snatch one and take a bite before our formidable dinner lady can slap my hand away or hit me over the head with the big brass ladle she's currently using to stir the mutton stew she's preparing for dinner.

"Oi! Make your own, cheeky," says Mrs Jenkins as she glares at the crumbs around my mouth.

"Any chance of a cuppa?" I plead. "I fancy dunking. I haven't dunked a biscuit in ages."

"There's the kettle, the aga's hot, but there's no water."

I grab a bucket from the cupboard, head out to the courtyard and draw some water from the well. It's crystal clear and ice cold. Back in the kitchen I fill the kettle and place it on top of the wood burning stove, which radiates a fierce heat.

"Why so serious?" asks the dinner lady as I warm myself, deep in thought.

"I don't want to lose this," I reply. She looks at me curiously, but I don't elaborate and she takes the hint and returns to her stew.

I make myself a cup of tea and grab another biscuit before heading back to the entrance hall and then up the main stairs.

I push open a door marked No Entry and enter the Ops Room. Most schools have Staff Rooms, but St Mark's is not most schools. Instead of pigeon holes and a coffee area, this room has a map of the British Isles covered in pins, and a notice board thick with accounts of missing children.

I am the first to arrive, so I pull up a chair and sit down, stretch my legs out in front of me and take a sip of my nettle tea. I wince involuntarily. I'd kill for a mug of Typhoo, but we've long since depleted our stocks of tea bags. Now if I want a hot drink my only option is home made herbal infusions. I tut. The Cull has turned us all into New Age hippies.

I dunk my biscuit and consider the map.

It is not a standard ordnance survey map; it does not show motorways, cities and county boundaries. Instead, it is hand drawn, with huge areas left blank and small handwritten notes that chart the limits of our knowledge. This is a map of the world left behind, a chart of rumours and hearsay, overheard whispers at market day, tales of powerful rulers and legends reborn. It is incomplete and surely inaccurate, but it represents the best intelligence we can gather.

Where a pre-Cull map would have read Salisbury Plain, this one has a small drawing of a mushroom cloud and the word FALLOUT written beneath it in red felt-tip. The areas which used to be called

Scotland and Wales now have big question marks over them because although we know there are power struggles going on there, we've no idea who's winning; the area around Nottingham shows a bow and arrow with 'The Hooded Man' written next to it. There are other, smaller pictures and names dotted about – Cleaner Town, Daily Mailonia, The New Republic of the Reborn Briton, Kingdom of Steamies – these are the major players, the mini-empires springing up across the land as alpha males assert their dominance and begin building tribes with which to subjugate, or protect, the survivors.

Beyond the shores of Britain some wag has written 'Here be monsters', but I reckon there are more than enough monsters already ashore.

I cast my glance down to Kent and the big red pin that marks the Fairlawne Estate, new home of St Mark's. There are no major players in this neck of the woods. A spattering of green circles mark the regular markets that have sprung up in the area. Unlike other parts of the country, the home counties have mostly reverted to self-sufficient communities, living off the land, trading with neighbouring villages, literally minding their own beeswax.

The alpha males who tried to set up camp in this neck of the woods were dealt with long ago, leaving room for looser, more organic development.

My eyes track north, to a big black question mark. London. We steer clear of it and, so far as we have been able to ascertain, so does everybody else we have regular contact with. Even the army, back before they were destroyed, were biding their time before wading into that particular cess pit. I think of it as a boil that sooner or later will burst and shower the rest of the country with whichever vile infection it's currently incubating. It disturbs me to be living so close to such a mystery, and I know that sooner or later I'm going to have to lead a team inside the M25. I don't relish the prospect.

I hear the bell ringing for morning break and then there's a cacophony of running feet, shouting, laughing and slamming doors as the kids race to the kitchen for biscuits.

The door behind me swings open. I can tell who it is by the lopsided footsteps.

"Hey Jack," I say, taking another sip of tea, hopeful that if I keep drinking I'll develop a taste for it in the end.

The King of England, Jack Bedford, drags a chair from the side of the room and sits down next to me, heavily. Without a word he leans forward, rolls up his left trouser leg and begins undoing the straps that secure his prosthesis.

"Still chaffing?" I ask.

He grunts a confirmation, detaching the fibreglass extension that completes his leg and laying it on the floor. He begins massaging the stump.

"It's not so bad," he says eventually. "But I've been reffing the footie. So, you know, sore."

"Come see me afterwards, I'll give you some balm."

"Thanks."

What he really needs is a custom-made prosthesis, properly calibrated. But the tech is beyond our reach. We scoured every hospital still standing and were lucky to find such a good match. I have no idea what we'll do if it ever breaks.

I like Jack. He's sixteen years old, his face ravaged by acne and his hair thick with grease that no shampoo seems able to shift. He keeps himself to himself, and has watchful eyes and an air of secrecy that I'm not sure anybody else has noticed. Only a select few of us know that he is the hereditary monarch, and we have no intention of telling anybody. Jack seems grateful for the anonymity. Nonetheless he has become part of the inner circle at the school, one of those boys that we adults treat as an equal. He's proven himself brave, loyal and capable.

"Anything new?" he asks.

"Yeah," I reply. "But we'll wait 'til the others get here."

"Fair enough."

The door opens again and Lee and his father, John, enter.

"I don't reckon it's likely," Lee is saying, but his father disagrees.

"Think about it," says John. "We know he likes the ladies, and he's got a violent temper."

"But we've no evidence he ever even knew Lilly," says Lee, taking a seat on my other side.

"Lee, she was his son's girlfriend."

Lee shakes his head. "No, I still reckon it's Weevil."

"Dream on," says John, with a laugh.

Neither Jack nor I have to ask what they're discussing. Our DVD nights have been dominated by season one of *Veronica*

Mars for the last two weeks and the whole school is trying to solve the Lilly Kane murder. With the internet consigned to history, no-one can hit Wikipedia and spoil it for everyone else, and I keep the discs locked in the safe so no-one can sneak down at night and skip to the end.

"You'll find out in two episodes time, guys," says Jack with a smile.

"May be a while though," I say. "We're nearly out of petrol for the generator. Can't have any more telly 'til we refuel."

Lee makes a pained face. "You're fucking kidding me. Really?"

I let him squirm for a second then smile. "Nah, telly as usual tonight, eight o'clock for the big finish."

"Bitch," he says, smiling, then he leans forward and kisses me. His jaw gives a little click as he does so, a reminder of the damage he sustained two years ago in the Salisbury explosion. He still has two metal rods holding the bottom of his face together. I kiss him right back.

Lee has just turned eighteen. I am ten years his senior. We've been lovers for six months and he makes me feel like a schoolgirl.

Jack rolls his eyes. "Get a room," he says.

When we break apart I catch John's eye, but his face is a mask, giving nothing away. I am still unsure how he feels about my cradle-snatching antics. Part of me couldn't give a damn whether he approves or not, but he's a colleague and an ally, not to mention my boyfriend's dad, so another part of me craves his approval. He's a hard man to get to know, John Keegan. A hardened veteran of numerous wars, he's seen and done some terrible things. He's undemonstrative but never rude; friendly but never familiar. He's fiercely devoted to his son, and Lee to him, but while they get along well and spend lots of time together fishing, playing football and running, there's a slight reserve to their relationship.

I know that Lee killed his mother – put her out of her misery when the virus was putting her through hell. He still hasn't told John this. I think John suspects and wants to talk to his son about it but has never been able to broach the subject. The secret hovers between them, poisoning the air.

"Where's Tariq?" asks Lee.

"Late as usual," I reply.

The door opens and Tariq strides in, chest out, confident, with a hint of swagger. The Iraqi is twenty years old, with hawkish features, thick black hair, eyes that seem to be permanently amused and a vicious hook where his left hand should be. The first person he makes eye contact with is John, and they share a nod of greeting. Before The Cull Tariq was a young lad in Basra, blogging about corruption and running from the militias. Afterwards, he and John led the resistance to the US occupation. John treats Tariq like another son, and Tariq does anything John asks of him, without question.

Lee and Tariq exchange greetings, but with more reserve. They are friends, and they've saved each other's lives countless times under fire, but Tariq doesn't entirely trust Lee. He thinks he has a death wish that could get everyone killed. I'm worried that he may be right.

Tariq pulls up a chair and sits beside John. The gang's all here.

I take another sip of tea. "Nope," I curse. "No matter how much I try to convince myself otherwise, this is rank." I spit the tea back into the mug and put it down on the floor.

"Okay," I say. "John?"

John gets up, steps to the front of the room and sits on the desk facing us.

"Couple of things," he says briskly in his thick Black Country accent. "We've had a response from the Hooded Man. He's invited an envoy to visit and discuss possible co-operation in the future."

"Do we have any idea who he is yet?" asks Tariq.

John shakes his head. "Haven't even got a name. My guess is that he's ex-military, but I don't know for sure. I did find out one thing though, and you'll like this – the man he deposed, who by all accounts was a vicious son of a bitch, was a Frenchman called De Falaise."

Tariq and Lee are agog. "No fucking way," says Lee, eventually. John just nods.

"Anyone care to fill me in?" asks Jack.

"We had a run in with him on the way back from Iraq. He's the reason I don't hear in stereo any more," says Lee. "Is he dead?" John nods again. "Then this Prince of Thieves guy's fine with me. Even if he does wear tights. Is there word on that, by the way?" John smiles and shakes his head.

"He's building an army of sorts," John continues. "Calls them Rangers. They're a kind of paramilitary police force and so far they seem to be doing a good job of keeping the peace. But it's still a power base, so there's every chance Hood could turn out to be just as bad as the man he kicked out, just more subtle."

"You still think we should send someone?" I ask.

"Oh yeah, but whoever you send should keep their eyes and ears open. If he's going to be a threat, we need to know. So far he doesn't know our exact location, and I'd like to keep it that way, at least for now."

I turn to the King. "Jack, you fancy a trip?"

He frowns. "Wasn't Robin Hood always fighting the king?"

"First off, he won't know you're the king," says Lee. "And second, no, he was fighting the king's brother. He was loyal to Richard. Did they teach you nothing at King school?"

"I missed the first year of Putting Down Rebellious Peasants."

"Has he been having problems with the snatchers?" I ask, bringing the conversation back on topic.

John shakes his head. "They know about them, but so far they're staying out of Hood's territory. I'd bet money that he's got some of his Rangers trying to track them down, but he's hardly going to tell us details of his operations." He pauses and takes a deep breath. I can tell he's about to deliver bad news.

"The second thing is that there's been another raid. A big one."

"Who?"

"The Steamies."

We're all shocked. The Kingdom of Steamies are a community that's grown up along the length of the old Spa Valley Railway. Their philosophy, handed down by their benevolent but bonkers leader, rejects all electrical power, relying instead on steam engines. It's like stepping back to the nineteenth century when we visit their domain, but most everywhere else is like stepping back to the fourteenth so they're ahead on points.

"How many?" I ask.

"They hit the Steamie settlement at High Rocks. There were eleven children there. All gone. They killed most of their parents in the snatch, too."

"That's a hell of an escalation," says Tariq.

John nods. "They're getting bolder."

"Did you track them?" asks Lee.

"Straight to the M25, same as always."

"Double the patrols," I say. "And enough with the rifles. Issue the machine guns. I'm not taking any chances."

"Done," replies Tariq, who is responsible for perimeter security. "That all, John?" I ask.

"Yeah, although I still think..."

"We should go after them."

"Sooner or later they're going to find us. I'd rather find them first."

"Duly noted."

There's a moment when I think he's going to challenge me, but he shrugs and resumes his seat. He's older than me, and far more experienced. But this is my school, and he accepts that – some days with better grace than others.

"Tariq?"

Tariq remains in his seat, I wonder whether out of laziness or some complex dynamic of male hierarchy that makes him uncomfortable taking the table his one time leader just vacated.

"I've been to three markets this week," he says. "Sevenoaks, Cranbrook and Crowborough. People are paranoid and there are a lot more guns being carried openly. There was a fight at Crowborough which ended with a man being shot. It was a misunderstanding, it seems. Someone trying to return a lost child got accused of abducting them. Tensions are high. When word of the attack on the Steamies gets out, they'll get higher. I didn't hear of any fresh raids, though."

"Lee?"

I know what he's about to tell everyone, so he turns away from me as he speaks. I stare at the thick line of baldness that runs down the back of his head, betraying the presence of a surgical scar. I bear a similar mark.

"I've been up to Oxford for a few days. A while back we heard of a group that had secured the Bodleian and was trying to start up a university. There are about fifty of them, all ages, scholars and students. The boss is a guy called Pearce – big, musclebound, ex-Para. He's an unlikely Dean of Studies, but from what I could tell he's passionately devoted to what they're doing and more than willing to kill anyone who threatens the project."

"Forces?" asks Jack.

"A team of six; four guys, two women. Hardnosed, well armed. Polite but not welcoming. They let me stay overnight, though, and while I didn't sound them out directly, I'd recommend making an approach."

"Why?" asks Tariq. "They're miles away."

"We're a school," I reply. "Where else would the kids go after they finish their studies with us but university?"

"There's more," says Lee. "Over dinner, one of Pearce's men offered up some intel on the snatchers. He says they've been increasingly active in East Anglia, and thinks they have a staging post in Thetford."

I rise from my chair. My stomach is full of butterflies because I know that what I am about to do puts everything I have worked to create here at risk. But I've mulled it over long enough. It doesn't really matter who these bastards are or why they're capturing children, they're expanding their area of operations and getting bolder. Sooner or later they're going to learn our location and pay us a visit. I don't intend to sit here waiting for them to arrive.

John's instincts are sound. It's time to take direct action.

"So that's where we're going," I say. "I want everyone out front this time tomorrow, full kit and arms. If these fuckers have a place of business, I think we should pay it a visit." I fold my arms and strike a resolute pose, accidentally kicking over my cold nettle tea as I do so.

"That's gonna stain," says Lee with a smile.

When the meeting's adjourned, the inner circle all head back to their allotted tasks. Lee is working in the garden today, Jack is doing an inventory of the armoury, Tariq is teaching creative writing to a classroom full of impressionable teenage girls who hang on his every word. John teaches PE and survival skills, but has a free day. He stays in his seat until the others have left, then leans forward earnestly.

"Good move, Jane," he says.

"But?"

"I want to set clear chain of command in the field. We've not gone looking for a fight in a long time and I want to be sure everybody knows how things work."

"I've told you before John, in here I'm the boss. But in the field you're in charge."

"And you'll have no trouble taking orders from me?" he asks, slightly dubious.

"None. You're a soldier. I'm a... I dunno what I am. I used to be a doctor, then I was a matron. Now, I suppose I'm a headmistress. Either way, you've more combat experience and training than all the rest of us put together. It's only right that you take charge when we're in action."

He nods, biting his lip. I can sense an unasked question.

"Do you think they're ready?" I ask eventually.

He shrugs. "Your guess is as good as mine," he replies. "Jack's pretty nimble on his leg. He's not going to win any 100 metre sprints, but he'll be fine. Tariq can still shoot straight and the claw's a nasty weapon if needed."

"And Lee?"

He pauses, trying to frame his question correctly. "The limp's almost imperceptible, his arm doesn't have full movement, but again, it's not a handicap. Physically, I think he's as healed as he's ever going to be."

"But psychologically?"

"He worries me."

"Still? It's been two years since Salisbury."

"But he won't talk about it. Anything that happened between The Cull and Salisbury is off limits."

"And that bothers you?"

"Doesn't it bother you?"

"No," I say firmly. "He wants to move on. I've told you everything I can about what happened during the year Mac was in charge, and Tariq filled you in on events at Salisbury. You know the facts. He was so angry all the time but it's faded now. He's calmer."

"I think that's got more to do with you than anything else," says John eventually. I just smile and he doesn't pursue the point. "Anyway, I want you to keep an especially close eye on him while we're out there. PTSD can manifest in unexpected ways. He's been fine here, it's true, but this is a sheltered environment and somewhere he feels safe. I was worried when he started going on field trips, but they've all gone smoothly. My point is he's not been tested. It's just possible he may fall to pieces the first time someone takes a shot at him. Or worse, see red and fly into danger without a second thought."

"I will, but I think you're worrying over nothing." It's a complete lie. Everything he's just said I've been thinking too. If I could think of a way to keep Lee out of danger, I'd take it. He's earned the break. But he'd be insulted and would insist on coming anyway so in the end it would probably do more harm than good. "Not exactly a crack squad of elite forces are we?" I say with a smile. "A one legged boy, a hook-handed man, a partially deaf limping potential headcase and a matron."

He sits back and crosses his arms. "Took out the whole US Army didn't we? I reckon a bunch of kidnappers won't be too much trouble."

But we both know it's bravado.

"While I've got you alone, John," I say. "Are you... I mean... me and Lee... is it?"

"Not my business," he says firmly. "He's 18."

"You don't mind, though?"

"That's irrelevant."

"Not to me."

He sighs heavily and his shoulders sag. For a moment the mask slips and I can see concern on his face. But it's not an unfriendly look.

"Honestly?"

"Honestly."

"All right then," he says. "I think you're gorgeous and clever and the best possible thing that could happen to my son right now."

"I hate to say this again, but... but?"

And then he says something that in one fell swoop fucks me up more than I could have imagined possible.

"Jesus, Jane, you don't half remind me of his mother when she was your age."

He rises from his chair, puts a hand on my shoulder for a moment, then leaves.

I sit there for on my own a long, long time.

God, I could kill a cuppa.

*   *   *

I worry about the perishability of rubber.

We've got a huge great pallet of condoms that we lifted from an abandoned warehouse. I remember when we found them, back on a scavenging trip when Mac was still in charge. I insisted we bring them along. At first Lee got a bit embarrassed – he was fifteen, after all – and then a bit annoyed.

"Why the hell would we want them?" he asked me.

I told him he'd understand eventually. I think he thought I was making fun of him, but I was beginning to worry about a residential school full of teenage boys and girls and the difficulty of stopping them shagging like rabbits every time they were out of a teacher's earshot.

Once I was in charge, I organised sex education classes and then made the condoms available to any child who wanted them. No age limit, no questions asked. Simply put, the alternative was lots of teenage mums. I may favour home births, birthing pools and all that jazz but if there are complications I've not got the kit to deal with them.

In post-Cull England, childbirth was once again almost certain to become a big killer of young women. I felt sure that sooner or later we'd hear of a communal birth centre being set up somewhere; it was inevitable. But until then, I wanted to keep pregnancies to a minimum, and sex ed. and free condoms seemed a pragmatic approach.

We've only had one unwanted pregnancy so far and thankfully the birth was textbook. Sharon from Bournemouth has a little boy called Josh and she's not telling anyone who the father is, although everyone knows it's a spotty little tike called Adrian.

This baby did something I'd not expected. It drew us all closer together, unified the school. Josh somehow became communal property, raised not just by Sharon, although I ensured she remained primary carer, but by the school as a whole.

The first time he crawled was during breakfast. He took off down the aisle between the tables to a huge round of applause and cheers from the assembled kids. Clearly, he's meant for the stage.

It was a special moment.

As the common room fills up for the evening's DVD I think of Josh and the effect he's had on us. What would the school do if he were taken? I don't mean if he died. It would be awful, but we're all familiar with death by now, and another reality of post-Cull England was that infant mortality was going to soar to... well, to the kind of levels seen in pre-Cull Africa. Death happens, you get over it, you move on.

I mean if he was snatched, spirited away, never to be seen again. It doesn't bear thinking about.

I dwell on this for two reasons.

Most importantly because the sell-by date on the condoms has just expired.

But more immediately, because children like Josh have been disappearing from homes and villages across the South-East for the last year or so. At first only a few, then more and more frequently and, after the incident at High Rocks, more violently. Someone is running an organised kidnapping ring and it's kids they're after. Chances are they'll eventually come for St Mark's.

I'm not a mother yet, I may never be. But these kids are all mine, in a way. And if someone's going to come and try to take them away at gunpoint, I'm going to stop them, or die trying.

Protecting them means leaving the school grounds, taking the fight to our as yet anonymous enemy. I've not left the grounds since I arrived here in a wheelchair, broken and battered after my time with the American Army. I don't want to leave. I have a kind of agoraphobia, I suppose. This is my home, my community, and the thought of leaving terrifies me. What if I inadvertently lead the enemy straight here? What if I have to watch Lee, or any of the others, die? I'm not a soldier, I never wanted to be a soldier, but that's what The Cull made of all of us. I've spent the last two peaceful years trying to pretend that my fighting days were behind me. But I was lying to myself.

I start the DVD then I head upstairs to strip and oil my guns.

CHAPTER TWO

The gun felt weird; a mix of familiarity and fear.

I settled into my position, feeling the early winter cold seeping up through my trousers from the damp carpet on the floor of the front bedroom. My gun-shot legs would ache all day after this, like an arthritic pensioner.

I rested my arms on the window sill of the old terraced house, carefully avoiding the few shards of broken glass still sticking up from the crumbling putty, and nestled the stock of the L115A3 sniper rifle in my shoulder, sighting down the barrel.

I'd taken it down the firing range a couple of weeks before, when I'd realised that a fight was inevitable. It had only taken me an hour or so to master it. My skills had not deserted me. It was the same weight as the L96 I had taken from the sniper who'd used it to put a bullet in my left leg four years earlier, but it had a silencer, a better sight, and it fired a higher calibre round – 8.59mm rather than the L96's 7.62mm. Basically, it made it much easier to hit the target, gave a near 100% certainty of killing them if I did, and a much greater chance of staying undetected after taking the shot. It felt like an extension of me, but one that I was not sure I was comfortable with, like how I supposed Tariq must feel about his hook.

I couldn't tell you whether it was fear, cold or anticipation that made my hands shake.

The pre-dawn darkness meant I would be invisible to the two men unless they were to turn their binoculars straight at me and, by some chance, pause to study the dark window for a moment. But right now they were pre-occupied with the strangers who'd just turned up on their doorstep unannounced and offered them five captive children. For the right price, natch.

"Do you have a preference?" I asked softly.

"Nah," replied Tariq, from the window to my right.

"I'll take the one with the beard, then."

"Okay."

It had been two years since I'd held a weapon with intent to kill. It hadn't been a conscious decision to avoid guns, but after Salisbury I'd spent so many months recuperating – learning to walk, to use my arms, to talk again – that target practice had been the last thing on my mind. Two years of nobody shooting at us had helped, too. But if I'm honest, I was wary of the things. I knew that my behaviour during and after Iraq had been erratic. I knew that Tariq was concerned about the risks I had taken, and those I might take again.

I shared his concerns.

"Three, two, one..."

I took a deep breath, held it, squeezed the trigger gently, put a bullet in the guard's heart and splashed his innards across a brick wall. He fell without a sound. I saw my dad catch and lower him to the ground. Then he stood and drew his sidearm. Tariq's shot also found its mark, and his target jerked backwards as the top of his head exploded. Jane flinched in surprise and failed to catch him. He crashed into the wall and slid down, staring up at her in reproach.

"Head shot?" I asked as I grabbed my heavy pack. "Flash bastard."

"Sight's high," replied Tariq as we got to our feet and picked our way carefully down the rotten, rickety stairs. We left our sniper rifles behind us. They were no use at close quarters, and if all went according to plan they would be collected for us. We pulled the straps of our SA-80s over our heads as we emerged onto the street. As I did so, I realised that my hands weren't shaking any more.

As we ran down the road, the five kids that Dad and Jane had been escorting were throwing away their handcuffs and pulling guns from under their coats. By the time we reached them, the team was ready.

Dad led the way into the compound.

"We're going to go with a variation of the Trojan horse approach that Jane used a couple of years back," my Dad had said, earlier that night. We had huddled around the feeble flame we'd just kindled in the fireplace of an abandoned farmhouse about a mile outside Thetford as he outlined his strategy.

"I had Rowles and Caroline with me then," said Matron, as if pointing out the flaw in his plan.

"There are nine of us this time. The odds are better," he replied, unsure what point she was making.

"You never met Rowles," I said.

Dad rolled his eyes and continued. "Jane and I will escort the younger children to the gate. You kids can stay bundled up in your winter coats, so there'll be plenty of places to hide your weapons. You'll be bound with what will look like handcuffs, but in fact..." He threw pairs of handcuffs to each of the twelve and thirteen year-olds we'd selected for this mission. The five children examined them and smiled one by one as they realised they were plastic toy cuffs, easy to pull apart but good enough to fool an unobservant guard in the half-light of early morning.

"Sweet," said one of them – a beanpole boy called Guria who had become de facto leader of the younger group.

"We know they keep two guards at the main gate but if last night was routine, they have no one else on the walls or, as far as we can tell, inside the compound," Dad went on. "They are not expecting to be attacked. Anyway, there's plenty of open ground between the gates and the nearest houses, so they'd see a frontal assault coming in plenty of time to sound the alarm.

"Jane and I will approach with the kids in tow and our hands up. They should assume we've come to sell them and let us approach."

"How do we deal with the guards?" asked Tariq.

"I don't want to get involved in close quarters fighting with the young ones around, so while we keep them talking, you and Lee will have to use the rifles to take them out quickly and quietly. The nearest house will provide a perfect vantage point. "I couldn't find any booby traps when I recced the area earlier, so you should be fine."

Tariq and I glanced at each other and nodded. "No problem," we said in unison.

"Once the guards are down, you kids take off the cuffs, get out your guns and scatter to the nearest houses. I don't want you inside the compound, because things could get messy, but if we need to make a quick retreat you can cover our withdrawal. Guria, you know how to use the sniper rifle, so you take up Lee's position."

"Fine," said Guria.

"Jane, Lee and Tariq, you'll come with me, inside."

"And then?" asked Jane.

"Then we improvise."

Dad went in first, Tariq followed, Jane and I brought up the rear. I watched Jane move as we entered enemy territory, marvelling at the change in her. I'd fought beside Dad and Tariq in Iraq and England, but Jane and I had only fought together once, very briefly, during the siege of the original St Mark's, three years earlier. I knew she was capable and ruthless, but I'd not seen this side of her in a long time, and even then I'd never had a chance to study her in action. I'd become accustomed to seeing the gentler, nurturing, matronly for want of a better word, side of her, during the past couple of years. I had mixed feelings about watching her creep into danger, all stealth and purpose. On one hand, I hated the idea of her being in harm's way. I wanted to protect her and keep her safe. On the other hand, *damn*, it was sexy.

She glanced back at me, perhaps sensing how closely I was watching her. She gave me a quizzical look then a quick, amused smile, as if she was reading my mind.

"Focus," she whispered. Then she turned away, back to the business at hand.

The wooden door in the old brick wall led directly into the playground of what had once been a primary school. We crept across a faded hopscotch cross that seemed to be pointing us to the main building – a solid, Victorian stone box with big, high windows which sat at the centre of a maze of single storey brick extensions built in the 1960s. The only sound was the crunch of gravel beneath our boots and the raucous crowing of a rooster, informing the world that dawn was nearly here. Anyone inside was obviously accustomed to sleeping through his daily performance.

Dad waved us towards a side door. We were still in the middle of the playground, as exposed as we could be, when the door handle turned. Dad didn't hesitate. He ran to the door, still totally silent, and was there with his knife drawn as it swung open to reveal a short, heavy-set man in a black jacket. The man was only half awake, mechanically going through the routine of opening up the building for the morning. He was so focused on his task that he didn't notice Dad's approach until the cold knife point brushed against his cheek. Dad grasped the man's top and pulled him outside the door, letting it swing to. We crowded around our prisoner as his surprise faded, to be replaced by amused defiance.

"How many of you, and how many kids?" whispered Dad as Tariq pulled a sidearm from the man's belt and shoved it into his own.

"Fuck off," replied the man, misjudging the situation entirely. He probably thought he could issue a few vague threats, put on a show of defiance, and then we'd knock him out or tie him up or something.

Dad considered his smug captive for a second, shrugged, and slid his knife between the man's third and fourth ribs, straight into his heart. The man never even had time to be surprised. He was dead before the blade came out again.

"Jesus," whispered Jane, involuntarily.

Dad lowered the body gently to the cold, hard tarmac, then flashed her a sharp look as he wiped his blade.

"Problem?" he mouthed silently.

Jane waited perhaps an instant too long before shaking her

head. They held each other's gaze for a second. She looked away first. Dad turned, pulled open the door, and led us inside.

Subconsciously I think I'd been expecting the building to have that familiar school smell, but instead we were greeted by the stench of rotting timber, pervasive damp and unwashed bodies.

We found ourselves in a corridor that stretched to our left and right, ending in double swing doors at each end. Wooden doors with glass panels led into what had once been classrooms. A notice board hung on the wall directly facing us as we entered. It still had water damaged paintings and faded crayon drawings pinned to it.

Jane gently closed the door behind us and Dad led us to the right, towards what had looked like the assembly hall from outside. No matter how softly we trod, the squeak of our boots on the linoleum sounded like a chorus of banshees. I nervously walked backwards at the rear of the group, covering the swing doors at the far end, expecting someone to come crashing through them at any moment, guns blazing.

We crowded around the hall doors. The windows had blankets hanging over them on the inside, so we had no idea what we'd be walking into. There was a heavy metal chain padlocked through the door handles. I took the metal cutters from my backpack and got to work.

"We go in quiet," whispered Dad as I tried in vain to cut through the thick steel quietly. "Jane, stay just inside the door and keep an eye on the corridor. Tariq and I will go right. Lee, you go straight ahead. We fan out. No shooting unless absolutely necessary – there could be children in here."

We all nodded.

I finished cutting and threaded the broken chain off the metal handles, leaving it in a pile on the floor. Dad gently pushed the door open and we crept into the darkness, the squeaks of our boot soles echoing against the rotting wooden climbing frames that lined the far wall.

Blankets had been taped over the huge windows that Jane and I walked past as we moved into the hall, but the first light of dawn sent dim chinks of light through the moth holes and gaps to illuminate a large floor space littered with small grey mounds.

It took me a moment to realise that these were sleeping

children, huddled on the cold, hardwood floor under ragged old blankets. There was no sign of any guards.

Dad waved me over to him.

"We've got to move quickly," he said. "The other exit is chained from the outside too, so we're stuck in a cul-de-sac. The second anyone walks down that corridor, we're trapped. You head outside and unchain the fire escape, that way we've got choices."

I turned on my heels and squeaked past Jane, down the corridor and back to the playground. Just as the exterior door swung closed behind me I heard a muffled shout of "Oi, who left the chain off? Jim? You there?"

I paused and considered my options, then drew my knife and crept back to the door, stepping over the cooling body of the guard Dad had killed only minutes before. I crouched down and peered through the glass panel, thick with grime and mildew. I could make out a tall woman walking down the corridor towards the hall. She was bringing a shotgun to bear, beginning to be concerned.

"Jim?" she said again, more quietly, wary and suspicious now.

I waited until she had just passed the door, stood up and grasped the handle. I'd have to be quick about this. I took a deep breath and swung the door open, stepped into the corridor and brought the knife to her throat in one fluid motion. She froze.

"To the hall, slowly," I whispered in her ear. She walked forward without a word. I pressed in hard against her back, feeling her body – warm, tense, slim and muscled. She was as tall as me, with dirty blonde hair, and she really needed a bath.

Jane opened the hall door and ushered us inside. She took the woman's gun away and gestured for her to sit on the floor. I could see children beginning to sit up across the hall, sleepy and confused.

"All yours," I said, and then I headed back outside to complete my task.

The sky was bright grey as I skirted round the outside of the building to the fire escape which was, as predicted, chained from the outside. I didn't bother being quiet this time. I chopped the chain and pulled the door open. It made an awful noise as it opened for the first time in years, but nobody came running.

By now there were children standing up, as Tariq moved quietly through the hall waking them one by one and telling them to wake their friends. There was a susurration of whispers.

The plan had been to take one captive for interrogation, rescue the kids, and try to get out of the compound without the alarm being raised. So far so good. I propped the fire escape open with a chair and ran over to Dad, who was kneeling facing the captured snatcher. Jane was still keeping watch at the door.

"I'll only ask you one more time," Dad said as I drew up beside him. "How many of you are there?

The woman, who I could now see was in her early twenties and had multiple piercings all over her face, clenched her jaw and stared ahead, defiantly. Dad shook his head and turned to me.

"Cuff her and bring her along," he said, then he went to help Tariq muster the kids by the fire exit. I pulled a set of genuine cuffs from my pack.

"Wrists," I said curtly. She held out her arms and gave me a sarcastic smile. I shook my head and indicated for her to turn around. She got up on her knees, shuffled so she was facing the wall, and put her arms behind her back.

I snapped the cuffs closed and used them to drag her to her feet.

There were about twenty children gathered by the door now, each with a blanket pulled tight around their shoulders. As I marched the woman across the hall towards them I could see that the boys and girls ranged in age from toddlers right up to fourteen or maybe fifteen year-olds. Every one of them looked hollow cheeked and had dark rings around their eyes where hardship and lack of food had taken its toll, but their eyes all told different stories, speaking of everything from broken defeat to spirited resistance. As I approached, one of them, a slight girl with a scowl on her face, stepped up to my Dad.

"Why should we believe you?" she said, folding her arms and sticking out her chin. "How do we know you're not just going to sell us yourselves?"

I could see that Dad didn't know how to respond to this. Even though he'd spent two years as a de facto staff member at St Mark's he still wasn't very good at talking to children. He tended to be brusque and uncomfortable around them. He wasn't unkind, but he didn't really understand that kids need to be handled with more sensitivity and patience than, say, a squaddie on a parade ground. He liked kids, he just didn't get them.

Tariq smiled and reached for the gun he had taken from the guard. He handed it to the girl, who took it warily.

"This is the safety," he said, demonstrating. "It's cocked and ready to fire now, so all you need to do is flick the safety off, point and shoot. But not at me, please. Okay?"

The little girl nodded at him in mute, wide-eyed astonishment.

"Good girl. I'm Tariq, by the way."

"Jenni," she whispered. "Pleased to meet you."

"And you!"

"If you've quite finished flirting, can we get a move on?" I said. Dad and I laughed as Jenni blushed bright red.

"Jane, let's go," said Dad.

She ran to join us and we led the children – cold, hungry, holding hands in a long chain, but quiet and co-operative – out of the hall and into the open. Tariq ran to the corner and peered around. He signalled the all clear and we moved as quickly as we could to the playground gate.

"One sound," I whispered to my prisoner, "and I'll slit your throat." Even so, I was surprised she didn't try and raise the alarm.

Dad pushed open the gate and stood watching the school for signs of pursuit as the children filed outside. When they were all out, and the gate was closed behind us, I gave a short laugh of relief.

"We're not clear yet," warned Jane, but I could see she was feeling it too. She smiled at me then ran down the road to get the minibus, which was parked down a side alley. It started first time and she drove quickly to the gate where we loaded the children inside.

When they were all safely stashed I leapt up into the front passenger seat with Dad and pulled the door closed. Just Guria and the other kids to collect, and we'd be on our way.

"Turn the heater on, I'm bloody frozen," I said. But Jane wasn't listening.

"Look," she said.

I glanced up and cursed.

Five men were standing in the road ahead of us, motionless, watching, waiting for us to make a move. They were dressed in camouflage gear. Dark green hoods obscured their faces. The outlying two had swords in their hands; the two inside them held strong wooden bows raised with arrows poised to fire. The middle one stood with his bow down, casual. Waiting for us to make the first move.

"And it was all going so well," muttered Tariq, over my shoulder.

CHAPTER THREE

"I'll handle this," says John.

But I've seen the way he handles things, and I'm not prepared to let him screw this up. This calls for diplomacy, not violence.

I'm out of the cab and walking before he can stop me.

The middle of the five men raises his bow, notches an arrow, draws the catgut back slowly and sights on me as I step into the road.

"Put your hands above your head and get on your knees," he shouts.

I put my hands up, but start walking towards them. I figure the last thing they'll be expecting is politeness, so as I approach I smile and say: "could you keep the noise down please, we're trying to stage an escape here."

I can see this throws him, and he doesn't try to stop me approaching. I stop about three metres in front of him, hands above my head, ensuring that my body language is as passive as possible. His arrow is still pointing straight at my head, and now the two men either side of him are aiming at the cab of the minibus behind me.

He cocks his head, inviting me to explain.

"At a guess, you're Rangers," I say. "From Nottingham, yes?"

He gives me nothing.

"My name's Jane Crowther, I run a school called St Mark's. You may have heard of us."

The man shakes his head once.

"Right, well, your boss invited me to send an envoy up to you last week. One of my people is talking to you guys in Nottingham right now."

He shrugs; what has this got to do with him?

"I imagine you're here to take down the snatchers and rescue the kids," I continue. "Thing is, we just did that. Or at least, we got the kids out of the building and into the minibus. Most of the snatchers are still inside, asleep. And the longer we stand around here making noise, the greater the chance of them waking up and starting to shoot at us. So can we please, *please* take this discussion elsewhere?"

He considers me carefully, then gives a tiny nod.

"Crossroads. One hour," he says to his men. Then he gestures for me to walk back to the bus. "I'll be right behind you," he growls. His men peel off and begin heading back into the shadows. I turn on my heels, but before I can start walking there's a sharp report, a dull impact, and a grunt. Instinctively, I drop to my knees and draw my weapon. I don't even need to look behind me to realise that the leader of the Rangers is slowly toppling backwards – I felt the spray of blood and brains splash across the back of my neck.

I can see Lee leaping out of the minibus cab while his father jumps across to the driver's seat and prepares to pull away.

But I'm confused. I scan the walls of the primary school and can't see anyone at all. The snatchers must still be in bed or, more likely, reaching sleepily for their guns now they've heard shooting. And then I process the fact that the blood hit the back of my neck. The bullet came from the other end of the road. I drop and roll, coming up facing the other way. I can see two Rangers bolting for cover in the terraced houses on either side of the road, and two more dragging their leader away by his wrists.

I'm totally exposed, a sitting duck, and I still can't see the shooter.

"No! Don't!" shouts Lee as he runs towards me. He dives sideways as an arrow comes whistling past me, meant for him. One of the Rangers is shooting at him.

"Dammit," I yell. "We didn't shoot your boss!"

And then I realise, with a sinking feeling, that we did.

"Guria, you fuckwit, where are you?" yells Lee as he staggers to his feet and scurries for cover.

I see a Ranger take aim at the minibus cab and I have no choice. I send two rounds past his head and force him into the doorway of the nearest house. I've just confirmed to him that we're the enemy. No going back now.

Before I can get to my feet and run to join Lee, there's a snapping noise and gravel spatters my cheek. Someone else is shooting at me. I'll be dead if I stay here another second, so I just get up and run as fast as I can for the nearest doorway, the frame of which splinters as I race through into the rotting terrace. Those bullets are coming from the other direction, which means the snatchers have woken up and decided to join in. I crouch inside the hall of the ruined house, trying to work out what to do.

I've got a kid gone rogue with a sniper rifle, misguidedly trying to protect me. There are at least four highly trained Rangers who now want to kill all of us. And there's an angry group of child-rustlers taking potshots at us from behind a big brick wall. Lee and I are trapped in houses on opposite sides of the street, there are four other armed children cowering in houses somewhere, and worst of all a minibus full of kids is smack bang in the middle of the crossfire. Would the snatchers shoot them rather than let them escape? I hear the engine revving. John isn't sticking around to find out. The minibus goes roaring past the house I'm sheltering in, making a break for it, getting the kids to safety.

The moment they're past I risk leaning out and sending some bullets back towards the snatchers. I get a vague impression of three of them lined along the wall. None of the Rangers are anywhere to be seen. I think only one of them is on this side of the street, which means three others are opposite me, with a clear shot if they want to take it.

There's nothing I can do here except get myself shot. Time to go. I race through the house, past an overturned sofa thick with fungus, through a burnt out kitchen, out the back door, down the old brick-walled yard, past the shed which used to be an outdoor toilet, and through the gate into the back alley.

Before I can get my bearings I hear the unmistakeable sound of a car crash.

Just for a second I catch myself wondering whether any day has ever gone completely to shit so quickly. But the answer, of course, is yes. Once.

Right – stop, think, prioritise.

Lee can take care of himself. Guria and the other four should have the sense to make their way out of the area, if they can avoid the Rangers. I have to worry about the minibus, because if John's wrapped it round a lamppost they could be injured. That's where I'm needed.

I run down the alleyway, away from the school, towards the ominous sound of a blaring car horn.

As I run, I expect to see a Ranger step out ahead of me, or hear one of the children calling for me to stop, but an eerie silence has fallen, broken only by that horn. The back alley is cobbled, with a gunnel running down the middle of it. I race past countless wooden yard gates, some hang off their hinges but most are still bolted shut. As I reach the far end of the alley I pass a row of garages and then I'm out into the street, skidding to a halt and trying to make it back into the alley without being seen. Because the minibus has driven head first into the grille of an enormous lorry, the first of a convoy of three, all boasting huge spray painted red circles on the side like some kind of logo. The street swarms with angry men carrying big guns.

I finally manage to stop about two feet away from a man who has his back to me. I take a step back; he hasn't heard me. I turn, planning to creep back into cover... and I'm staring down the double barrels of a sawn-off shotgun.

So there I stand, watching the steam from the ruined minibus curling into the air behind the head of this gunman, trying to think of something to say. But he finds his tongue first.

"Well fuck me slowly with a chainsaw," he drawls. "Look who it is."

"Oh great," I say when I've caught my breath. "And I didn't think today could get any worse."

He smiles, turns the gun around and slams the stock into my face.

The world goes black.

CHAPTER FOUR

I actually saw the muzzle flash as Guria took out the Ranger.

He was about halfway down the street, just behind the Rangers, in the top window. I opened the door and ran into the road, ignoring Dad's calls to stay put. I didn't really have a plan; I just wanted to stop Jane being cut to pieces in the inevitable crossfire. As the shot man fell, and Jane ducked, I saw one of the Rangers raise his bow to finish me off. I shouted at him to stop, but he wasn't having it. I dived out of the way and heard an arrow whistle past, far too close for comfort.

I was a dead man if I stayed in the open. I had no choice but to hare over to the nearest house and dive inside, sliding on my stomach over the slime that had accumulated in the once pristine hallway carpet. I stood up feeling soggy and sick. My best chance of ending this was to get to Guria and take over the rifle. He was about fifteen houses up on this side of the road. I glanced back out the door and saw Jane had made it to cover across the road. That was a relief. Then the minibus roared past me, bullets pinging off its roof as the snatchers joined the fight from their compound.

Events were moving too damn fast. I ran out into the alleyway behind the house and raced up to where Guria had been hiding. Somehow I managed to get all the way there before any of the Rangers emerged into the alley to make their own escape. Or maybe they were digging in for a fight.

I reached the kitchen door of what I was reasonably sure was the right house, and brought my SA-80 to bear. Guria was one of us, but this was the first time he'd fired in anger. I had no idea what state he'd be in when I found him, and I wasn't going to let him shoot me dead in a moment of hyper-adrenalised panic.

I grasped the old Bakelite doorknob and pushed. The door had been left locked but the wooden frame was rotting away; the lock fell off and crashed to the kitchen floor as the door opened with a wet smack. So much for stealth. I checked inside but there was nobody there so I stepped in and pushed the door closed behind me.

"Guria," I said, loud but not shouting. "You there?" There was no reply so I made my way through the ground floor to the foot of the stairs. There was a skeleton lying sprawled across the bottom steps, the black stain that had seeped into the carpet around it all that remained to indicate it had ever borne flesh.

I stepped over it and climbed the stairs, which creaked alarmingly. They could go at any minute; this house was not a safe place to be, even without the threat of being shot. In the five years since The Cull, the elements had started to eat away at the infrastructure that civilisation had left behind. The endless persistence of water, probing every crevice and crack, with no houseproud DIYers to hold it at bay with supplies from Homebase, had started gradually eating away the houses and schools, shops and offices, and all the places we'd built to shelter us from the cold. There was no-one still trying to live by scavenging the scraps of what was left behind – it had all been corrupted by time.

I reached the landing and spoke again.

"Guria, you there?"

There was no response from behind the door to the front bedroom, which was pushed to. Had I miscounted, got the wrong house?

I pushed the door and stepped inside.

"Guria?" I said softly.

I heard a crash in the distance and the sound of a car horn.

The boy was crouched at the window, still facing the street, grasping the sniper rifle. I could see he was breathing.

"Guria, you okay?" I stepped forward.

He turned his head, as if finally registering that I was there. He was white as a ghost, pupils dilated, staring into the middle distance. He was in shock.

"Oh, hi Sir," he said, as if from the bottom of a deep well. "I just shot someone."

"I noticed."

"His head kind of went pop."

"Yeah, they do that. Good shot, by the way."

"Like a melon."

"Hmm. Can you pass me the rifle?"

"Oh, do you want a go?" He stood up and turned, holding the rifle out to me.

"No, get away from the window!"

But it was too late. He turned sharply, as if he'd heard something, and then Guria, silhouetted in the window, looked down in puzzlement at the arrow shaft sticking out of his chest.

"Oh," he said, and dropped dead at my feet.

The Rangers weren't our enemy. This was all a horrible misunderstanding. There was no need for this to go any further.

I knew all this.

But I looked at the dead child lying at my feet, with his wide eyes staring at the ceiling as his brain slowly cooled and died, and I felt a hard cold certainty in my chest.

Calmly, I reached down, picked the rifle up and raised it to my shoulder. Keeping three steps back from the window, hidden by the shadows of the room, I raised the powerful sight to my eye and switched through the options until I hit the heat sensor. And there he was, the man who'd shot a thirteen year-old boy who'd been my responsibility.

Lurking in the shadows of the bedroom directly facing me, he had no technology to aid his sniping. He felt confident, secure in the murk.

I took careful aim.

"Not a mercy killing this time, Nine Lives," said the voice in my head that had remained silent for two long years.

"No," I replied out loud; the first time, I think, I ever answered him audibly. I squeezed the trigger, putting a high velocity round through the man's heart. He stayed upright for nearly ten seconds before he crumpled like a discarded puppet.

Confident that the immediate danger was past, I stepped forward and scanned the eerily quiet street. At one end the snatchers were emerging from the schoolyard gate, rifles and shotguns raised, looking bewildered, trying to work out what the fuck had just happened. At the other end the car horn still blared, and I saw a wisp of smoke drifting across the road mouth, evidence of whatever accident Dad had driven into.

There was no sign of any of the other Rangers. I assumed they were all hiding on the same side of the street as me. But the snatchers presented a tempting target. There were five of them now, in plain view.

I sighted on the rearmost. The cold hatred in my chest was still there, lending me an almost supernatural calm.

"Oh this is good. I like this," said the voice.

I counted to three and then caressed the trigger once before letting fly. Within five seconds four of the snatchers were lying on the ground – head shot, chest, chest, head. They lay on the cobbles, blood pooling and mingling, running to the drains. The last one standing was left alone, surrounded by the corpses of his colleagues.

"Let him sweat," said the voice.

I held my fire. The man didn't know what to do. He was waiting for the inevitable kill shot, shaking in terror. A dark stain spread from his crotch as he wet himself. He dropped his gun and raised his hands, staring left and right, desperately trying to find me, as if locating me would allow him to appeal directly for clemency.

It took more than a minute for him to decide to turn his back and run. I let him take two steps before I shot the cobbles at his feet. He stopped and fell to his knees then shuffled around to face down the street towards me again. He was crying, hands pressed together in supplication, his chin wobbling as he screamed for mercy.

I let him go on like this for a minute or two, regarding him dispassionately like I would an ant underneath a magnifying glass on a hot day.

Then I blew his heart out through the back of his chest.

"Phew. I don't know about you, Nine Lives," said the voice in my head. "But I've got a blue steel boner that a cat couldn't scratch."

I smiled; so did I. To my surprise, I was quite glad Mac was talking to me again.

That should have been the first clue that I'd crossed some kind of line.

I went down on one knee and leaned over Guria. I gently closed his eyes and brushed away a lock of hair that had fallen across his face.

"Sorry," I whispered.

My business here was done. I had three more Rangers to hunt down. I got to my feet, turned on my heels and stared straight down the shaft of an arrow, notched and ready to fly.

"Drop it, you sick motherfucker," said the Ranger.

CHAPTER FIVE

There's a hand shaking me, but I shrug it off and turn over, trying to go back to sleep.

"Jane, you need to wake up." The voice is soft but urgent, and the shaking resumes. I try to swat them away. I hear another voice saying "for God's sake," then feel a sudden sharp sting as someone slaps me across the face. I'm instantly wide awake. My head hurts like hell and there's something wrong with my nose. I don't even need to feel it to know that it's broken again.

I'm lying on a very smelly blanket on what feels like a camp bed. It's cold in here and the bright sun is streaming through the windows straight into my eyes. I take a moment to adjust.

"Welcome back," says Tariq as he bleeds into focus next to me.

The best I can offer as reply is a vague mumble that sounds like a question.

"Back in the compound. The school," says John, behind me, and then goes on to pre-empt all my questions. "There was a convoy of snatchers coming to pay a visit here this morning. Reckon they were coming to collect this month's cargo. Three trucks loaded with kids and heavily guarded."

"And muggins here drove into them headfirst."

"I wasn't expecting oncoming traffic," says John. "There's not exactly a major congestion problem these days."

I turn to look at John. Every tiny motion of my head hurts. When he swims into focus I see a huge livid rip across his forehead.

"Ouch," I whisper.

He winces, seemingly more embarrassed than hurt. "Yeah. Steering wheel. Knocked me cold for a while."

"And the kids? Hang on," I say, suddenly outraged. "Was it you who bloody slapped me?"

"They're fine," he says, ignoring my protest. "A bit shaken, but they're back in the main hall while the snatchers try to piece together what happened here. Someone took out all their people. They were lying in front of the gate when we walked in. Sniper, I think."

"Guria? Lee?"

"If I had to guess, I'd say Lee."

"How many?"

"Five."

"Jesus. He shot five of them when we'd already left?"

John nods and somehow manages to resist saying "I told you so."

"Anyway," he says, and I can tell it's an effort. "We can't worry about him now. Jane, one of the snatchers seemed to recognise you...?"

"Yeah. I met him about three years ago. He was part of a child trafficking ring near the school. I shut them down and took him prisoner. I was going to interrogate him and find out where the kids were going, but Operation bloody Motherland turned up and arrested me instead. They let him go."

By now my eyes have adjusted and I can see we're in what must have once been a classroom. There are a couple more camp beds against the wall and some discarded clothes and tins of food. This must be where three of the snatchers sleep. Slept.

I sit up, trying to ignore the pain in my head. I reach for my sidearm, but of course it's gone. So has the knife in my boot.

"They were pretty thorough," says Tariq, brandishing the stump where his hook should be.

The door opens and two men stand silhouetted against the rising sun. "Miss Crowther. What a surprise."

I recognise him from Olly's compound, the day Operation Motherland turned up and ruined my life. "Hello Bookworm. How's it hanging?"

He steps forward and grabs me by the hair, yanking me to my feet and dragging me from the room. Tariq and John make to intervene, shouting protests, but the other man fires a warning shot over their heads and they stand back.

I am dragged down the corridor towards the main hall and thrown, head first, through the swing doors. I crash to the floor, my vision blurring from the intensity of the migraine. But I don't hit hard wood. Instead, my hands and then my right shoulder crash into something soft, yielding and wet. I recoil, my hands sticky with blood. I've been thrown onto a pile of bodies, six in all.

I make to stand but I feel a boot on my shoulder, pushing me down. Then knees in my back and a hand on the back of my head, pushing my face into the gaping wound in the back of one of the dead snatchers. I gag.

"Who the fuck are you?" says a voice that I don't recognise.

I don't reply. The hand pushes my face deep into the gore. I feel my cheek scraping against a jagged edge of shattered bone. Christ, this guy's got a huge hole in him. That new sniper rifle is vicious.

"I won't ask again."

"I'm Jane Crowther. Pleased to meet you," I say, trying not to get blood in my mouth.

"You're sure this is her?" he asks. "She shut down Olly's supply line?"

"Yes, boss," I hear Bookworm reply.

"So what are you?" asks the man in a thick Scottish accent. "Some kind of vigilante?"

"Just a concerned citizen."

"Who goes around massacring people."

"Who goes around rescuing children from kidnappers."

He snorts, derisively. "We're not kidnappers, miss. We're saving these kids. Aren't we boys?" There's a chorus of muted giggles, although one guy looks uncomfortable, as if offended.

"Saving them from what?"

"Eternal damnation. Apparently."

"It doesn't do to mock the Abbot, boss," says the uncomfortable one, threateningly. The boss nods, suddenly serious.

"You're right, of course, Jimmy," he says solemnly, then winks at me, humouring his colleague. "Anyway love, we've got you and your two blokes. How many more of you are there?"

"Enough."

He shoves my head hard into the wound and suddenly I can't breathe, my mouth and nose blocked by soggy meat. He literally rubs my face in it, then lets go and stands back. I fling myself backwards, gasping for air, scrabbling away from the obscene mound of carcasses. I catch a glimpse of the children, huddled in the corner of the hall, watching wide-eyed, before I kneel and throw up, heaving long and hard until there's nothing left and I feel wretched and hollow.

I'm still kneeling there with my eyes closed, trying to quell the stomach spasms, when I hear his voice in my ear, speaking softly.

"Finished?"

I look up at him, and am surprised to see how handsome he is. I spit a potent mix of vomit and blood into his matinee idol blue eyes. He just laughs and backhands me, sending me sprawling.

As I lie there, waiting for a bullet to end me, I hear Bookworm say "I reckon Spider will want to talk to her," and my vision blurs, my blood feels like ice in my veins, my head swims and I begin to tremble.

He's alive.

"What did you say?" I rasp, eventually.

"I said our boss will want to talk to you."

"His name. You said his name."

"Yeah." Bookworm sounds confused.

"What was his fucking name?" I yell.

"Spider," says Movie Idol, curious in spite of himself. If his reaction is anything to go by, I must have gone as white as a sheet.

"Spider," I say. "Spider." And then I can't stop saying his name, it pours out of me in a hysterical flood of jumbled syllables. "Spider. Spider. Spider. Spider. Spider. Spider. Spider. Spider. Spider..."

He slaps me again and I fall silent. I barely even know where I am. All I can see is that face. All I can hear is that voice. All I can feel is the sick ache in my stomach as my brother looks down in surprise at...

"Yes," I say quietly, rising to my feet. "Yes, I think he will want to talk to me. I certainly want to talk to him."

Movie Idol narrows his eyes and smiles. "You got history with the big man?"

I nod.

"Fine, you just bought yourself a ticket to London." He turns to address the gaggle of gunmen. "Put her and the kids in the lorry."

Two guys step forward and herd us towards the fire escape. As I step outside I hear Movie Idol giving a final order.

"Oh, and kill those other two fuckers."

I try to turn and protest, but the tide of children sweeps me out into the playground.

There's nothing I can do.

We're herded through the playground and out the front gate into the street. Two big container lorries are waiting. Both have their rear doors open, revealing hordes of terrified children huddled together for warmth. There are six men with guns standing around the trucks, both preventing the children from running and keeping an eye out for attack. Every one of them is a plum target for a good sniper, but for some reason Lee isn't taking the shot. Suddenly I feel guilty – the only thought I've spared for Lee since the Rangers attacked has been to worry about his mental state; it hasn't occurred to me that he might be lying dead in one of these houses.

I turn to look back at the school, where John and Tariq are being executed, and I curse myself for being such a fool. Who the hell did we think we were to come charging in here and take these guys on? We're... Christ I don't know what we are but we certainly aren't soldiers, or even police. It's ironic that we managed to take out the entire US Army two years ago, but now we've been undone by a bunch of child snatchers in lorries.

Our escorts chivvy us into the back of the foremost lorry. As I step up to the ramp I slip in a pile of what smells like human shit. There are no seats in here, and a couple of buckets sit by the doors, empty but reeking of effluent. This must be the kids' toilets, and they've just emptied them in the street. The smell of unwashed bodies, open toilets and fear is overwhelming.

"Sorry it's a bit cramped," says the snatcher next to me, sarcastically. "But your man wrote off the third lorry, so we've had to shove its cargo into these two."

The mass of kids shuffle up to make room for us new arrivals. Just as I sit down I hear two muffled shots from inside the school.

I sit in that lorry, surrounded by despairing children who I am powerless to help, leaving behind two dead friends and a missing lover, on my way to be reunited with the cruellest sadist I've ever met, and I begin, to my shame, to cry.

As the lorry doors swing shut I catch a glimpse of Bookworm leaving the school, scurrying to the rearmost lorry, waving to his boss at the front to tell him the job is done. Then the doors close with a heavy bang and we're plunged into darkness.

CHAPTER SIX

"I'm not your enemy."

The Ranger didn't waver for an instant. "I said drop it."

We stared at each other for a moment, as I considered my options and he got ready to skewer me. I dropped the gun and kicked it over to him.

"Useless at close range anyway," I said.

He looked down at Guria's body and I saw the shock on his face.

"But he's..."

"Just a kid. Yeah. Shot him anyway, though, didn't you?"

"Never. Not to kill, anyway. Did he move just before he was hit?"

I nodded.

He flashed me a look I couldn't quite interpret then backed onto the landing and gestured me downstairs.

Five minutes later we were in the kitchen of another house, further down the street, where the Rangers had regrouped. The other four kids were there too, rounded up like I was.

As I entered the house one of the kids – I think his name was Wallis – said: "Hey, Sir, where's Guria?"

I just shook my head and let my captor push me down on the floor, where I sat cross-legged.

"So they call you Sir, do they, Son?" said a tall Irishman who seemed to have taken command. "Fancy yourself a General do you? Like it when children call you Sir? Make you feel important?" He was barely holding in his anger, leaning down, getting in my face, trying to provoke me.

"No, I just find that it helps maintain classroom discipline."

He pulled back his arm to slap me around the face, but one of his fellows grabbed it and pulled him back. He shook the guy off, but composed himself.

"Two of my friends are dead because of you."

"And one of mine, because of you. Plus, if that car horn is anything to go by, the rest may be in serious trouble." I allowed some of my anger to surface. "We had everything under control here until you fucked it all up, charging in and trying to lay down the fucking law. Who made you judge, jury and executioner?"

"I'm not the one who just gunned down an unarmed man."

"A kidnapper and a murderer. That lot have been stealing children from across the country for months now. They leave communities shattered, adults dead. And what for? Do you know? Do you know where they're taking the kids, what they want them for?"

"No."

"Neither do I. But I doubt it's anything good. So yeah, I shot them. It was the best way to ensure we had a clean getaway. If you hadn't butted in, it wouldn't have been necessary."

"So it's our fault?"

"Stop it!" shouted Wallis all of a sudden. We fell silent and stared at him, almost guiltily. "You're a kind of police, right?" He said to the Ranger, who nodded. "Well so are we, kind of. This is all just stupid. We're on the same side. The kidnappers are the bad guys."

There was a long silence, then the lead Ranger said, as calmly as he could manage, "Why the fuck did you shoot Grier?"

"It was a mistake. The boy with the sniper rifle... it was his first time in the field. He panicked. Must have thought he was buying us a chance to escape."

The Ranger closed his eyes and wearily massaged his temples with his right hand. "So Phil shot him."

"And I shot Phil."

"And these kids?" He gestured to Wallis and the others. "Is this their first time, too?"

I nodded.

"So you're what, an army of children?"

"We're a school, not an army. But we defend ourselves when we have to."

"You really think giving children guns is going to help?"

"Has done so far. You'd be in a US concentration camp by now if it weren't for us, mate."

He shook his head in disbelief. "Twelve year-olds with sniper rifles. Such a fucking mess."

"Guria was thirteen," said Wallis quietly.

"You know what," I said. "We can sort this out later. Right now I'm more concerned about my friends and the children they were trying to rescue. Can we work together?"

He considerd me carefully for a moment. "What you did, shooting those people in the street. That was not right in the head."

"Then sign me up for psychoanalysis, but do it later, yeah?"

He held my gaze, trying to decide what to do.

"Ferguson, we've got movement in the street," said another Ranger, poking his head into the room.

My interrogator turned to leave, then glanced back at me and nodded, indicating that I should follow.

"But this conversation is not over," he said softly as we walked down the hall to the front room. "Just paused."

"Hang on," I said. "I thought there were only five of you. Two are dead, that leaves you and the two in the kitchen. Where did this guy come from?"

"Josh here was on sniper duty himself, upstairs. But he held his fire until he was sure what was going on. Discipline and experience, see?"

We reached the window and peered through the tatty lace curtains. The children we had loaded into the minibus earlier were walking down the street in a tight huddle. It took a moment for me to work out what was happening, but then I looked closer and made out two men amongst the kids, scanning the houses on either side of the road carefully. They must have seen the bodies at the school gates and this new bunch of snatchers were using the kids as a human shield.

But worse – leading the group were my Dad and Tariq. Dad had a nasty gash across his forehead that had soaked his face and jacket with blood; Tariq had Jane slung over his shoulder, an unconscious dead weight.

I heard footsteps in the hall and turned to see yet another Ranger enter.

"The convoy's in the next road," the man reported. "The van drove straight into it. It's a write off, and I think the first lorry is too. They're disentangling them now."

"Thanks," said Ferguson, then he turned to me.

"Those people out front..."

"My dad, my friend and Jane. She's our boss."

He nodded and I could see that he was thinking hard.

"Well, we have to rescue them," I said.

Ferguson regarded me coolly. "Do we? Do we now?"

"For God's sake," I said, but then I took a deep breath and stopped for a moment before continuing as calmly as I could manage. "I've got to assume you came here for the same reason we did – to find out who the snatchers are and where they're taking the kids, right?"

Ferguson nodded.

"Okay, so we want the same thing. Track these guys, shut them down. Now you could try and take this lot, capture a survivor, interrogate them. But how many kids would die in the crossfire? Your only option is to infiltrate and collect intel."

"Go on."

"They're going back to the school. I've been in there. I know the layout. We go in and we eavesdrop."

"And free your people at the same time?"

"If the opportunity presents itself," I said, although I was quite clear in my own mind that I'd rescue them no matter what.

"If this fucker tries to stop you," says Mac, "you'll just have to kill him. His men would never know that it wasn't the snatchers."

The group in the street drew level with our house and paraded past silently. We watched them go, seeing the fear on the children's faces as they were marched down a shooting alley.

"Okay," said Ferguson eventually. "But just you and me. If we don't make it back, my guys will make sure your kids get home."

"Done." I held out my hand. He ignored it and walked past me, checking his weapon and barking orders.

By the time we'd got to the end of the alley, the snatchers and their hostages had made their way into the school. They made the kids carry in the bodies of the men I'd killed.

The wall that ran across the front of the school compound stretched down the sides too, but I'd glimpsed a wire mesh fence at the rear of the building. Ferguson and I broke cover, scurrying out of the alley and down the side of the school, staying in the shelter of the wall.

When we reached the corner I took out the wire cutters and within moments we had slipped into a playground. We darted from slide to roundabout to climbing frame until we reached the outbuildings.

There was no sign of movement at the rear of the school; everything would be happening in the front playground and the main hall, I guessed. We quietly tried all the doors and windows we could find. They were all locked, but time and neglect were on our side. I pushed one window gently and the whole frame came free and fell into the school. I gasped, waiting for a crash, but there was none. I peered inside and saw that it had landed on a mouldy blue crash mat. Ferguson and I climbed inside and found ourselves in a room full of soft foam wedges, mats and seats.

I clambered over the wet, squishy foam and cracked the door open. There was nobody in the corridor, so I headed into the school proper, with Ferguson close behind me. This part of the building had been left to rot, unlike the area around the main hall, which had obviously been inhabited since The Cull. We moved through the eerie, mildewed corridors stepping carefully to avoid the lino tiles which had curled upwards and made loud cracking noises if we trod on them. We came to a pair of swing doors and I peered through a frosted glass panel and saw movement very close. It took a moment to work out that there were two men standing just on the other side of the door. It looked like they were guarding a room.

I turned to Ferguson and indicated that he should look. He took my place just as there were sounds of movement in the corridor beyond. I could hear muffled shouts and then a gunshot. In sudden panic I lurched forward, gun at the ready, but he spun and put his hand on my chest and shook his head firmly.

We stood there for a moment, me desperate to see what was going on, he resolutely holding me back. He didn't see my hand slowly move towards the knife in my belt.

He held up his hand, releasing me and whispered: "We go around, through the window."

I considered for a moment, then nodded. So we went back the way we had come, back across the foam and out into the playground. Then we skirted the buildings until we were outside the room that was being guarded. I was surprised how calm I was when we reached it. Someone had been shooting in there, so there was every chance that Dad, Jane or Tariq was lying dead. I felt nothing but a fixed certainty that, even if one of them was dead, my gun and my knife would help me make it better.

I peeked over the window ledge and saw Dad and Tariq sitting on a camp bed, looking grim. I tapped on the glass lightly. Tariq jumped in surprise, but Dad just turned and smiled. They came to the window.

"Brace the frame," I whispered, miming how they should hold the window steady.

They looked confused, but nodded. Then Ferguson and I took up positions at either side of the window and pushed. We were in luck. The frame slowly slid forward and oozed out of the brickwork, entire. Dad and Tariq took the weight, carried it inside and laid it on the bed.

"Where's Jane?" I asked when they returned to the window.

"Just took her to the hall," replied Dad.

I reached into my pack, took out two Brownings and handed them to Dad and Tariq.

"Then let's go get her."

Dad shook his head. "No. There are too many of them." I made to protest, but he waved me quiet. "And there are children in there."

"We can't just let them drive off with her, for fuck's sake."

"We have to," replied Dad.

"You could shoot them all and rescue her yourself," said the voice in my head. I actually considered it for a moment.

"How many men in total?" asked Ferguson.

"Fifteen at least. It's some kind of armed convoy, collecting kids from staging posts like this across the country and shipping them into London."

Ferguson nodded. "They're more organised than we'd thought."

"Then let's kill them all, release the kids and go home."

Dad gave me an exasperated look. "Lee..." but he broke off when we heard voices at the door. Without a word, he and Tariq scuttled to the door and took up positions either side. Ferguson and I ducked down below the window ledge.

I heard the door open then a brief scuffle and a groan, then the door closed again. I looked up to see Tariq holding his gun barrel in the mouth of a spotty little man in a dark green hoodie.

"Sod this," I muttered, and climbed into the room. Ferguson followed me.

I pulled my knife out as soon as my feet hit lino, stepped forward and laid the blade across the captive's throat. Tariq removed the gun.

"You're here to kill us, right?" said Dad.

The terrified man nodded.

Instantly, Dad aimed his gun at the wall and let off two rounds.

"Now strip," he said. The terrified man undid the zip on his hoodie. "Quickly!"

"Good idea," I said, as I began unbuttoning my own coat. "I'll take his place and follow them back."

Dad shook his head. "No way, son. You're coming with me."

"But I'm the right height and build," I protested. "Neither of you are."

Dad looked past me, over my shoulder. "But I am," I heard Ferguson say, in response to my father's piercing gaze.

"Oh come on, we're going to trust this guy over me?"

"Yes," said Dad firmly. "I think your judgment is a little off."

"What the fuck is that supposed to mean?" I replied.

"I think maybe he's seen me," whispered Mac.

But Dad wasn't going to get into this now, and our captive was down to his underpants.

"If I get away with this, I'll stick with them until they reach wherever their base is, then I'll try and sneak away, head back to Nottingham," said Ferguson as he hastily pulled on a crusty pair of smelly combats. "You should join my men in the road and head there yourselves."

"And if you don't come back?" I asked peevishly. "If they rumble you the second you walk out of this room?"

"Then there'll be plenty of guys to take my place."

We heard a distant car horn.

"They're wondering where he is," said Tariq.

Ferguson pulled the hood over his head and headed for the door.

"Head North via Hemel Hempstead," says Dad as Ferguson makes to leave. "Look for us there."

"Will do," he replies.

"Good luck," I said as he turned the handle. He didn't acknowledge me at all.

We waited a minute, but we heard no shots and no commotion. Dad left the room and came back a moment later.

"All clear."

I ran into the playground just in time to see the trucks turning the corner at the end of the road. The engines faded away and silence reigned. Jane was gone.

I stood there for a moment, then I began walking to the gate. I would find my sniper rifle and go after her. Anyone who got in my way would die. Simple as that.

I felt a hand on my shoulder. I stopped but didn't turn around, afraid of what I might do.

"Lee." It was Dad.

"I'm going after her."

"Like hell you are."

"Don't try and stop me."

"There's a pile of bodies back there with bloody great holes in them."

"So?"

"Was that you?"

"Yes."

"And what threat did they pose to you? You shot them when we'd already left. They were irrelevant."

"They were scumbags who had it coming."

"So you're judge, jury and executioner now?"

"When needs must."

There was a long silence. "You're not going after her and that's final."

I burst out laughing and turned to face him, bringing my gun up until it was pointing right between his eyes.

"Really, Dad? You think you can ground me? What am I, twelve?"

He looked at me with such sadness in his eyes that for a moment I felt a stirring of... panic? Conscience? I ignored it.

"No, you're eighteen. But you're out of control. Your judgment is shot and you're a danger to yourself and to the people around you. I am your commanding officer and you will do as I say."

"Like fuck I..."

His eyes gave no warning, and he moved so fast and with such control that I was disarmed and lying face down on the concrete with his knee in my back before I knew what was happening.

"If I let you run around with a gun, how many more people will die? How long 'til you decide that Tariq's broken one of your rules and has to be taken out? Or me?"

"Not that long at this rate," I said. It was supposed to be a joke, but nobody was laughing. "If she's harmed in any way, because you stopped me going after her, I will kill you."

He considered me for a moment and then turned away.

"The awful thing is," he said softly, "I believe you."

I got to my feet and held out my hand for my gun. He considered me for a moment then handed it back. I shoved it in my waistband and then walked back towards the school.

"You'd better come up with one hell of a rescue plan, Dad," I said over my shoulder as I walked away.

CHAPTER SEVEN

It's cold outside, and there's no heating in the lorry, but the huddle of children produces a foul selling warmth that at least stops us getting hypothermia. There's no light either. Or seats. Five winters without maintenance have reduced Britain's roads to a long trail of endless potholes through which we splash and spring. So we bounce along in the dark, getting bruised and beaten as we crash into each other, or momentarily lift off then slam to the floor on our bony, undernourished arses.

None of the snatchers got into the back with us, so we're unguarded. But the heavy doors are securely locked from the outside, and even if we could get them open, we're hardly going to jump from a moving vehicle, are we?

I expected a flood of eager questions once the doors closed and we were momentarily unwatched, but these children have been broken. They sit silent and scared, clutching their blankets around their shoulders as if they were some kind of armour. One small boy keeps being shoved against me by the movement of the lorry. I try to talk to him, but he ignores me. Eventually

I put my arm around his shoulder and cuddle him in close. At least that way, I reason, we won't bang into each other so much. But his response to my attempt at comforting him is to bite my forearm, hard. I yell and snatch it back. Little beast.

"Hello?" I hear a faint shout from deeper in the bowels of the lorry. "Hello, is that the woman who came to rescue us?" It's a girl.

"Yes," I shout back. "My name's Jane. What's yours?"

There's no reply, but a few moments later I hear vague sounds of commotion and I realise someone is fighting their way through the crowd to get to me.

"Hello? Where are you?"

"Here," I reply, and I steer her towards me in the darkness until I feel small hands grabbing at my coat. I grasp her hands tightly. I fight down my fears and put on an upbeat façade.

"And what might your name be, young lady?"

"Jenni," she says, and thrusts a gun into my hands. "They didn't think to search us."

For a moment I'm too surprised to speak, and then I remember Tariq giving her the weapon back in the school hall.

"Oh Jenni," I say eventually. "You are my kind of girl!"

"Where are they taking us?" she asks. I can hear her trying to be brave.

"I don't know, sweetheart. I don't know anything." But that's a lie. I know Spider. I know what he's capable of.

I shove the gun into my trousers and pull my jacket down over it. They searched me back at the school; they've no reason to do so again.

"Where are you from, Jenni?"

There's a long silence, and I wonder if she heard me, then she says: "Ipswich."

"And how old are you?"

"Thirteen."

"So you were eight when..."

"Everyone died."

"And how have you lived since then? I mean, who's been looking after you?"

"Mike," she says, as if this explains everything. "But he's dead now." Her matter of factness stops me cold. I don't ask any more questions. She lets me put my arm around her though, and she nestles into my chest. She soon she falls asleep. I feel the slow rise and fall of her breathing as we rattle and bounce in the darkness. Eventually I rest my head on hers and I slip into a half-sleep. I have no idea how much times passes until the explosion.

In the enclosed space, the bang is deafening. It comes from the front, from the cab, and the lorry lurches violently to the left. We're flung into each other like some mad rugby scrum and there are cries and screams as the lorry tilts past the tipping point and slams down on its side. The doors at the back buckle and a chink of light breaks in. The lorry is still moving forward, crippled now, and we're bounced and jostled. Loud screams from the bottom of the human pile as children are crushed. The lorry jacknifes on its side and the cargo container sweeps in a wide arc then smashes into something solid. We come to a sudden halt and are all flung against the wall, compressed in an awful smashing of limbs. The doors crash open and children spill out of the container, tumbling helplessly onto tarmac.

There's a moment of stillness as our ears ring and we get our balance, re-orientating ourselves. Then the screaming starts again and there are children yelling for air, and for people to get off them, or just crying in pain as the inevitable broken bones grind against each other.

I've ended up at the top of the pile, so I scramble towards the doors as delicately as I can, but it's impossible. The mass of children heaves and shifts beneath me and I'm thrown off balance, unable to escape.

I hear the crack of small arms fire over the din. I can't locate where it's coming from, but it redoubles my determination and I ruthlessly scramble back to the top of the pile and out the doors, literally sliding out across the backs of children. I draw my gun as I do so. To my surprise I manage a relatively graceful landing as kids rain down around me, blinking in the sudden, bright afternoon light.

The gunfire is coming from my left. I spin and see the snatchers who've survived the crash, huddled behind the open cab door, firing up at concrete embankment. We're on an A road, in the suburbs of London, at a guess. Beckenham, perhaps? I glance around the container and see that the first lorry is still upright, parked a few hundred metres down the road. It is coming under heavy attack, many rocks and a few bullets pinging off its bonnet and roof. Before I can react, they pull away, cutting their losses, abandoning us.

Which isn't necessarily a bad thing.

The kids are still tumbling out of the lorry, all walking wounded. I briefly search for Jenni, but can't find her in the confusion.

Right, time to take control.

I have no idea who's attacking the convoy. They could be good guys, but they could equally be a rival bunch of snatchers. Until I know, I can't afford to start shooting. I look behind me. There's a side street with a pub on the corner. It's derelict and ruined, but it will have a cellar and that's our best chance of shelter.

"Listen," I shout. "Everyone into the pub. Quickly."

But it's no use. I have no authority here. These kids don't trust me, and why should they? They scatter in all directions, in ones and twos, pure panic. Scurrying for cover or making a break for freedom. I see one duo blindly racing past the snatchers towards the enemy guns. One of them is hit in the crossfire and drops, but the other keeps running and disappears into a tower block.

I feel a hand tugging my coat and I turn to find Jenni pulling me towards the pub.

"Come on," she says urgently. Then she shouts at the kids who are still pouring from the back of the ruined lorry. "Come on! This way!" Thankfully, some of them hear, and once they begin to follow us, the others fall in behind them. Jenni and I begin running towards the pub.

We're about ten metres from the door when a man steps out of the doorway. He's about my height, dressed in tracky pants and a thick, quilted coat topped by a beanie. His face is grimy and hard to make out. In his hands he holds a crowbar. He stands with his legs apart and starts smacking the crowbar into the palm of his left hand like a panto actor in *Eastenders* pretending to be a hard man. He doesn't slow me down. I level my gun at him as I keep running.

Two more men step out of the shadowy pub interior. They're also dressed in rag-tag looter chic, but while one of them dangles a bicycle chain from his right hand, the other has a gun aimed right back at me. Jenni and I skid to a halt, but the kids behind us are too panicked. They sweep past us and then veer right as they see the menacing figures before us.

Instead of heading into the pub the stampede takes off down the side street, leaderless, lost and running into the territory of god knows what kind of gang. I yell at them to stop, but nobody's listening.

"Leave the kids alone, bitch," shouts the man in the middle over the sound of pattering feet and, I realise, nothing else – the gunfire behind us has stopped.

"She's not one of them," shouts Jenni. "She was a prisoner, like us."

"Then she can drop the gun," replies the man.

I aim it at his head. "And let you take them instead? I don't think so. Stay close Jenni."

I notice that the tide of children is ebbing and that some of them have gathered around us. I glance down briefly and recognise a number of faces from the school. About five of the kids we tried to rescue have rallied to my defence.

"She's telling the truth," pipes up a boy so tiny he can only be about eight. "She tried to help us." I make a mental note to hug the life out of him if we get out of this alive.

"Doesn't matter," comes a loud voice from behind us. "She's still a fucking adult. You can't trust them. Everybody step away from her. NOW."

Such is the authority in this woman's voice that four of the kids peel away and begin running to catch up with their fellow escapees. It's only Jenni and the pipsqueak left.

I turn to face this new player.

In the distance I can see the snatchers lying dead in the road, and between us and them stands a group of ten children. And then I do a quick double take back at the pub doorway and realise that they're not men – they've got the slightly out of proportion, weed-thin tallness of teenage boys.

I look back at the group in front of us. They're all teenagers. Only two have guns, the rest brandish truncheons, chains and even pitchforks. One of the kids with a shotgun, a girl, steps out of the crowd and takes point. She's wearing a brown fur coat tied around the waist with a leather belt; she's got a grey hoodie on underneath the coat and she pulls the hood off, releasing a cascade of greasy red hair.

The sun is behind her so I still can't quite make out her face.

I lower my gun. "I really was a prisoner. I'm not of the snatchers."

She doesn't reply.

"Honestly, I'm trying to help these children," I plead.

The girl steps forward and suddenly I can make out her face. It takes me a second, but then I gasp in shock.

"Well you took your fucking time," says Caroline.

The scars on the right side of her face look like the worst case of acne I've ever seen. I remember the cleaner's shotgun blast peppering her with shot, seeing her fall, working all evening to sterilise and dress her wounds. Failing to save her right eye.

I don't know what it looks like under the eye patch she's fashioned from elastic and felt, and I don't ask permission to look.

She's taller but still very solid. She'd be pretty if it weren't for her injuries, and her hair is stunning. I spent so long looking for her; it's hard to believe she's actually standing in front of me.

The last time I saw her she was being taken into the hospital at the Operation Motherland base, Rowles at her side. I had assumed that was where she remained until the nuclear blast. But when Lee had recovered from his injuries enough to be able to communicate again, he told me that she wasn't there. The Americans knew nothing about her. She had vanished from under their noses even as Sanders and I were escaping in the opposite direction.

I spread the word that I was looking for her to all our contacts, but I never heard so much as a whisper. Her trail had gone cold by the time I knew to start looking.

I look at the short, square, scarred pirate Jenny in front of me, gun in hand, defiant, leading an army of children, and I feel a strange sort of pride.

"That's my girl," I whisper.

She hands me a mug of hot milk, which I take thankfully, warming my frozen fingers.

"Fresh water's hard to get here," she explains. "But there's a guy who comes to market with milk once a week, so..."

We're awkward with each other. Not quite sure what to say. We slip into survivalist small talk – where do you get medicine, what do you use for fuel, do you have a generator?

We're sitting on a ragged old sofa in the middle of a huge open plan office. Third floor, centre of the high street. The desks and chairs have been cleared away and the floor is a mad maze of old beds and sofas, with long clear runs where the younger kids race around, burning off the little energy they have.

It's a headquarters, of sorts. There must be thirty or so kids living here; closer to a hundred now we've rounded up most of the escapees from the convoy. My hands ache from all the stitching and splinting I've been performing on the injured from the attack. Medical supplies are non-existent, so I've been using all sorts of dodgy unsterilized kit. The sooner I can get these kids out of here and back to the safety of St Mark's, the better. We have enough supplies there to deal with the imminent avalanche of secondary infections. But for now, the last child has been mended and the majority of them are sleeping it off.

Caroline is the leader here, even though there are older, stronger kids in the mix. There are hulking great teenage boys who take orders from her without question.

It takes a while for me to ask the obvious question. "Where are we?"

"Hammersmith."

"Jesus, that far in? I thought this was Bromley. What's it like in the centre?"

"Church land. We don't go there."

"Church...? Never mind. Tell me later." Small talk exhausted, I lean forward and ask the big question. "What happened, Caroline? Where did you go?"

She looks down for a moment then, talking to her shoes, whispers: "Rowles?"

"He died, Caroline. I'm sorry."

She nods once. She knew the answer to the question before she asked it.

"He saved us all," I add. "Little madman took out the entire US army, if you can believe that."

She looks up, amazed. "What?"

I nod, smiling. "Nuked them."

Her mouth falls open in astonishment then she begins to laugh.

"He asked about you," I continue, smiling in spite of myself. "Wanted us to find you, tell you he loved you."

Gradually her laughter subsides and she wipes away a tear that could equally have been caused by hilarity as grief.

"He stayed behind so I could escape," she says eventually. "The surgeon who operated on me came to get me during the attack. Spirited me away from right under their noses."

"Where did he take you?"

"We spent a while in a house somewhere in Bristol, while I recovered. Just the two of us."

"Did he...?"

"Oh yes," she says matter of factly. "But, you know, could have been worse." She registers my look of horror and dismisses it with a scowl. "I'm still alive," she snaps.

"Okay," I say, eager to move on. "And then?"

"He traded me to a trafficker for a pallet of Pot Noodles and a bag of firelighters."

I stare intently at the floor, unable to meet her gaze. "I should have looked after you better," I say. "I'm so sorry. This is all on me."

I feel her hand on mine and I look up. She's not smiling, but she's not scowling either. "Not your fault. Move on," is all she says. But I'm worried for her. Caroline and Rowles were inseparable for a while. Kindred spirits. Bonnie and Clyde. But while she was brave, strong and ruthless to a fault, she didn't have the emotional detachment of her younger partner in crime. I remember the look on her face, the utter horror, when she accidentally shot a soldier who was trying to help us. Rowles would have shrugged and made some comment about tough luck; Caroline was devastated.

Yet here she is leading an army, battle scarred and hardened and not yet sixteen. I wonder if that vulnerable core has been entirely burnt away.

"I thought you'd died in the nuke," I explain. "It wasn't 'til much later that we discovered you weren't there. We searched high and low for you, I swear."

"I believe you. But once the traffickers had me, I was shipped straight to London."

"You escaped, though. I mean, look at this place. Why not come find me?"

"I was... busy for a year or so. And when I did manage to get away, I didn't escape alone. I had this lot to look after. And a war to fight."

"Against who? Who are these bastards?"

She regards me coolly for a moment then says: "Come with me."

As we walk out into the main street and down to the centre of town, we talk more, filling in the blanks. I tell her how I ended up in the van, about the snatchers and how they killed Lee, John and Tariq; she relates stories of all the times the church have tried to track them down or infiltrate them. There's a streak of ruthlessness to Caroline's tale – moles identified and shot no matter how young they may have been, lethal traps laid at freshly abandoned living spaces. She's been fighting a guerrilla war and she's been fighting dirty. I don't have the right to disapprove – she's kept these kids safe in the face of overwhelming odds – but there's a disquieting element to her stories. I can't decide whether her precautions and her summary justice were always justified or whether she's succumbed to paranoia. I remember how Lee was after the siege of St Mark's; reckless, too quick to fight when a calmer head could have avoided the need. I see a lot of that in Caroline. The sooner I get her back to the school, the better.

It's so long since I've been in a city that I've almost forgotten what it's like to be surrounded by concrete. Everywhere I look is evidence of The Culling Year. Burnt out cars and buildings, skeletons in the street, a wrecked van, turned on its side. Someone's gone mad with an aerosol too – up and down the high street, in big red letters it reads 'whoops apocalypse :-)' over and over again.

With no council maintenance teams to trim them, the trees are taking over. Tough grass is starting to force its way through the moss-covered tarmac, and foxes stroll blithely down the road eyeing us more with hunger than fear, as if calculating the odds of successfully bringing us down and making us their next meal.

As we walk and talk, Caroline notices me watching the foxes.

"Keep clear of them and they'll keep clear of you. Otherwise they tend to go for the throat. And if you hear a dog barking, go the other way. Don't let them get your scent. We've managed to trap and eat most of the local packs, but there are still a couple of nasty ones left. We lost a girl to one of them only last week. Seven, she was. Poor love wandered off and tried to play fetch with a Rottweiller."

We cross what would once have been a busy traffic junction and suddenly I realise that we're not alone. I become aware of shadows flitting underneath the overpass, and catch a snatch of raucous laughter somewhere up ahead, echoing through a deserted shopping mall. There are people here, all moving in the same direction as we are. Then we turn a corner and I see our destination: The Hammersmith Apollo. The sign above the entrance still reads "Oct 24/5 – Britain's Got Talent Roadshow!"

There's a small market outside, a pathetic collection of scavengers trying to barter remnants and relics for food. But there's precious little of that, just an improvised spit on which rotate a couple of thin looking pigeons. The smell isn't exactly appetising.

Caroline notices my disgust. "I know. You've probably got a big old vegetable garden and a field of sheep, huh?"

I nod.

"I dream about mashed potato," she says wistfully.

"Then why are you still here?"

"Because of him," she says, pointing.

I look up and see a huge mural painted onto the theatre wall. It stretches the entire height of the building and depicts a withered old man in glowing white robes. His balding head is ringed by a red circular halo and his hands are stretched out towards us in a gesture of welcome. Blood drips from his fingers. I suppose it's intended to be beatific, religious, holy. But to me it just looks fucking creepy, because standing around him, gazing up at him in awe and wonder, are a gaggle of children.

"The Abbot," says Caroline. "Come on, it's nearly time for the miracle" She leads me through the market and into the theatre.

Inside is a small wiry man with a little stall selling bags of KP peanuts. I gawp. "I know," says Caroline, registering my amazement. "He's here every time, and no-one knows where he gets them. People have tried following him back to wherever he's got his stockpile, but he's too slippery.

"Hey, thin man," she says cheerily. "Can I get a freebie for my guest here?"

The peanut seller smiles broadly and tosses a packet to me. "Anything for you, sweetheart," he says. Caroline blows him a kiss and we walk through the doors into the auditorium as I pull open the packet and inhale the salty aroma. Yum.

"We rescued his daughter – well, he says she's his daughter – from the snatchers six months back."

There's a big screen on the stage and a projector in front of it. A relatively large crowd – fifty or so people – has gathered in front of the stage. I hear the cough and splutter of a generator starting up and settling into its rhythm before the projector comes alive and beams snowstorm static for our amusement.

"So what are we going to see?" I ask through a mouthful of honey roasted heaven.

"Wait and see. It happens at the same time every fortnight," she says, as we take our positions at the edge of the crowd.

The television signal kicks in and we see a graphic of a red circle against a light blue background, and then the show begins. The miracle.

The broadcast is by a group who call themselves the Apostolic Church of the Rediscovered Dawn and they're – wouldn't you know it – American. Their leader is the creepy guy from the mural. An ancient, wizened old vampire who's survived the plague despite being – he claims – AB Positive. He provides a demonstration, mixing his blood with O-Neg taken from two acolytes who sport the dead-eyed grins of happy cultists, then holding it up to the camera as it clumps.

The crowd in the studio Ooh and Aah, gasp and clap, then they start singing some bollocking awful gospel shit. The crowd here, though, aren't quite so sold. I get the impression they're just basking in the glow of the television, reminding themselves of moving pictures and cathode ray tubes. The programme is irrelevant, but watching it evokes families gathered around the national fireplace watching *Big Brother* or *Doctor Who*. Happier, simpler times.

When the song has finished, the abbot gives a little sermon.

About children. It takes a few minutes for the penny to drop, and then I remember what the snatcher had said back in the school, about saving the children's immortal souls.

"Dear God," I whisper, my peanuts momentarily forgotten. "They're shipping them to America."

CHAPTER EIGHT

"America? You have to be shitting me."

"No, honest man. They got planes flying out of Heathrow and everything."

"But why?"

"New beginning. That's what the churchies say. We're rescuing the kids so they can go out to America and find the Promised Land or something. They've got it easy over there, you know."

"Really?"

"Yeah, still got electricity and supermarkets and all that stuff. So I heard."

"And the nukes?"

"Wiped out the political elite. Left a power vacuum that these Neo-Clergy have filled. And they've got everything just fucking sorted, man. Peace, love, charity, all that jazz."

Tariq looked at me over the top of our prisoner's head and rolled his eyes.

"Listen, pal, I don't know where you're getting your information but I know for a fact that America's political elite is alive and kicking."

"Yeah, 'course you do."

"Saw the President himself two years back, on a live... oh. Oh holy shit!"

"What?" asked Dad.

"What his aide said about children. Do you remember Tariq?"

"I was bit busy being shot, old chap."

"He said, now let me get this right... 'spied her rounding up the children'. It was the first thing I heard when I came round in Blythe's office."

"Well, that's our boss, isn't it," said our captive. "Spider. The big man."

"Spider? I thought he was talking about Jane. Spied her. Fuck, I'm an idiot."

"What are you thinking, Lee?"

"Don't you get it? That wasn't the bloody president. That was this Abbot guy pretending to be the President. He had Blythe running round at his beck and call, trying to take control of the UK so he could use the army to round up all the children and ship them out to the States."

"And he must have already had a guy on the ground starting the job," says Tariq. "This Spider bloke."

"Who's assumed control this end now that we've taken the army out of the equation. The President's aide told Blythe there was a bigger picture."

"This isn't a new mess at all, then," said Dad. "It's the same old mess."

"But with less impaling this time around. I hope."

"Yeah," said our captive cheerily. "The big man prefers crucifixion."

I clipped his ear.

"Um... I didn't follow half of that," said the guy who'd assumed control of the Rangers. "Can you start at the beginning?"

"Later," snapped Dad. "First of all, this little sod's going to give us chapter and verse on his boss's operation. Aren't you?"

"You betcha."

"Smart lad."

*   *   *

An hour later we were gathered in front of a classroom whiteboard as Dad talked us through a map of London that he'd put together during the interrogation.

"These guys are well armed, very organised and disciplined," he told us. "They've got a whole bunch of ex-special forces types running their operation, and they maintain a clear and functional command structure. The good news for us is that they mainly concern themselves with keeping order in London. The snatchers who operate outside the M25 are basically contractors. They're scavengers and lowlifes who work in teams to assemble kids in a number of compounds like this one, spread around the country. Then they're collected regularly by convoys, each of which is run by one overseer from central command who keeps them in line.

"They don't have complete control of London. South of the river their control is pretty much absolute. There are communities there who are actually giving their kids to these bastards willingly. It's an area of hardcore zealots and converts. Pretty much entirely hostile territory.

"North of the river the picture's less clear. It seems the population there is mostly controlled by fear and intimidation, although the battle for hearts and minds is ongoing. There's one major pocket of resistance around Hammersmith where – Lee, you'll like this – a gang of kids who escaped from a transport have set up a liberation army."

I smiled. "Nice."

"But according to our man here, there's a major crackdown planned for next week. They've tried to lure them out into traps or get someone on the inside, but it's never worked. They're going to go in hard and wipe them out."

"Not so nice," murmured Tariq.

"What about their command?" asked one of the Rangers.

"This is where it gets tricky. They've set up home in the Palace of Westminster and turned it into a fortress. Concrete barricades, electric fences, gun towers, searchlights. They've even got a minefield. And this is where their boss lives. Spider."

"What do we know about him?" I asked.

"He holds court from the speaker's chair in the House of Commons, but apart from that, nothing. No one except the very top echelon get to see him. But he's got a reputation for being utterly ruthless."

"There's a surprise," I said.

"And he keeps his men happy with a brothel he's set up in – get this – the main chamber of the House of Lords."

"Brothel?"

"Rape camp, really, I guess. A whole bunch of young girls who are at the men's disposal 24/7. He's got huge stockpiles of food and booze too. If you work for him, you eat and drink your fill and fuck any time you feel like it."

"Shit, where do I sign up," laughed one of the Rangers until his mates gave him death stares, and he muttered: "Only joking, geez."

"Twat," said one of his colleagues.

Silence fell as we considered the size of the task before us.

"So," said Tariq eventually. "We invade London, fight our way past a city full of brainwashed religious cultists, take on a private army, storm a massively fortified castle that's defended by highly motivated special forces, and kill this Spider fucker. Then we take a plane, fly to America, rescue all the kids and take down a church that effectively rules a continent."

"That's about the size of it," said Dad.

Tariq sniffed dismissively. "That's the problem with life these days. So few real challenges."

"So here's what we're going to do," Dad continued. "Tariq, you're going back to St Mark's. There's a chance that Jane might tell them where the school is."

"No fucking way," I shouted. "She'd die first."

"They might not let her, Lee."

"She'd never talk."

"We can't take that chance." He stared me down and after a long moment, I nodded. He was right. "Tariq, you go back to the school and put them on a war footing. We've rehearsed it often enough, so you know what to do. But be ready to mobilise, too. We might need you."

"No worries, boss," said Tariq.

"Lee, you're going with our Ranger friends here. Meet up with

Jack in Nottingham see if you can persuade the Hooded Man to lend us some troops. We'll need all the help we can get."

"He'll want to talk to you about our dead men, too, I reckon," said one of them, threateningly. Dad was instantly right in his face.

"If anything happens to my boy, there will be a very bloody reckoning in Nottingham. Do I make myself completely clear?"

The Ranger tried to stare him down, but failed. He looked away. "Whatever," he said. But he looked away first. Message received.

"And what about you?" I asked.

"I'm going to Hammersmith," he replied, stepping back. "If there really is an army of kids in there, they don't know an attack is coming. I can warn them and either help get them to safety or, more likely, help them fight. It's where my experience will be most useful. We need all the allies we can get if we're going to pull this off."

I was checking the saddle on the spare horse the Rangers were letting me ride when Dad took me to one side.

"What now?" I asked tersely.

He looked at me hard, as father and commander fought it out. "It's been two years since Iraq and Salisbury. You've not been in a fight since. You refuse to talk to anyone about anything that happened. And now, the first time we go into combat, you shoot six people – one potential ally and five irrelevances who didn't need killing."

"I disagree. They really, really needed killing. But I'm sorry about earlier. I wasn't thinking straight."

"I know. I'm sorry too. But I'm worried about you. You're my son and I love you but to be totally honest you scare me a little bit right now. I think your judgement is off."

"That why you're sending me on the diplomatic mission?"

"No, you were the logical choice. But I can't pretend I'm not glad of that."

"Can I have my weapon back?"

He sighed and handed me the handgun. "Just don't shoot Robin Hood, okay?"

We both sniggered in spite of ourselves. "Now there's a sentence

I never thought I'd have to say," he said, smiling.

We both stepped forward and embraced, awkwardly. "Good luck in London," I said. "I'll be at the rendezvous, whether he sends help with me or not."

He hugged me hard then let me go and stepped back.

"Be safe," he said.

I put my foot in the stirrup, swing myself onto the horse and trotted over to join Hood's men.

"We ride fast and we won't be making any concessions. So keep up or get left behind," said their leader.

"Don't you worry about me," I said.

"Oi!" it was Tariq, walking towards me, waving. I pulled the reins and steered my horse across to him.

"You off then?" he said.

"Yup. See you at the rendezvous."

He nodded then looked up at me, his face for once entirely serious. "She'll be fine, Lee."

"Let me worry about her," I replied. "You just keep the school safe. No matter what."

"Promise. Hey, you'd better hurry up, they're going without you."

I turned to see the Rangers galloping away down the road. I kicked my steed hard and took off after them, riding to beg assistance from a legend.

CHAPTER NINE

"He wears this black robe with a big hood. He never takes it off."

"So you never saw his face?"

"No, sorry."

"And his voice?"

"He didn't speak. He just nodded or shook his head when they asked him questions."

I put my hand on the arm of the little boy with the missing ear and say: "Thank you."

He nods and scampers off.

"I told you he wouldn't be much help," says Caroline. We're sitting on one of the sofas, back in the office building she calls home, watching the sun set behind the Lyric Theatre.

"And he's the only one here who's met Spider?"

Caroline nods. "He doesn't leave Parliament, and he doesn't show his face. Why are you so interested anyway? You'll never get near him."

"Someone said that to me once before, but I got close enough to ensure that he'll remember me for the rest of his life."

Caroline regards me curiously. "So you met this guy before The Cull?"

"I think so. No, I know so. It must be him. It all fits."

"And is he the reason you changed your name and went into hiding?"

I look up, startled. "How...?

"I heard you and Sanders talking after I was shot. You thought I was asleep. He knows you from before, doesn't he?"

"Yes. And it's knew, I'm afraid. He's dead too."

"So..."

"Yes, Spider's the reason I went into witness protection and ended up at St Mark's. But it's a long story and I don't really want to talk about it, if that's okay."

"Whatever. So the school's back up and running?"

"Yeah," I reply, grateful that she isn't pressing the point. "Sixteen staff now, seventy-three kids. It would be more if these bastards weren't spiriting them away."

Caroline stares intently at her hands. I can tell she wants to ask the obvious question but isn't sure how to.

"Yes," I say. "All of you. We've got plenty of room."

She looks up and beams. "There are thirty-four of us. Plus kids we rescued today."

"More the merrier," I say, smiling.

"We'll have to go out and around," she says, excited for the first time today. "Coz south of the river is churchland." She looks up at me and stops short, her smile fading. "There's a 'but' isn't there?"

I nod. "Spider. He and I have unfinished business."

"But... but that's mad. Even if you get in to see him, he's surrounded by a fucking army!"

"Oh, he'll see me, all right. And as for the army. Well, one thing at a time, eh?"

I take out my sidearm and chamber a round.

"You are fucking mental, Miss. If you go and get yourself killed, who's going to get these kids to safety? You owe them... you owe *me* that."

She's right, of course. I do.

I know the sensible thing is to get these kids back to St Mark's, meet up with Lee, try and recruit help from Nottingham and put together a properly formulated plan of action. I know this. But John and Tariq are lying dead in that school, and Lee is missing. For all I know, I could be the only one left of our team, and I'm closer to the heart of this mystery than anyone's yet got.

I can't turn back now.

I shake my head. "Sorry Caroline. I'll give you directions to the school," I say. "If I'm not back in three days, take these kids and go."

I lean forward and hug her tightly but she doesn't respond, shocked at my abandonment. "I'm so glad you're safe, sweetheart," I say. "I can't tell you how glad."

Then I let her go, stand up, and walk out of the building without looking back. I don't want to see the accusation in her gaze. I take a moment to get my bearings then take off down the high street, heading for the Thames. If I walk all night, I can be there by dawn.

It's a bitter night. Clear sky, full moon. The sun's not down for an hour before there's frost on the ground. I walk down the Thameside path in the half-light, listening to the lap of the waves as the tide drags the river down, slowly exposing the rubble of a thousand demolished warehouses and the rotting timbers of ancient wharfs and jetties.

I went on a walking tour of the Thames once, when I was a medical student at Barts and The London. The guide was an ancient old woman, eighty if she was a day, yet sprightly and funny and with a deep booming voice that always reached me, even when I was at the edge of the crowd.

A hundred and fifty years ago the exposed mudflats of low tide London would be swarming with mudlarks, even at this time of night, she'd told us. Children between the ages of eight and fifteen would swarm down to the edge of the retreating water, sometimes wading hip deep in mud laced with fresh effluent and the occasional bloated corpse, scavenging for lost trinkets and dropped wallets. Mostly, though, they just found lumps of coal which had fallen off the barges that passed up and down the river. They'd collect the coal in sacks and then take it to sell to a local dealer. If they were lucky, they'd earn a penny a day.

150 years of progress, of making sure that children were protected from that kind of existence – in the West, at least – and yet five years after The Cull, I'd just left a hundred and thirty children who were living together in a crumbling building, scavenging for food and clothes, barely better off than mudlarks. Most of them would probably never go to school or university, never learn about history or geography or medicine.

Human nature tells me that there are sweatshops in England now. Somewhere, someone will have rounded up kids to use in makeshift factories. It's inevitable. One day someone will let something slip at a market and we'll follow whispers and rumours and track them down. I know with absolute certainty that if I survive this week, one day I'll kick down the doors of an old warehouse and find a hundred emaciated, pallid children dressed in rags, making matches or shoelaces.

And I'll free them, and feed them and clothe them and teach them.

Right now, we are clinging to the scraps of knowledge and technique left to us by the dead, but when the last person who was over 16 during The Culling Year dies, it will be these children who inherit the ruins. It's vital we protect them. Give them a childhood and an education. If we don't, we'll be responsible for a new dark age.

I tell myself this, examine my motives for staying at St Mark's, rehearse all the arguments I've used to justify what we're doing, all the historical precedents that have spurred me on, all the smiles I've brought to the faces of children who would be dead without my intervention. But all of it, every laugh, every smile, just wilts when I think about the man I am walking towards. My grand mission to save a generation of lost kids was discarded, forgotten and irrelevant the instant I heard that name again.

I keep putting one foot in front of the other, forcing my way through the silent city, finally realising the true power of revenge.

It's still dark when I reach the reconstructed Globe Theatre. I'm amazed to see it's still intact, despite a thatched roof that's practically an invitation to arson. I'm walking past when I catch an echo of a voice. Faint at first but then, as I pass the wrought iron gates, distinct. Someone is reciting Shakespeare from inside the theatre, presumably on the stage. I stand and listen for a moment, surprised by the sudden, unexpected evidence of life. It's the only sound in the cold, calm night.

It's a man, young by the sound of it, and he's not following any play that I know. He skips from this to that – a comic monologue, a Hamlet soliloquy, a sonnet. After a few minutes, I sit on a bench and give myself over to this improbable voice. Was he an actor? If I enter the theatre, will I recognise him? "Oh you played whatshisname, on *The Bill*!" Or is he a young man who'd just been accepted to RADA and was about to begin a career that would make him a star, standing alone on a dark stage in the middle of a dead city, dreaming of a world where the sex lives of actors were the talk of every sitting room in the land?

He's good. Emotive. Strong, clear voice. I feel a sudden ache in my chest, and I stifle a sob that seems to have come from nowhere. I sit and listen to King Lear's death speech with tears pouring down my face. I have no idea why I'm crying, but I can't help it. The tears just flow out of me.

And as his medley of Shakespeare's greatest hits continues, this suddenly echoes from inside the wattle and daub walls:

"How couldst thou drain the lifeblood of the child,
To bid the father wipe his eyes withal,
And yet be seen to bear a woman's face?
Women are soft, mild, pitiful, and flexible;
Thou stern, obdurate, flinty, rough, remorseless.
Bid'st thou me rage? Why, now thou hast thy wish.
Wouldst have me weep? Why, now thou hast thy will.
For raging wind blows up incessant showers,
And when the rage allays the rain begins.
These tears are my sweet Rutland's obsequies,
And every drop cries vengeance for his death."

I have no idea what play it's from, but I hold my breath, transfixed, until it's finished. The tears turn to ice on my cheeks. When the final syllable fades I release a long, slow breath and rise from my seat.

I walk on, gun in hand, leaving the anonymous actor behind to conjure the spirits of the dead in an empty auditorium.

I have a job to do.

Lambeth Bridge is gone. There's just a spur of stone sticking out over the river, like a huge jagged diving board. I walk to the edge and look down into the water, rising now that the tide has turned, swirling and bubbling with the strength of the current. Fall in there, you wouldn't last long.

A corpse floats past, face down.

The sun is just edging over the horizon as I walk past Victoria Tower Gardens and reach the Palace of Westminster, the seat of British democracy. I stand and gaze in astonishment for a moment at the gun towers and fences, the thin strip of what looks like bare earth between the wire enclosures, and the sign that says 'minefield'.

On the grass at the centre of Parliament Square stand three crosses, with rotting corpses nailed to them. Some wag has scrawled INRI on the central spar of the middle crucifix. The victims hang there staring at the Houses of Parliament which now sport a huge red circle painted across the stonework.

The wrought iron fence that encloses the Big Ben end of the building has had gibbets attached to the stone corner posts. Only one is currently occupied, by what looks like a young girl. She is curled into a ball, naked and frozen. There are five heads stuck on to spikes along the length of the fence.

A bullet pings off the tarmac at my feet and I hear a high pitched laugh.

"You only get on warning shot, darling," shouts the gunman who's just appeared in the nearest watchtower. "And that's just coz you're pretty. Normally I just shoot people dead. Saving bullets, you see. Every slug gotta kill. Waste not, want not and all that."

"I want to talk to your boss," I shout back.

"You want to die?"

"My name," I yell, "is Doctor Kate Booker." That name feels strange in my mouth again after so long. "I know Spider from before The Cull. Tell him I'd like a word."

I look down at the red dot that's dancing around my sternum. "Trust me, he'll see me."

The laser sight disappears and I stand there waiting for fifteen minutes or so. Eventually, the large metal gate swings open and the man from the gun tower stands there, waving for me to approach.

I walk over to him slowly, full of confidence. I feel totally calm, but I know the nerves are going to hit soon and I'm trying to be ready for that.

"Follow me," he says, and he leads me across the lawn and into a cavernous hall, its walls made of huge blocks of stone and its massive wooden ceiling so big that it bleeds into shadow. Our footsteps echo as we cross the immense floor, passing plaques that tell us this is where Winston Churchill lay in state, and there is where William Wallace was condemned to death.

We ascend a wide stone staircase then turn left down a long corridor lined with epic pre-Raphaelite paintings. We emerge into a huge circular chamber with an unlit chandelier hanging above us. I remember this space from television, watching MPs stand here justifying themselves to the press. Four white statues stand silent in the gloom as we turn right and walk down another long corridor to two wooden doors.

The building passes in a blur of murals, stained glass, intricate mosaics and elaborately designed floor tiles. I concentrate on putting one foot in front of the other, keeping the lid tight closed on the terror that threatens to bubble up and engulf me. This whole place seems exactly as I would have imagined it pre-Cull. There is no evidence of this being the headquarters of a cult. They've kept the place pristine.

We pass through another chamber and walk past a statue of Churchill, sticking his big round tummy out at me as if it were a challenge. Then we pass through a gothic stone arch that seems shattered and wrecked, walk through some big doors and I find myself standing at the far end of the House of Commons. A very faint hint of orange dawn light seeps through the grimy row of tiny windows that provide the only illumination. Tiers of green leather benches rise to my left and right. Serried wooden balconies loom over the room, lending it the air of an arena, which I suppose it always was.

The doors close behind me, the loud bang as they shut jolts me. I spin around but my guide has gone. I am alone.

The room is totally silent, the backbenches deep in shadow. I walk forward on the lush green carpet, towards the table over which the party leaders used to squabble. I'm sure it has some pompous name – the Debating Oak or something – but I've no idea what it is. There are ornate wooden boxes on either side of the table, and I know these are called the dispatch boxes. Or are they? Weren't they the red cases they used to carry?

Oh, who cares.

It's smaller than I imagined, functional and unimpressive but I still feel as if I've wandered on to a film set. That this room should have survived The Culling Year completely intact is hard to fathom. I know there were riots and mobs, mass burnings and massacres on the streets near here. But I suppose the security forces managed to hold the line long enough for attention to focus elsewhere. I know at least one guy who thinks the Government are still here, hiding in air tight bunkers under the ground, waiting for a cure. But the air in here is dead. This is a museum. No-one will ever argue about defence funding in here again. Thank God.

I hear a faint rustle at the end of the hall ahead of me. A rat maybe? I stare into the shadows. A shape leans forward out of the darkness and – dammit – makes me jump and give a little squeal of surprise. Like a fucking schoolgirl.

It's a figure, dressed entirely in a black robe, hood down, sitting in the tall wooden Speaker's Chair. His face is hidden in the darkness, but I know it's him.

Spider.

I stand there, paralysed.

I'd pictured myself surrounded by his loyal troops, pulling out my gun and shooting him, then being instantly cut down, dying there but not minding.

Or I'd pictured myself being frisked at the gate, handcuffed, brought before him on my knees, forced to beg for mercy. But making my pitch well, securing a position as his official doctor, working my way into his trust and then striking the first time he dropped his guard, just a little.

Or I'd pictured myself held down as he raped me then slit my throat.

But this. Alone. Unwatched. Armed.

I reach down and pull out my gun, aiming it straight at the black space where I know his head is.

Neither of us speaks for a long moment.

But he doesn't move. Doesn't ring an alarm or shout for help. Doesn't raise a gun in my direction.

Instead, he laughs. Softly, genuinely. Then he leans back into the shadows, resting his head against the padded chair, waiting for me to make my move.

I step sideways, edging my way towards the gap between the table and the front bench.

"Remember me?" I say. I want to scream in his face, but there's no need to shout. Every whisper carries crystal clear.

No response. I reach the corner of the table and begin walking towards him, gun still aimed true.

"Remember Manchester?" Halfway, now. The outlines of his cloak emerging as I approach and the sunlight strengthens from above.

"Remember my brother?" And, oh yes, I yelled that. And here comes the anger and the terror and the nerves. My stomach floods with acid, my veins race with adrenalin. My hands shake with the force of it.

But I keep walking.

There's a step at the end, just in front of the chair, and I mount it, shoving the gun under the fold of his hood into the black space.

And there I stand, unsure what to do. He's just sitting there, waiting for death. Where's the catch? What does he know that I don't?

I stand there for nearly a minute, the only sound is our breathing – mine hard and ragged, his soft and calm.

Then he murmurs: "I remember, Kate. I remember it all."

That voice. I feel faint at the sound of it. My arm drops for an instant as I go weak. My knees try to buckle, but I force them to lock again. Raise the gun level.

Then he slowly lifts up his hood and pulls it back, revealing his face.

And suddenly it's eight years ago, I'm a completely different person, and the Chianti is warm on the back of my throat.

PART TWO

Kate gently lowered herself into the hot water, letting her skin adjust to the heat in tiny increments, her lips pursed with the pleasure of pain.

When she was fully submerged, only her head poking up through the bubbles, she lay there for minute or two with her eyes closed and focused on her breathing. She took long, slow, deep breaths and pictured the cares and stresses of her day dissolving out of her into the bathwater. Then, her heart rate slow, her head clear, she stretched out a languid hand for the glass of red wine perched on the windowsill above her. She took a sip and moaned softly in blissful contentment.

It had been an awful, wonderful day. Her first shift at A&E. She'd trained for years in preparation, and had some training yet to complete. But all that study, that sacrifice, the sleepless nights and double shifts, the practical exams and psychological probes, the stuck up consultants, insolent orderlies and endless, endless paperwork, had led her to this day; an afternoon spent dressing a huge abscess on the back of a homeless alcoholic who smelt like he slept in a supermarket skip full of rotting meat.

She was going to have to scrub herself raw to get the stench out. The smoke from her joss stick merged with the steam from the bath. It smelt the way she imagined a hookah pipe would, and it made her feel exotic and elsewhere. Plus, it masked the rank odour that still haunted her nostrils.

The flat was silent. The students upstairs, for all their exuberance, rarely partied until 4am. They were asleep, as was her flat mate Jill; a plain, bookish girl who kept herself to herself, liked early nights and slept with earplugs in. Kate liked being awake when everyone else was asleep. It made her feel secure, confident that no-one was watching or expecting anything of her.

The world was asleep, and Kate felt free as a bird.

When she heard the gentle knock at the front door, she initially thought she must be imagining it. But no, there it was again, louder this time. Her hard-won calm evaporated, but she decided to ignore the intrusive noise. It was probably just some pissed up student who'd got the wrong flat. Just ignore it, she told herself. They'll go away.

The knocking got louder and more insistent. Kate muttered: "La, la, la can't hear you." Then she heard the rattle of the letterbox and her name being whispered through it.

"Kit," said the voice. "Kit, I know you're in there. Open up."

Kate sighed. "For fuck's sake," she cursed under her breath as she lifted herself out of the foam. "What now?" She towelled herself down and pulled on her bathrobe, the moth eaten old silk one with the holes in it, and went to let in her brother, James.

"What bloody time do you..." Her half-angry diatribe died in her throat as she pulled the front door open and saw the woman.

"Thank God," said James. "Help me get her inside."

Kate's brother was not tall – about five foot seven – and the woman dwarfed him. He stood in the cold hallway, holding her up. Her head lolled on his shoulder and her feet dragged across the threshold as he and Kate manhandled the unconscious woman into the flat. James kicked the door closed behind him.

"Bedroom," said Kate.

They gently lowered the unconscious woman onto Kate's bed. Just for a moment, Kate hesitated. She looked at the woman's face in the light and was suddenly taken aback. Despite her height, this was the face of a child. Kate mentally re-categorised her – this wasn't a woman, not quite yet. If she was eighteen, it was only barely. This was a girl; a girl wearing white stilettos, stockings and suspenders, a red basque torn open to reveal her left breast, and nothing else. She had been severely beaten. Her hair was long and blonde, her cheekbones high and her lips full. Kate thought she looked Eastern European.

Her training kicked in. "Call 999," she said as she lifted the girl's eyelids and shone the bedside lamp into them, checking pupil dilation.

"I can't, Sis," said James, who fidgeted nervously at the end of the bed.

"Fine, then I will." Kate lifted the handset from its cradle on her bedside cabinet, but James scurried across and made to grab it from her before she could dial. They struggled for a moment before Kate let the phone go and returned to the girl.

"James, this girl needs a hospital," said Kate. "What the hell is going on here? Who is she?"

James was hovering at her shoulder, putting her off.

"For God's sake, sit down and tell me what's going on," she barked as she took the girl's pulse.

He lingered for a moment then went to sit at the foot of the bed, wringing his hands anxiously.

"I'm in trouble, Sis. Really bad."

"Save it," snapped Kate." The girl." Check skull for evidence of blunt trauma.

"Her name's Lyudmila. She's a prostitute. Kind of."

"Not your type though." Examine limbs and ribs for signs of breakage.

"She's from where I work."

"You're a student. You don't work, you scrounge."

He didn't say anything more except: "Is she going to be okay?"

Kate focused on her patient. When she'd assured herself that the girl was in no immediate danger, she pulled the quilt over her and left her to sleep it off.

She grabbed a pair of jeans and a t-shirt, ushered James out while she dressed, then joined him in the living room. He was boiling the kettle in the kitchenette. She nipped into the bathroom, collected her wine, then returned to the cracked leather sofa, tucked her legs underneath herself and said: "Get your tea. Sit down. Start at the beginning."

James plonked himself down at the other end of the small sofa, cradling the mug and biting his lip. Kate had seen her brother up against it more than once – the time he'd been attacked on the street by gay bashers; the day he was expelled from school – but this twitchy nervous wreck was barely recognisable as her flamboyant, devil-may-care, overconfident younger sibling. As he opened his mouth to speak she had an inkling that everything in her life was about to change. She felt a rush of butterflies in her stomach.

But before James could begin, there was another, louder knock at the door.

"Oh fuck," he whispered. His face went even paler, his eyes widened with fear and he stared at Kate like he'd just seen a ghost.

"Who is it?" she asked, but he wasn't listening.

"They must have followed me. Oh fuck oh fuck oh fuck." He leaned across and grabbed her wrist. "Don't open it. Just stay quiet, maybe they'll go away."

The knocking came again, louder this time.

"James, it's 4am and the lights are on. They know we're here. Who is it?"

"They're looking for her."

"Why? What are they going to..."

There was a sudden loud crash from the front door, which rattled on its hinges.

"Fuck!" Cried Kate, suddenly, finally, scared.

There was another crash and this time she could hear the wooden door frame begin to splinter.

The door to the second bedroom opened and Jill stood there in her sensible flannelette pjs, rubbing her eyes and digging in her right ear for her earplug.

"What the bloody hell's going on?" she asked sleepily.

Kate leapt up and reached for the phone. "Sod this," she said. "I'm calling the police."

"No, Kate, please," shouted James as he rose to his feet.

Another crash from the door. This time it flew open with a huge crack of shattering wood. All three of them turned to see an enormous man framed in the doorway.

With a square head and haircut to match, the man's shoulders were so wide he had to turn a little bit sideways and stoop to fit through the doorway. His suit was large and baggy, more like a tent, and he lumbered into the room, his eyes narrowed and threatening.

James stepped forward, putting himself in front of Kate and Jill. He hunched his shoulders like a dog that's about to be told off by a pack leader, lowered his head, held out his hands in supplication, and started to beg.

"Petar, mate, I'm sorry. I didn't know what else to do. Nate was out of it and Lyudmila needed help, y'know. At least I didn't go to a hospital, right? Right? I mean, I did good not to go..."

The man raised a huge, ugly paw and backslapped James across the face with such force that he flew sideways, crashing into the sideboard and collapsing to the floor in a dazed heap, the silhouette of the man's hand etched onto his face in livid red.

"Hey," shouted Kate, stepping forward and jutting out her chin defiantly. "You leave my brother alone."

He raised his other hand and gave her the same treatment. It felt like being hit in the face with a girder. It lifted her off her feet and sent her sprawling into the kitchenette, scrabbling for purchase on the lino.

It was the first time in her life that anyone had ever hit her. She sat there, stunned, so surprised and shocked that she had no idea how to react. Out of the corner of her eye she registered Jill stepping backwards into her room and closing the door. The giant ignored her, instead opening the door to Kate's room where the injured girl was still in the bed.

He looked inside, assured himself that she was in there, then turned and walked out. She heard him bark a terse order in a language she did not recognise, and then three men entered the flat. They wore similar suits to the giant, and their faces were hard and cruel, but that wasn't what made Kate cry out in fear.

All three of them were carrying guns.

Kate had never seen a gun before. Not a real one, not up close and personal. She'd seen them on telly, of course, and in news reports about gang violence. She'd been trained what to do if a gun was pulled in the hospital, but there was no panic button here, and no guaranteed minimum response time.

The sight of the small, black, stubby metal objects paralysed her. She knew exactly the damage a bullet could do. Her mind was suddenly filled with images of herself lying on the floor, bleeding out from ruptured arteries, lungs filling with blood, choking on her own fluids, twitching and convulsing as she voided her bowels, wet herself and lost control of her body, dying on a black and white lino floor in a pokey flat with the smell of a tramp in her cooling nostrils.

What the bloody hell had James got her mixed up in?

She instinctively crawled backwards into the corner, as if cramming herself between the MDF cabinets would help. One of the men went into her bedroom, another grabbed James and dragged him to his feet, the third came for her. By the time he reached down to take her arm, Kate was hysterical. She began kicking and screaming, flailing around with her fists and shaking her head wildly. She didn't see what hit her across the temple, but if she'd been able to think about it, she'd have realised it was the handle of the gun. Her head swam, her vision sparkled, she went limp with the sound of James's protests ringing in her ears.

She didn't entirely pass out, though. She remained vaguely aware as the man grabbed her wrists, spun her around and pulled her out of the flat by her ankles. Her head bounced off the doorframe with a horrible thud, scraping the back of her scalp so it bled through her hair; it was thickly matted with blood by the time they reached the lift.

She was thrown into the lift like a sack of rubbish and ended up in a foetal heap in the corner. As the doors slid shut, she finally blacked out.

In years to come, Kate would grow accustomed to waking from unconsciousness. The sharp pain in her head that revealed the site of the blow; the dry, metallic taste in her mouth; the shock of bright light; the fear that maybe this time some permanent damage had been done. The most important lesson she learnt, though, was not to panic. To take a moment to assess the damage, establish her capabilities.

The first time she awoke from such an ordeal, she didn't have this experience to draw on, so she sat bolt upright and looked left and right quickly, terrified. The sudden movement caused a spike of agony in her head, her vision blurred, and she slumped back down onto what she realised was a red leather sofa, groaning as the room span around her. She clutched her hands to her head as if that would stop the wild rotation of the room and make the pain go away. It didn't.

"Here, take these," said a voice above her. She squinted up and saw a man looking down at her. He had a glass of water in one hand and a packet of Nurofen in the other.

Slowly, she sat up and reached out for the medicine, gulping them down hungrily, and draining the glass of water. As she handed back the glass she instinctively opened her mouth to thank the man, but then realised her mistake.

"You're welcome," he said softly, with a smile. She registered an accent, but couldn't place it. Russian, maybe?

Kate wanted to run, to scream, to try and escape, but she

guessed she wouldn't get five metres. She leaned back into the comfy sofa and took in her surroundings.

The lighting was low and red. She was in a large room, a hall of some kind. No windows, so possibly a cellar. There were sofas and armchairs dotted around on the thick carpet, arranged in horseshoes with glass tables at their focal points. At the far end was a bar and on either side were raised platforms with metal poles that ran to the ceiling. She was in a strip club. An upmarket one, but not one of the majors. Probably central London. Even through the headache she knew what that implied about the management.

There was one more detail, too – handcuffed to the stripper's poles, sitting on the floor with their hands behind their backs, were James and Lyudmila. The girl was out for the count, but James was conscious. She couldn't be sure in the half-light, but Kate thought he'd been beaten up.

The man in front of her sat down in an armchair. He placed his arms on the armrests very deliberately, as if arranging himself like a work of art ready for display. His movements were precise and considered, but Kate did not think it was vanity. She got a sense that he was so full of anger or violence that even the simple act of sitting in a chair required titanic effort and conscious control.

This man immediately scared her more than anything else that had happened on this bizarre, awful night.

She forced herself to meet his gaze, but his eyes were lost in shadow. He was middle-aged, maybe in his forties. Short hair topped a high forehead above a long, straight nose and sensuous, amused lips. He was not overweight nor musclebound and he wore an expensive, well-tailored suit. He should have been attractive, but there was something cruel about that smile, and his body language screamed danger.

"What is your name?" he asked softly.

"Kate."

"Hello Kate. People call me Spider."

Of course they do, thought Kate. Can't have a criminal mastermind with a name like Steve or Keith. She almost voiced her sarcastic thought, but didn't, possibly because she was surprised to find herself capable of levity. She wondered if maybe she had a concussion, and then mentally chided herself;

of course she had a bloody concussion.

"Interesting name," she said. "Where's it from?"

His smile widened. "I am from Serbia."

"Oh."

"Have you ever been?"

Kate shook her head.

"It is the most beautiful country on Earth." He paused and Kate felt herself being appraised. "Maybe one day I will take you."

The way he said it left Kate in no doubt that the double meaning had been intentional. There was a long silence. No sound penetrated this room from outside. All she could hear was her own breathing and the soft hum of the ancient aircon.

"What do you do, Kate. I mean, for a living?"

"I'm a student doctor. You?"

"Oh, I do many things. Many things."

"Is this your club?"

He nodded. "And let me say, Kate, that if you ever tire of the medical profession, I am sure we could find a place for you here."

"If Lyudmila's an example of how you treat your staff, I think I'll pass."

"Lyudmila broke the terms of her contract."

"How?"

"She spat."

It took Kate a moment to work out what he meant, but when she did she felt sick to her stomach.

Spider leaned forward, gently intertwining his fingers and placing them on his knees.

"How do you know her?" he asked.

"I don't."

Spider looked puzzled and then surprised. He swore in Serbian and despite the language barrier Kate could tell he was amazed.

"You mean James brought her to you on his own?" he asked, openly astonished.

Kate didn't know what to do. If she said yes, would that make things better or worse? Eventually she nodded.

Spider turned to look at her brother and shouted. "Have you found a spine, Booker? I did not think you ever would."

"She... she was hurt, boss," wheedled James. "And Nate..."

"That useless junkie is gone. He works for the Albanians now."

"I know that, boss. But she was hurt, she needed to be looked after. I didn't know what else to do."

"So you took her to this girl?"

"Yes."

"And how..." Spider broke off and looked sharply back at Kate, then back at James. "Ha! She is your sister. You took Lyudmila to see your sister the doctor."

James hung his head in shame and then gave one short nod.

"Sorry, Sis," he said softly.

Spider turned back to Kate and leaned back in his chair again, once more placing his arms just so.

"I apologise for the way you were treated, Kate. I can see that this situation is not your fault."

"But?"

"But I hope you see that I am now in a very difficult position. The business I run is not, entirely, legitimate. There are people who would like to see me locked up. You have seen my face. You know my name. You can identify some of the men who work for me. You are a problem. I think it would be sensible for me to kill you."

"No! Boss, please!" yelled James.

As Spider rose from his chair, his precise movements made him seem almost robotic. He turned and walked over to James, who cowered on the floor. Spider stood above him on the stage and lashed out with his foot, kicking James hard in the face. It was a sudden, shocking action, an explosion of pent up rage. For an instant Spider's limbs were flexible, his neck was loose, his body fluent and fluid. Then, when the blow had been struck, he stood stock still and kind of settled, his body returning to repose, an act of conscious thought, re-imposing order on the chaos he worked so hard to contain within himself. His momentary loss of complete precision seemed almost not to have happened.

He spun on his heels, walked back to Kate, and resumed his seat.

Kate could hear her brother sobbing quietly.

She surprised herself by thinking how much she would like to kill this man.

"Who..." Kate's mouth was too dry to form words. She rubbed the sides of her tongue across her teeth to force some saliva into her mouth, then sluiced the tiny amount of liquid to the back of her throat, swallowing. "Who was Nate?"

Spider's eyes narrowed, calculating. "He was my doctor."

Even though she'd known what he was going to say, the fact of it chilled Kate to the core. This man needed a doctor on call all the time. Dear God, how many women... how many beatings?

"And he's gone now?" she asked.

Spider nodded.

"Then maybe I can help you. Take his place."

There was a long silence. When Kate had woken up this morning she'd known this would be a life-changing day. But not in her wildest dreams had she envisaged sitting in a strip club at the crack of dawn as a Serbian gangster considered whether to kill her or welcome her to a life of crime.

Spider rose again and walked over to Lyudmila. He stood over the unconscious girl, his back to Kate, for a long moment. He stood so still that you could have mistaken him for a shop window dummy. Then he reached into his jacket and withdrew something that Kate couldn't see.

The shot was deafeningly loud, totally unexpected. Kate screamed in spite of herself. Lyudmila jerked once, but other than that you'd never know that a small piece of metal had just evacuated her head. James cried out, a howl of horror and shame. Spider turned and walked over to him. His body language had changed again. Now he moved like a hunter, loose limbed and balletic.

Kate didn't have the luxury of going into shock. She leapt up from the sofa and ran over to them. Spider still had his gun in his hand, and he aimed casually at James's head. Kate flung herself between the gun and her brother.

She opened her mouth to speak, to beg for her life and James's. But she looked into Spider's eyes, able to see them properly, up close, for the first time. She instantly realised that it would be hopeless. There was neither pity nor humanity in those eyes. They were the cold, dead orbs of a predator, nothing more.

As she realised there was nothing she could do, Kate felt something inside her change. For the first time, she understood that her life lay entirely in the hands of another person, who would end it or not according to his whim. She was no longer in control of her own fate. Her life as she had known it was over.

This realisation lent her a sudden, deep calm.

She looked into those eyes. She did not beg, or plead or cry. She did not try to strike a bargain or make a threat. She did not try to seduce him or attack him. All of those things would have resulted, she knew with absolute certainty, in instant death.

She just said one word, calmly, simply and without emotion. "Please."

The barrista scooped the soy milk froth over the coffee with a long spoon, put a heart shaped flourish in the pattern then sprinkled it with chocolate.

"Two ninety-five," she said, her Polish accent impossible to miss.

Kate paid. She smiled at the young woman, lifted the two mugs and a small packet of biscuits, then walked back to the table in the corner where her broken brother sat hunched and sniffling. She placed the mug of coffee in front of him and took her seat, facing him across the small round table. Over his shoulder she could see people hurrying to and fro down Villiers Street, popping into Accessorize or Pret, enjoying the bustle and business of their daily lives. She envied their ignorance and felt as if she no longer lived entirely in their world.

Her hands were steady as she lifted the coffee mug to her lips. She was surprised by this, but reasoned that she would probably go into shock in an hour or so, when the adrenalin finally wore off. For now, she felt focused, purposeful yet slightly spaced out, as if she had just begun the long build up to a skull shattering migraine.

James, she could see, was already in shock. She'd been trained to deal with people brought into A&E like this; taught how to treat them while eliciting their story, gathering information to help with diagnosis.

"Start at the beginning," she said, more harshly than she'd intended. It seemed that when it came to her brother, her training didn't help

James sniffed, wiped his nose on his sleeve and took a sip of coffee. He looked up at her and she winced again at the marks on his face. His left eye was swollen shut, his jaw bulged and bruised, and his front left canine was a gaping, bloody hole. Say what you like about his personality, James had at least always been pretty. He'd always jokingly referred to himself as the lipstick half of any relationship. Certainly his boyfriends had always tended to be square-jawed gym bunnies. Kate suspected his pretty-boy days were over.

"I got into trouble about six months ago," he said, but then he ground to a halt, staring at the table top.

"James." He did not respond. "For god's sake James, snap out of it. I need to know what you've got me into and I need to know now. Just take it slowly and tell me the whole story from the start."

James reached across and placed his hand on hers, squeezing it tightly and taking a few deep breaths to calm himself. Then he looked up and smiled weakly.

"Okay. But if you tell Gran about this, I'll tell her what you did with Bobby Arnold on your fifteenth birthday."

"You bitch, you wouldn't dare!"

"Try me, toots."

They both laughed, but not for long. James opened the small packet of biscuits and offered one to her. She took one as he dunked his in his coffee.

"I dunno why you do that," she said, screwing up her face in distaste.

"What?"

"Dunking. All you end up with is soggy biscuit mush at the bottom of your coffee. It's gross."

He didn't respond and it soon became apparent that their reservoir of small talk was empty.

"I got in trouble, Sis. Big trouble. About six months ago. It was Phil. You remember Phil?"

Kate remembered Phil, all right. She'd known he was trouble the first time he turned up at the pub that Sunday night. Tall, muscled and totally in love with his own reflection, he was boorish, brash and bullying. James couldn't look at him without doing simpering puppy eyes. Kate thought that was the attraction – Phil had finally found the only person in the world who adored him almost as much as he adored himself. He didn't exactly treat James like shit, he didn't need to. It would have been redundant.

James practically lay down on the ground and begged Phil to walk all over him.

Kate loved her brother, but Jesus, his taste in men was worse than hers. Nonetheless, she couldn't work out how Phil would have led her brother to Serbian strippers.

"What, he dragged you to lap dancing clubs?" she asked, incredulously.

"No, don't be daft. Phil's problem was gambling. Spider doesn't just run that strip joint. He's got a casino, super illegal, in one of the arches underneath Waterloo station. High stakes, no IOUs. You know Phil worked for that big accountancy firm, right? Well his boss took him there one night after work. He'd never have been able to get in there on his own, but once he'd been vouched for, he started going there on his own. A lot. One night he took me along. It was fun, you know? He hit a winning streak and we walked out three grand richer."

"Oh James, tell me you didn't go back on your own?"

"I figured, you know, if Phil could do it..."

"You fucking muppet." Kate shook her head in wonder. "Every time I think you can't get any stupider, you lower the bar."

James stared at the table top again. "Yeah, that's right Kit, let's have another round of 'my little brother, the big gay loser'. That's exactly what we need right now. So fucking helpful." He made to stand.

"Oh sit down," she said wearily. "Fucking drama queen."

He planted his arse on the seat again, sullen and pouting.

"How much do you owe?"

"A lot."

"How much, James?"

"Twenty-three grand."

"Holy fucking Christ."

"I know, all right. I know. About four months back they grabbed me as I was leaving and took me back to see the boss. I swear, Sis, I thought he was going to shoot me there and then. I... I kind of begged."

"And he offered you a chance to work off the debt, yeah?"

James nodded. "He's into some seriously bad shit."

"No, really?" said Kate, finally starting to feel her cool slipping away. "The guy who just beat us up and shot a girl in the head for no reason at all? You think?"

"He's got the casino and the strip club, but there's more. Lots more."

"Like what?"

"Brothels. Well, not really brothels. More like, dungeons, really."

"What, for S&M?"

"No. Literally prisons where he keeps these girls locked up. They're all underground; railway arches, old sub-basements, places like that. There are about six or seven of them that I've been to and I know there are more. The high rollers at the casino, and the guys at the strip club who want to spend a little more cash when the doors close, this is where they go."

Kate felt bile rising in her throat.

"You've been there?"

"That's my job. I have to look after some of the girls. Bring them food and stuff. Keep them alive."

"Lyudmila?"

James nodded. "She was new. Arrived last week. These girls, right, they think they're going to get jobs here. There's a whole chain designed to get them to the UK. Guys who go around the villages in the Ukraine and Latvia, Siberia and places like that looking for teenagers. And I mean thirteen up, right? They say they're recruiting for cleaning jobs and hotel waitresses, that kind of thing. The girls pay a fee, or their parents do, and they're shipped over here and then they just... disappear."

"These dungeons..."

"It's not just sex, Sis. And it's not exclusively teenagers. There are young kids, too. And murder rooms. And then..."

Kate had heard enough. "Okay, okay. Shut up. Let me think."

"There was this guy, Nate. He did all the doctoring for them. But he was a junkie and he wasn't reliable, so last week Spider threw him out. Sold him to another gang, like. When Lyudmila got roughed up, I didn't know what to do with Nate gone. I'm so sorry for getting you involved in this, Sis. Really."

"I said enough," Kate snapped. "I need to think. Figure out the angles."

"There aren't any, Kit. This guy, he's smart and ruthless and he's got a fucking army working for him. He even gets a whiff of betrayal and we're dead. Both of us. Just like that. No warning, no second chances. And that's if he's feeling generous. Coz if he's not, we'll end up in one of those dungeons, Sis. And no-one – no-one! – gets out of them alive."

"There's always an angle, James. Always," replied Kate. But she wasn't sure if she believed it, not in this case. The only thing she knew for certain was that her stupid, self-destructive, funny little brother, who she loved more than anything in the world in spite of his manifest flaws, was in trouble and, like she had done all his life, she was going to have to rescue him from himself.

"Get me another coffee, eh. And a chocolate muffin." Kate handed James a tenner and sat staring out of the window as he went to the bar. It took a minute or two for her to realise that she was being watched by the man sitting at the window in Prêt directly opposite. When their eyes met he smiled and nodded slightly, then finished his coffee, left the shop and walked away.

"Oh James," she whispered. "What have you done?"

The next few days passed in a blur of A&E shifts and deep, dreamless sleep. Spider had said he would call when he needed her, but her phone didn't ring.

Jill moved out of the flat without warning two days after the invasion. Kate came home from a long shift and found the flat half empty. No note, nothing. Bitch hadn't even left the rent. So Kate dug out the most recent itemised phone bill and called every number she didn't recognise until she reached Jill's Dad, who was not amused to hear of his daughter's midnight flit. He promised Kate that his little girl would be at her door in an hour with the rent in full. She was too, sullen and angry and refusing to speak. She held out an envelope full of cash and the second Kate took it she turned on her heels and stalked away.

"Don't be a stranger," Kate yelled at her retreating back, laughing.

She didn't see the man who had been watching her, but she was constantly on the lookout for him. She was convinced she'd be seeing him again.

After a week she almost convinced herself it had never happened; that it was business as usual, that she hadn't been beyond the looking glass and seen a girl murdered. But then on

Friday, as she sat in her track pants and t-shirt eating Pot Noodle on the sofa, watching *Loose Women* on her day off, there was a sharp knock at the door. She considered not answering, but whoever it was would be able to hear her telly.

The giant stood in the hallway, waiting patiently.

"Boss says you got to come."

"Okay, give me a minute to..."

He reached in and grabbed her wrist.

"Now."

"Okay, Jesus, can I at least get my coat?"

But he was pulling her across the threshold. She tried to grab her keys from the hook on the coat rack before the door closed behind her, but he pulled her too firmly and the door swung shut.

"Fuck, how am I supposed to get back in without my keys, dispshit?" she yelled as he dragged her towards the lift. He stopped dead, turned and looked down at her. He didn't say a word, just stared until she said: "Okay, lead on." He turned again and started walking. Outside the air was chilled and Kate felt goosebumps rising on her bare arms as she was bundled into the back seat of a waiting car with tinted windows.

"Look at the floor," said the giant as they pulled away. Kate did so without question.

They drove for about forty-five minutes. When they pulled up the giant reached across and snapped a sleep mask across her face so she couldn't see a thing. Then she was shoved outside and led across what felt like a cobbled street and into a cold, damp space that she was willing to bet was a railway arch. She was led down steps into a narrow space with dead acoustics and dust in the air. Down a corridor, then left and right and left again, and more steps.

"Mind head," said the giant a moment after she scraped the top of her head on what felt like soft brick. She stooped as she was led down a narrow stone staircase. By now, she knew she was deep underground. Another corridor, still stooping. She felt, then heard a gentle rumble somewhere off to her left. It took a moment to realise it must be a tube train.

Kate heard a key turn in a lock followed by the squeal of old hinges, then she was shoved through a doorway and her sleep mask was ripped off.

She was in a brick-lined cellar, barrel vaulted. Narrow but long, it stretched away, its vanishing point lost in darkness. There was a pervasive smell of damp and a distant sound of running water. An oil heater blazed away by the door, so at least it wasn't cold, but in every other respect it was probably the least healthy place in London. Trying not to think about the horrors of Weil's disease or the agony of hypersensitivity pneumonitis, Kate noted the bed, table and wind up lamp, the bucket in the corner with a tea towel draped over it and, finally, the girl sitting on the chair, dead eyed and listless, sallow cheeked and pale.

Kate turned to the giant, who was bent almost double in the corridor outside.

"People pay to come down here?" she asked, incredulous.

"No," he replied. "She come up for work. Stay here rest of time."

"Okay, well that's got to change. You need to get her out of here now."

"You stop her coughing."

"I can't. Not if she stays down here."

"You stop."

"I told you, I can't. Even if I can alleviate her symptoms, they'll come back if she stays down here."

The giant considered this. "Stop cough. Only need to stop coughing for afternoon. After that..." He shrugged.

Kate sighed. "Okay, I'll need prednisone." The giant looked confused. "Give me a pen, I'll write it down."

He handed her a biro and a receipt. She briefly considered ramming the pen into his throat and trying to make an escape, but dismissed the idea as ludicrous. She scribbled the name of the drug and handed him the piece of paper.

"I come back in hour." He slammed the door closed. Kate was imprisoned.

She stood there for a moment, then the girl on the chair burst into a fit of awful, hoarse coughing that went on for over five minutes. Kate held her shoulders as the spasms wracked her. There were flecks of blood on the girl's lips when she finally finished. Her breathing was ragged and rasping.

"What's your name?" asked Kate.

The girl stared at her, uncomprehending.

"Do you speak English?"

No response. Kate pointed at her chest and said "Kate" then pointed to the girl, who just stared back at her as if she were mad.

"I feel like I'm in a bad Western," muttered Kate. Another ten minutes of trying failed to illicit any response. The girl was in deep shock, nearly comatose. There was no reaching her. Kate explored the depths of the tunnel, but found only rubble and rats. In the end there was nothing to do but wait for the giant to return. The girl had moved to the bed when Kate walked back from the far end of the tunnel. Kate sat next to her and put her arms around her bony shoulders. They sat there like that for a few minutes, then the girl rested her head on Kate's shoulder until she fell asleep and slumped into her lap. Kate sat there, with the head of this sick, lost, broken, doomed girl nestled in her lap. She stroked her lank, greasy hair and cried.

As much as she had been forced to confront brutal reality on the night she met Spider, it was during that long hour in that awful place that Kate changed forever. Parts of her psyche scabbed over and hardened, unexpected resolve made itself known, and the well of her compassion was exposed as deeper than she had ever imagined.

When the giant opened the door and handed her the drugs, it was a different woman who took them from him. Harder, colder, angrier and less afraid.

Kate administered the drugs and told the giant that she had done all she could. The sleep mask was replaced, and she was led away from a girl she was sure would be dead by nightfall.

A tiny part of Kate remained behind in that cellar. The tiny piece of Jane that had been born there left in its stead.

She was driven back to her flat, back to the world she knew. But it felt different. Distant. Changed forever. She walked up to her front door and reached into her pocket for her keys.

"Oh fuck it," she cursed, remembering that she had not had time to grab them. She stood and stared at the door and then stepped back and took a running kick at it. She felt the wood give and heard the sharp crack as it splintered. She kicked it again, and again, then shoulder charged it, yelling as she did so, smashing into the door time after time, hating it, wanting to annihilate it utterly, as if it was mocking her. The facia caved and split before, after one almighty crash, it flew of its top hinge and collapsed inwards.

Kate stood there, breathing hard, teeth clenched, eyes wide, her heart pounding, ignoring the pain in her shoulders and legs. She heard a slight cough to her left and turned to see the old biddy from flat four peering anxiously out of her door.

"What?" snapped Kate. The woman's head disappeared inside and the door was firmly closed.

"Didn't you just pay a lot of money to have that door fixed, Miss Booker?" said a soft voice to her right. She spun, suddenly alarmed. But whereas a week ago she might have given a tiny yelp of surprise and felt a jolt of nerves, now she didn't make a sound and stood ready to fight.

The man from the coffee shop stood there in the corridor. Short for a man, about the same height as Kate, he wore a black leather jacket, white shirt and blue jeans above waxed black Docs. He looked about forty, blonde hair slightly receding but not too much, with laugh lines around his mouth, and deep crow's feet framing his blue eyes. Kate's first thought was 'he fancies himself'.

"And who the fuck are you?" she snarled.

He reached into his jacket and pulled out a small leather wallet which he flipped open and held up for her to inspect.

"DI John Cooper. Metropolitan Police. Can we go inside and talk? That is, if we can get the door to close behind us."

He helped her prop the door back up in its frame and shoved a dining chair up against it to keep it in place, then sat on the sofa as she made him a cuppa.

Her mind was racing as she fumbled with mugs and teabags. She'd been considering going to the police, obviously, but Spider had been clear that James would die very slowly indeed if she did so. He had sources within the police, he said, and he'd know the instant she broke ranks. She had looked at her brother's pitiful, tear-stained face as he crouched on that stage, handcuffed to the stripper's pole, and she'd known that she had no choice. This organisation was big and complicated; there was every chance that Spider was telling the truth, that he did have some bent copper on the take. No, she'd decided that if there was a way out of her situation, she'd have to find it herself.

Nonetheless, she slowed her step ever so slightly every time she passed a Police Station, and felt a jolt of butterflies at the thought of stepping across the threshold and spilling her guts, of sharing the problem, making it someone else's.

The man on her sofa made her almost as nervous as Spider had. Her first thought was that she had made some stupid rookie mistake, given the game away without meaning too, drawn needless attention somehow. Her second thought was that he could be Spider's enforcer, sent here to warn her to keep her mouth shut.

She wasn't sure which outcome would scare her the most.

She took the two mugs through to the living room, handed one to Cooper and sat in the armchair opposite him, sipping her own. She couldn't think of anything to say, so she sat there as he studied her, waiting for him to make the first move.

"Is that brick dust in your hair? Been on a building site?" he asked, not unkindly. His accent was hard to place. He didn't have the Southern glottal stop or the rounded vowels of the North. He spoke precisely, his words chosen with care and delivered in RP, as if maybe he'd attended a posh school as a boy but had then had the edges knocked off his cut glass vowels by years living below his station.

Kate didn't reply, but she gripped her mug with tight, white knuckles.

"And you've got mould or something very like it smeared down the arm of your sweater." He cocked his head to one side and bit his lip thoughtfully. "Underground then. Maybe a railway arch or a cellar. Somewhere old, wet and crumbly, that's for sure. You smell a bit damp, if you don't mind me saying."

Still Kate did not say a thing, unsure where he was going with this.

"Could you lead me there, or did they blindfold you?" he asked.

The question was so bluntly put that Kate answered it almost in spite of herself. It seemed he already knew everything anyway.

"Blindfold," she said, her mouth dry. She took another sip of tea.

He nodded. This was the answer he'd been expecting. He considered her carefully for a moment and seemed to come to a decision.

"You are in very deep shit, Miss Booker. These are bad, bad men your brother's got himself, and now you, involved with. I take it you know the basics of their operation?"

Kate nodded once. She thought her face must be as white as a ghost's.

"Then you know that they eat people like you up for breakfast. You'll work for them as long as you are useful, but the first time you make a mistake, or they get suspicious of you in any way, or they just decide that they want someone fresh for their evening's entertainment, you will disappear as completely as if you had never existed."

"Why..." Her mouth was dry again. She took another sip of tea. "Why don't you just arrest them then? Isn't that your job?"

"It's not that simple. This gang doesn't exist in isolation. There's a chain stretching right across Europe. This is a huge operation, involving the police of twelve countries, many of which have police forces that see bribes as a normal part of their pay packet. Plus..." He hesitated.

"Plus?"

"Plus, there's someone in our own force looking out for them. I think. Perhaps. I can't prove it." He looked up at her, momentarily suspicious, as if asking himself why he was telling her all this.

"That's why I've approached you like this, at home. Anyway," he continued. "Recently we had a bit of a setback. Our... channel of information dried up."

"Nate, yeah? The doctor?"

Cooper looked shocked, as if he'd been caught out. Then he nodded, a little surprised she'd put a name to their mole so easily. "Loathsome little junkie, but easy to manipulate."

"Oh. I see. You want me to take his place."

Cooper sat back in his chair. "Where did they take you just now? What did you see?"

"Nothing useful. An old underground cellar. Damp, as you say. I could hear tube trains and, I think, a river nearby. But that could be anywhere in London, couldn't it?"

Cooper nodded thoughtfully. "And what did you do there?"

"Listen, my brother..."

"We know all about your brother."

"They told me they'd kill him, if I came to the police."

"Most likely. You too."

"Then what the fuck is with turning up at my front door? If anyone sees you... I mean, what kind of fucking amateur are you?"

Cooper smiled. Kate did not think it was particularly reassuring. "Spider doesn't have the resources to do keep you under surveillance. He relies on your fear to keep you in line. You were tailed when you went shopping yesterday, and they had someone in A&E two nights ago pretending to have food poisoning so they could see you at work, but they don't watch you all the time. By now they're becoming confident that you haven't gone to the police. And if you haven't gone yet, chances are you won't."

Kate sat there and suddenly felt ashamed and embarrassed. "I would have," she said. "Eventually, I would have. I've thought about it."

"But your brother."

"He's not the hardest of men. He's weak and stupid and his own worst enemy. But he's my best friend. I've had to look after him his whole life, get him out of trouble, keep him from being bullied. Jesus, the amount of times at school I had to fight his battles for him. I suppose I should have known that something like this was inevitable."

"We can keep him safe."

"Not your job, Mr Cooper. It's mine."

Cooper leaned forward in his chair, clasping his hands together and holding her gaze firmly. "If you help us, Kate, you have my word no harm will come to him."

Although this figure of authority was asking for her help, Kate felt as helpless as she ever had. If she agreed to inform for the police, she'd be placing herself and her brother in terrible danger. But if she said no... she thought of that poor girl in the cellar. Where was she now? Dolled up and drugged up, washed and brushed up and delivered to some hotel room for the pleasure of a banker or drug dealer who'd use her and then hand her back to her captors, dead or alive.

She stared deep into Cooper's eyes, seeking reassurance. He smiled at her, and she felt her resistance crumble.

"Okay, okay. What do I have to do?"

They didn't call on her for another two weeks. But this time she did not allow herself to pretend that life was normal.

At Cooper's urging, Kate signed up for self defence classes. Each day after work she would spend an hour in a draughty scout hut in Camden learning how to turn an opponent's weight against them, learning simple blocks and combos designed to prevent her from coming to harm and allow her time to run.

They didn't teach her how to collapse a windpipe with a single punch, or how to twist a neck and break it, or the places on the body where the lightest blow could cause the most damage. She was a doctor; that stuff she already knew. But knowing and doing are two different things and she knew she lacked the control to throw those kind of punches. Still, she trained and practiced and worked out. The face of the girl from the cellar hovered in front of her as she pounded the treadmill and worked the punchbag.

She would look at herself in the mirror before bed and laugh humourlessly. Who did she think she was, Rocky? She was a not very tall young woman, slight and delicate. All the training in the world wouldn't enable her to inflict so much as a single bruise on the giant. But nonetheless, she trained and practiced and focused.

If any of those bastards tried to make her the main attraction rather than the attending doctor, she'd let them know what a big mistake they'd made.

Then, one Sunday night as she sat vacantly watching some telly programme that passed through her eyeballs and out the back of her head without touching the sides, there was a knock at her yet-again rebuilt door.

Kate took a moment to slow her heartbeat and take a few deep breaths. She told herself she was in control as she rose and grabbed the bag she had left by the door especially for this occasion. One more deep breath and then she opened the door.

Her brother stood there with a bottle of wine and a box of chocolates.

"Hey, Kit," he said, bashful at disturbing her.

"Oh James, not tonight, eh. I've got an early shift tomorrow."

He shuffled his feet. "Sorry, Sis. I've got no choice."

Suddenly Kate realised that, despite appearances, this was not a social call. "Right. I'll get my coat." She turned away but he put his hand on her arm.

"We don't have to be there for an hour or so. That's why..." He held up the bottle of wine.

Kate sighed, stepped back and ushered him inside. "You know where the glasses are," she told him as she closed the door and put the bag back in its place.

He made small talk at first. "How's the hospital... you met a new bloke yet... going to get another flat mate?" That kind of thing. Kate indulged him until he finally ran out things to say. At this point he'd normally reach into his seemingly endless collection of anecdotes and start telling dodgy stories about this or that night on the town and the disreputable character he'd hooked up with. It was only when the silence fell that Kate realised she'd not seen James hold court like this for months.

"I'm not much of a sister, am I?" she said.

"What?"

"I should have noticed something was wrong. I should have asked about it."

"Don't be daft. You've been up to your ears with training."

"Still." The silence that fell then seemed like it would swallow them whole, and they stared into their wine glasses.

"James, how does this end for us?"

He looked up and his face said it all.

"Why haven't you gone to the police?" she asked.

He shook his head. "Too scared. Why haven't you?"

"Don't tell him," Cooper had told her two weeks earlier. "No matter what. I know he's your brother and all, but from what I can gather he doesn't seem the kind who could keep a secret."

Kate gave James a look that said 'why do you think?' and he nodded. "Right."

"I have an idea, though," she said. "Something we can do to help ourselves."

"Hit me."

"I've considered it."

She got up, grabbed a notepad and pen from the kitchen counter, and sat down again. "I want you to tell me everything, and I mean absolutely everything that you know about their operation. Dates, times, locations, personnel. Everything."

He looked wary. "For why?"

"Insurance."

"Oh, Sis, that's not..."

"Do you trust me?"

"With my life."

"Then spill."

So he did, until eventually he checked his watch and told her it was time to go.

It was a cold, clear night, cloudless and silent.

The yard was lit by sodium lights mounted high on the posts that marked out the limits of the chain link fence. Huge containers were piled high in blocks, forming a kind of maze. The fleet of articulated lorries that ferried them across Europe and beyond were lined up near the entrance, seeming naked and unwieldy without their cargo. The pungent stink of rotting vegetables and the cry of hungry gulls betrayed the presence of a tip nearby.

Two portacabins, one on top of the other, sat at the heart of the maze. Their lights were on and Kate could see movement inside as she and James walked towards them.

James didn't knock, he pushed the door open and they stepped into a fug of warm, damp, gas-heater air that smelled of stale coffee and cigarettes.

The giant was sitting on a tatty old armchair which seemed comically small for him. His knees were up around his ears. A group of four crowded around him, sipping coffee from plastic cups and smoking. They were talking and joking in what Kate assumed was Serbian.

Kate was relieved that Spider wasn't present, even though she'd known he wouldn't be. Cooper had told her he normally ran things from Manchester.

The giant unfolded himself and rose as the siblings entered. The men fell silent, watching them with eyes that betrayed only the barest smidgin of interest. Each of them glanced briefly at

James and then shifted his attention to Kate, sizing her up and finding her either adequate or wanting, depending upon their taste. One of them smiled at her, revealing crooked yellow teeth. She ignored him.

"You have the medicine?" asked the giant.

Kate held up her bag. He seemed content. He handed James a clipboard and a large manila envelope. Her brother took it without question.

"Come on," he said to Kate, and led her back outside to a set of stairs that led up to the portacabin above. A young man stood outside the door, on guard. He unlocked the door as they ascended and ushered them inside. Kate heard the door lock again once they were in.

The small room held eight women and girls. All were sitting on the floor, crowded around a gas heater, warming their hands. They wore simple, functional clothes and had obviously not washed in days. There was a pungent smell of BO.

"Hello ladies," said James, smiling. Kate was disturbed at how easily he slipped into this role. She wondered how many times he had done this before. "If I can please have your passports and travel documents."

One of the women, the oldest of the bunch, maybe twenty or so, Kate thought, translated James' request to the other, and they each reached into their pockets and produced their passports. Kate thought the meekness with which they did this spoke volumes. These girls were scared. They hadn't admitted it to themselves yet, but they knew, deep down, that something had gone wrong, that they had been fooled, that something awful was about to happen to them.

James collected the passports and visas cheerfully, placing them in the manila envelope. He turned to Kate as he did so. "Best get on with it, Kit."

Kate crouched down and opened her bag. Inside were the syringe needles and ampoules that she had stolen from the hospital. Vitamin shots, wide spectrum antibiotics and, as ordered, mild sedatives. She told the girls to roll up their sleeves. Again the oldest one translated.

"What is that?" she asked.

"Nothing to worry about," Kate lied, feeling a tiny part of her die as she did so. "Just vitamins and stuff. Something to give you a boost. You've had a long trip in that lorry."

The woman was suspicious but there had been that faint air of resignation to her question which betrayed her powerlessness. Kate gave each of the trafficked women a shot.

While she did this James got each woman to stand up as he examined them, scanned a list of outstanding requirements on the clipboard, and decided which of the various distribution points they would be transferred to. The skinny one with the blonde hair was pretty enough for the high rollers, so she'd go to London. The three chubby ones were disposable but functional, they could go to Manchester. There was a special request for a young girl for extraordinary duties. James picked out the redhead, who couldn't have been more than sixteen, for this role.

Kate felt sick as she watched him do this.

James tried to present a cheery front as he consigned these women to their various fates. He knew what he was doing; choosing which ones would be raped, which would be murdered, which would vanish into the cellars, and which in the penthouses. But he didn't want them to know what was going on, so he smiled and joked, even though he knew most of them didn't understand what he was saying.

When the allocation was complete, and the injections had all been administered, James told them it was time for sleep because they would be collected early in the morning. He turned off the light as he left them to snuggle together for warmth on the floor, under ragged duvets.

Kate and he went back downstairs, handed the clipboard to the giant, and waited as he studied it. Eventually, he nodded.

"Good," he said. Then he allocated each of the four men a girl or two to transport. James was also given an assignment, driving to Manchester. Kate was dismissed.

The men left and went up the stairs to collect their by now unconscious cargo. James hung back, drinking coffee with the giant.

"I thought you were driving one of them?" she asked.

James stared at his feet, unable to meet her gaze.

"I am," he said. "But they'll... they'll be a while."

The giant laughed. "This is not real man. Not like girls." He laughed again, as if this was the funniest thing in the whole wide world.

Kate wanted to grind broken glass into his face.

"Can I go?" she asked.

The giant nodded. "Get more medicine. More girls next week," he said, and he waved her aside, dismissing her.

Kate stepped out into the night and walked steadily and carefully until she turned a corner and was out of sight. Then she placed her hands on her knees, bent double, and vomited until there was nothing left to come up.

She wiped her mouth on her sleeve, stood upright, and walked out of the yard in search of a taxi.

"You really shouldn't have gone to all this trouble," said Cooper, with his mouth full. Kate laughed.

"If my Gran knew I was playing host to a Detective Inspector and not feeding him, she'd have a heart attack. She feeds everyone who ever knocks on her door. Doctor, postman, Jehovah's Witness, she doesn't care. Even if I call her and say I'm stopping by after dinner at a fancy restaurant she opens the door and says 'ooh love, you're looking a little peaky, I've done your favourite, corned beef pie!' And she'll sit there and watch me eat it, no matter how full of Sunday lunch or curry I am."

"And you've inherited her compulsion?"

"It what we do oop North, DI Cooper. Just because you Southerners think hospitality begins and ends with a twist of lime in a G and T, doesn't mean we're so stingy."

"Well this pasta is great, thank you. I'm not sure what my boss would say. He might accuse me of taking bribes."

"It's not *that* good."

"I'm a copper, Miss Booker..."

"Kate, please."

"I live on pies, chips and coffee, Kate. You may not believe me, but I used to be lean and toned. It's only since I joined the force that I've got so flabby."

Kate didn't think he was flabby. Fancies himself, she thought again, but not unkindly. Fishing for compliments.

"What did you do before?"

"I was in the army."

"Really? I wouldn't have pegged you as the soldier type. What were you, admin or engineer?"

Cooper hesitated. "Not exactly."

"Man of mystery, huh."

"Something like that."

He finished his bowl of pasta and swilled it down with a gulp of lager. Kate collected their crockery and put the kettle on. Cooper browsed her bookcases while she made coffee. Once he'd taken it, he sat down, the informal air almost, but not entirely, banished. She sat opposite him.

"You gave the girls the injections?" he asked.

Kate nodded.

"How many?"

"Eight. Three for Manchester, two each for London and Birmingham, one for Cardiff."

"Good. We'll track them to their destinations."

"And then do nothing because you're waiting for authorisation." The bitterness in her voice was hard to disguise.

"It won't be long now, I promise." He paused and Kate could tell he was considering whether to tell her something. He put down his cutlery and leaned forward across the table intently. "We're tracking a lorry full of girls at the moment. The Ukrainians, for once, actually tipped us off when it left. So far we've managed to keep track of it all the way to Dusseldorf. If we don't lose it before it gets here, we should have the whole trail mapped out clearly. Then we can wrap it all up in one fell swoop."

"That's brilliant!" said Kate. Cooper looked down at the table. "But?" she asked, dreading his answer.

"They've decided the south coast ports are getting too dangerous. We think they're coming in via Grimsby and straight to Manchester."

"And that's a problem, why?"

"We don't have anyone on the inside in Manchester." He looked up at her and took a deep breath. "We don't think they have a pet doctor up there yet, though."

"Right," said Kate, not quite following his logic.

"And in the next few days he's got a massive shipment of girls arriving there, the first to go direct, bypassing London."

"Which would mean they'd send for me to help process the girls."

"We hope so, yes."

"And you'd follow me so I could lead you straight to them?"

"That's the general idea."

Kate considered this for a moment. "I'd still be in there when you stormed the place, right?"

Cooper held her gaze firmly. "It's the only way. You'll be away from home so they'll let you sleep the night there, I guess, before driving you back."

"Oh great. That's just what I want, a night stuck in a portacabin with those bastards."

"Which is why we'll take them as soon as you lead us there."

"And how exactly will I do that?"

"You'll need to carry some kind of tracking device."

Kate shook her head firmly. "They frisked me last time. They'd find something like that."

"This will be well disguised. Trust me, they'll have no idea it's there."

"Wait a minute. You'll take them as soon as I get there? You mean I'm going to be in the middle of a police raid?"

"Don't worry. I'll be there and I'll make it my first priority to get you to safety."

Kate did not feel reassured.

"So I should expect to get a phone call in the next couple of days," she said.

"Yeah."

Cooper considered her, biting his lip. "I've still not told my boss about you, you know. I'm keeping you completely off the books. With the operation nearing completion, the risk of a leak from within the Met is too great. I still don't know who Spider's got on the inside and until I do, I'm playing my cards very close to my chest."

"But surely the operation you're proposing is going to require a lot of manpower."

"Yeah. I'm bending the rules a bit there." Kate waited for him to elaborate, but "it's not exactly ethical" is all he said.

"Fuck ethics," said Kate, suddenly impassioned. "If this works, you'll be in a position to shut him down for good."

Cooper smiled. "Let's hope so. As they say in all the good movies: so now we wait."

"However shall we pass the time?"

Cooper looked surprised and Kate cursed inwardly. Too obvious. Inappropriate. Stupid. Damn.

He registered her embarrassment and smiled. "I have an idea or two."

Kate lifted her face out off the blue crash mat and groaned.

"This," she said pointedly, "was not what I had in mind, Detective Inspector Cooper."

Cooper laughed as he bent down and held out a hand. She grabbed it and allowed herself to be helped to her feet.

"Again, Sanders. And stop going easy on her," he said.

"Sir," said the massive, muscled soldier who had just thrown Kate to the floor like she weighed less than a feather pillow. "Now remember what I said, Miss Booker, duck under the attack, grab, pivot and throw."

"Soldier, you're three times the size of me. I don't have to duck under your attack, I just have to stand here and let it pass over my head."

The soldier smiled and held out his great meaty hands, ready to attack once more. Kate sighed and prepared to meet his attack. She placed her feet wide apart and raised her own hands, practically doll like in comparison. "Come on then, let's..."

But he was already moving, and once again Kate didn't manage even the most rudimentary defensive manoeuvre. She was face down on the mat again before the second was out.

"Perhaps we should..."

"No," said Kate firmly as she peeled her face away from the sticky plastic. "Let's go again." She got to her feet. "You really know how to show a girl a good time, Cooper," she said. The policeman just smiled and waved from the bench at the side of the dojo.

Five more attacks, five more humiliations until finally, on the sixth go around, she managed to get a hand to his wrist and a shoulder to his stomach. She tried the lift, but it was like trying to topple a solid granite statue. After straining for a few moments, she gave up and allowed herself to be flattened once more.

"Better," said Sanders. "Anyone not trained would have been thrown by that."

Kate scowled at him. "The men I'm dealing with are ex-Serbian military, Sanders, and one of them is even bigger than you."

Sanders cast a curious glance across at Cooper, who nodded once.

"Right," said the soldier. "In which case, I think we're taking the wrong tack. Tell me, Miss Booker, have you ever fired a gun?"

"She won't be armed, Sanders," said Cooper. "Too dangerous."

"Still, they'll be carrying guns, yeah?" Sanders countered.

Again Cooper nodded.

"Then it can't hurt, can it? Come on Miss Booker, let's get you kitted up."

Sanders led Kate out of the gym and across a sparse concrete courtyard ringed with old single storey buildings. It was about midday, but although Cooper had driven her here some hours before, she still had little clue where exactly here was. It was only when she saw a group of men in the distance, running into woods dressed entirely in black, carrying guns, that the penny dropped.

"Not exactly an engineer," she muttered as she entered the long building that housed one of the SAS firing ranges.

"Why did you do that?" Kate asked as they pulled out of the driveway, several hours later.

She had been thrown and chased, beaten and bruised, and taught how to shoot a variety of weapons. She had, she reluctantly admitted to herself, rather enjoyed firing guns. The power of it was exciting.

"If anything goes wrong, you could find yourself in the middle of a firefight. It's important you be ready."

"Of course I'm not ready. You think a day like that is all it takes to get me ready for a warzone?"

"No," replied Cooper quietly. "But it's all I could think to do."

Kate blushed, ashamed. "Thank you."

"You're welcome."

"So were you one of them, in the army?"

"If I had been, I wouldn't be able to tell you. And if I were to cash in some favours by asking old friends to give you a workover, then it would have to be a very well kept secret indeed if I wanted to avoid having my bollocks cut of and fed to me by big men in balaclavas."

Kate couldn't tell whether he was joking or not. "My lips are sealed."

"Good. But remember what you learned here today. It could save your life."

"You promised me…"

"That nothing could go wrong. I know. And it shouldn't. But there are always factors that can't be foreseen."

"Cooper, can I ask you something?"

He nodded, keeping his eyes on the road.

"Why is my brother really working for Spider?"

"What do you mean?"

"He's a student. He's nothing special. He has no special skills or contacts. There's nothing he can do that one of Spider's normal henchmen can't. I'm a doctor, I understand why I'm useful to him. But James?"

There was a long silence as Cooper kept his eyes on the road. Eventually he said: "Spider is gay. And he likes them pretty."

Kate hadn't thought anything about this business could make her feel any more wretched. She had been wrong.

They drove the rest of the way home in silence. Cooper pulled up outside Kate's building as the clock on the nearby church struck eight.

"Home sweet home," he said.

"Want to come in for a nightcap?"

He turned and looked at her, lips pursed, appraising. "No, Kate. Best if I don't. Maybe once this is all over…"

"Right, yes, of course. I only meant a coffee anyway. I'll see you soon, I guess."

"Definitely."

"Okay, off I go. And thanks, for today."

"You're welcome."

Four days later, Kate was sitting in the back of a Ford Focus on the M1 north. The giant was crammed into the front passenger seat and the yellow toothed man who kept smiling at her was driving. The stereo was playing some awful Euro-pop.

The rain was coming down in sheets and the windscreen wipers were barely able to cope as they weaved in and out of the traffic. She didn't envy anyone who was trying to follow them through this deluge. She resisted the urge to check the mobile phone in her pocket. The transmitter inside was working, Cooper had checked it himself yesterday. All she could achieve by fingering it was to draw attention to it, which was the last thing she wanted.

Somewhere out there in the downpour, Cooper and his team were gathering, ready for the kill. After her visit to Hereford, Kate had a suspicion that she knew what Cooper had meant by 'bending the rules'. She had seen footage of the Iranian Embassy siege. She knew what to expect and she knew what to do. She was pretty sure that she'd be seeing Sanders again by the end of the day and that thought reassured her; he inspired confidence somehow, even more so than Cooper.

Everything was going to be fine, she told herself. This has all been planned by professionals. Nothing can go wrong.

The giant turned in his seat and looked back at her. He held out his hand.

"Give me phone," he said.

"Sorry?" she asked, taken by surprise.

"Phone."

"Why?"

He didn't say anything, just kept his hand held out, impassive.

Kate gulped and reached into her pocket, removing the phone and handing it to him.

"Careful with it, eh? That's top of the range," she joked, trying not to reveal her sudden terror.

The giant wound down the window and tossed the phone out onto the motorway. The window closed with a soft buzz of internal motors.

"What the fuck was that for?" she yelled.

The giant turned again and held up a little black plastic box with a small LED that flashed red. "Boss not like bugs," he said, matter of fact. Then he turned back and returned to staring out at the lorries as they sped past, each carrying a cloud of spray behind it.

Kate sat there knowing with total certainty that she was a dead woman.

Two hours later they pulled up outside a huge Victorian warehouse in Moss Side. Kate knew where they were because the giant had not told her to look at the floor and had not bothered with the sleep mask. That they didn't take such rudimentary precautions confirmed to her that she was not going to be allowed to walk out of wherever they were taking her.

The giant unfolded himself into the street and pulled her door open, ushering her inside the warehouse through big black wooden doors. The rain was still pouring, and the air was saturated with the hoppy aroma of a nearby brewery.

The ground floor was massive and unsegregated. Racks of cheap clothing stretched away on all sides into the gloom. The giant led Kate to the stairs and they went up two storeys. The second floor was also full of cheap clothes, this time in piles on tables, being sorted by a small group of women; Kate guessed Somali but she couldn't be sure. This floor had a wall running across it, and the giant led her to a small door which, incongruously, had a keypad lock. He typed in the code and the door clicked open.

The other side of the door was a different world. Kate walked from a low rent sweatshop into a plush corridor decorated with velvet wallpaper, laid with deep red carpets and decorated with modern art prints and photographs, all soft core, nothing too obvious.

The next door led into a lobby area that felt more like a lounge or a bar. Leather sofas and armchairs dotted the room, ringing small round tables with table lamps on them, casting a soft glow. There was an unmanned bar in the far corner..

"Sit," said the giant without looking at her. She did so as he left by a small door beside the bar, going deeper into this hidden world.

Kate sat there, collecting her thoughts. The transmitter was gone, so all Cooper knew was that she had been taken. He'd have no idea where she was now unless he'd been able to physically keep the car in sight at all times. She figured the torrential rain made that unlikely.

She was on her own. There was no cavalry coming.

Worse than that, Spider would know by now that she had betrayed him. He might react in a number of ways. He could kill her outright, but she thought at the very least he'd want her to examine the new intake first. Alternatively, he could disappear her into his system, send her to some dank cellar or a dungeon somewhere to be kept on ice ready for a client who fancied a girl who'd put up a fight. That seemed most likely. After all, she was a resource he could use to turn a profit.

She told herself to stay calm and clear headed. As long as she was alive, there was a chance she could find a way to alert Cooper.

The wild card here, she knew, was her brother. What might Spider do to him?

She didn't have to wait long for an answer.

The internal door swung open and Spider entered. He was wearing a different but equally well cut suit, this time of dark purple. His face was impassive and he moved with controlled, almost robotic precision. He walked behind the bar without acknowledging her, took a glass from beneath the counter and poured himself a whisky before looking up at Kate.

"Drink?" he said.

Kate considered for a moment before nodding. "Red wine, please.

He took a wine glass down from a shelf and began to open a bottle.

"I thought we had an understanding, Miss Booker," he said as he pulled the cork out with a soft pop.

Kate thought it best to stay silent.

"I thought that you understood the consequences of betrayal," he continued, pouring the wine into the large glass.

"My lieutenant thinks I should give you to him. He thinks it would be fun to rape you while strangling you. Although he enjoys fucking them, I think he does not like women very much. He likes to cut them with the bayonet his grandfather used in the Second World War. He keeps it very sharp." The glass full, he put the bottle down, walked over to Kate and handed her the drink. "Does that sound like an appropriate punishment to you, Miss Booker?"

She took the glass and had to put it down immediately, as her hands were shaking too badly to hold it steady.

Spider remained standing, looking down on her. "I worry,

though, that if I were to let him have his way with you, you would not learn your lesson."

The internal door swung open again and Kate stifled a cry of fear as she saw her brother being led into the room by the giant.

He saw her and smiled. "Hi Kit," he said. Then he registered the fear on her face and the single minded focus with which Spider was regarding her, and his step faltered.

"I think," said Spider quietly, "that a different punishment would be better." He turned to James and smiled. "Hello, Booker."

"Hi Boss," said James, giving the most unconvincing smile Kate had ever seen.

"James, how long have you been working for me?"

"Ooh, six months now, I reckon."

"Six months." Spider nodded. "You have been a good worker."

"Er, Boss," said James, trying not to let his fear show. "What's up?"

"Your sister has betrayed me to the police. She tried to bring a transmitter here with her."

Kate met James' eyes and she saw all the hope vanish in an instant, replaced by total despair. Spider reached into his jacket and pulled out a huge hunting knife, shiny and sharp. He turned and walked over to James and caressed his cheek with the sharp edge, tenderly.

"I like you, James," said Spider.

"I, I like you too, Boss," James stammered.

"You have kept me amused far longer than most lovers, but I don't think you do like me. Not really," replied Spider, who was now standing pressed up close to James. "I think you are scared of me. And that is how I like it. The one thing my lieutenant and I have in common is that we both know there is no enjoyment to be had from fucking someone who is not scared of you."

Kate found her voice at last. "Stop this. Please," she said, rising to her feet. "He's done nothing wrong. It's me you've got the problem with, Spider. There's no reason to hurt him."

"What do you think, James?" asked the Serbian, standing behind the terrified young man, chin resting on his shoulder, knife pressed up against his temple.

James had nothing to say.

"Do you think I should kill you? Or perhaps your sister?" There was no reply. "Petar wants her. You know what he would do to her."

Tears began to stream down James's cheeks but still he stayed silent.

"You still need me to examine the new shipment of girls," said Kate, desperately.

Spider shook his head. "Once I learnt of your betrayal I diverted that container. To the bottom of a river."

"I'll tell you anything you want to know," said Kate, using the only bargaining chip she had left. "I know the policeman who's running the operation. I can lead you to him."

"Do you mean DI Cooper?" he laughed. "We know all about him. What else you got?"

Kate had nothing else.

"Thought so," said Spider.

Then he pushed the knife through the thin bone plate on the side of James head, straight into his brain.

She doesn't remember what happened next. All that survives is a sound; a low keening that goes on forever and ever. The second the knife went in, the world went black and her mind stopped creating memories.

The woman who gradually became aware of her surroundings however many hours later was a different person. Someone as yet unnamed. Someone at whose very core nestled a cold, hard knot of calm determination and resolve. Someone with only one thought in her head.

Vengeance.

The world came to the woman a piece at a time.

First it was the faint smell of burning hops. Then the sound of her own breathing. She floated in a dark void, examining the smell and the sound for a long time before her body began to send back signals that told her she was lying on a bed. Then there was a taste of stale wine and bile. Finally, she opened her eyes.

The world looked... different. The room was monochrome – black walls, white nurse's outfit hanging from the white hook on the inside of the door, shiny grey buckles on the straps that adorned the sturdy black wooden cross, white trolley with black implements strewn across it – whips, dildos, clamps and catheters. But even despite the lack of colour, the woman who awoke on that bed (and was it a waking, truly? Had she been asleep or just comatose? Had she really opened her eyes or had her optic nerves instead rebooted themselves after a long shutdown?) somehow knew that even had the room been painted in fluorescent colours they would have seemed muted.

The way she saw the world had literally changed.

The bed springs creaked as she sat up. She had been expecting a headache, but her head was clear and her senses were sharp. There were no windows in this dark place. The only illumination came from four uplighters, one in each corner of the room.

She stood up and checked the door, knowing it was locked but determined to be thorough. She then turned to assess the room, methodically cataloguing its contents in her mind, searching for a means of attack or something she could use to defend herself.

She noted the absence of panic, but did not think it worthy of further examination.

The trolley offered the best hope, but there was nothing there that could be of genuine use. The cat o'nine tails lacked the sharp stones that would have rendered it really painful, and she did not think beating a man around the head with a giant black rubber cock would do anything but provoke laughter.

Perhaps if she pushed the trolley itself at whoever entered, it would unbalance them long enough to give her an opening. But when she tried to move it forwards the wheels squealed alarmingly and refused to move.

She made no further progress before she heard a key turn in the lock. She stepped away from the trolley and into the only really clear area in the centre of the room. If she was going to fight, this was all the space she would have to do it in.

The door opened and the giant stepped inside. The woman who was no longer Kate abandoned all thought of fighting.

He closed the door behind him, not bothering to lock it. He knew there was no way she was getting past him.

She stood there, impassive, as he removed his jacket and hung it on the hook, covering the nurse's outfit. He then removed his shirt, revealing an acreage of tattooed chest that was twice the woman's width from shoulder to shoulder. He hung the shirt over the jacket.

He stepped forward and reached out his huge right hand, wrapping the fingers around her throat and lifting her off the ground with a single outstretched arm. He brought her face close to his as she choked. She felt his warm breath on her cheek as he examined her closely. Then he relaxed his grip and she collapsed in a heap at his feet, gasping for air. He turned his back on her, stepped to the door and removed a huge bayonet from the inside of his hanging jacket.

"Stand," he said. The woman did so.

He stepped forward and inserted the bayonet under the bottom of her t-shirt. He ripped the blade upwards and the cloth parted before it like butter meeting a hot knife. The bayonet was so sharp, she thought, you probably wouldn't realise you'd been stabbed until you looked down and saw the hilt sticking out.

The blunt edge felt cold against her skin as it rushed up from her belly to her throat.

When the t-shirt had been split from waist to neck, it fell off her. She stood in her bra, facing this enormous man, knowing exactly what he intended to do to her, and still she felt no fear.

She remembered the dojo, she recalled the moves she'd been taught in a draughty hut in Camden, and she knew that all that training was useless. If he came at her with some momentum, she could perhaps have used it against him. But the room was too small; he had no need of speed. If he had been smaller, she could have tried to throw him from a standing start, but she hadn't been able to throw Sanders who, big as he was, was slight in comparison.

Her best chance, she realised, was the bayonet.

"Rush a gun, flee a knife," Sanders had told her. "If you run at a person who's trying to shoot you, you force them to fire quickly and without time to aim properly. You have a better chance that they'll miss you than if you turn and run. But a knife is different. It's only lethal in close quarters and once you've got a hand to it, it can move both ways. You'd be amazed how many stab victims are killed with their own blades."

The woman focused all her attention on the blade. This man

was too strong to wrestle with, but even so she had a slim chance of turning his weapon against him. To do that she had to know exactly where it was, how it was angled, where it was pointed at all times.

He reached down and unbuckled her belt, pulling it out in one fluid movement, cracking it like a whip, and tossing it over his shoulder into the corner.

He angled the knife down, inserting the point inside the waistband of her jeans, directly below her belly button.

Then something distracted him. A distant rumble. The floor shook briefly. There was a scream somewhere far away. He glanced over his shoulder instinctively, even though the closed door and windowless walls offered no vantage.

When he turned his attention back to the woman he noticed she had taken a step backwards. He looked down and registered that she had something in her right hand. Something long and thin. Something dripping.

He took a step towards her and felt his centre of gravity shift in an unsettling way. There was a soft wet sound and he felt pressure on his foot. He looked down to see his entrails spooling out of his belly and falling to the floor like a coil of steaming, lumpy rope.

Still looking at his feet in wonder, he saw a hand enter his field of vision and felt it punch him on the breast. The hand withdrew and he opened his mouth in astonishment as he realised there was a black metal handle sticking out of his chest.

How the fuck had that got there?

He reached down and grabbed the handle, pulling it and exposing the blade of his grandfather's bayonet. It emerged from his heart smoothly, without a sound. The room span and he felt something hit him on the back of the head. He wasn't conscious long enough to realise that it was the floor.

The woman reached down and took the bayonet from twitching fingers, then stepped over the giant corpse and opened the door. Somewhere in the distance she could hear gunfire.

She walked out of the room, blade in hand, spoiling for a fight.

As she moved down the corridor, she could still hear occasional bursts of gunfire somewhere below and ahead of her. She didn't know how, but Cooper and his men must have found the warehouse. This mean that time was not on her side. She had to find Spider before Cooper did.

The corridor ran the length of the building along its external back wall. Tall metal framed windows ranged to her left, a collection of doors to her right. A quick glance outside told her that it was late evening and she was at least one floor above the lobby bar.

The door at the far end of the corridor burst open and the man with the yellow teeth came running through with a sub machine gun in his hands. Without noticing the woman, he turned and entered the first door. The woman heard a girl's scream and then a burst of gunfire.

She began to run. The man stepped back out of the room, the barrel of his gun smoking. He turned to walk towards the next door and then stopped in amazement as he registered a woman in a bra running towards him with teeth bared. It took him a second to react, but he soon brought the gun to bear.

"Rush a gun, flee a knife," the woman muttered to herself as she barrelled forwards. The sound of the shots was deafening in the enclosed corridor, and she felt hot air stream across her right shoulder as the distance closed. Then there was a sharp sting in the same shoulder but she ignored it as she crashed into the gunman, flinging him to the floor. The bayonet clattered out of her hands as they fell. She wrestled with him for a moment and then, realising the madness of this, sat up, straddling him like a lover. Again he took a moment to react to this unexpected move, a moment in which she reached down, grabbed his gun, reversed it and used the butt to send the bones from his nose shrapnelling into his frontal lobe.

She leaned across him, grabbed the bayonet again then stood, blade in one hand, gun in the other. She checked the gun once, recalling Sanders' tuition, recognising the vital parts. She pointed it at the chest of Yellowteeth and squeezed the trigger. A stream of bullets thudded into him.

The woman nodded, satisfied.

She heard a door open behind her and she span around, raising the weapon. A teenaged girl peered out at her, eyes wide with fear. The woman lowered the weapon.

"You speak English?" she asked.

The girl nodded. The woman handed her the bayonet, and the girl looked at it in wonder.

"Take this," said the woman. "Stick it in any man you meet who's not wearing a uniform. Understand?"

The girl nodded.

"Good, now get everyone in these rooms into the dungeon at the far end. Lock the door. The keys are in the pocket of the dead man you'll find in there. Don't come out until the shooting stops. Can you do that?"

Again the girl nodded. "You've been shot," she whispered.

The woman looked at her shoulder and registered a small hole at the top of her arm. She fingered it, and found the exit wound. The bullet had gone straight through and missed both bones and arteries. She didn't feel any pain, though she knew that would not stay the case for long.

She turned, jumped over the corpse of Yellowteeth and ran out the door. She had wasted enough time.

She emerged onto a darkened dance floor with swing doors at the far right. She ran diagonally across it. As she reached the halfway point the doors swung open and three men ran in. All were in civvies and all carried guns.

Their eyes took a moment to adjust to the darkness, so by the time they realised they were not alone it was too late. The woman sprayed the doorway with bullets and the men jerked and dropped. She kept running, jumped over them and flew out the swing doors, ready to fire.

Behind her, in the corridor where she'd killed Yellowteeth, she heard shattering glass as Cooper's men came in through the windows. So now they were ahead of her and behind her. She gritted her teeth.

She had to get to Spider first.

She ran down an empty staircase keeping the gun aimed at the bottom in case anyone else came running through. There was another soft explosion on the far side of the building as she reached the bottom and turned to find herself facing another corridor and another row of rooms.

These doors were open. One, about halfway along, had a single bloodstained hand stretched across the threshold.

The woman walked down the corridor checking each room for survivors. Despite her focus, she knew she would have to help any wounded girls she found, even if that meant letting Spider escape.

But Yellowteeth had been thorough. Each room held at least one dead girl, some as many as three. No-one was to be left alive who could testify against them. No witnesses, no descriptions. The woman reached the end of the corridor with something approximating relief and pushed through into the lobby bar.

A patch of darkness on the carpet was the only evidence that someone had been stabbed in the head here not so long ago.

There was a burst of gunfire from somewhere close, beyond the opposite door, then heavy footsteps on the stairs behind her. She scanned the room in desperation. Had they already captured him? Had the bastard escaped her?

Out of the corner of her eye she caught a glimpse of something that didn't seem right, so she turned and realised that there was another door, slightly ajar, behind the bar. It was flat and featureless, disguised as part of the wall, which is why she had not seen it earlier. She ran to it and pulled it open, squeezing through and closing it firmly behind her. Cooper and his team would probably not see the door on their first pass, especially if they were still encountering resistance. If Spider had come this way, she would be the only person in pursuit for now.

The woman smiled, but it was not like any smile Kate had ever worn.

She scampered down the dark, narrow stairs. A small landing with another discreet door marked the ground floor, then the steps continued down into the cellars. The woman saw a glimmer of light ahead and slowed. She turned the corner at the bottom and found herself in a long, low featureless brick corridor, painted black. There was no light here, but she could make out a fading glow at the far end, betraying the presence of someone fleeing with a torch. She took off in pursuit, catching only vague impressions of rooms off to her left and right, each marked by a low, round arch and some brick steps going down into a chamber. The squalid cellar entrances smelt of blood, shit and fear.

The woman barrelled on through the darkness, turning the corner at the far end to find a dead end and an old metal grille in the floor. It was still open, and the glow of the receding torch seeped out of it. She did not even look down into the sewers before jumping.

She splashed into cold, lumpy water that came up to her waist.

The sewer was a round tube of Victorian brick. The current was strong, swollen by the heavy rains, and the water swirled and eddied, trying to pull her feet out from under her. The floor felt slimy beneath her feet and she knew that if she lost her footing she would be in big trouble.

She held the gun high above her head and waded forward, following the fading light around the curve of the tunnel.

She had only progressed a few metres when she stepped into space, a breech in the sewer floor, like a pothole. She unbalanced and fell backwards, disappearing into the raging torrent and being carried forward at speed. She lost her grip on the gun. Flailing around in the darkness, she broke the surface once, twice, gasping for air as she hurtled along.

For the first time it occurred to her that she might die down here.

She lost all sense of orientation. Down was up, left was right. The water roared in her ears, she saw flashes behind her closed eyes and felt the dizziness of impending unconsciousness.

Then she hit something. Something soft, which fell ahead of her, and then she and this object were tumbling together in the water. Something hard hit her on the side of the head; was that the torch or her gun? Just as she thought she was dead, the water threw her out into a void and she fell, momentarily free, drawing ragged, desperate breaths.

She splashed down into a lake of some sort and fought to the surface. There was no light down here. The torch had gone. She floated there, treading water as it swirled around her, calming herself, listening intently, trying to filter out the sound of the waterfall that had deposited her in what she assumed was some sort of junction.

She had not fallen down into this pit alone. The person she had collided with must be here too, somewhere in the darkness.

"Spider," she shouted. Her voice echoed back to her a hundred times. This chamber was big and arched. "Spider!"

She waited, feeling the fatigue in her legs as they kicked against the tide.

"Miss Booker, you surprise me," came the reply at last, his too calm voice seeming to come at her from every direction.

She turned left and right, trying to get a bearing on the bastard.

It was no use; he could have been anywhere.

"If I could see you, I would shoot you," he said, seeming more in control. Had he made it out of the water on to some ledge? He didn't sound like he was swimming any more. "But I suppose I will have to settle for leaving you here to drown. Goodbye, Kate."

Kate, thought the woman. *Who's Kate?*

"I'll find you," she screamed. "No matter where you fucking hide, I'll find you."

"No," came the reply, fainter now, moving away. "I will find you, if you survive the day. Trust me."

"Spider?" she yelled. "Spider!"

But there was no reply, only darkness and water and white noise.

A council worker found the woman later that night, unconscious, half dead, suffering from hypothermia, washed up on a brick shore half a mile under the city. Her body was swarming with rats. When he managed to wake her, she couldn't tell him her name. Delirious, she muttered incoherently about webs as he radioed for assistance.

Two months later, a nondescript car drove through a pair of wrought iron gates and down the driveway of a minor public school in Kent. It parked behind the main building and two people, a man and a woman, got out.

He wore a smile that spoke of familiarity and nostalgia. Her face betrayed no emotion at all.

"This way," he said, and walked towards the rear doors, his feet crunching on the gravel.

She did not follow him immediately, pausing to take in her surroundings. The sports fields stretched away ahead of her, bordered on all sides by thick woods, lush green in the summer heat. The sky was blue and the air was clear and smelt of pine needles and fresh water. The only sound came from the soft rustle of the leaves in the gentle wind.

"You coming?"

She turned and trailed after the man, who pushed open the door and entered.

The building was impressive and old, but not as old as some public schools. This was a Victorian edifice, imposing and solid. The inside reflected this, with dark wood panelled walls, tiled floors and portraits of illustrious benefactors with big sideburns hanging on the whitewashed walls.

The man led her deep into the silent building, up a small back staircase once meant for servants, to a small door in the east wing. He opened the door then handed her the keys.

"Welcome home," he said.

"It's not my home, John."

"It is now," said DI Cooper. Then he added, smiling: "Matron."

The woman slapped him playfully on the arm and allowed herself the tiniest grin as she stepped over the threshold into the flat. It was pokey but cosy. An small open fireplace sat in the middle of the far wall, with a flower print sofa and chair in front of it. There was a dresser, a bathroom with an old enamelled bath, a kitchen that barely had standing room for one and a bedroom with a single bed and wardrobe. The woman sighed and walked over to the living room window. The view of the fields and woods, with the thin skein of the river glinting on the horizon, was beautiful. This was a good place; quiet and peaceful, isolated from reality. The outside world would not bother her here.

"Yeah, it'll do," she said eventually, heartened by the green and the sun. It was hard to feel too low on such a gorgeous day. But she knew that looking out of this window on a cold, grey winter's day would be a very different prospect.

She heard a click from the kitchen and the rumble as the kettle began boiling. She stayed at the window until the man tapped her on the shoulder and handed her a mug of strong hot tea. She thanked him and sat on the sofa. He sat opposite, on the armchair, sipping his own brew.

"So this is where you went to school, huh?" she said.

"Yeah. I'm on the alumni committee and everything."

"I thought places like this only turned out lawyers and bankers."

"Oh no, soldiers too. There's a cadet force here."

"Seriously?"

"Once a week they dress the boys up in uniforms and teach them to shoot things."

A flash of unease passed across the woman's face.

"Don't worry," said the man. "Matrons are exempt. You won't ever have to hold a gun again, Kate."

After a short pause she said: "It's Jane, remember? I'm supposed to be Jane now."

"Sorry, I know. But not forever. Once we catch the bastard you can go back to being Kate again."

The woman did not correct his misapprehension.

"The boys arrive tomorrow," he continued. "Then you'll be up to your elbows in Clearasil, TCP and black eyes."

"Can't wait." Another pause, and then: "Do you have any idea where he is?"

The man shook his head. "If I had to guess, Serbia."

The woman nodded.

"Were there any biscuits in there?" she asked. "I fancy dunking."

When Cooper had gone, the woman drew a bath and gently lowered herself into the hot water, letting her skin adjust to the heat in tiny increments, her lips pursed with the pleasure of pain.

She floated, weightless, closed her eyes and concentrated on her breathing. She took long, slow, deep breaths and pictured the cares and stresses of her day dissolving out of her into the bathwater.

But there were no cares and stresses to disperse. It felt as if there was nothing in her at all. She was hollow.

The woman considered the emptiness dispassionately, turning it over in her mind as one would a vase or an artefact unearthed at an archaeological dig, feeling its weight and form, assessing it.

"Jane," she said out loud. "Jane Crowther. Matron."

She said the name in different ways, trying different intonations, a question, and answer, a hail, a statement.

"Jane. Jane. Jane."

It felt strange in her mouth. But it felt good on the inside.

Yes. She would be Jane now, the woman decided.

And it was right that she should be empty, she concluded, for that was what a newborn was – a vessel waiting to be filled with new experiences.

The woman who was now Jane ducked her head under the water for a moment and concentrated on the still warmth, the only sound her own heartbeat. Then she pushed her head back up to the air and took her first breath.

PART THREE

CHAPTER TEN

The implications of what I'm seeing overwhelm me.

I stand there holding the gun, frozen in wonder and horror as the events of eight years ago spool through my head like a movie. Each event, each conversation, is suddenly reinterpreted with new and sinister emphasis.

It this is true then that means... which means that... in which case...

I stagger back from the Speaker's chair as if hit, almost losing my footing. I think maybe I let out a cry.

"Surprise," says the man in the cloak.

The sound of his voice brings me back to the here and now. I refocus my attention on him, steadying my wavering hands and aiming the gun right between his eyes.

"Oh Kate," says John Cooper. "Is that any way to greet an old friend?"

CHAPTER SIX

CHAPTER ELEVEN

I was a little nervous when I rode into Nottingham.

The castle was impressive and welcoming, although they insisted I leave my gun with them for the duration as, apparently, no firepower was allowed in the town. Hood had his own band of merry men and there was a family atmosphere that reminded me a little of St Mark's. I had some concerns when I saw the army of Rangers training in the grounds, but those fears were dispelled when I met the man and his entourage. These were obviously good guys, which was a blessed relief.

Jack had been there three days already when I arrived and he was fitting in nicely. There was something of the chameleon about Jack. He was good at blending in, finding the right tone to strike in a particular group or environment. In Nottingham he was blokier, more one of the lads than he was back at school. It had worked. He had met Hood a couple of times and been greeted with cautious warmth. As we'd discussed, Jack had proposed an arrangement whereby either of our settlements could, if seriously threatened, send a messenger asking for aid which would be immediately rendered.

Hood seemed open to the idea, but it was still early days. Jack was taken aback when I turned up intending to ask him to deliver on his end of the bargain so quickly.

"I don't know if he'll be up for that. Things aren't exactly quiet around here," Jack told me as we walked around the castle boundary on the day I arrived. "There's some nutty cult on the rise and it's got them a bit spooked. Plus, you know, they had a hard fight against that French geezer so they're cautious about going looking for trouble."

"Geezer? Really, Jack? Geezer?"

"What?" he replied, I thought slightly shiftily.

I laughed. "Was that the commonly accepted term at Harrow for French psychopaths?"

"No," he said, straight faced. "The accepted Harrovian term for a French psychopath was Le Geezer. But, you know, I didn't want to confuse you with the complicated foreign lingo."

"Right."

He gave me a sudden appraising stare, as if trying to work out what I was getting at which, since I was just joking, made me wonder what he thought I was getting at. I shook my head and filed it under the category of 'Jack being odd'.

"Anyway," he went on, "they've got quite a force of Rangers. As you've found, they don't carry guns, just knives, swords, bows and arrows, quarterstaffs. Proper mediaeval stuff."

"So where," I interjected, "did all De Falaise's firepower end up?"

"I asked that, but they're not saying."

"'Cause we could use it, if they'd let us."

Jack shook his head firmly. "No chance. Hood has a thing about modern weapons. If they had an arsenal somewhere, he's either destroyed it or put it somewhere no-one else can find it."

I nodded. "So how many men can he spare us?"

Jack winced. "I don't know if he's willing to spare us any, but I got the impression that the best we could hope for is maybe five or six."

I looked up at the castle walls, where we'd seen at least fifty Rangers being put through their paces. "Fuck, really? That's it?"

"He said he has to make the cult his top priority. Plus..." Jack trailed off, seemingly unsure of what to say next.

"Yes?"

"Well, what happened in Thetford? 'Cause whatever it was, those Rangers you came back with kind of hate your guts."

"Things got complicated."

He waited for me to say more, but I kept my mouth shut. Even I wasn't entirely sure what had happened back at the compound. I kept replaying the moment I killed the begging snatcher, trying to reconstruct what I was thinking at the time, trying to work out whether it was justified. But I came up empty handed time and again. It was like I hadn't been me at all when I pulled the trigger. I was beginning to suspect that I couldn't recall what I'd been feeling because I hadn't felt anything at all. And that scared me.

We rounded a corner and found ourselves back at the castle gates. Jack saw this girl called Sophie, who he'd been mooning after, with a total lack of success on his part and no encouragement at all on hers, and took off to resume his charm offensive.

I went to find Hood.

The living legend was pacing up and down in front of a map of the area, which was hanging from the wall of what used to be the visitor's centre.

Courteous yet taciturn, he had a weather-beaten face that spoke of a life outdoors. He seemed uncomfortable inside and, every now and then, I caught him flashing tiny glances at the walls as if suspicious or resentful of them. I don't think he realised he was doing it.

He indicated that I should take a seat in one of the moulded plastic chairs that were piled up in the corner.

"Tell me about De Falaise," I asked, substituting curiosity for small talk.

He regarded me coolly. "Like a good war story, do you?" The implication was unspoken but clear.

"My Dad and I had a run in with him, back in France," I explained. "I'm deaf in one ear because of that bastard."

He looked surprised and I admit I felt a little pleased with myself. I got the impression he was not an easy man to surprise. I realised that something about his quiet authority made me want to impress him.

"You were in France?" he asked. "What were you doing there?"

"Making my way home."

"From?"

"Iraq."

Now he was really surprised. I intended to leave it at that, just be enigmatic and cool, but I felt a sudden need to confess. Something about this strange, solid man made me want to unburden myself to him.

Hood pulled up a chair and sat opposite me as I talked, listening without comment as everything that had happened to St Mark's since The Cull poured out of me. The choices, the killing, the monsters and heroes. As I spoke the sun went down until only a solitary candle lit the room, catching the lines on his face until it seemed I was speaking to a statue or a demon. Hood had an amazing quality of stillness. I don't think he even blinked while I spoke, and I spoke for a long, long time. In that quiet, half lit room it was as if there was something not quite natural about him, something more than human. Or maybe something less.

When I had finished – and I was completely honest about what had happened in Thetford – I fell silent and waited nervously for his response. He sat there, impassive, for what felt like a lifetime.

"Have you told you father this? Or Jane?" he asked, the voice seeming to come from the very fabric of the building.

"Some of it," I said. "Not all."

He rose from the chair and walked across to me. He laid his hand on my shoulder and looked down into my eyes. There was such compassion in them, but no pity. I felt a lump in my throat and realised I was about to cry.

"You should."

"I..." I found it hard to form feelings, let alone words to express them. "I want..."

"I know what you want, son. But I can't give it to you."

He turned and walked to the door then paused and said, over his shoulder: "You can have a team of men. My very best. They'll be at your disposal from dawn tomorrow."

He half turned and looked back at me through the gloom.

"And Lee, if things go badly, send word if you can," he said. "If it's at all possible, I'll come."

Then he opened the door and left.

I sat in that chair watching the candle flicker against the darkness until the first hint of light crept across the horizon. Then I wiped my eyes and made ready for war.

CHAPTER TWELVE

Tariq felt the frost crunching beneath his feet as he walked across the grass towards the school. The air was crisp and cold but the sky was clear and the sun shone strong but heatless.

He loved this place. All his life he had dreamed of escaping from Basra, of never again seeing dust or sand or dun coloured buildings. This place, with all its rain and greenery, its tall palladian columns and huge windows, was as far away from his birthplace as he could imagine. When he had lain in his bed at night as a boy, this is what he had dreamed of. Another man might have felt a twinge of guilt when he realised that, in some ways, The Cull was the best thing that ever happened to him. But not Tariq. He rarely dwelt on the past and seldom paused to examine his motives or feelings. He lived in the moment and he liked it there right well, thank you very much.

As a teenager he had pictured his future as a journalist in the UK, lobbing perfectly formed gobbets of vitriolic prose at Saddam and the Ba'athists over the internet. But he didn't mourn the loss of his dreams and ambitions. He was a teacher now, and a member of a community that had taken him in and made him part of a family. He would settle for that and count himself lucky.

He'd fight for it, too. Fighting seemed as natural to him as breathing. He had stood in opposition to someone or something his entire life – Saddam, the militants, the Americans. It was only in the last two years that he'd had nothing to fight. Peace had brought its own challenges, though, not least the loss of his lower left arm after the Salisbury explosion. The pain had gone now but he still felt occasional flashes of feeling in his missing fingers, and the stump itched like hell if he wore his hook on hot days.

He raised the artificial limb and flexed the metal claw. It made a soft clicking sound as he did so. The younger kids called him Captain Hook, but he didn't mind that. He'd even play along sometimes, bellowing a piratical "ARRRR!" and chasing them down the corridors as they screamed with terrified delight.

The thought of anyone taking them away and making them slaves caused an old familiar anger to rise inside him. He'd almost missed it.

He pushed open the doors and walked inside. The first person he met was Green. Tariq thought Green was a bit odd. Gawky, with acne scars and floppy blonde hair, he was very quiet and reserved in company. But give him a classroom of students or, better still, a gang of people wanting to put on a play or a musical, and he was driven, focused, funny and inspirational; a natural performer. Tariq had assumed he was gay, but recent rumours suggested otherwise. The oddest thing, though, was that he didn't take part in any of the military training exercises. Matron had exempted him, and only him, from all such activities. She'd never told Tariq why. She'd just said: "He's earned it."

Green nodded a greeting as Tariq entered, then smiled in relief as the four kids he'd brought back with him shuffled past in search of baths and bed. But his face fell as he realised no-one else was following on.

"That's it?" he asked.

"Call an assembly, ten minutes, dining hall," replied the Iraqi. "All kids of ten and up. I need to get some food in me first."

He hurried off to the kitchen and left Green to round everyone up.

* * *

Tariq had been a leader before, in Basra. Giving orders came easily to him, and he felt no nerves as he stood in front of over forty children and twelve adults.

"Hands up everyone who was at the original school during the battle with the Blood Hunters," he said.

About twenty hands went up.

"And how many were here when we moved from Groombridge?" About thirty.

"And how many of you want to move again?"

There was a murmur of disquiet.

"Because there's a chance we're going to come under attack. And I, for one, am not running and hiding this time!"

He was hoping for a chorus of "Damn straight!" but instead Mrs Armstrong spoke up from the back.

"Why not start at the beginning, eh, love? Tell us where the others are."

Tariq looked down at his audience and shook his head in wonder at his own stupidity. These weren't his fellow rebels from Basra, these were bloody kids, and he had started off like he was a sports coach gearing his team up for a big match. What was he thinking?

So he told them, honestly, without sugar coating it or hiding anything, exactly what had happened and what they had learnt at Thetford.

"We've prepared for a siege, over and over," he said in conclusion. "You all know your roles and positions. My job is to make sure that this place stands firm, no matter what. And with the defences we've got and the strategies we've drilled, anyone who attacks this place is going to find they've bitten off more than they can chew."

He fell silent then, waiting for some kind of response.

"No," came a voice after a moment's silence. It was not shouted, but it was spoken forcefully. It took Tariq a second to realise that it was Green speaking.

"You want to say something?" asked Tariq.

Green got to his feet and gestured to the podium where Tariq stood, asking permission to address the room. Tariq nodded and stepped aside, surprised.

Green cleared his throat and looked at his feet as he prepared to speak. Then he looked up and addressed the room.

"Somewhere in London there's an army of kids fighting a war," he said. "Kids like you and me. Kids who should be here, with us. We've been looking for allies recently, building trade relationships with the Steamies and the rest, and trying to arrange mutual defence pacts with Hood and Hildenborough. We know some of the people we encounter may be hostile or dangerous, but we keep looking for allies who can help us.

"These kids in London don't know it, but they are already our allies. Because they're us. They're you and me and her and them, if we'd never found this place. If Matron hadn't stuck her neck out and fought for us. If Lee hadn't seen off Mac. If Rowles hadn't sacrificed himself to keep us safe.

"If not for their efforts, we would be those kids. Scared, alone, fighting a war against kidnappers. Or worse – shipped to America already, where God knows what would have happened to us.

"And how do we repay the sacrifices our friends have made to keep us safe? We hide here and hope the bad guys don't come looking for us? Well, yeah. Of course Matron and Lee want us to do that. It's natural. They've fought hard to keep us from harm, to create this place for us. They don't want to risk it or lose it. Of course they want us to stay here and protect this perfect haven they've built.

"But the thing is, they've also taught us by their example. And their example teaches us a different lesson.

"It tells us that the only safety worth having is the kind you fight for.

"It tells us that sitting around waiting for other people to look after you is asking for destruction.

"It tells us that protecting people weaker than ourselves is the most important thing we can possibly do with our lives.

"They're out there now, fighting for us. God knows where Matron is, or what's happening to her. Lee's dad has gone to London to try and lead a gang of kids against an army that will almost certainly kick their ass. Lee's gone riding off into potentially hostile territory with a bunch of men who we don't know he can trust.

"And we're supposed to sit here and let them do all this for us because it's what they would want us to do?

"Fuck that.

"Fuck hiding.

"Fuck defences.

"Fuck keeping a low profile.

"If we want to justify what they've done for us, we don't do it by staying here and letting them risk their lives for us again.

"We do it by joining them.

"We do it by fighting for ourselves.

"We do it by going to war.

"We've spent all this time looking for allies to help us, and now we've found some. But they need our help instead.

"So tomorrow, instead of running all the drills we've rehearsed a thousand times, I say we get kitted up, arm ourselves, and take the fight to the enemy. We go to London, we meet up with John and this resistance army in Hammersmith, and we shut these motherfucking nutjobs down and bring those kids here, to safety, where they belong.

"Who's with me?"

Tariq stood, mouth gaping open in astonishment, as the whole room rose as one and began cheering. Green stepped down from the podium and walked across to him.

"They're all yours," he said with a smile.

CHAPTER THIRTEEN

Caroline rubbed the sleep from her eyes and sat up.

"What?" she mumbled.

"There's a man," said the young boy who had just shaken her awake.

"What kind of man?" she asked, reaching for her jumper.

"Soldier," said the boy.

Caroline was instantly awake. She pulled the jumper over her head, grabbed her jeans and got to her feet.

"Where?"

"He was at the market just now."

"Just now? What time is it?"

"I dunno," shrugged the boy. "Sun's up."

"You know the rules about going to the market on your own," she scolded.

"Didn't go on my own," he pouted. "Went with Jimmy and Emma."

"Who are how old?" she asked, rhetorically. But the boy had stuck out his lower lip and refused to make eye contact.

Caroline shook her head wearily, wondering when she ended up a mother.

"Okay," she said. "So this soldier, why come tell me?"

The boy sulked a little bit more then finally muttered, petulantly: "He was asking about us."

"Did anyone tell him anything?"

The boy shook his head.

Caroline reached down and began secreting her arsenal of knives about her person, then she grabbed her shotgun and ran for the door.

The man was not very subtle.

It was not uncommon to see people dressed in combat gear, especially these days. But something about the way he wore it told you that it was more than just an affectation. This man was a soldier born and bred; his bearing and body language proclaimed it like a loudhailer. It was something about the way he looked at things. You could see him scanning the environment, calculating routes of ingress and egress, assessing the potential threat of everyone who passed his eye line, turning his body every now and then to make sure his awareness was 360 degrees. He was armed, too, with a machine gun strapped across his chest; his hand was always on it, ready for action.

This man was alert and dangerous.

And looking for her.

She thanked Tom, the potato seller, for allowing her to shelter under his awning as she observed the man, then stepped out into the open square.

The man clocked her instantly, as she'd expected he would. She stood there and deliberately met his gaze, then nodded right, indicating a side street down which she then walked. He followed her a moment later.

They met in the quiet street, surrounded by burned out cars and looted shops. She had the shotgun raised and ready to fire as he stepped into view.

"Hands down," Caroline said.

He let go of his gun and let his hands fall to his side. Caroline considered shooting him there and then. Even talking to this man was a risk, but after a long moment she decided to let him speak.

"Who are you and why are you looking for me?" she asked.

"My name's John. I heard there was an army of kids here, fighting the snatchers. Is that you?"

He had a Midlands accent, and something about his tone of voice made Caroline feel that perhaps he wasn't the villain she'd been expecting.

"Maybe. Maybe not."

"I'll take that as a yes. Good. I have news for you. And an offer."

"I'm listening."

"At dawn tomorrow you are going to be attacked by the church. They know where you are and they've decided to finish you off."

"How the fuck do you know that?"

"My friends and I captured a bunch of them two days ago. One of them was very talkative."

Caroline digested this information for a moment, then asked: "Offer?"

"I want to help."

"How?"

"I've got a lot of experience of fighting in urban environments. I can help you, teach you how to give them a very memorable welcome."

"My mum always warned me to be careful of things that seem to good to be true," said Caroline. "Why would you do this?"

He shrugged. "Because it's the right thing to do."

Caroline snorted derisively.

"I represent a place, a safe place," said the man, undeterred. "A school actually, where a bunch of us look after kids."

Caroline sneered. "Right," she said. "And that doesn't sound at all creepy." She stared hard at this man, trying to work out if he was telling the truth. Despite her sarcasm, she was surprised to find that her initial instinct was to trust him.

"This school have a name?" she asked.

"St Mark's."

Caroline suddenly felt sick. First Matron and now this guy? This was too much of a coincidence. Matron had gone looking for Spider only yesterday. They must have captured her and tortured her until she told them where Caroline and her kids were hiding.

This guy, Caroline realised, was a church infiltrator.

And she knew how to deal with infiltrators.

"You don't say," said Caroline. "And you run this school, do you?"

"Me and some others."

"What's the name of your Matron?"

He narrowed his eyes, curious at this unexpected question. "Jane," he said eventually. "Jane Crowther."

"And you are?"

"I told you, I'm John."

"John Keegan?"

The man's face betrayed his surprise and he nodded. Caroline walked forward, 'til the barrel of her shotgun was less than an inch from the soldier's chest.

"Where is she?" she asked.

"What?"

"Where are you holding her?"

"I'm sorry, I don't..."

"Guys!"

Ten teenaged boys stepped out of doorways and from behind cars, carrying their weapons in plain sight, encircling Caroline and the man.

"Take the gun off," she barked.

"Listen, lets rewind a bit, I don't think we..."

"Take. It. OFF!"

He did so, letting it clatter to the tarmac from where it was retrieved by one of the boys, who gripped it excitedly. Caroline saw the realisation flash across the man's face – that he had miscalculated, was outnumbered and surrounded. She followed his eyes as they darted left and right, assessing which of the boys he should go for and which route of escape he should take back to the market. She saw his posture change ever so slightly as he prepared to make a move.

So she stepped forward and brought her knee up hard into the man's bollocks, doubling him over with a whoosh of escaping breath. *Let's see you make a run for it now*, she thought.

"Jane left here yesterday, heading straight for you bastards," she said.

"No, wait..."

"She told you where we were, didn't she? Jesus, I don't know what you did to her to make her give us up, but I know her. She'd have to be half dead before she told you anything that would lead you to me."

"You've got it wrong..." the man gasped through his pain.

A tall boy stepped forward and cracked the man hard across the head with a truncheon. He crumpled to the ground.

"Don't answer her back, fuckhead," the boy shouted.

"Luke," said Caroline, addressing the boy. "Get back to the others, tell them to pack up and move out. We're not waiting, we're going now."

The boy nodded and ran off down the street.

Caroline knelt down beside the man.

"What was the plan, eh?" she asked. "Infiltrate us, let us think you'd help us fight the church and then lead us into a trap? Box us up and ship us out, problem solved?"

The man looked up at her. "I'm telling you the truth, I just want to help," he said, his voice rough with pain. "How do you know Jane? When was she here?"

"I know her, you bastard, because she's my friend. And she tricked you. That's the best bit. She may have led you right to us, but she fucked you up at the same time."

"I don't..."

"John Keegan's dead, motherfucker. She told me herself." Caroline laughed, but there was no real humour in it. "She told you to pretend to be a dead man because she knew it would tip us off. So you lose, asshole. She was too clever for you."

"No, wait, I see what's happened here..."

Caroline stood up, levelled the shotgun at the man's head, and blew his brains all over the street, even as he tried desperately to cling to the cover story she'd so easily seen through.

"Back home, now," she ordered, and the boys took off down the street.

Caroline stayed for a moment, looking at the corpse of the man who'd tried to win her trust. She had a moment's doubt. What if...?

But she shook her head. No.

"Joke's on you, churchman" she said, and then she ran after her friends.

John Keegan's body lay in the street until nightfall, when the foxes and the dogs fought over it.

The foxes won, and dragged it hungrily away.

CHAPTER FOURTEEN

"I always thought you kind of fancied me, Kate," says Cooper, after swilling down the last mouthful of turkey with a swig of Chablis. It's the first thing he's said since I entered the room, escorted by two guards, and sat down to dinner.

The spread was impressive and smelt incredible. I considered refusing to eat, sitting there with my arms folded, defiant. But that would have been self defeating. I practically lick the plate clean, despite the nausea that his proximity provokes.

I consider correcting him, telling him I'm Jane now. But I pause for a moment as it occurs to me that the distinction is no longer so clear cut. Not now, not with this man sitting across the table from me.

"I did," I reply. "But I always had really, really crappy taste in men."

"Had?" he asks, amused.

"I've had better luck since the world ended."

"So I gather."

"Excuse me?"

"I heard on the grapevine that you hooked up with my old mate Sanders." He leans back in his chair, smug at my surprise.

"Oh yes, I've been keeping tabs on you, Kate. Or, rather, my friends have."

"The Americans."

He nods. "I couldn't believe it when your alias cropped up. I tried to tell Blythe that he'd got the wrong end of the stick, but he didn't buy it. He was so convinced you were some kind of spook."

I have a fork. If I launch myself at him, I've got a better than even chance of getting it through his eyeball. But he knows that I won't. The reason I can't kill him now is the same reason I couldn't shoot him in the Commons. I need answers. Unfortunately, I don't know how to begin asking the questions.

I can't tell whether he's changed in the last eight years, or whether the version of him I met before The Cull was a carefully constructed act. Is this the real man? He's not that different. Speech patterns and body language are the same. The smile, the eyes, the good natured air of vague sarcasm – it's all exactly the same.

"You have so many questions for me, don't you?" he asks.

I nod.

"Then hit me. I'll fill you in." He dabs his lips with a napkin and pushes his chair back from the table, stretching his legs out and linking his fingers behind the back of his head. The midday sun is streaming through the lead latticed windows along the riverside wall of what used to be the Speaker's Cottage. It casts his face into sharp relief.

I try to form my first question, but I come up blank.

"Let me get you started," he says, smiling, for all the world the image of the genial, helpful friend. "Spider is dead. He died that very day."

The same day I did.

"How?"

"I garrotted him."

"Why?"

"He had outlived his usefulness."

I shake my head. "No, sorry. You have to go farther back."

"The clues are all there. You work it out. The point is that the man who killed your brother is dead."

"But you let me think he was still alive."

"Yes, I did. Listen, your role in leading me to his base of operations in Manchester was invaluable. I'd been trying to get a bead on that place for months. Little bastard wouldn't tell me where it was. That was the problem, really. He'd decided not to trust me any more. Thought he could go it alone, run the business without my help and protection. Or, most importantly, without paying me my cut."

"So you taught him a lesson."

"Just so. The idea was that he would kill you himself. I planted that really obvious bug in the phone, assuming he'd find it and shoot you. How was I to know he'd go and kill your brother instead? That was a shock, I can tell you, to find out you were alive. I couldn't just kill you, not after that. It would have aroused too much suspicion. So I managed to wangle you into witness protection."

"And of course my absence protected you, not me."

"Exactly."

"You must have needed someone else on the payroll, someone at Hereford."

"Natch."

"And another bug besides the one in the phone."

"In your shoe, set to become active after a couple of hours so that it would avoid detection."

I nod, dotting Is and crossing Ts in my head. "So you ran Spider's operation, he was just a front?"

"Uh-huh."

"And now...?"

"Now I don't need a psychopathic Serbian mass murderer as my mouthpiece. There's nobody to stop me running my business just the way I want. I use his name though. It had kudos in certain circles. Even after The Cull, there were people who knew the name. It made things easier."

My mind works furiously, piecing it all together.

Cooper must have met Spider when he was in Serbia with the SAS during the Balkan conflict. Spider was probably already running some kind of organised crime ring, maybe even a trafficking route. Cooper offers him a way into the British market and they go into business together. Then he leaves the army and joins the police, managing eventually to get himself assigned to the case, making sure no-one gets close to his operation. This all works nicely until, one day, Spider gets cocky and tries to shut him out and run a Manchester 'branch' all on his own. He must be watching Cooper, making sure he isn't followed. That must be a very complicated game of cat and mouse. No matter what Cooper tries, Spider outwits him.

Cooper needs a way in that Spider won't see coming. And then I turn up, eager little lamb, and lead him straight there. Cooper uses a few of his mates from the SAS to storm the warehouse. At least one of them must have been on the take.

(Sanders? No. I dismiss the thought. Couldn't have been.)

God knows how he spun that one, but he must have had some way to get his bosses to swallow it. He shuts the warehouse down and then hides me away in St Mark's where I can't be any threat to anyone.

Cooper sits opposite me, studying my face as I process everything he's told me.

"You're wondering who you can take revenge on now, aren't you, Kate?" he asks. "Spider's dead, and even though I duped you, I was not directly responsible for James' death."

"Indirectly, though. You planted the fucking bug."

He shrugs. "Kate, he was dead the moment he caught Spider's eye and you know it. The bug was an excuse on a particular day. If it hadn't been that, it would have been something else."

He's right. I do know it.

I consider the man sitting before me and I'm confused. Spider was obviously a monster. Everything about him screamed danger – the way he looked at you, the way he moved, the way he spoke. He was a predator, a shark, a psychopath.

But Cooper is different. Kate never had a moment's unease about him. He was jovial and pleasant but inspired confidence. And he still has an easy capability about him. He doesn't seem unhinged or mad, scary or dangerous at all. He seems like a bloke. Just an ordinary bloke.

He thinks of people as goods to be traded, commodities whose profit potential can be realised – but his manner gives no hint of the pitiless void at the heart of him.

"I spent so long fantasising about what I'd do to that man, if I ever had the opportunity," I say.

"I bet you did. But I'm not him."

"No, you're not. You're the man who used me, set me up to be killed and then condemned me to a life ruled by a lie."

"Mea culpa."

"You're also the man who trafficked vulnerable girls into hell."

"That too."

"Why?"

He shrugs. "Because I can," he says, a parody of abashed modesty, like a cocksure young man admitting to sleeping with a friend's girlfriend; he knows it was wrong but he actually also thinks it was kind of cool.

"But surely you must have realised it was wrong?" The words feel foolish and naïve, but I want an answer.

"The world was built on slavery, Kate. How do you think this country got built? Or America? Or Rome or the pyramids or anything lasting? What I did, what I do, is perfectly natural. The slave masters of the past were pillars of the community, members of guilds and lodges, knighted and rich, the toasts of the town. Why shouldn't I be?"

I look at this man I once invited into my bed, and I feel sick to my stomach. Spider may have been a monster, but he wasn't the worst of it. Not by a long shot.

"I never took advantage. It's important you realise that," he continues. "I busted countless drug dealers in my time. They all had one thing in common – they were users too. The ones who didn't get caught, the smart ones, stayed clean. It was the same with me."

"So that makes it all right then?" I am on the verge of shouting. I take a deep breath.

"I trafficked them into the country, I set them up, sourced the clients and took the money," he says, for some reason intent on justifying himself to me. "But never, not once, did I ever take advantage of one of them. That would have left me vulnerable, you see? There was no room for emotional attachments on the job.

"I had a girlfriend. That surprises you, doesn't it? Jenny. Nice woman, worked for HBOS. Thought I was a dull copper, which kept me safe. And her."

It takes me a moment or two to collect my thoughts.

"All right, morality aside, how did you pull this off?" I gesture to the building around us. "How did you end up here?"

CHAPTER FIFTEEN

My double life ran like clockwork after you helped me sort out Spider. I found a new front man, someone else within the organisation. You never met him. He became the new Spider. It became a title rather than a person, which served me well. It made it clear to the new guy that he was disposable, and it allowed me to continue to use the, shall we say *brand awareness* that Spider had created amongst our clients and competitors.

I considered coming down to school and finishing you off, you know.

Really. You were a loose end. I hate loose ends. But in the end I figured it was riskier to break cover than leave you to rot.

Did you enjoy being Matron? What am I saying, of course you did – the world's ended and you're still doing it!

I had a fifteen year plan. Worked it out while I was undercover in Sarajevo, back in the day. I won't bore you with the details, but it worked, was working, would have worked.

Three years to go when the fucking Cull hit. Three years and then I'd have packed my bags and vanished off the face of the

Earth. Nice little mansion in South America, I reckoned. Get fat, raise a few kids.

Best laid plans, eh.

They knew a lot earlier than they let on. About the blood type thing. Since I'd been in the army, my medical details were on record. I was contacted when the press were still talking about bird flu. Recalled to Hereford.

There was this soldier, Major General Kennett.

Really? What was your impression of him?

Ha! Yeah, I agree actually. Decent bloke. Capable. Prissy, though. Couldn't make the hard decisions.

He briefed us. Not completely, obviously, but he told us we were immune and that it would get bad enough that there might be a breakdown of public order. We were going to be the last line of defence when the police and regular army were no longer able to cope.

Operation Antibody it was called.

I know. Laughable.

They knew, though, the Government. Makes me wonder how long they'd known by then. What they knew about where it came from.

I've searched this place and Number 10 top to bottom more than once. Nothing. No clue at all. I thought there may be some evidence at the MI5 or MI6 buildings, but all the interesting parts are still sealed up. I don't reckon we'll ever know how it started or where it came from.

Who cares now anyway?

Once I was drafted again, my main concern was the organization. I kept in touch with my new Spider by phone, trying to maintain control. I got regular reports as things fell apart but eventually I lost touch with them all.

My network was gone, my resources were gone and I began to suspect that the money I had accumulated would soon be worth less than nothing. All that effort, for what?

So we were broken into teams and dispatched across the country to key installations – nuclear power plants, arms depots, local governments that kind of thing.

I was part of the London team. We were all Regiment or ex-Regiment; the best, you know? Our job was to protect the Government.

At first it was pretty easy. The regular security teams were bloody good. We just shadowed them, learning the ropes. Then when one of them went down, one of us would step into the breach.

They'd done the same in Government, you know. Formed an inner cabinet. The handful of O Neg MPs, some immune peers and a few other top dogs. They were running things long before the rest of the real cabinet fell ill. It was like the ones who knew they were going to survive just started ignoring the ones who were doomed, as if they were already dead.

Some of my colleagues thought it was callous, but of course it was the sensible, expedient thing to do.

The armed forces were recalled from abroad and the O Negs were weeded out. That's when the word spread, you know. Someone in the army worked it out and told the press.

Anyway they formed these units of immune men and women. Army, police, fire and medical. All the emergency services. Even the BBC were sorted out, a core team of broadcasters who could keep a skeleton news service on air until there was no-one left to watch it. But there weren't enough of us to go around, so they had to be concentrated in one place. One safe haven where there would be enough immune people to stick it out until it was all over and retain order and civilisation amongst themselves.

It was a good plan. It's what I would have done. They made one crucial mistake, though. They chose the wrong place to make a stand.

They chose London.

Why do – sorry, did – all politicians have such a love affair with London? I never understood it. Obviously what they should have done is taken off for somewhere remote, rural. I actually said this to the PM once.

Sorry? Oh yes, he was immune. I know, what are the odds! Things would have gone very differently if he hadn't been. There'd have been an almighty power struggle. But because he was top dog, and he knew he was going to survive, he was able to lay down the law pretty much unchallenged. He was a subtle fucker, too. Lots of backroom deals went down before the rest of Parliament worked out what was going on.

So, yeah, I told him he should move everyone out to Macynnleth or some other alternative energy centre or something. And it's not as if he didn't think along those lines, 'cause the plans for Operation Motherland were drawn up at around this time, so they knew the advantage of being away from the urban centres, they knew the risk of secondary diseases and riots and all that stuff.

But he was determined that they had to stay put, right here in the Palace of Westminster, barricading themselves in like it was Fort Apache.

"The people need to see that we haven't deserted our posts," is what he told me.

And of course once the news got out about the virus and what it was really doing, the riots began.

I thought I'd seen desperation before, during the siege, but this was a whole other order of magnitude. The savagery of it was...

We set up concrete barricades along Whitehall, blew Westminster Bridge, put up gun emplacements in the cathedral. Put a ring of steel all around Parliament Square and kept them out. Hundreds of thousands of them. It would never have worked in peace time. We'd have been overrun. Tear gas and water cannons, even rubber bullets wouldn't have kept them out.

We had live ammunition, though. And grenades and tanks.

There came a day when it was obvious that we were going to be stormed, that Parliament was going to fall. I was with the PM when he made the call to shut down the BBC. He insisted he had to close them down before we opened fire on the crowds. Didn't want news of the massacre to spread. I thought that was stupid – the more people knew, I reckoned, the better. Spread a little fear, show them we mean business. But he wouldn't have it.

I think he was ashamed of the order he was about to give.

I was given the job of leading the team that flew to White City. There was a tent city outside Television Centre, as if people wanted to be close to some symbol of order and safety. The good old BBC, they'll look after us. You know, I think there was more faith in them than in Government at that point.

They let us in because they thought we'd been sent to protect them. When we ordered them to go off air they refused.

So that's where the massacre began. I must say it was a very odd feeling, kind of surreal, shooting Jeremy Paxman in the head.

We took some fire too. God knows where they got guns from, but they put up a good fight. Kate Adie may have been in her sixties, but she shot two of my men. And fucking Andy Hamilton stayed on air on Radio Four the whole time, but we'd cut the lines to the transmitter, so no-one heard his final broadcast. I let him live, actually. He always made me laugh

Once they were down I radioed in and the shooting began back in Whitehall. By the time we got back it was mostly over. There were bodies everywhere. I remember flying over Trafalgar Square and seeing it thick with corpses, like a human carpet.

Sorry? No, not at all. It was necessary. I thought so then and I still think so. Needed to be done.

The problem was that the PM's power base wasn't as strong as we'd thought. There were some people in cabinet who tried to stop him giving the order to open fire. While I was busy at the BBC, these dissenters tried to stage a coup. Some of our guys, SAS bodyguards, joined in. Said they couldn't carry out an order like that.

Wimps.

It was a hell of a fight. By the time we got back the PM was already dead, killed in the initial confrontation. Despite that, his supporters were winning. The coup was botched and the rebels were executed on the spot.

But the next day something unexpected happened. Kennett turned up with a force of soldiers, and told us that we were under arrest. Following illegal orders, he said. Took some balls, I reckon, for him to stand up to us. There were eighteen of us, entrenched, all Regiment. He knew that we wouldn't just roll over, and he knew he couldn't force us to hand over our weapons. So he basically turned his back on us, threw us out of the army, said we'd all been dishonourably discharged and would not be welcome at Operation Motherland HQ.

Then he buggered off to Salisbury and left us in charge of the wreckage.

The only one who left with them was our mutual friend Sanders. One of the rioters had managed to hit him with a rock while he was on the barricades, so he'd been out of action when the order to fire was given. Lucky bastard had a get out of jail free card. I reckon he'd have opened fire like the rest of them, but later that day he swore to me that he wouldn't have.

You think so? Well, I suppose you got to know him a little better than I did.

Anyway, with the PM dead, most of the cabinet wandering around like headless chickens, and the bleeding hearts executed, I saw my chance and took control. It wasn't hard. I had the most experience of command. I acted like I was the boss and they fell into line.

But Central London was empty. Those left alive fled the centre after the massacre, and the virus was still finishing its work.

I was the ruler of a ghost town.

I didn't have grand ambitions. We fortified our position as thoroughly as we could, gathered up all the food we could find, and waited for the virus to burn itself out. That was a long winter. Quite boring, actually.

By the time spring came I'd worked out a new plan. I divided the city into quadrants and we began clearing it. Emptying the roads of cars, dragging all the bodies to mass pyres, stockpiling fuel and resources. We did that for a whole year, one street at a time. Reclaiming the heart of the city.

The Army stayed away. I knew they were collecting weapons from all around the country and building their great depot on the plain, but they didn't want to get involved in London. Kennett left it to us. Probably figured that time would only make him stronger and us weaker. He'd have been right too. I'd consolidated my position but I had no real power base because nobody would come into the centre any more. I think Kennett would probably have come for us eventually, and I'd have been toast. If it wasn't for the American.

I bet you encountered a lot of religious cults in the last few years? I expected the same thing to happen in the outskirts of London, but they all unified behind one preacher. I first heard about the American three years ago. He'd built up quite a following in West London. I found out later that he'd flown into Heathrow and started preaching at the first settlement he found. He taught people how to tune into the broadcasts.

That's right, yeah. The Miracle.

So he gathered a huge following very quickly and then one day he and a gang of his followers walked into my territory and said hello. I think his acolytes were supposed to intimidate us.

They were all dressed in army surplus and carrying shotguns.

They nearly wet themselves when they realized who we were.

He didn't, though. He stayed very cool.

So I let him talk. Gave him dinner at Number 10, allowed him to make his pitch. I needed allies, after all. He showed me the broadcast and I was impressed. I didn't think this Abbot guy was the new messiah but I could see how people could want to believe he was.

I wasn't convinced they were a real force, though. I mean, a bunch of religious nutters run by a Yank didn't seem like much of a threat to Operation Motherland. But then, after dinner, the yank took me down into the cellars of Number 10. There was a door down there that I'd not been able to breach. The keypad was still active, run by some distant power source, and I'd had no joy with the code.

But this guy knew it. That's when I really started paying attention. I asked him who he was, but he just smiled. To this day he's never told me, but he must have been CIA, probably based here before The Cull. He knew all sorts of crazy shit, let me tell you.

The bunker down there is pretty extensive, with lots of comms equipment. He took me to an office, which I think was the PM's retreat in the event of a major attack, and said to pick up the red phone on the desk.

I did so, and after a second's silence I heard someone saying my name.

The voice at the end of the phone said he was the President, that he was working with the Abbot, and that they had managed to restore rule of law. He wanted to know if I was the de facto PM, so of course I said yes.

Long story short, he had a proposal for me. If I would start exporting children to the US, he would send their army to back me up.

Now look at this from my position. On one hand I have a power base but no power, and the British Army knows where I am and is almost certainly getting ready to come and flush me out. On the other, I'm being offered the support of an entire army that will *do as I say* as long as I provide them with the resource they require. Can you think of anyone better suited to round up the kids and ship them abroad? I mean, it's kind of top of my CV, isn't it?

So I told the President about Operation Motherland. Where they were and what they were doing. I told him if he wanted my help, he would have to eliminate them first.

He put me in touch with Blythe in Iraq and the rest you know. I realised that once Kennett was out of the way, I would have to deal with Blythe, but at least initially he'd be on my side. I'd have time to work out a strategy to deal with him.

And then, hallelujah, the Yanks took out Kennett and his forces, but managed to get themselves wiped out in the process. I'm not ashamed to say I did a little jig when I heard about the nuke. Couldn't believe my fucking luck. The biggest single threat to my power base had been neutralized and there was no fall out.

Well, not for me, anyway. Ha ha.

At that point I could have told the President to go fuck himself, but the thing was I kind of enjoyed being back in the trafficking business. It gave me something to do, and it meant that my sphere of influence spread. People started to become afraid of me, to respect me and my forces. Me and the Yank still work together. He takes care of the religious stuff – brainwashing the plebs and spreading the word – while I take care of logistics and manpower.

Pretty much the entire territory inside the M25 is mine now, and soon we'll start moving outside. I actually had your school down as my first port of call. Once I've dealt with a little problem in Hammersmith tomorrow, maybe we'll take a trip there together.

What? Oh, didn't I say?

How do you think the Abbot stays alive? Blood transfusions, Kate. Daily. Fresh, young, healthy blood from universal donors.

He's basically a vampire.

And Britain is his blood bank.

CHAPTER SIXTEEN

"Attacking that convoy had seemed like such a good idea at the time," said Caroline, shaking her head in frustration. "This is like herding cats."

The army that she'd accumulated during the previous year were pretty well drilled. They followed orders and knew when to shut up. The hundred or so kids that they'd released from the convoy, on the other hand, were a gaggle of confused, impulsive, homesick brats with snotty noses and bad attitudes. Trying to smuggle them out of the city without drawing attention would have been hard enough, but doing so while they fought, cried, wandered off or kept nipping into abandoned buildings in search of a bed, was driving her nuts. She had to keep reminding herself not to be angry. They were hungry and tired, and it was a freezing cold night.

While she mostly managed to keep a lid on her anger, her fear was growing unchecked. They needed to get a move on. It would be dawn in an hour and they weren't far enough away from their old nest yet. The trail would be fresh and easy to follow. The churchies had jeeps and helicopters. It had taken Caroline six hours to move the kids about a mile north; it would take their pursuers two minutes to cover the same distance.

"Luke," she called. The gangly teenage boy who served as her lieutenant was at her side in an instant. He was a year older than her but he was puppy dog loyal and hard as nails. "I want you to take Andrew, Melissa and Lizzie, and scout ahead. Find us somewhere to hole up. Somewhere defensible, okay?"

He nodded, gathered up the other three kids and ran to the end of the road, scanning for activity, then ducking out of sight. They were travelling parallel to the main road out of Hammersmith, using the residential side roads as cover. The idea had been to go north 'til they crossed the M25, then swing west and circle round until they were above Kent before heading south to the school. At this rate, she realised, it would be a death march. She was rapidly coming to the conclusion that they would have to find somewhere safe to stay out of sight while a couple of them made the journey. That way the school could send a lorry to collect the kids. That is, if the school was still there. Caroline was sure that Matron had given up their Hammersmith base, what if she had given up the school too? She dismissed the thought, not because she didn't think it likely, but because there was nothing she could do about it. If the school was gone, she decided, they'd just have to go to ground in the countryside. There'd be plenty of places to disappear.

Those kids who'd been with her for a while were trying to keep the new arrivals quiet as they neared the street corner. Caroline was in front, gun at the ready, when she heard a single shot echo back to her from the road ahead. She spun around waving frantically, indicating for the kids to scatter. Her 'soldiers' immediately began shushing the kids and herding them into the abandoned houses. In one minute the street was empty, the fear of imminent discovery managing what she'd been trying for hours to achieve – keeping the little brats quiet so she could think. She could see the pale faces of her guys at the doorways of the houses they'd taken shelter in, standing guard, waiting for her to make a move.

She gripped the gun tightly and ran to the pavement, pressing herself into the shadows and creeping forward so she could peer round the corner into the next road.

Her heart sank as she saw a pair of dual-cab pickups on the road, their roof-mounted spotlights picking out her four friends, who were down on their knees with their hands behind their backs. Each vehicle carried a team of four heavily armed men, three of whom were advancing with their guns trained on the captives. The road was wide and open, and the cars and kids were in the middle of a huge junction, providing almost no cover. She couldn't get close to them without being seen by the two men who were standing in the open backs of the vehicles, scanning the area for possible attack.

They were too far away for her to hear what the men said when they reached the four kneeling children, but she could tell they were shouting. Andrew was typically defiant and shouted back, which earned him a gun butt in the face and then, once he'd fallen over, a hard kick to the solar plexus.

Caroline clenched the gun tighter, so wanting to blow that fucker's head off but seeing no way to do so without leading them right to the children she was trying to protect. She was about to turn away when first one lookout then the other went rigid and dropped like stones off the sides of the vehicles on to the road. Caroline hadn't heard any shots. What the fuck had just happened?

The men interrogating her friends didn't seem to know either. At first they just looked confused. One of them walked to the nearest car to see what was going on. Just as he rounded the cab he dropped too, silent and instant. Caroline realised they were under attack, but she still had no idea by whom, or how. She was still too far away to approach unseen, even with this distraction. If she made a play, there was still a better than average chance that she'd be cut down. She bit her lip and, fighting down her instinctive desire to wade into the fight, waited to see how this would play out.

The engines of the vehicles revved as the two drivers indicated their desire to leave. The two men still in the open hesitated, unsure, and then ran – one to each cab. Neither of them made it. This time, as the second one fell, Caroline caught a glimpse of something sticking out of his chest. She couldn't be sure at this distance and in this light, but she thought maybe it was an arrow.

The drivers didn't wait another second. They screamed away at speed, racing to escape this silent attacker. One of them made it, but the other began swerving wildly from left to right before smashing straight through the frontage of an old pub, erupting into flames. The archer must have managed to shoot the driver through his windscreen while he was moving. Shit, this guy was good.

The other pickup squealed around a corner and vanished into the night as Caroline broke cover and ran to see how her four friends were doing. Andrew was sitting up, his face a mess of tears and snot. The other three were getting to their feet, mouths open. Caroline went and inspected one of the dead churchies. Sure enough when she rolled him over there was a thin wooden arrow buried deep in his chest. It had been painted black.

"That's mine," said a deep voice behind her and she spun, instinctively raising her weapon as she did so.

Since there were no streetlights, there were few shadows for the archer to step out of. He just sort of materialised out of the darkness. Dressed head to toe in dark green, he held a wooden bow in his right hand. A quiver of arrows stuck up over his left shoulder.

"The beauty of arrows, you see, is that they're recyclable. Shoot a bullet or a cartridge, like the one that shotgun of yours fires, and it's gone forever. But an arrow..." He stepped past her, reached down and yanked the wooden shaft from the dead man's chest. It came out with a soft squelch. "That can be used again."

"Who are you?" asked Melissa, who was now standing behind Caroline.

"My name's Ferguson," said the archer in a thick Irish accent, as he wiped his arrow clean on the dead man's jacket. He stood up and slotted it back into his quiver, ready for another day. "I'm a Ranger." He seemed surprised that this pronouncement was greeted with silence. "From Nottingham," he added. And then: "I'm with Hood."

He stared at their blank faces, waiting for the spark of recognition. Nothing.

"I can see we need a better publicist," he said, smiling.

"Thank you," said Andrew, now on his feet.

"You're welcome. You know what would be a good way to

thank me? Getting this young lady to stop pointing a shotgun at me."

Everyone stared at Caroline, who held her gun steady. "Hood?" she said. "Robin Hood in Nottingham?" The sarcasm dripped like honey.

"The very same," said the archer.

"Right. And you're, what, one of his Merry Men?"

The archer shook his head "No. I'm one of the Sullen Men. The Merry Men are, you know, merrier than me. They crack more jokes."

Caroline could see her friends smiling, but she didn't follow suit. "Why should I trust you?"

The archer indicated the dead bodies of the churchies that littered the crossroads, the look on his face saying 'you want more proof?'

"Bit convenient, though, isn't it? You just turning up like this, just in time to rescue us from the bad guys. Almost like it was staged."

"Caroline, seriously?" said Luke.

"Think about it, Luke. Perfect way to gain our trust. What if Matron didn't tell them where the school is? This would be a perfect way to infiltrate us and get us to lead them straight there. They've already tried it once, remember."

"He killed them, Caroline," said Melissa.

"Yeah, and wasn't that easy?"

"You think they let him?" Andrew's tone of voice betrayed the incredulity he and all his friends were feeling. Caroline didn't understand why they couldn't see it.

"They're fucking churchies, guys," she said. "Probably think they're martyrs, seventy-eight virgins waiting for them or something." She glanced at their shocked faces. "What, you doubt my judgment now, after everything we've been through? Don't you see this is what he wants? Turn you against me, let you lead him to the school and then it'll be a fucking army of snatchers turning up at to carry us off. We should just kill him and move on."

Luke stepped forward and gently laid his hand on the barrel of her shotgun. "Too paranoid, Caroline. I don't buy it."

The archer wisely stayed silent, watching Caroline closely, waiting to see how this would play out.

Caroline clenched her jaw. She could just pull the trigger, finish this guy regardless. It was the safe thing to do. It was necessary, she knew that. Why couldn't the others see it? Once he was dead they'd fall into line, they'd have no choice. Who else was going to shepherd them to safety? They'd realise eventually that she was right. She squeezed the trigger gently.

"No!" shouted Luke, pushing the barrel down as the gun went off. The cloud of lead pellets embedded itself in tarmac. The archer didn't even flinch.

Caroline spun fast, dropping the gun and drawing a knife from her belt as she did so. The blade was at Luke's throat before he could step backwards.

They stood there, frozen, for a long moment. Luke was scared but defiant, sticking his chest out and staring Caroline down. Eventually she withdrew the knife and resheathed it.

"Traitor," she spat. Then she turned on her heels and stalked off into the darkness, away from her friends and the children who were beginning to emerge from hiding to see what was going on.

She needed to be alone.

Ferguson found her an hour later.

The shop downstairs had been looted clean, but the flat above it, although long abandoned, still had some stuff lying around that no-one had bothered to cart off. She lay on the double bed, ignoring the smell of mould, and took another swig from the bottle of whisky she'd found down the back of the sofa.

She disregarded the soft knock at the front door. It was open anyway, and she knew it would just be one of her friends come to coax her back. She already knew she was going to relent, but she allowed herself the luxury of sulking there in the darkness, knowing that she was being self indulgent but needing to be persuaded, needing someone to make explicit how much she was needed and valued.

She didn't look up as someone entered and sat at the foot of the bed. Which is why she was so surprised when they began talking and she realised who it was.

"How long have you been looking after them?" asked the archer.

She thought: *I don't recognise your right to ask me that.* She didn't reply.

"It's not easy, being a leader," he said. "Managing people, trying not to let them down, making decisions when they're too stupid or lazy to make them for themselves."

"They're not stupid," muttered Caroline. "They're just kids."

"True. But how old are you?"

"Fuck off." She took another swig.

"Not old enough to be drinking that, that's for sure."

"Touch my bottle and I'll slice your fucking hand off."

"Wouldn't dare. Your deputy told me where you're making for."

"Then he's a blabbermouth twat who deserves everything he gets."

"You kiss your mother with that mouth?"

She looked up, open mouthed, then she threw the bottle at his head. He swatted it away.

"Sorry," he said, seemingly genuine. "It's just something you say, isn't it?"

"Not any more," she growled through gritted teeth.

"No, I s'pose not."

There was a long awkward silence before Caroline said: "What do you fucking want, anyway?"

"This school you're heading for, St Mark's."

"What about it?"

"Luke says their matron was with you. Is that right?"

"Like you don't already know," she muttered darkly.

"Is what he told me correct – did she go to the centre to kill Spider?"

Caroline glowered at him, then eventually nodded once.

"And you used to know her? You were at the school?"

Again she nodded.

"Right. Well that's good, because you see I met some of their people. Three guys – Lee, John and Tariq. Do you know them?"

"I knew Lee for a while. Never met his dad or the other one. They're dead, anyway. The snatchers killed them when they captured her."

Ferguson shook his head. "No, they didn't. I was there that day. I was in the other lorry, the one you didn't manage to liberate – good job, by the way. We faked their deaths so I could get inside Spider's organisation."

Caroline shook her head. "No, don't believe you."

"They're still free. By now they should have got word to my boss. We're going to bring these bastards down, Caroline. And you can help us."

"No, Matron said they were dead. She said she knew they were dead."

Ferguson paused, slightly thrown by her insistence. Caroline heard the edge of panic in her voice and tried to damp it down without success.

"I promise you, Caroline, they're alive. The school is safe, and my boss will be sending help. I've been in Westminster for two days. I've mapped the layout, the disposition of their forces, their timetables. Everything. I need to get this information to my people so we can mount an assault..."

"What did he look like?"

"Sorry?"

"John. Lee's Dad. What did he look like?"

"Um, medium height, brown hair and eyes. Strong chin. I dunno, I didn't study him. Why?"

Caroline felt like wetting herself. She tried to rationalise it, to tell herself that no, she had been right, the man she'd killed had definitely been an imposter. But she knew.

Oh God, she thought. *What have I done?*

CHAPTER SEVENTEEN

By the time we reached Hemel Hempstead my arse hurt like hell. I'd done plenty of horse riding after The Cull, but not so much since Salisbury. I had shooting pains in both my legs, souvenirs of the times they really were shot, and chaffing in places that, thank God, had managed to avoid being shot so far.

I got down from my horse feeling like an old man, walking bow legged and grunting the way oldsters do when they get up from an armchair.

"Behold, the mighty warrior," laughed Jack as I hobbled towards him.

I let my horse loose to graze on the patch of grass by the car park of what used to be the West Herts College.

"Tease me again and I'll shoot you in both legs," I snapped. "See how you like horse riding then."

He patted his steed on the flank and it trotted off to graze alongside its fellows.

The sun was setting. It had been a cold, rain-drenched ride

and although the downpour had finally ended, the evening temperature was dropping fast.

"Is it open?" I asked, indicating the double doors that led into the main college building.

Jack nodded.

"We'll sweep it first. Just in case." This was Wilkes, leader of the six Rangers that Hood had gifted us.

Tall and solid, he was a no-nonsense Yorkshireman with ruddy cheeks and jet black hair. He'd hardly spoken to me since we'd been introduced, except to make clear that he and his men were here to help, but they'd do so on their terms and wouldn't be taking any orders from me. I didn't argue. I figured once they met Dad they'd fall into line, recognising the value of having a trained soldier in command.

The five men with him talked and joked amongst themselves, but gave me a wide berth. At least they weren't openly resentful, like the ones who'd ridden with me up from Thetford, so I supposed that was progress of a sort.

I stepped back and let them enter first, with swords drawn. Jack and I stood outside feeling foolish and cold. Five minutes later the door swung open again and one of them ushered us inside.

The college had been trashed, but there was still plenty of wooden furniture for us to chop up for firewood. Within the hour we had a big bonfire in the car park. We gathered round it for warmth and shoved foil-wrapped potatoes into the flames to roast.

No one came to investigate the fire. If there were people still living in the vicinity, they stayed away.

"I thought they'd be here by now," I said as I watched the flames consume a pile of old lab tables. "The snatchers were due to attack the kids in Hammersmith yesterday. If Dad got them out in time, they should be here."

"You think they might be having to fight their way out?" asked Jack.

"Could be," I replied.

"So how long do we wait?"

"We go at dawn, I reckon. If they're besieged, they'll need us."

"Oh yeah, you eight guys are a hell of a rescue force."

I span around, startled by this new voice. Tariq stepped into the firelight, gun in hand, smiling broadly.

"Don't move!" came a yell from the other side of the bonfire.

"Relax," I shouted as I got to my feet. "He's with us."

"What happened?" asked Jack, as anxious as I was at seeing Tariq here. "Did they attack the school already?"

Tariq shook his head, then indicated behind him with his hook. I stared into the darkness and realised that he was not alone. About forty children I recognised stepped forward into the orange light. They all wore their camo gear, their faces streaked with shoe polish, their hands full of hardware.

"We decided," said a boy I was shocked to realise was Green, "to bring the fight to them."

"That fucker shot me. Shove a knife in his throat would you, Nine Lives?"

I ignored the voice in my head as I approached Green, who sat on his own at the point where the fire's warmth ceased to give protection against the frost that was settling on the hard ground.

"Hi," I said. "You mind?" I indicated that I'd like to join him, and he waved me forward. I sat down next to him, watching the crowd mingling around the fire.

"You want to know what made me change my mind. Why I picked up a gun again and joined the team," he said. It wasn't a question. "Honestly, I don't know." There was a long pause as he considered.

"Partly it's because I feel like a grown up now," he said. "I know I'm strong enough that no-one could make me do the kind of things Mac made me do when I was part of his team."

"That was what you were afraid of?" I didn't know whether to be insulted or not. Did he really think that Jane or I would ask him to do something he didn't feel okay with?

"You don't know what it was like," he said, staring off into the distance. "You always played things your way, but I liked being a follower. It made me feel safe. It's attractive, you know? Allowing something else to make all the decisions, ceding your free will to someone else."

It wasn't attractive to me. In fact it was baffling. But I'd seen enough cults and armies to know that what Green was describing was more than simply common.

"If you do that," he continued, "then the person who's in control can make you do anything, anything at all, and you never think about the morality of it. You rationalise it away and say that it's their fault. You're just following orders. No blame attached. It insulates you."

"But you did question it," I pointed out. "You turned on Mac. You shot him dead, mate."

"Not soon enough." He sighed. "But afterwards, when he and the school were gone and we'd relocated, I decided to treat it like a drug. I though I had to go cold turkey. No guns. No power to give orders. No clique or gang. I would be completely independent. That way no-one could ever get their hooks in me again. I couldn't fall off the wagon, be seduced into letting someone else tell me what to do."

"So it wasn't fighting you were afraid of, it was following orders?"

He nodded.

"And you don't feel that way any more?"

"No. I trust you and your Dad, and Jane and Tariq. You're good people. Plus, I know now that it wasn't a drug. I won't have a relapse because I changed when I shot Mac. It's taken me a while to realise it, but I'm a different person now. There's nothing left of the boy I was. His vices aren't mine. His weaknesses, either."

He turned his head and looked me in the eye. "Think back Lee," he said. "To who you were before The Cull. Is there anything about that person that you recognise when you look in the mirror?"

I shook my head. "No."

"Me neither. I'm a man now," said Green, turning back to the fire. "I know my mind and I know I'm capable of choosing for myself. And right now, I choose to fight. I owe it to Matron, and to all the kids I teach."

"No, really, just stab him would you?" said the voice. "Pious little shit."

"Thank you," I told Green, pretending I didn't hear a dead man whispering in my ear. "I won't betray your trust."

Green smiled into space. "You'd better not," he said.

*   *   *

Eventually everyone else left to spend the night in the beds at the nearby hospital. I stayed put and watched the fire burn. I knew I should try to sleep, that going into battle tired is suicide. But there was no point even closing my eyes. Ferguson hadn't made contact, Dad was missing and Jane was captured.

I didn't know what to worry about most – my Dad fighting off a besieging army, Jane being tortured by a monster who treated people like dirt, or our chances of getting cut to ribbons by landmines and gun towers sometime around teatime the next day. Whichever way I turned, things looked bleak.

As the sun rose I heard the distant engine of a lorry. I grabbed my gun and ran to the main road, careful to stay out of sight as the noise grew louder. A minute or two later a removal lorry, huge and unwieldy, rolled down the road. As it passed I caught a glimpse of the driver and ran out, waving my arms and shouting. He must have seen me in the rear view mirror because the lorry pulled up and Ferguson jumped down from the cab.

I ran to met him.

"Is my Dad with you?" I asked.

He shook his head. "I found the kids, though."

"The ones in Hammersmith?"

He nodded. A girl jumped down from the other side of the cab. Short and stocky, with an eye patch and long red hair, there was something vaguely familiar about her.

"Hi Lee," she said as she walked to Ferguson's side. My face must have betrayed my confusion, because she added: "Caroline."

"Bloody hell," I said, astonished. "We looked for you everywhere."

"I know. Matron told me."

"What?"

"Lee, did you get to Nottingham?" asked Ferguson.

"Um, yeah, there are some of your mates in the hospital. Just down the road on the right." He took off past me to compare notes with his colleagues. Caroline walked to the back doors of the lorry and opened them, revealing a small army of children huddled in the back.

"Caroline," I asked. "Have you seen Jane?"

She nodded, and something about the way the blood drained from her face told me that she did not have good news for me.

CHAPTER EIGHTEEN

"I meant to ask," says Cooper as we walk the corridors of power. "Were your people responsible for taking the plane at Heathrow last week?"

"Someone took a plane?"

He examines my face closely to see if my surprise is genuine. He decides it is, and he nods.

"Yeah, a bloody 747, no less. A woman and a bloke killed a bunch of my guys and flew to New York leaving me with four months worth of children backed up at the airport."

"I came here to kill you," I suddenly blurt out, frustrated by small talk.

"No, you came here to kill the man who killed your brother. Your surprise prevented you from killing me. And now I've answered all your questions, you have all the facts at your fingertips. So you have a choice."

"Which is?"

"Join me or die," he says slowly, rolling his eyes, as if explaining something very simple to an idiot.

"But why offer me that choice? Why not just kill me? What makes you think I won't pretend to join up in order to save my life until I can find a way to betray you?"

He sighs and looks up at the ceiling, shaking his head at my obstinacy. "I like you, Kate. Always did. You've got, what do they call it? Pluck, spunk, guts."

"God, you really are a public school boy, aren't you?"

"Plus, you know, you're not bad looking all told."

"Oh thanks," I say, then a thought occurs to me. "Christ, you're not saying you want to go steady?"

"Don't be silly. I'd wake up with a knife in my heart."

"Trust me, it wouldn't get that far."

"Pity," he says with a wink, as he walks away. I trail after him as he promenades through his echoing palace, confounded. I just can't work out why I'm still alive.

"This is the central lobby," he says as we enter a huge chamber with four corridors running off it at each point of the compass. A massive chandelier hangs above our heads and statues regard us gnomically from the shadows. "Directly above us is a big tower and in it there's this huge metal contraption, like an engine," says Cooper. "No-one has any idea what it is. You see, when they were building this place they gave the contract for the central heating to a guy who said he had a revolutionary new system that he would install. Once he was done all they had to do was switch it on and voila, nice warm Palace. But when they opened it for use they switched it on and nothing happened. So they called for the guy to come explain and he'd gone. Legged it with the money! So no-one knows if this machine above is a real central heating system that turned out not to work, or a huge fake thingy put there to make the con look good!"

As he talks I realise he's enjoying himself, holding court, having an audience. And then it dawns on me that I haven't seen him speak to anyone since I arrived. He's barked orders, taken reports, had brief conversations about logistical issues, all with his fellow ex-SAS inner circle or the newly recruited chancers and religios. But I've picked up no sense of camaraderie, no friendship, just cold business.

"Jesus fucking Christ," I say as it hits. He turns to look at me.

"What?" he asks.

"You're lonely. That's it, isn't it? It's lonely at the top for the poor slave trader. You don't have any friends, only subordinates and acolytes. You don't want a girlfriend, necessarily. You just want someone to talk to."

He says nothing, but the smile has gone from his face, the mask has dropped and there's a warning in his eyes. He doesn't try to deny it, though.

"So you think I'll just hang out with you while you tell me top Parliament facts, and bitch about how hard it is pimping for a vampire? You think we'll end up buddies? That I'll gradually come to understand, to empathise and commiserate? And how do you see this ending, huh? Will I fall into your arms and soothe away your ennui, finally won over by your dignity and..."

A single, shocking slap to the face silences me. But only for a moment.

"You are fucking deluded, you know that? Look at where we are. Look at what you do. You're the fucking King, Cooper. You don't get to have friends. You get to have subjects. You don't get understanding. If you're lucky, at best you get loyalty, at worst obedience through fear and then betrayal. That's the job, your majesty. Fucking live with it."

I fall silent, breathing hard, furious and defiant.

He waits for a moment, although whether he's waiting for me or him to calm down, I'm not sure.

"You just demonstrated exactly why I want you around Kate," he says, his face full of something like admiration.

"What, 'cause I think you're pitiful?"

"No. Because you kept talking even after I slapped you." He turns on his heels and walks away briskly. "Try anything clever and you'll be shot," he says over his shoulder. "See you at seven sharp for dinner."

So here I am, given the run of the Houses of Parliament. I'm not alone, though. I've got a shadow; a bored looking soldier who lurks around corners and watches from a distance in case I try and scale the barbed wire fences, stroll through the minefields or jump into the river... actually, that's not a bad thought.

I gaze out of a first floor window, considering the current of the Thames. I can see it swirl and roil beneath me, strong, tidal and deadly. Freezing cold, too. I dismiss the idea. It would be suicide. I glance at the ornate cornices that decorate the outside, wondering if maybe I could climb down at low tide. But no. Again, suicide.

A rope perhaps? I file that thought away.

I notice a sign directing me to the House of Lords and I figure I may as well take a look. I'm surprised to find a guard on the door. He sits on a chair staring into space, not enough wit even to read a book to pass the time. As I approach I wonder if he's in some kind of coma, but he looks up as I reach for the doors.

"You got the boss's permission to go in there?" he says, his voice a low moan of thoughtless boredom.

"No. Do I need it?"

He purses his lips and shrugs. "Knock yourself out," he says. "The one with the tattoos swings both ways. You clean up after yourself, though. If you damage anything, I mean. I'm not bloody doing it."

I have no idea what he's talking about, but I push open the door and enter the second chamber.

I'm greeted by a young black woman in a short black dress.

I stare at her for a moment, in surprise. Then my gaze moves past her to take in the room beyond. There are about twenty women here, all dressed casually. The upper benches have been made into little nests, with blankets and pillows and piles of clothing. It only takes me a moment to work out what I've walked into.

"Hey Jools, we got fresh blood!" yells the woman in front of me. A short Asian woman steps down from her nest and walks across the floor towards me. All eyes are on me.

Jools stands in front of me, hands on hips, assessing me.

"You a bit scrawny," she says. "They'll feed you up, tho. You got a name?"

"Jane. I'm, um, not... Are you the boss here?"

A chorus of cackled laughter makes me blush. "Look behind you, sweetheart," says Jools. I turn and there, written across the doors in white paint is the legend: "We are your lords now. Bow down before us."

"Only boss here is Spider," she says. "But he visits me more than most, so I got his ear, like. You know?"

A woman on the bench behind her laughs and says: "you got his cock, more like!" More laughter from the ranks.

I can't help but assess Cooper's preferred concubine. My height, small hips and breasts, but a pretty heart shaped face. A woman, but girlish. Tough though, streetwise.

"So that makes you, what, top dog in the harem?" I ask.

"Summat like that, yeah. So we'll get you a bed sorted then you can tell us your story."

"No," I say hurriedly. "I won't be staying."

She cocks her head and narrows her eyes, all welcome swept away by sudden suspicion.

"That so."

"I'm a doctor," I say, as if that explains anything.

"Shit, I was an MP," comes a voice from somewhere to my left. "Don't make no difference here."

"I mean that I'm here to help. How many of you are there?"

Jools doesn't answer.

"Are you all well? When did you last have a check up?"

"We're all clean, if that's what you mean. If we weren't, we'd be in the river."

"That's not..." I'm too uncomfortable to know what to say. I'm out of my depth here.

"How many of you are there?" I ask again.

"Eighteen," says Jools.

"Okay. Thanks. I'll, um, I'll see you around I guess."

Jools steps forward and gets right in my face, chin up, eyes wide. "Not if I see you first."

I can't get out of there fast enough.

Yet as I walk away from Cooper's rape room, it occurs to me that there are nineteen women in that room, and the ones who haven't gone all Stockholm will be very angry indeed.

I have nineteen potential allies on the inside. It's not much, but it's a start.

There is a special quality behind the eyes which all the men who work for Cooper have. Something cold and dead and hidden. Every one of them has it. The guy following me around Parliament is the same. It makes sense, I suppose; to be the kind of person who treats other people as cattle you must either have to kill some part of you off, or be born without it in the first place.

Whatever that part of a person it is – compassion, empathy, simple kindness – it dies easy. All it takes for it to wither away is peer pressure and time.

"What did you do? I ask him as I open my bedroom door in the morning and find him standing outside, patient as stone. "Before."

He shakes his head, unwilling to discuss it. I don't think he's one of the original SAS team. I wonder who he was, and I wonder what changed him. School teacher who watched his pupils die, perhaps? Accountant who found comfort in ledgers and spreadsheets but feels cut adrift in a world without numerical order? Drug addict forced to go cold turkey? Or just a family man who held his wife and children as they bled out?

He's a pretty nondescript bloke. Not a muscled heavy or a lean military type. He's in his early forties, slight spare tyre around the waist (which testifies to how well they eat here), receding hairline, pallid skin. The threat that he implies comes not from physical strength or bullish machismo; it comes from the way he looks at me as if I were a tiresome detail, a turd laid on new carpet by an eager puppy which has to be cleaned up. Just a bit of business.

What would his pre-Cull self have done if he had known what he would become? Rub his hands in glee or put a rope around his neck and end it all?

What would I have done, had I known who I would become?

I've not slept a wink. All night I've lain in bed staring into the darkness, trying to work out a strategy but I've got nothing.

No-one's coming to rescue me. I guess the kids we brought with us to Thetford may have made it back to the school and told them what happened, but their standing orders are to fortify and defend. There's no-one there with the authority or gumption to attempt a rescue. Anyway, it would be suicide.

Cooper still doesn't know where the school is now. The Yanks will have told him about Groombridge, but they never learned about Fairlawne, so it should be safe.

Unless I tell him. Maybe that's what he'll do – wait until he's bored with me and then torture me to get the location of the school. Rich pickings for him there.

I may have to work out a way to kill myself. But I'm not there yet.

Not quite.

CHAPTER NINETEEN

It didn't take long for Wilkes and Tariq to start arguing.

"I've been trained for this, mate."

"In peace time. I led the resistance against the American Army in Iraq. I have experience that you don't."

"Of getting everyone under your command killed."

"John delegated command to me if he didn't make it."

"You aren't the boss of me, mate."

"I'm not your fucking mate."

And so on until eventually Caroline shouted: "Oh why don't you just whop your cocks out right now and we can see who's biggest?" which made Jack snigger but didn't exactly help.

"Listen," I said to the council of war gathered around the fire. "We all agree we need a clear chain of command. Yes?"

Wilkes, Ferguson, Tariq, Jack and Caroline all nodded. Green just stared into the flames.

"And we all agree that if my dad were here, we'd be happy to let him lead us because of his experience and training?"

Again they all nodded.

"So we should make finding him our first priority. We know he was on his way to Hammersmith to meet up with Caroline. For some reason he never got there. We have to track him down. We can't win this fight without him."

"Lee, we have no idea where he is or what happened to him," said Tariq. "I want to find him as much as you do, but we have no leads and we don't have any more time. Jane is on the inside and God knows what they're doing to her. We have to get her first."

"Don't you think I want her safe?" I countered. "But we have no chance if we keep fighting amongst ourselves like this. We need a strategy and a leader. Dad's the only one we would all agree on."

"We could vote," said Jack.

"What?" asked Wilkes, incredulous.

"He's right," said Caroline. "We could vote. Elect a leader."

"I won't take orders from him," said Tariq more apologetic than angry.

"Then we don't vote for a leader," continued Jack. "We vote on a plan. Chances are we're going to need to break into at least two forces anyway. As long as each group has a leader who agrees to the plan, we're fine."

"I'm not going into battle with a strategy voted for by children," said Wilkes.

"We may seem like children to you," I said, trying to keep the anger out of my voice, "but between us we've seen more combat than you."

"Do you have a better suggestion for breaking this deadlock?" asked Caroline.

Wilkes considered for a moment, then shook his head. "What do you think, Pat?"

"If we can come up with a plan we all agree on, it sounds sensible to me," said Ferguson.

I leant over and whispered in Jack's ear. "Well done, Your Majesty, you just convened your first Parliament."

We took the discussion inside then, to one of the lecture halls of the old college. Ferguson drew a map of the enemy stronghold on the whiteboard. His attention to detail was impressive. He picked out the fences, minefields and gun towers, as well as various internal details such as where the children were being kept, and the location of the Lords' brothel.

There came a point where the level of detail began to disturb me.

"Question," I said as he picked out Spider's sleeping quarters. "How the hell did you get inside, collect all this intel and then get out again without being caught?"

"With great care and a little help."

"From?" I tried not to sound too suspicious, but failed.

"Once the lorries arrived at Westminster I got straight out and ran inside, shouting that I needed the loo. If I'd hung around, they'd have realised I wasn't their man. I'd been in the Palace of Westminster once before, on a tour, so I vaguely knew where I was heading. I made straight for the Lords." He looked expectant, waiting for us to realise something. When none of us did, he said: "The brothel."

"Jesus, Pat," said Wilkes.

"If I'd tried to hang around making sketches and stuff, I'd have been caught," Ferguson explained. "The only chance was to get in and out as quickly as possible. So I went straight to the brothel and told the guard on the door that I was a new recruit and I'd been waiting all week for some loving. He let me in, no problem."

"You sick..." began Caroline.

"Let him finish," said Tariq.

"There's about twenty women in there. Well, women and girls. They have these kind of bunks set up on the benches. Some of them got up and came over to me, but most just lay there hoping I wouldn't pick them out. I pushed the eager ones aside and picked out the youngest and most frightened girl there. I figured maybe the confident ones may not have been exactly trustworthy. The girl led me to a little nook behind the speaker's chair where there was a mattress.

"Her name was Tara.

"And there, in total privacy, where no-one would disturb us, I got her to tell me everything she knew about the snatchers' operation. Layout, routines, names – everything. I got lucky picking her; she paid attention.

"When she'd told me all she could, I went out the main doors again. I found an office overlooking the river – luckily it was low tide, so I climbed out and down to the shore."

He noted my look of disbelief.

"I used to be a rock climber, okay?"

I hold up my hands. "Ok."

"I was inside for forty minutes at the most. Then I waited 'til nightfall, found an eyrie in one of the buildings on Parliament Square, and spent a day mapping the external defences and noting their patrols.

"Big Ben still chimes, you know. All their scheduling hangs off it.

"Happy?"

I nodded. "Sorry. Force of habit."

"Don't worry about it," he said, and went back to giving us the lowdown.

It was sundown again before we all agreed a plan of action. After that there was nothing to do until morning. Tariq came and found me as I lay on a hospital bed, failing to sleep.

"So what do you think?" he asked as he sat on the next bed.

"I think it's a crazy plan, but it just might work!"

"Ha, yeah, reckon that's about it."

"What do you think, Tariq?"

He bit his lower lip and held my gaze. "I think it's the best we can do in the circumstances."

"But...?"

"But I wish John was here. What do you think can have happened to him?"

I shrugged. "God knows. Caroline says he never reached them, so somewhere between Thetford and Hammersmith something went wrong. As soon as we're done with the snatchers, I'm going to retrace his route. For all we know, he could be lying in a ditch with a broken leg or something."

"Why not go now?" asked Tariq. "We can handle the assault. You go find your dad."

I regarded him coolly. "Still don't trust me in a fight, huh? Still trying to get rid of me."

He hesitated a moment, choosing his words carefully. Then he said: "Do you remember when we rescued Jane back at Groombridge, the day John was shot?"

I nodded.

"You were... I don't know what you were like. Those Yanks were shooting at you and just walked towards them like you were bulletproof."

"So?"

"You're not bulletproof, Lee. And neither am I. I stood with you, followed your lead because I had no choice – it was either that or leave you to die. But I was sure we were dead men."

I shook my head, unsure exactly what he was getting at. "We weren't though," I said. "We won that fight."

"God alone knows how. We should have been killed a dozen times over that day. Luck like that doesn't hold, Lee. Sooner or later it runs out. You acted like a mad man. That's fine if it's only your life you're risking. But it was mine too."

"What's your point, Tariq?"

"My point is that tomorrow you're going to lead a team of children into battle against the fucking SAS and I want you to realise that you're not invincible. If you go wading in there like the Terminator, it's not just your life you'll be throwing away."

"Did I ever tell you about Heathcote?" I asked. Tariq shook his head. "He was one of my school mates. The Blood Hunters held him captive during the siege. I took a knife and slit his throat just for a chance to get close to one of the bad guys. Sacrificed him in cold blood. I'd do that a hundred times over if it meant winning."

Tariq stared at me, his face a mask. I couldn't tell if he pitied me or feared what I might do. Then he stood up and walked away without a word.

I lay back down on the bed and closed my eyes, willing myself to sleep.

But the sound of Heathcote's screams, and the hot slick feel of blood between my fingers, kept me awake 'til dawn.

CHAPTER TWENTY

It began to snow heavily as they split their group into three.

The younger kids who had escaped Hammersmith with Caroline were taken back to St Mark's in the removal van, driven by one of the Rangers. They had no place in a battle, and they'd be safe back at the school.

Lee, Jack and Ferguson had taken off on horseback at first light, heading for the Thames, their saddlebags heavy with ordnance.

Everyone else had piled into the three school minibuses Tariq had used to bring the team from St Mark's. They headed west, to Heathrow.

The ranks of Caroline's little army had been swollen by a bunch of the older kids from the convoy they'd attacked. There were nearly fifty of them now. Wilkes, who was in joint charge of this part of the operation alongside Tariq and Green, had insisted that there be an age limit. They'd fought over that for an hour until they'd agreed that any child under thirteen was not to be involved in the fight.

The other bone of contention had been firearms. The team from

St Mark's had brought crates of various types of gun with them, and plenty of ammunition. Caroline felt strongly that every child should be given a gun, but no-one agreed with her. Too risky, they said. More chance of them shooting each other than the bad guys.

In the end they'd compromised. Only those kids who'd been trained would carry machine guns and grenades, which meant all the St Mark's lot. Her lot would be allowed handguns if they were sixteen or over. The younger teenagers could have knives, clubs, bats or that kind of thing, and they were to stay behind the kids with guns, as a second wave to mop up stragglers. Wilkes was unhappy with this compromise, but Lee and Jack insisted that the children be allowed to fight. It was, Lee said, their fight in the first place.

Caroline was relieved when Lee left. There was something behind his eyes that she didn't trust. Right up to the moment she met him again she had been unsure what she would say.

"Hi Lee, long time no see. By the way, I executed your dad the other day."

"Wow what a co-incidence bumping into you! 'Cause, you see, I bumped into your dad a few days back. Yeah. Blew his brains out."

"Lee, I don't know how to tell you this, but your dad's dead. The churchies got him."

That last one had been her favourite. Blame it on Spider, get Lee fired up for the attack, make it personal. But it turned out he and Matron were together now (and by the way, euw, she was like, ten years older than him) so he had a personal stake in the attack already. Anyway, if she told him that, he'd press her for details and she was sure he'd have worked out she was lying sooner or later. Being caught in a lie like that would be worse than just staying silent.

She told herself that she was being silly, that he was an ally and a friend. But she looked into his eyes and was absolutely certain that if he knew what she'd done, he'd kill her on the spot.

So she'd played dumb, denied all knowledge.

"No, no-one approached us. We left 'cause Matron told us where the school is now and we decided to risk the journey."

She crouched behind the enormous wheel of a 747 on a

Heathrow runway, wet through and chilled to the bone, but she counted herself lucky to be there. Lee had believed her and had decided to go looking for his dad only after they'd brought down the snatchers. Plus, he was off with the Rangers leading the other pincer of the attack, so she didn't have to be around him. More importantly still, the other kids who'd witnessed John's death weren't around him either. She'd not yet had a chance to take them to one side and brief them, tell them what had happened, make them swear to keep it secret. She'd have a chance to do that now, though, before they met up with Lee again.

Assuming he didn't die in the coming battle. Which, she realised guiltily, would solve a lot of problems for her. For a moment it occurred to her that if things went her way, she might get the chance to shoot him in the confusion. Friendly fire. No-one would ever know it had been deliberate. She pushed the thought aside, pretending she hadn't had it, shocked at herself.

But she had to admit, it would be convenient.

She banished the thought and focused on the task at hand. In the near distance stood a row of lorries. She counted thirty-four in total. All had the familiar red circle of the church sprayed onto their sides. They were neatly lined up in the shadow of an enormous hanger. This was their target.

Caroline watched Tariq and Wilkes as they ran from car to car through the car park that sat between the taxiway where she crouched, and the hanger.

There was one guard patrolling lazily in front of the huge sliding doors that once allowed airliners in for servicing.

When the two of them were at the very edge of the car park, Wilkes drew back the string on his bow and sent a thin shaft of wood straight through the Guard's heart. He dropped without a sound.

He and Tariq broke cover, racing for the small, human-sized door that sat in the middle of the plane-sized one. When they got there they stood on either side of it, ready to deal with anyone who came out. Wilkes waved to Caroline, who in turn waved to the kids and Rangers sheltering behind the concrete wall at the end of the line of planes. As per their orders, they didn't run out. Instead they walked en masse, with Green and two Rangers at their head, older kids at the front, younger ones at the back.

When they reached her, Caroline joined them at the front. The army of children walked towards the hanger, silent and full of purpose. When the whole group stood united, she, Wilkes, Tariq and Green checked their watches and began a countdown. Then Green and Wilkes broke right while Tariq and one of the other Rangers broke left, slipping around the edges of the hanger with five armed kids in tow.

Caroline took up a position beside the door, alongside a Ranger, waving the remaining kids back against the hanger doors. The snow fell silently as they stood there, breath clouding the air, waiting for the exact moment. Eventually, after ten minutes had passed, Caroline raised her right hand and counted down from five with her fingers. When the last finger made a fist, she took hold of her machine gun, stepped back from hanger door and, in tandem with the Ranger whose name she still hadn't bothered to ask, kicked it open and went in shooting.

The second they burst into the hanger Caroline realised they'd made a massive mistake. All their planning had been based on the idea that the kids would be sleeping on the cold floor of the cavernous, empty space.

But in the centre of the concrete expanse stood the biggest plane Caroline had ever seen. A guard was already running up the staircase to the door in its nose. It was the only staircase running up to the plane – the doors at the midpoint and rear of the plane were closed.

Underneath the fuselage, Caroline saw Wilkes, Tariq and their teams bursting in from the two rear doors, similarly amazed at the scale of their miscalculation.

The kids were on the fucking plane.

Caroline was closest to the moveable metal stairs and she put on a burst of speed as she registered the situation, racing to get within firing range before the guard could make it inside the plane and close the door. He had made it as far as the top step before she managed to get a bead on the man, and sent a stream of bullets thudding into him. The guard cried out, spun and toppled down the stairs; a dead weight and an obstacle.

Caroline kept running, aware of the kids streaming into the hanger in her wake.

"Don't let them close the door," came a distant, echoing yell from Tariq.

"Well, dur," she muttered as she raced towards the metal stairs.

As she reached the foot of the stairs she jumped over the still twitching corpse of the guard she had shot and began pounding up towards the door, which began to swing closed ahead of her. The men closing it were well protected behind its bulk, and she'd climbed only a few steps before she realised there was no chance at all of reaching the door in time, or getting a clear shot at the men who were closing it.

She dropped her gun and it swung free on its shoulder strap as she reached into the pocket of her fur coat and pulled out a grenade. She bit the pin and pulled it out with her teeth, never breaking her upwards stride as the gap between door and fuselage narrowed. She took three more steps and then stopped, drew back her arm and threw the grenade as hard as she could towards the tiny gap. It soared through the air and straight through a space merely twice its width.

The door slammed shut amidst a chorus of shouts from inside. There was a loud clang as the door lock was engaged and then immediately disengaged. The door began to swing open again, ever so slowly.

Then the grenade exploded, blowing a huge gaping hole in the side of the plane, sending the door, and various body parts, flying over Caroline's head. The shockwave picked her up and tossed her backwards off the staircase into the freezing cold air high above the concrete floor, which rushed up to greet her as she screamed.

CHAPTER TWENTY-ONE

"They blew the bridge because the point where it meets the bank is their weakest spot," said Ferguson.

I panned across with my binoculars to focus on the jagged outcrop of stone that marked the opposite side of the now destroyed Westminster Bridge. I could see immediately what he meant. At the foot of Big Ben there was a patch of open ground between the wall of the Palace and the edge of the bridge accommodating some steps that led down to a tunnel entrance. The tall black fence that ringed the Palace only came up as high as the bridge, which meant that you could get inside by laying a plank of wood across the gap and leaping in. Obviously not an option when the CCTV systems were all working, but now it seemed eminently doable.

"It's called Speaker's Green," explained Ferguson.

"What's that tunnel entrance?" asked Jack.

"Westminster Tube. There are tunnels direct from the station into the Palace and that big building opposite it, the one with the black chimneys. That's Portcullis House where the MPs offices used to be. There's a tunnel running from there under the road into the Palace as well."

"In which case we should go in underground, through the tube," I said. "They blew the bridge but they didn't blow the tunnels, did they?"

"They didn't need to," the Ranger replied. "Once the pumps shut down, the tube tunnels all flooded. The old rivers that run under the city reclaimed them. If we had scuba gear, maybe, but even then it'd be madness."

"So we go in over the fence there?" asked Jack.

"It's an option, but it's the wrong end of the building," said Ferguson. "If we go in there we have to travel the whole length of the Palace to get where we're going, which massively increases our chances of discovery. No, our best way in is there. The Lords Library."

He pointed to the opposite end of the Palace, to the huge tower that marked its southernmost point.

"There are only two places where the Palace backs directly onto the river, and that's the towers at either end," he explained. "In between there's a bloody great terrace between the wall and the river. What we have to do is get on the water, moor at the foot of that tower, and climb in one of the windows. It's our best way of getting in undetected."

"I don't know about you, mate, but I'm not Spider-Man," I said. "There's no way in hell I'm going to be able to scale that wall."

"What we need," said Jack, "Is one of those grappling hook gun thingys that Batman uses."

"Nah," said Ferguson, smiling. "We can do better than that."

Ten minutes later we climbed down from our vantage point through the ruined interior of St Thomas' Hospital, emerged into a street buried under a thickening carpet of snow, and set off in search of a dinghy.

"Whatever you do, don't fall in, okay?" said Ferguson unnecessarily as we climbed into the small inflatable that we'd found in a River Police station half a mile upstream. "The water is freezing and the current is deadly. If you hit the water you're dead, simple as."

"But we're wearing life jackets," I pointed out.

"Don't matter," says the Irishman. "You probably won't be strong enough to swim to the shore. You'll stay afloat, but you'll freeze to death before you hit land."

"I thought Irish people were cheery, optimistic types," said Jack as he climbed carefully into the rubber boat.

"What the fuck ever gave you that idea?" asked the Ranger, untethering the boat and pushing us away from the shore.

"Um, Terry Wogan?"

Ferguson clipped his ear and handed him an oar. "Row, you cheeky sod."

There was no moon, but the world was clothed in white and the sky was still thick with falling snow. The current took us quickly and we floated out into the Thames.

"We can't use the engine, 'cause they'll hear us," explained Ferguson. "And we don't have an anchor, so the hardest thing will be to bring ourselves to a halt long enough to climb out. When I give the signal, you two need to start rowing as hard as you can against the current. Got that?"

Jack and I nodded as Ferguson used his oar to steer us as close to the bank as possible. Although the blizzard was providing us with the best possible cover, there was no point in taking foolish chances; the further out we were, the easier we would be to spot.

I was astonished at how fast we moved, and we were floating alongside Parliament within ten minutes. As we neared the farthest tower, Ferguson gave the signal. Jack and I dipped our oars and began paddling frantically against the tide, trying to slow us down. The Ranger took his bow and notched an arrow. Attached to the shaft was a small metal grappling hook from which trailed a slender nylon rope. Despite all our efforts, we continued to sweep down the river, but Ferguson did not allow himself to be distracted. As we reached the tower he let the arrow fly. It soared away into the white and although we listened, we never heard it land. But the rope didn't tumble back to the water.

He grabbed the end of the rope and looped it through one of the metal rings on the rim of the dinghy and pulled. I sighed with relief as the rope went taut and he pulled us in to the edge of the river, where the dinghy nestled underneath the concrete lip that marked the ground floor of the Palace. He tied it off and Jack and I gasped with relief as we dropped our oars. My arms were burning from the effort of rowing against a current that laughed at my exertions.

We looked up at the blue nylon rope that trailed up into the night sky. The snow was so thick now that the top of the tower was lost to view. The rope seemed to rise up into nowhere. We all pulled on the rubber-coated climbing gloves that Ferguson had looted for us from a sports store on our way into town, and put on the strange climbing pumps which were soft and lacked soles, but had rubber moulding all over, for purchase.

"Climbing in these conditions is extremely dangerous," said Ferguson. "So we'll go in the first window we come to. Take your time, don't hurry, and remember – there's no safety rope, so whatever you do, don't lose your grip."

I handed him the heavy kit bag that was the key to our success. He slung it over his back, took the rope in both hands and launched himself off the dinghy. He scrambled up over the concrete lip in no time at all. We waited until we heard a muffled crack and saw shards of stained glass tumble past us into the water. I gestured for Jack to go first.

He nervously followed Ferguson, but whereas the Irishman had been speedy and confident, Jack was all over the shop. His prosthesis slowed him down, and his fibreglass foot scrabbled uselessly against the wet concrete and he slipped backwards more than once as the nylon rope got wetter and more slippery. Eventually he also disappeared over the concrete lip and the rope went slack indicating that he'd made it inside.

I grabbed the rope and pulled myself up. Every set fracture and old bullet wound protested as I hauled myself skywards, but I focused on doing everything slowly and carefully, and managed a steady, unwavering ascent.

When I crested the concrete rim I saw a gothic arched hole where a stained glass window had nestled. I reached up to grab the window sill and two things happened in quick succession: there was a burst of gunfire from inside the room, and Jack crashed out of the window to my right, flying backwards in a cloud of glass and lead, clutching Ferguson's black kit bag, plummeting soundlessly.

I braced my feet against the stone, looped the rope around my left hand, reached into my coat, pulled out my Browning and

then pushed up with my legs, propelling my head and shoulders
in through the gaping stone window frame, firing as I went.

CHAPTER TWENTY-TWO

Caroline hit the floor hard with her right shoulder, which made an awful crunching sound. She rolled with the momentum, tumbling like a drunken acrobat.

She screamed as she hit, but it was more battle cry than fear. There was anger in it too, that none of them had reckoned on so obvious a reversal of fortune. That plane was huge and made a perfect billet. Somebody should have worked that out.

When she finally stopped moving and skidded to a halt, she hurt everywhere. She just wanted to lie down, close her eyes and rest for a while. But she did what she always did in moments like this: she asked herself what Rowles would do. As soon as she asked herself that question, she opened her eyes, gritted her teeth, gripped her gun and got the fuck up.

Her shoulder was useless and there was something pulled in her left leg; her hearing was muffled and... *woah*... her balance was a bit off. But she limped back towards the plane, ignoring the pain.

The kids were pouring up the stairs and through the jagged blackened hole that denoted where the door had been a minute ago. Small circular windows ran the length of the plane on two levels, which meant that this plane was a double decker. The windows along the lower level were lit by the strobe flashes of gunfire; the upper windows revealed blurs of movement but no fighting yet.

She felt a hand on her shoulder and she whirled, gun raised. It was Tariq. He was looking at with concern and his lips were moving.

"Speak up," she said. "Part deaf. Explosion."

"I said are you okay?"

"What do you bloody think? Come on." She turned and kept moving towards the steps. Tariq fell in beside her as Wilkes and the ten kids that had come in the other end streamed past them towards the stairs. Caroline glanced up at Tariq, who waved them past, obviously determined to stick with Caroline.

"I don't need a baby sitter," she said.

"Well I do," he replied, still focused on the stairs ahead. "And you're the designated adult."

Caroline smiled as she swung the gun back up to her hip.

"This plane is huge," she said as they reached the foot of the stairs. The last few kids were disappearing into the belly of the plane above them.

"A380," said Tariq. "Biggest airliner ever made. Lap of luxury."

A huge explosion blew out the rear doors and a man dressed entirely in black and with an Uzi in his hand, tumbled backwards out of the resulting gap in the fuselage, arms flailing. He fell onto the concrete head first, his brains and lungs suddenly finding themselves colocated.

"They do know we want some of them alive, don't they?" asked Caroline as she dragged herself up the stairs.

A man appeared in the hole above them, firing back down the body of the plane. Caroline hardly blinked as she squeezed the trigger and cut him down where he stood.

"I don't know, Caroline. Do they?" asked Tariq as she stepped into the plane.

She glanced down at the dead snatcher then looked up at Tariq and made a sad face. "Sorry," she said.

Tariq tutted as he stepped across the jagged metal edge. "Just don't let it happen again."

They turned and walked into the passenger section, guns raised, and all their wisecracks died unspoken as they beheld the carnage before them.

The two aisles were littered with corpses of children and snatchers alike. The air was thick with cordite and the walls and ceilings were sprayed with blood.

Caroline couldn't have told you whether it was her post-explosion balance problem or the sight of that charnel house which caused it, but she turned, bent over and was violently sick.

"Fifteen of our children dead," said Tariq as he sat down next to her in the business class compartment an hour later. "Seven of yours, eight of ours. Plus the thirty-two kidnapped kids they blew up in their attempts to escape."

Caroline shook her head in disbelief. "And?"

"Two of the Rangers are down."

"Wilkes?"

"No, he's fine."

"What about captives?"

"Two. Wilkes is just getting started on them. Thought you might want to come along."

Caroline thought about this for a moment and decided that no, she really just wanted to sit here drinking this nice wine she'd found in the galley.

"Drinking before noon?" asked Tariq.

"Unless you have any other painkillers to hand, I'll stick with tried and tested if that's okay with you."

The Iraqi reached out and took the bottle from her. She glared at him, eyes narrowed.

"No, it's not okay," he said sternly. "The only thing worse than a sixteen year-old girl with a gun and an itchy trigger finger is a drunk sixteen year-old girl with a gun and an itchy trigger finger."

"Jesus," said Caroline as she stood. "Listen to Jeremy fucking Kyle. Fine, I'll lend a hand."

She limped past him and climbed the staircase to the luxury cabins that sat on the floor above.

She pushed open the cabin door and found Wilkes and Green

standing over two men sat on the double bed, hands tied behind their backs.

"Have they agreed to help yet?" she asked.

Wilkes shook his head. "Not yet, but they..."

Caroline pulled a kitchen knife from her belt and before the Ranger could stop her, she leaned forward and thrust it deep into the heart of the captive nearest to her. His mouth formed an O of surprise and he let out a strangled gasp, then his eyes rolled back in his head and he slumped against the wall, stone dead.

Caroline pulled out the knife, wiped it on the sleeve of her coat and turned to the other man on the bed.

"We can do this without you, you know," she said calmly. "Your only chance to live another minute is to agree to help us. Otherwise we'll go to plan B. What do you say?"

He nodded in mute horror. Caroline patted his cheek chummily. "Good man."

As she withdrew her hand she noticed that she'd smeared his face with blood. She pointed to her cheek. "You've got a little spot there," she said, helpfully. Then she walked out, passing Tariq who stood in the doorway, slack jawed.

"Fucking hell. That girl scares me," said Green once he'd got his breath back.

"Oh, I dunno," said Tariq. "I kind of like her."

Caroline limped down the stairs. When she reached the bottom she heard heavy footsteps following behind her.

Wilkes emerged and grabbed her arm, pulling her through business class and into the cockpit. He slammed the door and stood before it, arms folded, face red with fury.

Caroline remained composed.

"The last time an adult locked himself in a room with me, I cut out his heart with this knife," she said. "So be aware, if your hand goes anywhere near your zip, you'll lose it. And I don't mean your hand."

Having dragged her in here to give her a piece of his mind, Wilkes found himself momentarily speechless. But he found his tongue eventually.

"Did you see the body count out there?" he asked.

Caroline nodded.

"Those were children," said the Ranger. "Children! They should never have been put in that position. A battlefield is no place for a child. We can't go forward with this plan, not after this. I'm calling it off. I'm only sorry I didn't do this sooner, then maybe some of those kids would still be alive. But this ends. Now."

"Oh really," replied Caroline, her voice dripping with sarcasm. "Well that's good to know. Pass that message on to the snatchers, would you? Give them a good talking to about it. I'm sure they'll stop the kidnapping then."

"Fighting them is a job for men," said Wilkes.

"No, you sanctimonious fucker, it's a job for boys and girls," yelled Caroline. "It's not grown ups they're kidnapping. It's kids. This is our fight, their fight. Not yours. You're the outsider here." She stabbed him the chest with her index finger, jutting her chin out and shouting in his face. "Since The Cull I've met one – ONE! – adult who hasn't tried to fuck me over. Every other predatory bastard out there thinks I'm either cattle to be bartered for food or a warm body to use and toss away. So don't you fucking dare, Mr high and mighty grown up man, tell me that children have no place on the front line. Because it's you lot who've bloody put us there. And believe me: every adult we meet is going to regret standing by and letting that happen. What does the bible say – The children shall inherit? Well that starts right now and you're either with me or against me. So shut up and help or fuck off out of my way. Because I promise you, if you try and stop me I will kill you dead."

She was breathing hard and furious when she finished her tirade, staring into Wilkes' eyes, all challenge and fire.

He stepped to one side and let her pass without saying a word, knowing that there was nothing he could possibly say.

They got all the children off the plane and gathered them together on the hangar floor. Green had done a head count and taken note of all their ages, so again they divided them by age. There were 132 kids under 13 amongst the 298 surviving captives. Green wanted to give one of his rousing speeches, but Tariq shook his head.

"Just let them choose," he said.

So the 166 remaining kids were given a choice to join the fight or leave with the youngsters. 45 of them chose to leave, too traumatised by the massacre they'd just witnessed. They joined the younger kids in two lorries and were sent back to St Mark's, driven to safety by the two surviving Rangers.

A third lorry, driven by one of the older kids, carried the corpses back for burial.

That left 121 new recruits who were again divided by age. 52 of them were over 16, and they were each given a firearm and an hour's group training in the hanger. The rest were set loose in the airport on a mad scavenger hunt for weapons; they returned with an impressive array of metal bars, chains and knives.

The sun was setting when they gathered by the lorries that were painted with the red circles. Wilkes stepped forward and shot the lorries up a bit, making it look as if they'd survived an attack. Then the army of children hid their weapons under their clothes, piled into the containers and got ready for war.

As Tariq watched the kids climb into the containers he felt a tug at his jacket and turned to find a familiar face looking up at him.

"They won't give me a gun," pouted Jenni.

Tariq smiled, glad to see she was still alive. "That's because you're still only thirteen."

"But you gave me a gun before and I managed not to accidentally shoot anybody with it" she said. "Please, Tariq. Pretty please."

He reached into his kitbag and handed her a Browning. "Okay, but don't tell the guy with the bow and arrow, all right?"

The girl went up on tiptoes and kissed Tariq on the cheek. "You're a sweetheart," she said.

The Iraqi was surprised to find himself blushing. Jenni secreted the gun inside her coat, but didn't move to join the other kids in the lorry. She glanced around furtively, as if looking for someone, then pulled him down the side of the lorry, out of sight.

"Listen," she said. "There's something you should know about John Keegan..."

The surviving snatcher was installed behind the driver's seat of the lead vehicle. He was in his mid-thirties, solid and capable looking, dressed in combats. Tariq thought that if he'd had to kill one of the captives, this is the one he'd have killed; the one Caroline stabbed had been snivelling and broken. This one was more composed. The Iraqi sat beside him, knife in his lap.

"Here's what you have to do," he said. "You lead the convoy to Parliament. If we're challenged when we arrive, you say Heathrow came under attack by unknown forces and you managed to escape. All we want to do is get inside the perimeter fence. Once we're in, I swear you'll be free to go. Understand?"

The snatcher nodded and turned the ignition.

They drove through the night, making slow progress down roads clogged with vehicles abandoned by the fleeing masses during The Culling Year.

The snow came down in thick, solid looking flakes, reducing visibility and making the going harder as they progressed. For a while Tariq thought they wouldn't make it, but as the day drew to a close they pulled up outside the tall black metal fence that ringed the Palace of Westminster. Big Ben loomed above them in the blizzard, marking the time as twenty past seven. They were actually a little early but that was okay.

The light was pre-dawn murky and the air was thick with snow as the snatcher honked his horn.

"Remember, once we're in, you can go," said Tariq, knife in hand. "Just don't try anything."

A minute later there was a knock at the window. The driver wound it down.

"What the fuck you doing here, Tel?" asked the guard, shivering despite the thick puffa jacket he was wearing.

"We had a bit of business, mate," said the snatcher. "Someone attacked us at the airport. Had to evacuate. Let us in, will you, I'm bloody freezing."

"You and me both. All right, put them underground." The guard stepped back and waved them forward.

The gate swung open and the three lorries pulled into the courtyard. The snatcher swung the lorry round and drove down a concrete ramp into the underground car park. He pulled into a bay and switched off the engine. The other two lorries pulled up alongside.

Tariq opened the door and stepped out. He gave the thumbs up to Wilkes, who sat in the cab of the adjacent lorry, looking unenthusiastic.

But Tariq's triumph was short-lived. There was a cacophony of boots as men streamed down the ramp.

Tariq stood frozen to the spot as the lorries were encircled by ten very well armed, very angry looking soldiers. The guard from the gate stepped forward and met the snatcher who had driven the lorry, by now out of the cab and running to meet his comrades. He took a gun from the guard and walked up to Tariq, smiling.

"I didn't give the pass word, dipshit," said the snatcher. "What, you think we're amateurs? We're SAS, pal. And you are really going to regret fucking with us."

CHAPTER TWENTY-THREE

I can hear Big Ben chiming midnight as I lie in bed, unable to sleep.

I've been given a room in the Speaker's Cottage. It's luxurious, furnished with lovely antiques that have been polished to a fine lustre, and the flock wallpaper feels expensive. The bed is huge and comfy, the eiderdown deep and warm. The window looks out over the river and catches the rising sun in the morning. It's a very nice room indeed.

But it's a gilded cage. Cooper sleeps next door in an even more opulent chamber, and when he escorts me to bed in the evening he locks my door so I cannot sneak out and kill him as he sleeps.

I lie awake listening to the creaks and echoes of this old building as the night cold grips its bones. I can hear Cooper pacing the floor. He's not exactly walking up and down outside – he ranges wider than that – but every few minutes his soft footfalls pass by my room and I hold my breath, listening for the key in the lock. So far he's always kept walking, but this time around he's stopped outside my door.

Silence falls as I lie there, holding my breath, waiting for him to enter or leave. He's been there for five minutes now. What is he doing? Listening at the door? Wrestling with his conscience? Plucking up the courage to come in? The silence lasts so long that I begin to doubt what I heard. Maybe I just didn't hear him leave. He can't have been standing out there, motionless, for so long, can he? That's paranoid.

Yet I feel that just by listening for him I've been drawn into a deadly game of cat and mouse. I consider getting out of bed, creeping to the door and peering out the keyhole. But if he hears me moving around that may catalyse a decision, lead directly to him entering.

So I lie here, listening to the sound that is no sound – the sound of a man trying to decide my fate.

I was surprised when I found the women in the Lords. Not because I didn't realise such a place probably existed – armed men who run internment camps have always kept women for their use, from the comfort women to the women kept alive for 'special duties' in the concentration camps. No, what really surprises me is that Cooper visits them himself. He had been so insistent that he never had any of the women or girls that he trafficked before The Cull. I believe him, too. Now, it seems he no longer feels the need for such restraint. He even has a favourite. I wonder what insight Jools might be able to give me into the real man.

I resolve to go and talk to her again in the morning. My movements around the Palace are not restricted, but I am closely watched and another visit to the Lords risks arousing Cooper's suspicion. Still, I need allies, and those women are the best I can hope for right now.

I hear a sound outside my window, like a sharp crack. The air is thick with snow and all sound is muffled, so I have no idea where it came from or what it was. A drifting boat bumping against the embankment, perhaps?

There are no more sounds and I realise that it distracted me. Has Cooper crept away while I wasn't paying attention?

The silent waiting resumes. Another five minutes pass and I can feel my eyelids starting to droop in spite of myself. Sod this, I think. I'm going to sleep. I turn over, pull the eiderdown up to my cheek, and close my eyes.

The instant I do this I hear a loud banging on the door of the cottage. My eyes snap open. I hear Cooper turn and walk away from my door – so he was still there! – and go to answer. I have a feeling that whatever has occurred may provide an opportunity, so after a second's consideration I jump out of bed and pull on my jeans, jumper and shoes.

I tiptoe to the door, grabbing a glass from the dressing table as I do so, placing it against the thick wood, trying to hear what's going on. It's hopeless, though; all I can hear is the muffled drone of their conversation.

Then there are hurrying footsteps coming my way. I leap backwards as the key is thrust into the lock. I stand in the middle of the floor, fully dressed, no point trying to pretend I was asleep. The door opens and Cooper stands framed there for a moment, surprised to find me up and about. His surprise soon passes.

"Kate, I need your help," he says. "Come with me, please."

Over his shoulder I can see one of his goons standing expectantly in the hallway, machine gun at the ready.

"Help with what?" I ask, not moving.

He pulls a handgun from his waistband. "You'll see," he says. He steps forward, grabs my wrist and pulls me after him.

"Hey!" I protest, but he spins and snarls at me with such menace that I'm momentarily silenced. Even when he slapped me he seemed in control, but in this brief instant I catch a glimpse of a different Cooper – furious, savage and ruthless, almost feral.

Ah-ha, I think. There *you are!*

He drags me down a small winding back staircase to the ground floor, through a series of carpeted corridors – green carpet, meaning we're in the Commons – then into the corridor that joins Commons to Lords, through the central lobby and up to the closed doors of the Lords itself.

There are six or seven of his soldiers gathered at various vantage points, all with their guns trained on the doors. The air smells of cordite. Unconcerned by the fact that his men are staying in cover, Cooper walks right up to the doors, still pulling me behind him. He stands in front of the doors for a moment then kicks them open and strides into the ornate, high-ceiling chamber.

The women are gathered in a line on the back bench to my left. They're all sitting bolt upright with their hands upon their heads, eyes wide and fearful. In the middle of the room, on the big red cushion they call the woolsack, stands a man in a hoodie with a bow and arrow. The string is taut, the shaft of the arrow aimed straight at Cooper's heart. My mind races. This is one of Hood's Rangers. Have they decided to take Cooper down? Is this the beginning of an assault? I feel a momentary rush of hope but then damp it down. There's no firing from anywhere in the building, no sounds of combat or attack. No, this is one man. Here to deliver a message, maybe?

It occurs to me that it might actually be Hood himself.

Cooper pulls me to his side, wrapping his left arm around my throat and holding his gun to my temple.

"Drop it or she dies," he yells.

The hooded man stands there, unmoved. He doesn't say a word.

Cooper lifts the gun an inch and fires a round just over my head, deafening me and making me yelp in surprise. I inwardly curse myself for being such a wuss. This is the point where I should bite his wrist or stamp on his foot, distract him for a moment and run for it. But there's a small army behind me and only one man ahead.

"I dunno who you think I am, but I have no idea who that woman is. Why should I care if she lives or dies?" The Ranger has a thick Irish accent. Not Hood, then. He's a bit shit, too, 'cause I've never met him before in my life but already I can tell he's bluffing.

Cooper drops the gun so it's pointing at the floor. For a moment I think he's backing down but then, the instant before he fires, I realise what he's about to do.

"No," I shout, but my cry is drowned out by the percussive blast that sends a small lump of lead into my right foot.

I scream in agony and go limp, unable to stand. Cooper's arm is tight around my neck, holding me upright. I begin to choke. As the blood pounds in my ears and my vision blurs I hear a voice shouting:

"All right, all right! We surrender!"

Lee?

CHAPTER TWENTY-FOUR

"I'm sorry about that, Kate," said the man I assumed was Spider as he handed Jane the syringe.

She took it without making eye contact and stuck it into her ankle, depressing the plunger. A few moments later her shoulders relaxed as the morphine did its work.

I knelt on the hard tiled floor of the central lobby with my hands on my head, fingers interlaced. The muzzle of a rifle rested gently on the nape of my neck, ready to end me if Spider gave the order. Ferguson was on his knees next to me in the same predicament. I'd counted seven soldiers in the lobby with us, mostly dressed in black or combats, all heavily armed. I could tell they were proper soldiers, not followers who'd joined after The Cull; something about their bearing and expressions told me they were professionals.

Corridors ran off the circular lobby in four directions, and white statues stood against the walls, regarding us coldly.

Spider was physically unprepossessing. Of slightly less than average height, he had blonde hair and blue eyes but lacked

Brad Pitt's good looks. He didn't have that quality of madness about him that Mac or David had possessed, nor the world weary doggedness of Blythe. He seemed kind of ordinary.

I didn't doubt he'd have killed Jane, though.

Ordinary, then, but dangerous.

"Do you have a surgeon?" asked Jane through gritted teeth. She sat on a chair against the far wall, white as a sheet.

"I'm afraid not," he replied, seeming genuinely apologetic. "We make do and mend."

Kate grimaced. "Fine," she said. "How about antibiotics?"

"Yes, we have those."

"Good. I want to get over to St Thomas's, I can patch myself up there, assuming any of the equipment still works."

"I'll detail one of my men to take you there now." The boss nodded to a soldier to his left, who stepped forward and helped Jane to stand.

She hopped away but just before she left the lobby she turned and said: "Oh and Cooper?"

Spider, who had been staring at me intently with a nasty smile on his face, looked away.

"Yes Kate?"

"If you hurt either of them. At all. I will kill you."

He laughed. "Oh Kate, please. You didn't manage to exact revenge last time. What makes you think you'll manage it this time?" He paused for effect, then said: "Don't worry. They'll still be here when you get back. Probably."

She limped around the corner and Spider turned to us again. He knelt in front of me.

"Five years I've been running things here," he said. "Five years. I have a team of highly trained, heavily armed special forces at my disposal and an army of daft religious nutters out there who think I'm the representative of the Messiah. In all that time I've had plenty of people try to break out of here, but no-one's ever been stupid enough to break in before. Why on God's Earth would you do such a stupid thing?"

"Good question," I answered.

"It wasn't rhetorical," he said, allowing an edge of menace to creep into his voice.

"Should I call you Spider or Cooper?" I asked.

He appeared to consider this seriously. "You can call me Cooper," he said at length.

"Well, Coop, I guess you could say I have a compulsion."

"What would that be, then?"

"I feel compelled to hunt down murderous bastards and wipe them out."

He narrowed his eyes and pursed his lips, considering my admittedly weak bravado.

"And how's that worked out for you?"

"Well, three years ago me and my friends managed to wipe out a cannibal cult that was terrorizing the countryside. Not as well armed as you guys, but they were all naked and bathed in fresh human blood, so they were a little scarier, I think."

"Good for you."

"And then of course there was the Americans."

"Excuse me?"

"The American army invaded a couple of years back. You may have missed the memo."

"No, no, believe me, I got that one."

"They didn't last long."

Cooper barked a sudden laugh and clapped his hands.

"Are you trying to tell me," he said, "that you single-handedly fought off the US Army?"

"Not single-handedly, no. I had a twelve year-old boy helping me. But essentially, yeah."

"And how did you do that, exactly?"

"We nuked the fuckers."

"You nuked the fuckers."

"Yup."

He stared deep into my eyes. I stared back and smiled.

"You know," he said. "I almost believe you. And this is how you go about killing bad guys, is it? You wander into their bases with some stupid plan and get yourself captured?"

The soldiers standing around us sniggered.

"Um, actually yeah, it kind of is."

"And then what do you? Manufacture some miraculous escape? Call in the cavalry? Light the Bat-signal?"

More laughs.

"No, I just wait."

"For?"

"A mistake."

He leaned in close 'til I could feel his hot breath on my face. "I don't make mistakes, kid."

He held my gaze for a moment then asked: "So how do you know Kate? No, wait, let me guess. You're one of the boys from St Mark's, yes?"

I nodded.

"I used to go to school there," he said. Which teachers survived The Cull?"

"Bates and Chambers."

"Didn't know Bates. Liked Chambers, though. Maybe I'll have him over for dinner once I've taken the school."

I shook my head. "Nah, he died a while back."

"Pity. Where is the school now, by the way? I sent a team there last year and it was just a burnt out wreck."

"We're somewhere you'll never find us."

"I could torture you. You'd tell us eventually."

"I was waterboarded in Iraq, pal. Bring it on."

Again he laughs. "Iraq, now? I can't decide if you're a superhero or a fantasist or both. You're certainly entertaining, I'll give you that. Final question: how long have you and Kate been together?"

"If you mean Jane, she's my Matron and that's all."

"She may be Jane when she's at school, but here she's Kate. Trust me on that. And you're lying, but I don't hold it against you. I should probably keep you alive, use the threat of killing you to make her tell me where the school is. But something tells me that you're more dangerous than you seem. So, firing squad at dawn, I reckon."

I just smiled at him. Our part of the plan may have failed, but if Tariq and the others kept to their schedule, they'd be here before dawn. I looked sideways and saw the snow falling through a far off window and bit my lip.

"Dear God, you're amateur," said Cooper as I glanced back at him. "Never played much poker did you?"

He stood up then and turned to one of his soldiers.

"These two aren't the whole story. There's someone else coming, another attack. They're supposed to be here by dawn but he's worried they won't make it because of the snow. Spread the word to be ready."

Cooper looked down at me contemptuously. "I used to be a copper, lad. I know all the tells."

He turned to Ferguson. "And you, Green Arrow, what's your story?"

Ferguson didn't say a word, he just stared straight ahead, jaw clenched tight.

"Smart man," said Cooper after a moment's silence. "I'll tell you what I think. I think you're one of these Rangers I've been hearing reports about. I think you've teamed up with these school runts. Quite the little power base. My question is this: is the next attack your lot?"

Ferguson stayed silent.

Cooper clapped his hands once, as if about to sum up at the end of a staff meeting. "Right then. Lock the boy up. Take the man and start chopping bits off him until you find out everything you can about his organisation. When Kate gets back, bring her to me. Double the patrols and issue extra ammunition."

He turned his back on us and walked away.

"I'm off to bed," he said cheerily. "I want to be fresh for the firing squad."

CHAPTER TWENTY-FIVE

Caroline felt like crying.

She'd spent so long fighting these bastards, trying to keep the children safe, trying to avoid ending up exactly where she was now – locked up, weaponless, powerless, cattle waiting to be shipped to the slaughter.

When the lorry had come to a halt she'd given the order for the kids to get their weapons out and be ready. They'd crouched there in the dark waiting for the back of the container to open, ready to pour out and finally take their revenge. But when the doors swung open she found herself staring down the barrels of about fifteen machine guns. She heard gasps and cries of alarm from the children ranged behind her. There was a moment of stillness during which Caroline was sure they were going to open fire, kill them all there and then. But the moment passed and one of the soldiers ordered them to get out one at a time and throw their weapons on the floor as they did so.

Caroline was at the front, so she got down first and tossed her gun on the ground. She was then frisked and sent to stand in the corner where she was covered by two guns. The children in both lorries went through the same procedure until they were all standing together, penned in, surrounded by guns.

She looked for the adults – Tariq, Wilkes, Green – but they were nowhere to be seen. They must have been taken away the second they arrived. She wondered if they'd been shot already. She tried to reassure the other children, but half of them were from St Mark's and didn't know who she was.

"Why should we listen to you?" sulked one boy, and she didn't have an answer for him.

She wanted to tell them that all was not lost, that they were only half the attack and if they just held their nerve, Lee, Ferguson and the kid with the limp would be coming to rescue them. But the soldiers could have overheard her, so she kept her mouth shut.

When the last of the children had been unloaded, the soldiers marched them up the stairs into the Place of Westminster. They went down a narrow corridor lined with heavy wooden doors and were herded into a big room dominated by a series of tables arranged in a square. Each sitting had a computer screen mounted in it, so Caroline reasoned it was some kind of committee room.

When all the children had been crammed inside, one of the soldiers stepped forward to close the door.

"For you, Tommies, ze var is over!" he said as he pulled the door shut. She heard some of his colleagues laugh as the door slammed shut and the lock turned.

She turned to see her army. An hour ago they were a heavily armed bunch of feral kids ready to kill any adult they encountered. Now they were just a bunch of scared, powerless children, jostling for space in a too-small room.

Behind them, huge leaded windows reached to the ceiling. The first light of dawn broke over the buildings that ranged along the opposite bank of the river.

"Um, milk, two sugars," said Tariq. And then, instinctively, without thinking: "Thanks."

Green flashed him an amused look. "Tariq, mate, they're going to kill us. I Don't think we should be thanking them for putting sugar in our tea."

Wilkes just glowered.

"Who said anything about killing you?" said the man who entered the room, rubbing sleep from his eyes and yawning. He turned to the soldier who was pouring tea for the prisoners. "Bill, did you say we were going to kill them?"

The soldier shook his head. "No Sir."

"Thought not. Carry on. Oh, and a tiny splash of milk and one sugar for me too while you're at it. Ta."

The man sat at the head of the conference table and leaned back in his chair, rubbing his hands through his bed hair. He looked at Green. "You're English, right? And you, your accent is... what?"

"I am Iraqi," said Tariq, proudly.

The man nodded. "You have a touch of Black Country in your accent, though. Learned it from squaddies, at a guess. Yes?"

Tariq nodded.

"You can call me Spider, I'm in charge here," said the man as he reached out to take the mug of tea his subordinate was proffering. He stirred it thoughtfully. "You gentlemen would be the second pincer of the St Mark's attack, am I right?"

The three captives sat silently.

"Yes, I am," said Spider. "I noticed that when I said that, you gulped," he nodded at Green, "and you glanced ever so briefly at the table," he pointed at Wilkes. "Dead giveaways."

He took a sip of tea. "So let me fill you in. Your advance team botched it. One of them is floating out to sea, the other two – Lee and one of your colleagues", he indicated Wilkes, "are in custody as we speak. My men have been torturing the Ranger but he's stayed silent. So far. Master Keegan is languishing in a committee room, contemplating his fate. I intend to have them shot in," he glanced out of the window at the pink light bleeding across the rooftops, "ooh, about half an hour."

The soldier placed mugs of steaming tea in front of the three captive men.

"You three have a chance to avoid being executed," continued Spider. "If, and only if, you answer all of my questions quickly and completely."

Tariq folded his arms and shook his head. "No chance."

"But they're quite simple," replied Spider. "For example,

number one: were you really responsible for the destruction of Operation Motherland and the American army at Salisbury?"

"Oh, hang on, wait a minute, I know this one," mugged Tariq, scratching his head, scrunching his eyes up and thinking hard. Eventually he opened his eyes and beamed in triumph. "I know. The answer is: yes we fucking were! How many points do we get? I want lots of points for that one!"

Green stifled a laugh. Wilkes continued to glower.

"And you, funny man, would I be right in thinking you met Lee in Iraq?"

Tariq nodded.

"So, not a fantasist after all," said Spider thoughtfully, sipping his tea. "Good. Next question. I understand your role in this abortion of a plan. Trojan horse, army of children. Very Lord of the Flies. But what was the role of Lee and his team? I know your attack was planned for dawn, so what were he and the Ranger going to do during the night? What trap were they planning to spring? Or were they just a diversion in case you couldn't get in the gates?"

Tariq smiled, holding Spider's gaze, giving nothing away. He shook his head slowly.

"Sorry mate," he said. "Don't know that one. Ask me something about movies. I'm good with movie questions."

"All right," said Spider, putting down his tea. "Here's one: you know that moment in the final act of an action movie, when the wisecracking hero gets captured by the bad guy who interrogates him but, realising he's getting nowhere, tells a lackey to kill the supporting character and then leaves the room enabling the hero to overpower the lackey, escape, and win the day?"

Tariq's smile faltered for a moment, and something behind his eyes changed. Then the smile returned, although it was sadder than before, knowing and resigned. He took a deep breath and nodded.

Spider put his tea down, reached into his trouser pocket, pulled out a handgun, raised it casually, and shot Tariq right between the eyes.

"My question is this," said Spider as the gun smoke drifted across the table. "Why does the bad guy never just shoot the hero himself?"

The Iraqi sat there for a moment, his eyes wide with surprise, the smile still fixed on his frozen face. Then he crumpled forward, his shattered skull hitting the table with a solid crack. Blood pooled around his head as it shook and juddered then eventually lay motionless.

Spider moved his arm slightly to the left so the gun was pointing at Green.

"I'll ask again," he said. "What was their role in your attack?"

Green sat transfixed, staring at his dead friend, tears pooling on his eyes.

Spider reached up and ostentatiously chambered a round.

"Diversion," whispered Green after a moment. "They had a bag of grenades. They were going to set off some explosions at the south end of the complex when the kids came through the gates. Draw your forces away."

Keeping the gun trained on Green, Spider turned his gaze to the soldier by the door.

"We didn't find a bag of grenades, did we Bill?" he asked.

"No," replied the lackey. "But the one who went out the window, he had a big kit bag with him. That was probably it."

Spider lowered the gun and nodded satisfied. "Good," he said. "Now if only your smartarse friend there had told me that earlier he could have enjoyed, oh, another half an hour of breathing."

Spider stood up and walked to the door. "Put these two in the Moses Room with the boy, then assemble a firing squad on Speaker's Green."

"And the body, Sir?"

Spider glanced at Tariq's corpse absent-mindedly as he walked past. "Oh toss it in the river."

CHAPTER TWENTY-SIX

I sat beneath the huge fresco of Moses bringing the tablets down from Mount Sinai, and made an accounting of all the ways in which I had fucked things up. It was a pretty impressive list. Dad was missing, Jack was dead, Ferguson and I were prisoners, and Matron had been shot. With our part of the attack prevented and Cooper expecting trouble, there was a very good chance Tariq and Caroline's forces would be wiped out the second they arrived.

It looked like Tariq was right. I would shortly be getting everyone killed.

"Feeling sorry for yourself, Nine lives?" Mac whispered in my ear. "Don't be pathetic. Take your lumps. This is the third time you've gone strolling into enemy territory. The third time you've baited the bad guy in their lair. How did you think it would end? Did you really think you were invincible? Frankly, I'm surprised he didn't shoot you dead in the Member's Lobby. He looked the type."

I paced the room, ignoring my internal heckler, looking for a way out. But the place was buttoned up tight. There were guards outside and nothing in here I could use.

Eventually I sat down in the chairman's seat at the head of the huge square of tables, put my feet up on the polished desk surface, and tried to sleep.

I couldn't think of anything else to do.

"How the fuck do you sleep at a time like this?"

The voice startled me awake and I jerked in alarm, unbalancing my seat and toppling myself in a heap on the floor. That such a quality piece of slapstick didn't illicit any laughter was my first clue that things were even worse than I realised. When I'd gathered my wits and looked up to see Green and Wilkes standing over me, I felt a knot of fear solidify in my stomach.

"Surprise," said Wilkes dourly, pulling out a chair and sitting down wearily.

I scrambled to my feet, the implications racing through my head. All my questions died in the face of their presence as one by one the obvious answers presented themselves. In the end there was only one thing left to ask.

"Where's Tariq?"

When Green also took a seat, not meeting my eyes, that answer also became apparent.

"How?" I ask eventually.

"Spider," said Green.

"Short guy, blonde?"

Green nodded.

"His name's Cooper," I said. "Spider's his stage name. Cooper sounds a lot more ordinary, doesn't it? Less menacing, more suburban. Call him Cooper, robs him of some of his power, I reckon."

"Whatever you fucking call him," growled Wilkes through gritted teeth, "he shot your pal in cold blood less than five minutes ago."

"I don't think he likes you," whispered Mac.

"Where are the kids?" I asked.

"No idea," said Green. "They took us away before they opened the lorries. I reckon they've got them locked up somewhere. That's assuming they didn't just leave them in the lorries and drive them back to Heathrow."

I shook my head "Not in this snow."

"Did you not hear me?" barked Wilkes, red in the face and suddenly furious. "Your friend is dead, Keegan. Does that not register?"

To be honest, it didn't. I'd seen so much death, lost so many friends and comrades, Tariq's death just added a digit to the death count. I didn't think anybody's death could affect me any more. Maybe even Jane's. I knew I'd do anything to save her, but if I imagined her death it left me cold. I knew that whatever happened I'd just carry on living. I didn't think I could be any more damaged than I already was.

"Jack's dead too," I said, as if it were an answer to his question. "We were caught before I even got in the window. He ended up in the river. Did you know he was the rightful King of England?"

"What?" Wilkes looked at me as if I was a madman.

"No really. King John. Honest," I said. "He was being looked after by the military when we met him. He kept it very quiet, though. Didn't want anyone to know. Just wanted to be one of the gang. Someone out there became the monarch earlier tonight. But whoever they are, they'll probably never know."

Wilkes shook his head in disbelief. "You are a bunch of fucking loonies. How the hell did we ever let ourselves get involved with you? I should kill you right now, you little shit."

"Easy," said Green, his voice stern with warning. The sight of this slight teenager telling this burly Ranger to behave was laughable, but such was the authority in Green's voice that Wilkes just clenched his jaw and turned away in disgust, done with the pair of us.

"Ferguson's alive too, in case you were wondering," I said. "I think they're torturing him at the moment, trying to get intel on your lot."

Wilkes didn't say a word.

"Fine, you have a good sulk," I said. "Green and I will try and come up with a plan to get us out of here."

Green laughed. "We'd better be quick," he said. "They're assembling a firing squad right now. The guy who marched us here said we'll be dead on the last strike of eight o'clock."

"There's still Jane," I pointed out.

"You saw her?" he asked.

"Yeah, she was here. She got shot by Cooper and went to a

hospital to patch herself up. She knew his name, and he called her Kate."

"Kate?"

"Hmm. It's her real name, from before she came to work at St Mark's. She was there under witness protection. And Cooper said he used to be a copper. I wonder."

"You think they knew each other before The Cull?"

I nodded. "It's possible. I didn't get the impression she was a prisoner here. Not like you'd think, anyway. Jane's our ace in the hole. When she gets back, she might be able to influence Cooper somehow. I don't know."

"You're clutching at straws, kid," sneered Wilkes. "We're dead. Simple as."

As if to prove his point, the door to the committee room swung open and a tall soldier stood framed in the entrance.

"Up," he barked.

We all got to our feet and shuffled towards the door.

"Get a fucking move on," shouted the lackey.

As we walked down the long corridor between the Lords and Commons, on our way to be executed, I was surprised to find that I wasn't nervous. I recalled the terror I felt when the Blood Hunters wrapped that noose around my neck and dropped me into space, or the fear when Blythe pulled the lever of the electric chair, or the desperation when I realised Rowles was about to blow us to dust. The urge to live, the fear of death, were strong in me then.

But now I just felt numb, empty, resigned. Maybe even a little relieved. I'd been shot before and it hadn't started to hurt until a good few minutes afterwards. The nice thing about a firing squad is that there aren't any minutes afterwards. I reckoned it'd be a painless death, give or take. And once it was done there'd be no more fighting. I wouldn't have to bury any more friends. I wouldn't have to sit Dad down and explain about Mum.

It's not as if I was looking for an opportunity to die, but I admitted to myself that I wasn't that upset about the prospect of it. Tariq had been wrong, I realised as I walked. I didn't wish for death. I was simply indifferent to it.

We passed through a stone archway out into the cold dawn air.

The patch of grass that sat between the walls of the Palace and the edge of Westminster Bridge was almost knee deep in drifted snow. A gaggle of armed men huddled against the wall, smoking cigarettes and gossiping quietly. They fell silent as we processed into the yard.

The man walking with us waved for us to line up against the metal fence, facing Parliament with the river at our left.

We crunched over to the fence and stood there, unsure exactly what to do.

There was an awkward silence as we stood there facing our executioners, who looked everywhere but at us, unwilling to risk meeting our gaze.

"Look at us," shouted Wilkes after a minute that seemed like an hour. "Fucking look at us!"

One by one they obeyed, and as they did so I saw their expressions harden, their faces set. These were not the kind of men to have doubts. When it came to the crunch, they were stone cold.

"Lovely day for a shooting," said Cooper as he strode into the yard. Jane limped behind him, her foot encased in a blue plastic cast. She looked at me and her face crumpled. I'd not seen her cry in so long. I wanted to run to her but I knew I wouldn't get two feet.

"Cooper, please," she said, choking back tears. "I'm begging you, don't do this."

He turned, raised his hand and slapped her hard across the face. She reeled.

"Fucker," I shouted, stepping forward. A stream of bullets thudded into the snow in front of me and I looked left to see one of the soldiers waving me back to the fence.

"I'll do anything you want," begged Jane, trailing forlornly after the man who held our lives in his hands.

He stopped when she said that, a terrible smile creeping across his face. He turned back to her again, slowly this time, full of menace.

"And what, exactly, do you think I want from you Kate?"

She stepped forward, her red, tear-stained face contorted into a grotesque parody of pleasing. She reached out and stroked his chest.

"I can be anything you want, Cooper," she said. "Anything at all. Just please, don't kill them."

For the first time that day I actually felt an emotion – pure, burning fury. I bit back my protest and clenched my fists, rooted to the spot.

Cooper reached out a hand and stroked Jane's cheek once, gently. Then he leaned forward as if to kiss her, stopped an inch from her lips and said: "Just another whore, then."

He stepped away, turned his back on her and barked an order to his soldier.

"Put her with the men."

"Sir?" asked the guy who seemed to be second-in-command, surprised by the order.

Quick as lightning, Cooper drew his sidearm and shot the man twice in the chest.

"I said, put her with the others," he yelled as his lackey toppled backwards into the snow.

Another of his men, eyes wide with alarm at his leader's sudden, shocking loss of composure, stepped forward, grabbed Jane's arm, and dragged her over to us.

She took her place alongside me, facing the firing squad. I reached out my hand and our fingers intertwined and grasped tightly.

She leaned over and tried to whisper something to me, but the huge bell in the tower above us began to chime.

The soldiers began to line up.

The first strike of eight o'clock sounded, sonorous and familiar.

They checked their weapons.

The second chime of the hour.

They all flicked off their safety catches.

Third chime.

Cooper bent down and lifted the machine gun from the corpse of the man he'd just shot.

Fourth chime.

He joined the line of executioners.

Fifth chime.

He flicked off his safety catch.

Sixth chime.

He raised his weapon.

Seventh chime.

He shouted "Make ready!"

I turned to Jane and embraced her, clasping her tightly to me,

ready for death, eyes closed, ears ringing.
  "I love you," I whispered as the clock struck eight.

CHAPTER TWENTY-SEVEN

I balance the torch on the table then take the scalpel and carefully slice down the side of my shoe, just above the bit where it meets the foam sole. Every tiny movement sends a shock of pain through my foot, so I go slowly. I'm in a small office, sitting in a padded chair, foot up on the table in front of me.

St Thomas' hospital has been pretty much gutted. When The Cull hit, I was safe at St Mark's, riding it out behind thick metal gates in the middle of the countryside. I can't imagine what it must have been like here in a hospital. The flood of sick people, all dying, incurable, hopeless and doomed. The doctors, succumbing themselves one by one but trying to keep the service going as long as possible, filling the beds and trolleys and corridors with sufferers, all hooked up to drips. At some point they must have started euthanizing people, adding extra morphine to the intravenous bags, putting people out of their misery. I imagined the final deaths, when there were no more doctors left, the last surviving patients lying here in a building strewn with corpses, feverish and delirious, dying mad and raving.

In our hunt for medicine we came across a small supply room in which sat a skeleton. It wore a white coat and a bottle of pills lay beside its outstretched hand. A doctor or nurse, immune but broken by the horror of it all, retreating into a darkened closet and gulping down pills to make it stop.

I looked at that skeleton and thought that could have been me, if my brother had never got involved with Spider, if I'd completed my medical training, become a doctor. I'd have been on the front line of the hopeless war against the AB virus and it would have killed me, indirectly but inevitably.

I don't allow myself the luxury of envying the corpse in the store room. Instead, I grab a scalpel and blade, a bottle of antiseptic, a needle and thread and some gauze bandages, then I limp across the hall to an office where I can work.

The blood-soaked shoe drops off my foot and hits the floor with a wet slap. The sock follows suit. I'm gritting my teeth in agony as I work, but I stay focused. Lee is alive and I have to get back to him. I'm the only hope he has.

When I heard his voice echo out of the Lords I felt a powerful rush of joy and horror. Joy that he was alive, and horror that he was surrendering to Cooper. I've already lost one man I loved to Cooper's schemes. I refuse to lose another.

In one respect being shot in the foot was a blessing. Had I been upright when I'd heard his voice I'd probably have burst into tears and run into his arms like a teenage girl in a pop video. But I was already crying in pain and I couldn't walk, so that wasn't really an option. I tried to play it cool, not let Cooper see how much I cared for Lee. I treated him like he was just another kid from the school. But I think Cooper knew; I think Lee's reaction to seeing me shot gave the game away.

I probe the small hole in the top of my foot. The bullet had passed straight through, right next to the bones that run to my big toe. Luckily it's not hit any of them, so I'm not going to be crippled. The damage is to flesh and muscle only, so if I can sew it shut, sterilise and bind it, then it should heal all right. If I stay off it for about a month, that is.

As I sew the wound closed I say to my guard through gritted teeth: "I'll need a cast. Go through the store rooms, there should be some somewhere. Hard plastic shell, foam lining, velcro straps, shouldn't be hard to miss."

The guard lingers, unsure.

"Oh for God's sake, I'm hardly going to be running away am I? Just fuck off and find me a cast, will you?"

He grunts and leaves. I glance out the window.

The moon is just starting to wane, and the snow is still coming down. We took a jeep across Waterloo Bridge to get to the hospital. The snow was so deep it was hard to drive, and I wonder if we'll find it as easy to get back. I know I've got to hurry. Cooper could be torturing Lee right now.

I splash some more antiseptic on the closed wound and stifle a cry of pain. The morphine's beginning to wear off. No chance of finding any of that here, it will all have been cleared out long ago. I bind my foot tightly and then grit my teeth and try to stand. It feels like someone's shoved a knife through my foot and every time I take so much as a fairy step they twist it savagely. I collapse back into the chair. No use pretending. I'm hobbled. The cast should help, though. Where the fuck is that squaddie?

I hear the door swing at the end of the corridor. Thank fuck for that.

"Did you find one?" I shout. There's no reply, but I hear footsteps crunching in the broken glass and detritus that litters the corridor. They sound strange, as if the person is limping, and each alternate step sounds hard and heavy, like a peg leg pirate. The footsteps get closer until I see a figure come to a halt in the darkness outside the room. Whoever they are, they're too short and slight to be the squaddie. The figure stands there, arms by their side and I make out a knife hanging from their right hand. I feel a shock of fear. Then I shine the torch on the figure and gasp in surprise.

"Hello Jane," says Jack.

I fire off a thousand questions. How did Lee and the others survive Thetford? Where are they all now? He answers me impatiently until my enquiries are exhausted and I ask him to find me a cast for my foot.

"Will this do?" asks the boy king as he appears at the door again a few minutes later, holding a blue foam cast.

"Yes!" I shout, and grab it off him. I gingerly place my foot in it and pull the Velcro straps tight. Once it's secured I stand up, waving away Jack's offer of a helping hand. I take a step and, while it hurts like hell, it's more bearable.

"Thanks, Jack, that's much better."

"You know," he says with a wry smile, "you could just cut it off. I hear they can do wonders with prosthetics these days."

I look down at the piece of table leg and foam that he's gaffer-taped to his stump.

"How did it break?" I ask, walking out as I talk. Together we hobble down the corridor, two cripples together, both too proud to join arms for mutual support.

"Lee, this Ranger bloke and me, we're climbing into Parliament, right? Up a rope, from a dinghy on the Thames," he explains. "It's bloody tough going for me, but I manage it. The Ranger, his name's Ferguson, he helps me in through the window. So he turns back to help Lee climb up, and I grab the kit bag. But as I do that, two soldiers come into the room and tell us to put our hands up. Ferguson spins around, fast as you like, and he's just a blur, right, all martial arts and stuff. But one of the guys manages to shoot me. I'm standing right in front of the window and I bring the bag up as a shield, but the bullets shatter my prosthethis, I lose my balance 'cause the bag's so heavy, and I go flying back out the window."

We reach the top of the stairs and finally admit that we need help, so we link arms and begin going down the stairs sideways, like some ridiculous quadrupedal crab.

"I swear, I thought I was, dead. But dumb fucking luck, I land flat on my back in the dinghy. The bag knocks all the air out of me and I'm laying there, pinned down and legless, gasping like a guppy. And I can hear shooting from above me, right, so I reckon Lee's gone in the window. I roll the bag off, get my breath back, and try to climb up and help. But it was hard enough when I had the prosthethis; it's fucking hopeless with one leg.

"Eventually the firing stops and I wait for Lee or Ferguson to call down for the bag, but they don't. So I reckon they're dead or captured, yeah?"

"Captured," I say as we pause to catch our breath on a landing. The corpse of my guard lies on the floor beside us, staring at the ceiling in surprise. My torch picks out the dark stain that marks where Jack's knife punctured his heart. "They're not dead yet."

Jack smiles. "Thank fuck for that."

I kneel down and rummage through the dead man's clothes until I find the keys to the jeep. I also take his machine gun, sidearm and a nasty looking knife. Jack and I link arms again and resume our ungainly descent.

"So I figure our mission's a bust," he says. "But I reckon I can still be useful, right, so I untether the dinghy and manage to row to a mooring and haul the bag up onto the embankment up these old stone steps. I figure I can flag down the others and give them the bag."

"Others?"

"Yeah, Tariq, Green and this crazy girl who says she knows you."

"Caroline?"

"Yeah, that's her. They've got this army of kids and they're gonna turn up at dawn, get inside the gates and then storm the place."

I stop dead in amazement and he topples forward, unbalanced, and slips down a few steps before he grabs the railing and manages to stop himself.

"But that's suicide!" I say.

"It wouldn't be if Lee and I had managed to pull off our little plan," he replies, righting himself and flashing me a sour glance.

"Which was?" I ask. "What was in the bag?"

So he tells me what their plan was. I stare at him for upwards of a minute, running it over in my head.

"That," I say eventually, "is fucking genius."

Ten minutes later we hobble out into the snow. My feet sink in it halfway up my shins, and it's still coming down.

"So where did you stash the bag?" I ask as we crunch across to the jeep.

"I was waiting halfway down Whitehall when I saw you being driven past," says Jack. "I just buried the bag in the snow and took off after you. I followed the tyre tracks. Sorry it took me so long. I'm not as light on my feet as I used to be."

"You and me both."

I pull open the driver's side door and clamber in. I tentatively depress the accelerator with my knackered foot. It hurts, but the cast makes it doable. Jack climbs in the other side. I turn the ignition and gun the engine. The wheels spin uselessly in the snow for a few moments and I fear we're going nowhere, but eventually they find purchase and we slip-slide away.

Without the orange streetlights making everything look slightly disco, London seems pristine and beautiful in the moonlit snow as I fight the wheel back to Westminster.

"The snow is our best friend," I say as we come down the Strand past Charing Cross station. "The guard has a little booth by the gate. He's expecting me back, and in this weather he won't be able to make us out properly from where he's sitting. There's a good chance he'll just pop the gates and wave us through."

"You don't want to wait and hook up with Tariq?"

I turn left onto Whitehall.

"Why should we? If we can get inside before they arrive, you can still fulfil your part of the plan. I'll stall Cooper and keep Lee alive until things kick off, then it's every man for himself."

"Here," shouts Jack. I slam on the brakes and we spin through 360 degrees before we stop. Jack lurches out into the snow and walks to the side of the road where he digs out the kitbag and limps back.

He tosses it in the back seat and gets back in. Another wheel spin, another moment of fear, but the four wheel drive doesn't let us down. I turn the jeep back the right way and we head off again. As we approach Big Ben I note the time: ten past seven. There's a faint hint of dawn across the river as we pass the road that runs to the ruins of Westminster Bridge.

A minute later we pull up to the gate. I flash my headlights and honk the horn once.

"Be lazy," I mutter. "Just this once, be lazy." I have the sidearm ready in my hand, just in case.

The gate swings open, pushing a tide of snow away into a thick drift. I send up a prayer to numerous gods, drive through the gate and down the ramp into the underground car park.

I pull into an empty space and switch off the engine.

"You know where you're going?" I ask.

Jack nods, resolute but nervous. "I think so."

"You can do this, Jack," I say. "Everything depends on you now. Go slow, go quiet, but get there. When was the attack scheduled to start?"

"The first strike of eight o'clock."

"Then get moving, and remember: every year the monarch should come to the Lords to make their speech saying how things are going to be different from now on. This is your chance. Make it good."

He nods, grabs the bag, and climbs out. In moments he is lost to the subterranean darkness.

I wait for a moment, gathering my thoughts, preparing. Then I too get out of the vehicle and walk into the Palace of Westminster, knowing there's a good chance I will never walk out again.

I limp as fast as I can to the Speaker's Cottage. There is no guard at the door, and all is silent when I enter. A sudden thought grabs me, so I hobble as softly as I can – not too difficult on this deep carpet – across to Cooper's bedroom door. I take the cold brass doorknob in my hand and turn it ever so slowly. It rotates without a squeak, the door is unlocked. Careless, Cooper. Thought that since I was out of the way and guarded, that he could relax a little.

I push the door open. The well-oiled hinges do not betray me. In the half light I can make out his bed. There, fully clothed above the covers, Cooper snores gently.

I can't believe it can be this easy. I glance over my shoulder, wary of sudden discovery, of a soldier who will leap out of the shadows and shout "fooled you!" But there's nobody. I step forward, drawing the knife from my belt as I do so. Normally I would have gone for my gun, but something in my subconscious diverts my hand to the hard metal blade.

I advance towards the bed. One strike, swift and sudden, and it will all be over. He lies on his side, his right temple presented as if offered to the knife.

I stand above him and raise the blade but before I can strike the door to the cottage clatters open and a soldier bursts into the hallway. Cooper starts up in sudden surprise, woken from deep sleep. He registers me in the darkness. I plunge the knife down with a scream, but the moment had passed. He's too fast for me. He spins sideways and the blade hits the eiderdown, sinking deep into feathers and mattress.

"Freeze!" comes a voice from the doorway. I let go of the knife and slowly raise my arms.

Cooper scrambles across the bed to the other side, where he switches on the bedside lamp. He's genuinely shocked, the first time I've ever seen him on the back foot.

I have no idea where it comes from, but I snarl at him, hissing like a cat, feral, furious and thwarted.

"Kate," says Cooper, panting with sudden exertion. "You are endlessly surprising." He turns to address the soldier in the doorway. "Report."

"We got them, Sir. Two lorries of kids. Armed to the fucking teeth. We've got their leaders downstairs now."

Cooper nods, arranging his clothes, making himself presentable. "Good. Keep Miss Booker here until I return."

He leans forward and picks up the knife. As he does so he notices the guns and wags his finger like a teacher remonstrating with a naughty pupil. He holds out his hands and I pass him the firearms. He shoves the handgun in his trouser pocket.

"I'll deal with you later," he says, then he strides from the room, closing the door behind him as he goes. I throw myself upon the bed, furious at myself for wasting such a golden opportunity.

I sit and stew for twenty minutes, trying to come up with a plan. Now that Tariq's forces are captured, Jack's diversion is the whole of our attack. It's not going to be enough.

If I do manage to slip away when Jack makes his move, I need to know where to go.

Twenty minutes later Cooper returns, smelling of gunpowder.

"What have you done with the children?" I ask the second he enters.

"They're safe, don't worry. They'll be held until the snow clears then we'll just ship them straight back to Heathrow. I must say, your friends are a resourceful bunch. Their plan was a good one, and it almost worked. But my men are better."

He sits on the edge of the bed and throws the handgun onto a dressing table. I see the top slide is retracted, indicating it's been fired. He follows my gaze.

"You really should have told that Iraqi not to be such a smartass," he says by way of explanation.

Oh no. Tariq.

He nods in response to the look on my face, and he taps the spot between his eyes.

I fly at him, fists swinging, teeth bared, but he bats me away as if I were a kitten. I tumble to the floor, my foot burning with agony.

"You know, Kate, I think I made a mistake with you. I thought perhaps we could be friends. I see now that I was naïve."

I spit in his face.

He wipes it away with a sneer. "Your friends are no use to me. The kids I can use. But the adults..." he shrugs. "I think it's time to end this."

He reaches out and grabs my arm, pulling me to my feet. "Follow me," he says and walks out of the rom. I hobble after him. I have to buy some time for Jack.

"What are you going to do?" I shout after him.

"A ten gun salute, I think," he says over his shoulder.

He hurries down the staircase to the front door. I limp in pursuit.

"Why kill them? They're no threat to you now." I know that sounds lame, but even if he pauses for a second to argue with me, it'll be a second gained. He sweeps out the front door, passing a guard from whom he grabs a fresh sidearm.

I trail after him, beginning to beg. He ignores me. He turns a corner and I hear him declaim: "lovely day for a shooting!"

I follow him outside into the stark white dawn. I see Lee, Green and a Ranger lined up against the fence, a group of armed soldiers opposite them. Oh god, it's a firing squad. My knees momentarily go weak with fear.

"Cooper, please," I say, choking back tears. "I'm begging you, don't do this."

He slaps me, Lee protests and a soldier opens fire. For a sickening moment I think he's shot Lee, but it was just a warning shot.

I'm crying now, pleading with Cooper, barely even conscious of what I'm saying. I step forward and come on to him. I'm sick at myself as I stroke his chest, all the time driven by the voice at the back of my head saying "just play for time, just play for time."

Cooper shouts an order then shoots one of his men, and the next thing I know I'm being dragged across to the fence and stood up next to Lee. I reach out and grab his hand.

I lean towards him and whisper: "be ready to run" but my voice is drowned out by Big Ben's insistent chime.

The men line up. Cooper joins them. They raise their guns as the clock counts down the final seconds of our lives.

Where the fuck is Jack?

I turn to Lee and we embrace.

Dear God, I may actually die here.

He whispers something to me, but I can't make it out.

Then my senses explode in fire.

CHAPTER TWENTY-EIGHT

As the final chime pealed I heard a deafening burst of machine gun fire. I braced for the impact, but there was none.

My ears rang as the shooting got louder. Then I felt a hand on my shoulder.

"Put the woman down and fucking run!" yelled Wilkes above the cacophony.

I opened my eyes, totally confused. Jane was already pulling away, dragging me along the edge of the fence to a stone alcove in the far wall where we could shelter.

I tried to make sense of what was happening. Cooper and his men were ranged along the far edge of the fence, backs to the river, engaged in a fierce firefight with a group of young women who were shooting at them from the covered stone walkway down which we'd been marched minutes earlier.

I glanced ahead and saw a figure beckoning us to a doorway. I thought my mind must be playing tricks on me, because it looked like Jack. Jane pulled me sideways as a stream of bullets whipped past us, cutting a straight line in the old stonework. We scurried through the doorway and behind a stone wall, under cover. Green was already there, gun in hand, raining fire on the pinned-down firing squad. Wilkes hurried in after us.

Jack shoved a gun in my hand and smiled at me.

"What the fuck is going on?" I shouted above the din.

"I landed in the dinghy," he shouted back. "I had the bag. Jane got me back in. Voila." He indicated the groups of armed women and beamed.

It takes a minute for the penny to drop. Somehow Jack has pulled it off and completed our mission – he's got the kitbag of guns to the women held captive in the Lords and turned them loose.

Jane turned, popped her head above the parapet and sent a burst of fire towards the bad guys. Then she ducked back under cover, leaned over to me and kissed me long and deep.

We only broke apart when there was a huge explosion from behind us. I peered over into the yard to see the last of Cooper's men pouring through a gap in the wall. They must have blown it open with a handful of grenades so they'd have somewhere to retreat. The snow-covered grass was littered with corpses and red with blood.

I turned to the group that ranged along the walkway.

"Jane, do you know where the kids are being held?"

She shook her head. "One of the committee rooms is all I know."

"We need to find them as fast as we can," I said. "There aren't enough of us to win this, and we're too concentrated. Can you lead us there?" Jane shook her head.

"I know where they are," shouted one of the women Jack had released from the Lords. I waved her over to me. She was gaunt and thin, pretty but tiny and undernourished. She had fire in her eyes, though, and she held the gun firmly and with confidence.

"And you are?"

"Jools," she said. "I heard some noise from one of the rooms we passed on our way here. I reckon the kids are in there."

"Get them out, get them armed," I said.

She nodded and smiled a grim smile that promised horrible death to anyone who got in her way. I decided I liked her.

"Come on girls," she yelled, and she took off at a run. The women streamed after her, free and armed and hungry for vengeance.

Jane pulled herself upright and hobbled into the snow to check the bodies. As she did so I turned to Wilkes and Green.

"Wilkes," I said, "you should find Ferguson, okay? I don't know where they took him, and he's likely to be in a bad way, but they may decide to just finish him off, and we could use him." I noticed he didn't have a gun, so I took one from Jack and handed it to him. He looked at it suspiciously, then nodded to the weapon.

"Fine," he said. "Just don't tell the boss about this, right?"

"Promise," I said, remembering Hood's feelings about firearms. He took off after the women into the Palace complex.

"You two, with me," I said, then I followed Jane into the snow. Green and Jack followed behind.

"Is Cooper here?" I asked.

Jane shook her head.

"Okay," I said. "We're going after them, through that hole in the wall. Green and I will take point, Jack you follow close behind and take care of Jane."

"I don't need taking care of, Lee," she said, momentarily indignant.

I stepped forward and kissed her nose. "Don't be daft. You've got a fucking hole in your foot."

I raised my gun to my shoulder and moved to one side of the hole in the wall. Green came up close behind me.

"You ready for this, mate?" I said, still unaccustomed to seeing him with a gun in his hand.

"Fuck yes," he said resolutely, which was good enough for me.

I lifted my hand and counted down from three then slipped sideways through the wall into the House of Commons Library tower, gun high, ready for anything.

Caroline heard the shooting and the explosions and became frantic. The attack was going ahead after all. They were supposed to be part of it, trapping the bad guys between two pincers and bottling them in. If there was only one wave of attackers, the soldiers would be able to dig in, fight back or escape. There'd be no-one to outflank them.

She began banging on the committee room door and yelling: "We're in here!"

A boy grabbed her shoulder from behind. "What are you doing? Are you trying to get us all killed?"

She swatted him away and kept banging on the door.

"Shut the fuck up!" came a yell from outside. That must be the guard.

"Come in here and make me, dipshit!" she yelled back. Then she turned to the assembled throng behind her and said: "When he opens the door we charge him. There are way too many of us for him to hold off, okay?"

A few children began fighting their way to the back of the crowd, scared now that things had come to a head. But the majority stood ready, nodding and squaring up, ready to run.

Caroline kept yelling until she was cut off by a burst of machine gun fire right outside the door. Something hard slammed into the door and she heard it fall to the ground. Was that the guard?

Moments later the key turned in the lock. Caroline held up her hand to hold the children back, telling them to wait for the right moment.

The door swung open and there, standing over the guard's corpse, were fifteen young women carrying machine guns.

"You lot ready to fight?" asked the woman at the front.

There was a brief pause then the children yelled en masse and poured out of the room looking for something, anything – anyone – to destroy.

The riot had begun.

Wilkes acted on instinct. He had no clue where they might have stashed Ferguson, but he figured it would be somewhere underground. He didn't know why, exactly, it just seemed appropriate; you didn't torture people in daylight, it was a dark, subterranean activity.

So he ran through the building, hearing gunfights all around him and a huge screaming furore to his right that sounded like the scariest borstal in the world at playtime, until he found a staircase to run down.

The gun felt odd in his hand. The boss had strict rules about firearms and even though he knew that he would be mad to toss it aside, it felt wrong to be carrying it. Just before he found the staircase he ran past a huge glass case mounted on the wall and stopped to gaze in wonder. Ranged within the display case were five beautiful shiny swords. The plaque underneath read 'Lieutenancy swords'. They must have been used for ceremonial events, like the opening of Parliament. He doubted they were sharp, but he smashed the glass with his elbow and reverently lifted down the big central blade. Its hilt fitted his hand like a glove and the elaborate silver designs that protected the swordsman's hand glittered in the light. He knew the names of each individual metal curlicue like a litany – contre-guard, anneau, pas d'ane, quillon, écusson. He smiled as he felt the weight of the sword against his palm.

He shoved the gun into his pocket – no point throwing it away just yet – grabbed a second sword, and ran down the stairs, a blade in each hand. Cold steel, he decided, felt much better than a firearm.

The cellars were a maze of tiny winding passageways, and Wilkes checked each door, finding pokey offices, store rooms, and finally a bar. The door opened from the inside just as he was reaching for the handle, so he stepped back and raised the blades. One of Cooper's men stood in the doorway, weapon raised, but the sight of a man with two swords took him by surprise. That instant of confusion was all Wilkes needed. He lunged forward, both swords level, and felt both the steel blades slide through the man's clothing and body smoothly and with little resistance.

So they were sharp after all.

The guard went rigid and the machine gun fell from his hands. The two swords were the only thing keeping him upright as blood poured from his mouth and his eyes rolled back in head.

Wilkes executed a perfectly poised fencing retreat, withdrawing the swords in one fluid motion, letting his skewered opponent crash to the floor, then he leapt over the body into the bar.

Here he found Ferguson tied to a chair, his face a mass of bruises and bloody, stripped of his shirt, his chest a dot-to-dot of cigarette burns.

He cut through the plastic ties on the ruined Ranger's hands and knelt down so they were face to face, hoping against hope that his friend had not been broken by his ordeal.

Ferguson looked up, swollen eyes full of fury. He asked for

water, his voice a faint whisper. Wilkes found a pitcher of water on the bar and gave it to him. Ferguson gulped it down then stood, a trifle unsteadily. He held out his hand and Wilkes passed him his shirt and hoodie. Ferguson dressed himself carefully then looked down at the dead body of his tormentor, machine gun laying beside him, ready for use.

Ferguson looked up and held out his hand.

"Sword," he said.

Green and I advanced through the wreckage of the Commons Library. Jane and Jack hobbled after us, covering our rear and sides.

"Remember," I said quietly as we picked our way across the rubble, "his core team were SAS. They know more about close quarter combat than all of us put together. Our only hope is to contain them, pen them in, give them nowhere to run. If this turns into a running fight, they'll pick us off easy."

The explosion had set fires in the old wooden building. Already flames were licking at the bookcases that lined the walls. Huge, heavy, leather bound copies of Hansard began to smoulder.

"This place," said Green, "is going to go up like a candle. We don't need to follow them in there, Lee. We can just stay outside and wait. The fire will force them out."

I looked down the long corridor ahead of me – a shooting gallery if ever I saw one – then back to the burning room. He was right.

"Back outside, now," I yelled, and we retreated to Speaker's Green. Burning pages began to rain down from the walls as we backtracked.

"We need to think this through," I said, turning to Jane. "Do you think he'll stand and fight or run for it?"

"Fight," she said firmly.

"Good, then what we have to do..."

My voice was drowned out by a roar somewhere off to our left. I glanced at the others in confusion then ran through the snow, underneath Big Ben and into the yard. A tide of children was pouring up out of the underground car park. At their head ran Caroline, a machine gun in her hands. The women from the Lords brought up the rear, yelping and whooping and firing in the air.

I tried to wave them down, to prevent them hurtling headlong into the Palace, but there was no stopping them. This wasn't an army, this was a mob and God help anyone who got in their way.

Caroline ran over to me as the mob streamed into the building, screaming and yelling and tearing the place apart, every one of them carrying a club, chain or gun.

"Not quite how we planned it," she said to me, panting and excited. "They left all our weapons in a pile in the car park, so we just collected them."

"We need to come up with a strategy for this, some plan..."

Caroline cut me off with a derisive laugh. "Forget it," she said. "Genie's out of the bottle, Lee."

I stood there, frustrated at the way the situation had slipped out of our hands so quickly.

"Fuck it," said Jack. "Let's follow them." He didn't wait for my assent, he just stomped off. Caroline went with him, Green shrugged as if to say 'what can you do?' and followed suit. I turned to Jane, who was looking anything but excited by this turn of events.

"Problem?" I asked.

He face clouded. "I don't want anyone getting to him before I do. Cooper's mine," she said. Then she too limped after the others.

I watched her walk awkwardly until she reached the door to the building – ripped off and smashed to pieces.

"I see what you like about her," said the voice in my head. "She's feisty."

Jane stopped and turned to look at me.

"Are you fucking coming, or what?" she shouted.

I walk through the Palace of Westminster with Lee at my side, trailing in the wake of the mob.

My foot pounds agonisingly as we shamble through the corridors of power. Everything has been ripped apart. Shattered wood panels litter the carpet, paintings and murals have been smashed and shattered.

The Commons is a scene of total devastation. The plush green leather benches have been slashed and the stuffing lies everywhere, mirroring the snow outside. The Speaker's Chair lies broken next to the upturned debating table. Centuries of tradition reduced to firewood in a few minutes.

A soldier lies sprawled in the middle of the floor. His head has been bashed in with a dispatch box that lies next to him, its lid snapped off. There are two children on the stairs that lead up to the back benches. I hurry over and kneel beside them, but they are shot to pieces and beyond help. One, a young girl, is a stranger to me, but I recognise the boy from St Mark's. I close their sightless eyes and stand, gripping my gun tightly, eager for retribution.

The row of grimy windows at the top of the chamber to our left begins to flicker orange as the fire sweeps parallel to us. It won't be long before it reaches this chamber.

We emerge into the Member's Lobby. Marble figures lie on the ground, arms broken, heads smashed off. We pass a group of four kids toppling a statue of some long forgotten administrator, his outstretched finger hectoring and stern; it snaps off as the figure crashes to the tiles.

Ahead there is gunfire and shouting, explosions and screams, and the constant angry roar of children on the rampage.

There are a series of loud reports down the corridor to my right. I spin to see a soldier backing away, firing a handgun as he goes. Then it clicks uselessly, the ammunition exhausted. He throws the weapon at whoever is advancing towards him, then turns to run in my direction. I raise my gun to cut him down but before I can fire a tall figure bursts into the corridor in a flurry of limbs and steel. The soldier raises his arms to protect himself, but the swordsman brings his blade down in a sweeping arc and cleanly severs the man's head from his body. It rolls towards me, the cadaver toppling to the floor behind it. The swordsman stands upright and walks towards us, dripping blade at his side. His face is a mass of bruises.

"Ferguson, is that you?" says Lee.

The figure nods as he reaches us. One of the four kids, finished with the statue now, runs forward and kicks the soldier's severed head as if taking a penalty. It soars into the air and narrowly misses a second sword-bearing Ranger who emerges from the corridor and ducks in alarm as the head flies past, breaking the window on its way out.

"Fucking hell!" swears the Ranger. He turns and shouts at Ferguson. "We're supposed to disable when possible, Ferguson. You know the boss doesn't like us killing if we don't have to."

Ferguson turns and stares at Wilkes who immediately puts his hands up.

"But, you know, do what you feel, pal," he says sheepishly.

The kids laugh and high five the head kicker, then they take off towards the Lords, following the sounds of the fight.

Lee, the two Rangers and I follow on behind.

As we walked through that corridor something strange happened to me. I felt my pulse racing, faster than it had even when I was lined up in front of the firing squad. My hand started spastically clenching and unclenching on the stock of my gun and Mac began to shout at me.

"Come on Nine Lives, what are you doing straggling at the back?" he bellowed. "Fucking get in there. Crack some skulls. Come on, for fuck's sake."

I tried to ignore him but he was too loud, too insistent. The desire to kill grew so strong that I could barely hold myself in check.

"Stay with her," I said to Wilkes. Then I looked at Ferguson as if to say 'you coming?' He nodded once, and we ran ahead, into the fray. I heard Jane shouting at me to be careful, but it barely registered.

We came to the Lords and found the doors smashed open. The noise from inside was indescribable. As we entered we found the mob of children, nearly all of them, I reckon, formed into a circle. Some were standing on the red leather benches to get a better view of the makeshift arena they'd constructed on the floor of the house. They were literally baying for blood, chanting, cheering, jeering and yelling. I fought my way through the crowd to the front edge and found two of Cooper's soldiers – big, burly men in black combats, shaven headed and scary – standing with their backs to each other, circling around and around waiting for the crowd to surge forward and tear them to pieces. They were bleeding, desperate and cornered.

The men were unarmed, and the children had enough weapons between them to gun them down a hundred times, but it seemed the crowd was eager for a more primitive spectacle. They were hurling anything and everything they could find at the men – books, computer equipment, chairs, heavy wooden boxes. The men were, I realised, being stoned to death. I felt a surge of excited bloodlust and ran out into the lobby where I had passed some more shattered statues. I grabbed a heavy, sharp piece of marble and ran back, fighting my way through the crowd to the front again, cradling it in my hands.

The men were batting away the objects that were flying at them, but they couldn't get them all. A gold finial smashed into the face of one of them and he reeled backwards. The children cheered as blood began to pump from his nose. He stopped for a moment and bowed his head, wiping the blood onto his sleeve. I smiled as I stepped forward, raised the heavy stone block, and brought it crashing down on the man's head, feeling his skull crack and crumble beneath it.

"Yeah!" cried Mac. "That's more like it! Kill the bastard!"

The man slumped against me, blood spurting from his head, spraying all over me. I brought the rock down again and again, splashing his brains all over my chest. The children cheered and stamped their feet. The other soldier stepped forward, holding out his hands. I'm unsure whether he was begging for mercy or trying to get me to stop. I brought the stone down one more time and the man collapsed to the floor. I dropped the stone on what was left of his head, drew my gun and shot his colleague in the face. There was a huge cheer from the crowd as the man's head jerked backwards and he toppled to the floor.

I raised my blood drenched arms, gun in hand, and I roared. The crowd echoed my triumph. If I registered the horror in Ferguson's face, Mac's encouragement was enough to make me to ignore it.

"Come on!" I cried.

The crowd of children parted before me then fell into step behind as I ran past the broken golden throne and out the rear doors into the Royal Gallery – a long corridor lined with opulent paintings of heroic military scenes from the nineteenth century. I ran at the head of the mob down that hall towards the doors of the Queen's Robing Room. The doors were slightly ajar, but there seemed to be nobody ahead of us, so I ran headlong toward them.

Only when I was two thirds of the way down the hall, with a hundred screaming children behind me, did the doors suddenly swing open to reveal four men, two standing, two kneeling, machine guns raised. And standing in between them was Cooper, smiling as he saw us approach.

"Fire!" he shouted.

The four machine guns opened up simultaneously.

It turned out I was right – being shot multiple times doesn't really hurt. It's like being punched by someone wearing boxing gloves; you feel the impact in your torso but there's no pain, just a sudden pressure and shocking push backwards as you absorb the momentum of the bullet as it spins into your flesh, tearing and ripping and smashing its way through you.

I hit the tiles hard and slid forward on a tide of my own blood.

All I could hear was gunfire and screaming.

And then, as silence fell inside my head, Mac whispered one word, clear and calm.

"Gotcha."

CHAPTER TWENTY-NINE

I hear the volley of gunfire and the sudden change from yelling to screaming as I pass the threshold of the Lords.

Ahead of me I can see the mass of children pouring past the Queen's chair, waving their weapons in a frenzy. Suddenly the tide turns and they back away and turn to run towards us. The children at the back are taken by surprise and some fall to the ground to be trampled by the mass panic that sweeps over them.

I try to wave them down, to get them to stop and regroup, but they're like a herd of panicked cattle – unthinking and unstoppable. Wilkes pushes me hard, flinging me onto the front bench, saving me from being trampled in the rush.

When the stampede has passed, I pull myself off the bench and see Wilkes picking himself up across from me. We can hear the commotion of the retreating mob behind us, and the groans of the injured and dying ahead.

"Put that bloody knife away and pick up a real weapon," I hiss at Wilkes, annoyed by his sword. He nods reluctantly and pulls a handgun from his pocket with his left hand, although he keeps the sword raised in his right. We advance either side of the throne into the corridor beyond.

The long, wide room is strewn with bodies. The air is thick with smoke so it's hard to make out the far end, where Cooper and his men must be. The light is streaming through the windows behind them, casting their shadows into the smoke, making them seem ghostly.

I turn to Wilkes.

"Find someone, anyone, and go around. Get behind them."

But before he can move there is a cry from the far end and the sounds of a struggle. The shadows dance and writhe in the smoke, there is a brief burst of gunfire, then footsteps on the tiled floor as someone comes running towards us.

"Stay right there!" I yell. The running man stops dead as the smoke begins to clear.

As the scene fades into view I first make out Cooper, standing about a third of the way to us, holding a handgun. He stares at me and snarls, a cornered animal. Then behind him I gradually make out four of his men, kneeling with their fingers laced behind their heads. Standing behind and above them are Green, Jack, Jools and some of the other women from the Lords, who have managed to outflank them.

"You're trapped, Cooper," I say, sighting my gun carefully on his chest. "There's nowhere for you to run. Your army's defeated, your prisoners are freed, your Palace is on fire."

He looks left and right desperately, searching for an escape route, but there is nothing. Then he looks down at his feet, at the dead and dying, and he barks a short, humourless laugh.

Quick as a flash he drops to the floor and grabs one of the shot children, dragging them to him and then pulling the body to the side wall.

I nearly scream as I realise that the bloody mess he's dragging is Lee.

My knees give way and I crash to the floor as I cry out. It sounds like someone else. Surely that scream of anguish can't have come from me?

In a moment Cooper is sitting with his back to the wall, legs wide, with Lee slumped back against his chest as a human shield.

My breath comes in short, ragged gasps and I try to focus

through my tears. Lee is still breathing, I can tell that, but he's been shot multiple times, across the chest and abdomen. He is literally soaked in blood from head to toe.

His head lolls back against Cooper's chest and his eyes open, rolling wildly, confused and in shock.

Cooper brings his gun up, presses it against Lee's temple, and stares at me over my dying lover's shoulder.

"He's still alive, Kate," he says, no longer shouting."There's a chance you could save him. Get him to St Thomas's quickly and you never know."

Lee's eyes focus on me and his face forms a question. Then he looks down at the forty or so dead and dying children that litter the floor before him and his mouth hangs open.

"What did I do?" he whispers as he surveys the carnage. He looks up at me with eyes clouded by tears and blood. "Matron, what did I do?"

I hear myself sob. This isn't the resolute warrior Lee has become. He just sounds like a frightened child.

I take a deep breath and force myself to take control. I slowly rise to my feet.

"Okay," I shout. "If you let him go, I promise you can walk out of here."

"Like fuck he can!" It's Jools, shouting from the far room, bringing her gun to bear on Cooper. "That rat bastard is mine."

"Julia, darling," says Cooper. "I didn't know you cared."

He takes the gun away from Lee's head for an instant and fires a single shot towards the far room. The gun is back at Lee's temple before Jools' lifeless corpse hits the ground. Jack cries out in alarm. There are shouts and screams both ahead and behind me.

Lee's looking left and right, starting to focus, starting to get a sense of his situation.

His eyes focus on the far wall and he seems to study the painting that dominates it. I glance right to see what he's looking at and realise it's a huge representation of the death of Nelson, who lies cradled in Hardy's arms, much as Lee lies slumped in Cooper's.

He smiles, and blood bubbles from his lips. Then he turns and looks at me.

For a moment I'm back in Manchester, staring into the eyes of my brother, seeing the realisation of his own death so clear.

Lee mouths words, trying to tell me something, but I can't make out what it is.

I cry out. "No!"

But his awful sad smile widens.

Then he lifts his right hand, grabs Cooper's gun, still tight against his skull, slips his finger inside the trigger guard and pulls.

There is a single shot.

Then many.

CHAPTER THIRTY

They counted twenty-three dead soldiers, forty-six dead children and three young women in their final sweep of the Palace of Westminster. Plus Lee, of course.

Some of the soldiers' bodies had been horribly mutilated. One had been literally torn apart. Green chose to believe it was the women from the lords who did that, not the children.

He organised teams to recover all of the bodies from the building – all their dead, that is. They left the snatchers to burn, and buried their dead in Parliament Square.

When the mob finally burnt itself out they gathered in the road outside, dazed by what they'd done, slowly coming down like clubbers after a great night out. Green addressed the crowd, telling them about the school, offering a home to all those who wanted to come with him. Anyone who wanted to return to the communities they were snatched from could come back with them too, he promised to arrange safe transport home.

A bunch of the comfort women elected to come with them, but a group of nine children refused to come along, insisting that they could look after themselves, distrustful of all adults even still. He let them go.

The fire spread more slowly than expected, but the entire Parliament complex was ablaze by the time they loaded the remaining children back into the lorries and set off for St Mark's through the snow.

As they reached the edge of the city two of them parted company with the main convoy. Jack led a small team to Heathrow where they spent three busy days siphoning off aircraft fuel, laying charges, planning the biggest explosion since Salisbury. When they pulled out of the airport, they left a huge conflagration behind them. All the planes burned, the runways a mass of unuseable craters. Nobody would be flying children to the US from there ever again, and neither could the American Church land and start again. In the week that followed, they took care of Gatwick and Luton before returning to St Mark's.

Wilkes and Ferguson, who had taken off back to Nottingham once the battle of Westminster was over, had promised the Rangers would take similar steps at Birmingham, Manchester and Leeds airports. Obviously there were still local and military airfields the church could use, but they agreed this sent a strong message and was worth the effort.

Jane took no part in any of this. She sat silent, comatose, her eyes fixed on some distant point. She let herself be led into one of the lorries, compliant, like a puppet or a doll.

When they got back to the school she took to her bed and stayed there. She would eat when she was fed, sleep when the candle was blown out, wake when they opened her curtains.

But that was all.

It was as if she wasn't even in there anymore.

EPILOGUE

Caroline opened her good eye and winced. It was hard to divorce the pounding in her head from the pounding on the door of her small room. The walls glowed orange, lit by the dying embers of the fire that kept ice from forming on the inside of the windows on these long, cold nights.

Even through her hangover, Caroline knew instantly what was occurring.

Someone was having a baby.

"Okay," she shouted wearily. "I'm coming." The hammering stopped and she heard footsteps scurry off down the corridor outside.

She rubbed her head and reached for the glass of water that she always kept on her bedside cabinet. She gulped it all down, wishing there were still such things as aspirin or Nurofen.

"What's going on?" murmured Jack, rolling over and nuzzling into her neck.

"The baby's coming," she whispered. "You go back to sleep."

He mumbled something and rolled back again, pulling the blankets tight to his neck. Within moments he was snoring softly.

Caroline reached across and stroked his hair tenderly before bracing herself and swinging her legs out of the warm cocoon of the bed into the freezing night air. The rug protected her feet from the worst of the cold as she pulled her jeans and sweater on. Her breath misted the air in front of her face as she added central heating to the list of things she would wish for if she ever found a lamp with a genie in it.

She sat back on the edge of the bed, pulled on her slippers, then hurried to the door and emerged into the first floor landing of Fairlawne, the new home of St Mark's.

The school she had returned to six months previously was very different to the one she had left two years before that.

It wasn't just that they were in a different building now; the sudden influx of new children had shifted the balance of the place. The easy cameraderie she remembered from their time at Groombridge was gone. There were new cliques and new gangs, new classes, new troublemakers and new favourites.

New names on the memorial wall, too.

With so many of the adults dead, they had too few staff to deal with the new intake. Although a bunch of the women who had been kept prisoner in Westminster turned out to be naturals, they couldn't replace what the school had lost. Green seemed to be in twenty places at once – breaking up fights, teaching classes, organising the repatriation of rescued kids, tending to the wounded and damaged. He was magnificent, holding the school together almost single-handed.

It felt as if the whole school were in a kind of shock, perhaps from the children's realisation of their own savagery during the battle of Parliament, or perhaps from the loss of so many friends and teachers.

Caroline felt it too. St Mark's was holding its breath, unable to relax, waiting for something to happen.

The winter had been unbelievably long, harsh and fractious. The fireplaces burnt twenty-four hours a day and the snow seemed never ending. They'd had little contact with the other communities they'd befriended. Travel was arduous in those conditions, so they became isolated. The whole school suffered from cabin fever. Tempers were short and food was scarce. There were so many new mouths to feed that the supplies they had laid in were inadequate, so they ended up slaughtering more of their livestock than they could afford. Caroline knew that by the time spring arrived they would have depleted all their meagre resources. They would have to work hard all summer – and pray God it was a good harvest – to lay in enough to see them through another winter.

The rumour had spread that the world was entering a nuclear winter caused by some distant cataclysm; another Chernobyl or a nuclear skirmish. But even as the winter entered its sixth bitter month Caroline was sure spring would come again; the snow would melt, the blossom would appear, the flowers would bloom. They had to.

On one of the very few times the school had been visited by traders from Hildenborough they heard that the Abbot had made his final broadcast, murdered on air by a Brit. The Church had been defeated at home and abroad. They were safe again.

Even in the cold darkness, some children were congregating on the landing as Caroline hurried to the birthing room, woken by the screams, emerging to see what was going on. She ushered them back to their beds.

She paused of the threshold of the room, disturbed by the noises coming from within.

Ever since she'd arrived here, Caroline had spent at least an hour a day in this room, sitting beside the bed, reading out loud. Mostly Jane Austen, keeping it light. Sometimes, less often, she had just sat and talked. Once she had confessed to the murder of John Keegan and broken down in tears. As she'd cried into the eiderdown she'd felt a hand on her hair, stroking it softly. It was the only sign of understanding she'd had in all that time.

Matron hadn't spoken a word since that day in Westminster.

Now Caroline stood outside Matron's room and heard her screaming her way through labour. It felt odd to hear any noise coming from that mouth.

She stepped inside. Matron was sitting up in the bed, legs splayed, face red, breathing hard. She reached out her hand when she saw Caroline enter, so she stepped forward and held out her hand in turn. Matron grasped it tight and pulled the girl to her side. They stayed like that, hands locked firm, as Mrs Atkins oversaw the birth.

All the noises that Matron vocalised were primal. They were roars and cries and groans and screams. Not one word passed her lips – no fucks or shits or Jesus holy motherfucking Christs.

It was an animal birth.

The baby was born as the first light of dawn crept in the window.

Caroline held the child as Mrs Atkins cut the cord. She gasped in wonder at the tiny, blue screaming thing in her hands. So light and so angry at being removed from the nice warm place that was all it had ever known.

She laid the newborn on Matron's naked chest and pulled the sheets up to protect it from the cold. It fell silent immediately, eyes open, comforted by the warmth of its mother's skin and sound of her heartbeat.

"It's a boy," said Caroline.

Matron looked up at Caroline and smiled through her tears.

"I know," she said. "His name's Lee."

Later, Caroline walked out of the room into the half-lit hallway and told the lingering children the good news before ushering them back to bed.

She walked down the stairs and out the front door to watch the sun creep over the snow covered treeline. Despite all the losses of the last few years, all the terrible things she had done and had done to her, the hardship of their lives and the endless winter that had enshrouded them for so long, she knew, with absolute certainty, that she was where she belonged, safe and loved.

As her eyes filled with tears, she caught the first faint hint of spring on the air.

THE END

SCOTT ANDREWS has written episode guides, magazine articles, film and book reviews, comics, audio plays for Big Finish, far too many blogs, some poems you will *never* read, and two previous novels for Abaddon.

He lives in a secret base hidden within the grounds of an elite public school which serves as a front for his nefarious schemes to take over the world. His wife and two children indulge him, patiently.

You can contact him at www.eclectica.info, where you'll find all sorts of nonsense.

THE AFTERBLIGHT CHRONICLES

Now read the an exclusive story set in the *Afterblight Chronicles* universe...

THE AFTERBLIGHT CHRONICLES

SIGNS AND PORTENTS

PAUL KANE

WWW.ABADDONBOOKS.COM

In this place, he could see the past, the present... and the future.

Mostly the future. Incredible as it seemed – to him as much as anyone – visiting this land had granted him access to things that hadn't happened yet; that *might never* happen if he was able to prevent them. It had helped him many times, warning him about his enemies, saving his life on numerous occasions. Never, though, had he found himself flying before. It wasn't flying as he'd known it when he flew with Bill, though – into Nottingham to take the castle from the Sheriff, then taking control of the chopper himself to save Mary. Nor when he'd been delivered to the forest (again by Bill), half dead, after the assault on the Tsar's army.

This time Robert was flying without the aid of any kind of mechanical device. The wind catching his trousers and top, tugging at his hood. He felt like Superman, arms out in front, zooming through a clear blue sky with cotton wool clouds. He squinted, seeing a couple of specks ahead of him: the only things marring his view. Specks that grew in size quite rapidly.

They came up on him fast and Robert saw now they were two gigantic birds – their wingspans huge. Like a cross between mighty eagles and vultures, they began to snap with their beaks, attempting to grab him. Robert twisted this way and that, and it was only now, as he dived forwards, that he realised he wasn't really flying at all – he never had been.

He was falling.

Head down, he aimed for the closest bird and reached out. His hands found purchase, clutching at the strange feathers, and he was able to swing himself up and onto its back. The other bird was swooping in to attack, just as Robert was standing – bracing himself against the wind. He ducked, narrowly avoiding the sharp talons. Seconds later he was up again, his trusty bow in his hands. An arrow was nocked, the twine pulled back as far as it would go. He was trailing the second bird's progress beneath the first, and he let go when he was sure of the shot. The arrow found a home in the bird's left wing but it kept on coming, under and up again, swooping in as Robert readied himself for another pass.

This time as it tried to grab him, Robert's aim was jostled by the bird underneath him turning, attempting to buck him off. He had to reach down and grab a handful of feathers again just to stop himself from falling.

By this time the second bird was circling below again, and as Robert rolled across the back of the first, he leaned over the side and fired. The bird was hit by its second arrow, between the shoulder and the neck. This appeared to do more damage, because the bird spun off to one side.

It was time to end this, to put them both down.

Robert stood once more, feeling like he was on some kind of bouncy castle – the kind he'd used to hire out for Stevie's–

He shook his head: though he didn't consciously try to keep thoughts about his late son out of his mind, it was so hard to think about him without remembering the... other stuff. The stuff that followed: the coughing up of blood, watching him slip away like Joanne and–

Robert gritted his teeth, aimed, and fired two more arrows directly into the chest of the creature about to attack one final time. It reared up with those deadly talons and then just fell away out of sight. The bird Robert was riding bucked again, and he had to let go of his weapon this time in order to hang on. The bow dropped away, just as the other bird had done moments before.

Could he ride this creature to the ground? Robert looked over the side and couldn't even see the earth beneath him... His answer came anyway, when the bird flipped over, rolling deep to try and dislodge him. When that didn't work, it started craning its neck around to peck at its unwelcome human passenger. Robert reached down and found the handle of his sword, which he drew, lashing out at the bird.

A couple of his blows found their mark, leaving long lacerations that wept blood. But when the bird jerked again, Robert knew he had to act. He stood and plunged the sword into its head, through its skull and out under its chin. Like the other one, it started to dive almost immediately, and Robert was at last thrown from his perch. The bird fell faster than him, leaving Robert to witness another preview of things to come: of what would happen to him as he plummeted through these clouds.

He still couldn't see the ground, but as he passed through the last wisps of whiteness, he saw the vast expanse of a forest below – *his* forest: Sherwood. The rational part of his mind knew where he really was and what was happening to him, but as always this felt so real (and hadn't he read somewhere once that if it happened to you here, you felt it in the real world?). He was falling, picking up speed as he went – and now he could see the damage those birds had done to his home below, bending and breaking branches as they plummeted through the trees.

Robert would make significantly less of an impact, but he'd be just as dead when he hit: splattered red over the rich greenery. Robert crossed his arms over his face – like that was going to be any protection – and braced for his crash.

But it never came. He'd closed his eyes, not wishing to witness his own end, and when he opened them again he was standing in the forest. It was as though he'd been safely deposited there, a huge hand reaching out from the clouds to place him safely on the ground like the gods of ancient Rome or Greece moving their subjects about. Or some other gods? Those who protected the forest's favourite son? Who'd kept him from harm not only with these warnings, but by renewing his energy when it was lacking. No sooner had he thought this, than he felt energised again and began to run through what had become his natural habitat after he'd retreated there because of–

Robert pushed himself harder, in an effort to push aside those memories again. He was a different person now, in a different world, with different responsibilities. He had married again, adopted another son who looked just like Stevie would have done if he'd survived (though wasn't him, Robert was at pains to keep reminding himself). That didn't mean you forgot the past – this place wouldn't let you, apart from anything else (and Robert more than anyone understood the importance of looking back to see the way forward).

But it did mean you learnt to make your peace with it.

He forged on, faster and faster: the forest feeling good beneath his feet. As he ran, though, he forced himself to take note of his surroundings; of what Sherwood was trying to tell him. It was then that he saw the cobwebs between branches; why hadn't he noticed them before? They were larger than you'd find in the average home or shed, stretched between oaks and birches. Here and there he saw birds – much smaller than the ones who'd attacked him in the sky – trapped in the strands like flies in any ordinary web.

Robert felt compelled to keep going rather than explore what might have caused such a phenomenon. It wasn't until he got deeper into the forest that he saw something that gave him pause. Cocoons; lots of them. Big and long, hanging from the trees. They looked like they were about to break open at any moment and butterflies would emerge. Except that the closer he got, the more he could see of them – and the less they looked like cocoons at all. These were people (men to be precise) covered in webbing, as if they'd met another superhero – Spider-man, rather than Superman this time – and come off worse.

Robert started towards them as he saw the victims struggling inside. He quickened his pace, rushing to help. But as he reached them something happened to those trapped inside. Each one in turn spontaneously combusted, bursting into flames that should have set the forest alight.

He couldn't see where the fire had come from, but it no longer frightened him as much as it had done in the past; flashing back to when those men in yellow suits and gasmasks had torched his house with flame-throwers.

Something was moving through the forest, something big... Robert looked up to see it brushing the tops of trees, this thing: bending them over so that they whipped back once it had passed by. He also heard the dull roar of the creature that had probably set fire to the webbed men.

He continued through the forest, knowing he could do nothing for those who'd been roasted alive. As he did, his pace quickened again – running *towards* the enormous thing he'd only caught a glimpse of, flashes of red between the trees.

Then, to his right, something else – almost as big – was making its way through the foliage. Could these be the two birds he'd thought he'd killed, only wounded and rampaging through Sherwood? But why the webs, why the fire? He caught sight of a hairy leg, possibly the thing that had incapacitated those other men. The closer he looked, though, the less he saw: he wasn't *supposed* to see any more yet. Didn't need to know what the hell it meant, just like with the birds... (Was he going to be attacked by huge eagle-vulture things? It was never that simple – always a metaphor for something else.)

The huge things were turning and moving on, away from him. All his senses were screaming 'let them go', but Robert couldn't. He chased after them, speeding up again – speeding up because, as he looked down, he found that he had not one pair of legs but two. Not feet, but hooves.

If he'd had hands, and he could reach up, he would have found antlers on his head, too. It wouldn't be the first time that had happened.

There were figures in the trees, men – *living* men this time. Soldiers, dressed in familiar grey garb. The Tsar's troops, the ones he'd defeated at the battle just outside Doncaster, that Dale and the others had seen off at Nottingham Castle. This was slipping into the past again, because there were also the Servitors they'd faced the previous year, hiding behind and flitting between the trees in their red, hooded robes.

But was it the past, or still the future? Were both of these threats about to rise again? Robert just had time to note that the grey uniforms were not quite the same on these soldiers before the rumbling in the forest returned. He assumed it belonged to the monsters again – because that's all it could be. But actually it was coming from man-made things, jeeps and tanks: more like the dangers he knew and had faced before. Where were his friends, he wondered, the people he loved and cared about? Why wasn't the forest showing him them?

Show me more...please! How can I be expected to do anything about all this unless–

The light was growing dim inside Sherwood, night falling... or something else. Robert, the stag-thing he'd become, looked up and saw the shape of the shadow falling over his beloved forest – could even see the outline, and the struggling brightness on either side.

That wasn't the only thing wrong, though. When Robert dragged his attention back down again, he saw another fire. Only this one had a spit over it; the kind you'd normally roast pigs on. This time, however, there was an all too familiar animal strapped to it. The antlers scraped the ground as the spit was turned by unseen hands, round and round, cooking over the fire.

As everything grew darker, Robert was suddenly aware that he had no form. That his perspective had shifted, and rather than watching the poor animal's flesh burn, he was actually *on* that skewer himself: the heat tremendous.

The shadows coalesced, forming a shape: a man appearing ahead of him. Robert didn't feel as though he should fear that shadow man, yet he sensed this figure would prove the most dangerous of all the enemies he'd face. Would do more damage than the rest put together, because he was following his own agenda.

The shadows were drawing in around him, and Robert realised that the edges were closing in. He was blacking out from the heat, could smell his own fat as it sizzled and popped.

When all he could see was darkness, the pain finally too much, he prayed that he would wake from this dream quickly.

Or he might never wake from it at all.

The heat was intense, but then it was meant to be.

It *had* to be for this to work. The man sitting cross-legged, naked apart from a small loincloth, breathed in the blistering air – mixed with spices he'd added to the fire beneath the stones. It wasn't the only way for him to connect with those beyond this realm, with his guides and with his gods. He could have walked out into the wilderness, for example, fasted or starved himself to reach this state. But he knew the task ahead would require both strength and for him to begin as soon as he was able.

Inside the lodge, he'd waited until the walls began to disintegrate. Not literally, and not the walls that he'd built – but rather the walls of this reality, allowing him to talk to those he obeyed.

Those who had a special destiny in mind for him.

He saw a green land – and at first he thought it might be up in the mountains near where he'd been born and raised, the hunter's skills coming as naturally to him as eating or sleeping. But this was far away, across the ocean. To reach it he would need to fly – like a huge black bird, stretching his wings, soaring high and fast. This was where he would begin his quest, that's what he was being told: the voices of his ancestors singing to him. So it was where he began his vision quest as well, looping down into that forest to explore.

He made his way through, just as much a spirit here as those who called to him. But there were forces trying to prevent his progress: he felt that too. Other spirits that dwelt within this particular domain, that were the representatives of the local gods. Nevertheless, he saw it here: what he was looking for.

In the middle of a clearing was a huge totem pole, cut from wood not of this forest. It was made up of a number of animals: a bear, a snake curled round the width of the pole, a wolf, buffalo and a bird – its wings unfurled. The eyes of the creatures all glowed, but it was the stone at the top of the totem itself that caught his attention. That was his goal on this particular expedition, and as soon as he recognised this it began to move, loosening from its housing; moving forwards to float in front of the totem. The animals came to life then, the bird flapping its wings, the snake uncoiling, the wolf hopping down, the bear and buffalo beginning to walk.

He watched this all with fascination – knowing they were the ones who'd guided him on this quest, who'd kept him free from harm up to this point (especially when it came to the plague that had killed so many others of his brothers). The stone continued to hover in the air, and when it flashed so too did each of the animals' eyes. It was the true stone of power, and when brought together with the others on his quest...

The animals all went their separate ways and he knew he had yet to trace all of them (though since what was known as The Cull, he had been quite busy in that respect). But his next task would be the recovery of the greatest of all the stones of power assembled here: which was even now floating in the air, pointing to the direction where it lay. The means to recover it would bring him to this forest, but where it actually was – that was another matter. Back across the ocean again, over land that was still foreign to him, but he knew took him even further east. A collection of countries that in total didn't even make up a fraction of the landmass his people had once claimed as their own.

He flew after the stone, which had settled in an icy, snowbound place. The dead stood frozen on the streets, decomposing slowly because the elements wouldn't let them go quickly or kindly to their rest. This was where he would begin his quest. The seat of 'power' for a ruler, the second such of his kind.

Without warning, he was yanked back, as if he was on a giant piece of elastic – pulled back to that forest, to stand in that clearing again. Only now, instead of the totem, he saw a man. The man he would soon have to face if he was to possess the stone. The man who would be the means to this end, because someone else wanted to possess *him*.

He stared at this person, dressed in green combats and a hooded top – bow and arrow primed and pointing at him. The Hooded Man possessed great strength, anyone could see that, but the seeker of the stones could also tell that it wasn't all his own. Like him, Hood had help... from the spirits of this place, almost as ancient as those from his own religion. In fact, couldn't he actually feel some kind of kinship with this person – a hunter just like him, just as skilled in the bow (*more* skilled perhaps? There was only one way they'd find that out).

He wasn't sure whether the Hooded Man could see him or not – it was a very rare thing for this to be a two-way vision – but he was taking no chances: he didn't want to tip off his opponent in this particular game of chess.

"Fulfil your destiny, Shadow," he heard as he was scrambling to leave the spirit world. "Do not fail us."

He wasn't about to – and just as the arrow the Hooded Man was pulling back was let loose, Shadow broke free of the vision, blinking to refamiliarise himself with his surroundings. He had no idea how much time had passed since he first entered, but felt parched and would need to re-hydrate himself right away, but his first step on this new mission had been taken. He felt a sharp stab of pain in his arm and looked down. Just below his shoulder was a wound. He might have scraped it on one of the rocks as he was attempting to exit the other reality, or maybe...

Shadow shook his head. It couldn't be.

He'd dismissed the notion almost as soon as he was clear of the lodge. It wouldn't be the last time he'd need to come here, for one thing he needed to learn more about his potential target – the person who stood between him and his prize – but he'd certainly be more cautious next time. Shadow would not underestimate his prey, for to do so would result not only in his end, but more importantly the end of his quest.

As he drank from the water bottles he'd left by the side of the lodge, Shadow thought about where he was heading next. His services were needed, but he'd better wrap up warm where he was going...

The runes had told her much.

Alone in the great hall she now called her own, she'd cast the stones upon the table in front of her, watching intently as they fell, examining the markings on each in the flickering candlelight. She'd done a simple line spread, a Celtic Cross pattern and finally – the most revealing, as always – a lifetimes spread: showing her previous and future lives. What kept appearing over and over was the symbol of *Raido*, or communication.

There was a need for her to connect with someone, and soon.

Tell me somethin' I don't know, she thought to herself. She'd been trying to connect and communicate since she was a little girl. But the time was coming around, of that she was sure. Her previous life, if read symbolically, had encountered great tragedy – *two* great tragedies to be precise, here represented by the symbol *Nauthiz* – but for a reason. The obstacles she'd put in front of herself, as well as those the world had thrown at her; necessary pain to bring her to this point in her current life. Her future life, the runes told her, was starred by the symbol *Gebo*: a partnership!

She'd encountered many such promises of this in her life, and all of them had come to nothing. This time, everything pointed to it being 'the one'. The thing that she'd been told about when she was in her teens.

Taking out the tarot cards now, she wanted to double check. Placing them in the spread she'd been taught all those years ago, she turned them over one by one to reveal the pattern of her future. Would it have changed since the last time she did this? She doubted it very much, the signs and portents then had been too strong. Turning over the 'significator' she saw the root of the thing she was seeking: a pair of naked figures, hand in hand with a crude representation of Cupid behind. *The Lovers.* It revealed what her heart desired more than anything, a unity she'd yet to feel with any of the other men she'd shared her life – and her bed – with. In spite of how very close she'd become eventually to all of them (they were all on... 'speaking' terms still) there just hadn't been the one that the cards back then had spoken of, had suggested to her.

The card on top of this was the opposition to her heart's desire, the main thing blocking it. And with one turn she saw what might stand in her way. A picture of a woman closing a lion's mouth – showing her power over nature. The card of *Strength*. She was calming the beast, just as she might calm the passions that were necessary for this plan to work. Letting out a snort, the woman turning the cards carried on with her reading.

She revealed the next one as the best that could be achieved if she just let things go ahead at their own pace: *The Star*, indicating that recent difficulties would soon be a thing of the past. Even if she did nothing, she would still get what she wanted.

The next turn showed her what was surrounding the matter in hand, what had already happened. Here she was greeted with a card that depicted a wheel covered in symbols, around which winged creatures floated. *The Wheel of Fortune.* The flux of human life and continual motion of the universe, symbolic of new beginnings. There had certainly been plenty of those since her rebirth (before and after the virus struck). She sensed another new birth on its way: the death of an old life and the beginning of a new one... but a *shared* existence. (She dismissed the other reading of this card which hinted that plans made could easily change at the last moment...)

The ensuing card showed her what had recently happened or was *about* to... A solitary man, head bowed and alone in his cave. *The Hermit*. He would soon call on her and represented another obstacle she had to get out of the way before being able to move ahead with her schemes. He would not – or she should say, his masters would not – be impressed with what she must do to draw *him* here. It mattered not.

Next was the future – something she was uniquely comfortable with. A place she'd been able to see, hoped to change, even before she'd learnt these ways. It showed a man suspended by ropes: *The Hanged Man*. She paused, frowning. This one was new, meaning a period of suspended action before things began to slot into place. She could wait, though; she'd waited this long, after all.

Turning over another card, she knew this one represented her. There were two stuck together, and she peeled them apart – one the *High Priestess*, the other *Empress*. Both made sense: she could be either... or both. Or one, *then* the other. That was more likely – yet wasn't there a nagging doubt now as to which one she *should* be? Because the next card was meant to represent something that might have an impact on the situation... Quickly, she turned this over and found the card depicting a jester. If she took this to be the proper card, it meant someone might not be able to see the wood for the trees. Or a risk would have a probable good outcome. Should it have been that card, or the previous one? Damn it all, she should know these things – she could *see* into the future, after all!

It was *The Fool* (she chose not to think about who might actually be the foolish one), so she moved on to the next card drawn: her hopes and fears for that future... It made more sense now, because she'd drawn *The Sun*. This would indicate she was content with her lot; a hope, but also a fear in case things didn't happen the way she wanted it to.

Finally, she got to the last card – the culmination of everything in front of her. She sensed even before she turned it over that it was *The Emperor*. The card she'd been seeing in her readings since she was a child. The card that represented the man she would marry (and *remain* married to...). Who she would join with on this plane, instead of having to content herself with talking to the ghosts of former husbands and lovers.

The Widow turned it over anyway, just to see the man's face. Sat on the throne with a sword in his hand, the Emperor to her Empress. The man who would come to her. She knew also that the next card she would place down on top of that, looking into the future, was *The World* they would rule together. But she looked no further than that – prevented herself. (Because had she done so, she might have seen those other cards of the Major Arcana – as incredible as it was for her whole draw to be so significant – *Death*, followed by *The Devil*: which could, of course, be interpreted as simply a new beginning and having to make difficult decisions, not necessarily a bad thing in itself – and not, surely not, a clouding of judgement).

Sweeping up the cards, The Widow drew them again by candlelight. She'd draw them until it was time to give the order for her men to attack one particular, special convoy, and she'd carry on drawing the cards until the large, olive-skinned man (her Hermit) came to speak to her at that castle.

But before she shuffled, she took one last look at *The Emperor*. The man she loved more than life itself and who *would* love her in turn.

A man who'd soon swap his hood for a crown.

Who would sit by her side and rule this entire planet one day...

He'd thought about that day often (especially after what had happened to them in the wake of the virus and The Cull). He remembered feeling elation initially, because he'd been called out of class, told he'd been sent for and could leave early – in the middle of the afternoon – and that meant he'd avoid the pummelling that was coming from Bevin and Lloyd, two of the ugliest brutes ever to walk God's earth. With less than a single brain cell between them, they more than made up for this in brawn. He'd once seen Bevin – all cropped hair and ink tattoos – break a first-former's leg by knocking him to the floor and stamping on it. Lloyd had stood by and laughed, then kicked the screaming kid in the stomach for good measure. Both had lied when questioned about their whereabouts while the crime was being committed, backing each other up.

A beating like that was waiting for *him*, too. That was his future, he'd been promised. It wasn't as if he'd actually done anything to them; you didn't need to. Bevin and Lloyd had their own unique way of picking their victims. Totally random and known only to them. The fact that he was the fattest lad in the year meant he was an automatic target, mind. In fact, he was surprised he'd escaped being picked on by them up till now. All the other bullies in that year and above (or below) had given it a go. Today was simply his turn, after school, as they'd taken great pleasure in telling him at dinnertime, knocking the crisps he was holding out of his hands. "You look like you could manage without them, lardie," Lloyd had sniggered.

Now both boys watched as he left the classroom, and he risked one glance back – knowing that this was only a postponement. Yet still he was filled with elation that his torture had been delayed. It was soon replaced with guilt when he found out exactly why he'd been summoned. "It's... it's your brother," the deputy head, Miss Anwyl, told him. He'd gulped, knowing it wasn't good news.

He'd had mixed feelings ever since his older sibling, Gareth, had been diagnosed. The poor sod had come down with a blood disorder way before it was 'fashionable' to do so when the virus hit. The disease of choice in his case was leukaemia.

He'd kind of looked up to Gareth, in a way you do to big brothers, but there was also a healthy dose of jealousy mixed in. Gareth did well at school, was good with his hands – he could fix anything, which was why he spent so much time with Dad in the garage and shed. Gareth was Dad's favourite, there was no doubt about that: the golden boy.

And while sometimes he'd wished that he was an only child, he'd never have wished *this* on Gareth. Especially as it didn't make any difference afterwards. Didn't make his Dad love him any more, or want to spend time with him (apart from when he reluctantly took his second son to those rugby matches). There was certainly never any wish for his brother to contract a terminal illness, to put him out of the picture.. .permanently.

But, as he was given a lift to the hospital by the neighbours who'd fetched him from school at his parents' request, then walked into the ward again – only the second time they'd let him visit since Gareth was hospitalised – he began to think that was a strong possibility. When he arrived at the room itself, his Mam and Dad were there, crying. His Nan – his only surviving grandparent – was sitting in the chair opposite and looked like someone had punctured her, letting all the air out. His family. The only people he'd ever relied on, and probably the only people he ever would: 'united' in misery and mourning. His brother was still, eyes closed, and he could see that there was no heart-rate on the monitor.

When he asked what had happened, his father shot him a vicious glare. "What do you think's bloody well happened? He's dead... My son is dead..."

Not being one to show his feelings, his Dad stormed out, leaving his Mam to come over and give him a big hug. "He doesn't... doesn't mean to snap..." she said in between the sniffles. "He's just... just..." She began crying uncontrollably, and his Nan had to get up and take over, taking her daughter into her arms. His Mam said she didn't want to be in that room right now, so the two women followed his father, leaving him inside – alone – with his deceased sibling.

Perhaps they thought he needed time to say goodbye; perhaps they weren't thinking at all. But for a good five or ten minutes (which actually felt like five or ten years) he was left with the body. Except Gareth wasn't as dead as they all thought he was.

"Hey little brother," Gareth's voice floated across the room. "How're things?" His eyes were open and he was sitting up, elbow resting against the pillow.

"You... you can't be..." He looked back at the door which his family had just walked through, about to call them back. Or call a nurse; a doctor: someone. They'd made a mistake, all of them. Gareth was still alive.

"Don't bother," said his older brother. "There isn't time. I just needed to talk to you, that's all. There are things we need to discuss."

His mouth fell open, but in spite of himself he found his legs moving, carrying him closer to the bed. "What...?"

"Listen to me," said Gareth. "You'll be the only son left when I've gone. And when the time comes, you'll have to be the man of the household."

"Dad's the man of the house," he'd replied, a fact that had been drilled into him since childhood.

"He'll need your help, little brother. They all will. Something bad's coming, but..." Gareth smiled; it was a chilling sight.

"But out of it will come something good. You'll have to step up. Remember what Mam always said about you, that you'd be important one day. That you'd *be* someone..."

That was true, she was the only person who ever had. But still he shook his head. He'd never amount to anything, and it was even more ludicrous to suggest that his dad would come to rely on him. He'd never relied on anyone, *ever*.

"You listen to them, though," Gareth continued. "Because they'll know things that you won't. There'll come a time when you'll need to listen to the warnings, do you understand?"

He shook his head; had no clue what Gareth was talking about. The fact that this was the most he'd said to him in ages was also throwing his concentration.

"You probably won't remember much about this talk in the meantime, but you will then. When they begin to tell you... things." Gareth grinned again. "About the threat you'll face."

Threat? Was he talking about Bevin and Lloyd? About the fact that he was going to get his head kicked in eventually, that they'd wait for him to return?

"An even greater threat than that, I'm afraid," Gareth told him. "In the meantime you'll just have to *endure*. But listen to what Dad says when he takes you to the matches. Listen and you'll understand what you must become. See you around, little brother..."

He turned away then, determined to fetch someone now to see to Gareth. Maybe they could give him medication, help him hang on for a little while longer. By the time he looked back again, Gareth was gone: adopting the same position he'd been in moments ago. He looked strangely at peace this time, though, as if he'd got what he needed to off his chest.

No-one believed the fact that Gareth had woken again to speak to him – they just thought he'd made it up. His Mam cried and his Dad took the strap to him for upsetting her (and upsetting *him*, though he'd never admit it). But what with everything that was going on during the funeral week, they forgot about this pretty quickly. What's more, Gareth was right: so did he.

When he returned to school eventually – he was allowed a bit of time off under such tragic circumstances – Bevin and Lloyd hadn't forgotten their promise. Nor did they make allowances for the fact he'd just lost his brother. "So what?" Bevin spat in his face. "We still owe you a pastin'."

He'd taken his lumps, and more besides, until the day when he wouldn't take anymore. The day Gavin had talked about, after the virus, when his family had come to rely on him...

But that was another story.

He remembered that talk, though, finally – after the shit hit the fan. It triggered something in him, something connected with those rugby matches. Something that made him recall his Dad's chants at them: *"We are Dragons! We are Dragons!"*

It would give him his name, and eventually his power. But he also remembered Gavin's words about listening to his family because they'd know certain things when the time came.

About a threat that would challenge everything he'd built up since the virus and The Cull.

A threat the Dragon needed to stamp out before it cost him dearly...

He hadn't thought about that time in his life for years.

Lying by the side of the desert road after the strike, after seeing so many of his men blown to pieces. After being thrown clear of the Land Rover Defender by the explosion itself, his ears still ringing from the blast. Henry had returned to consciousness in waves, blinking and seeing only a blue sky; which swiftly turned black, as the trails of smoke rising from the vehicles – including a Ferret Armoured car and a FV107 Scimitar CVR – drifted across. He'd tried to move, conscious that he was still weighed down by his helmet and backpack. Then he'd felt the searing pain in his leg, waking him fully.

He hissed through his teeth, spitting out blood as he did so.

A mortar or rocket based-system (probably a Howitzer), combined with an RPG attack proved that absolutely nowhere was safe over here at the moment. He'd figured that out as soon as he'd stepped off the transport. The campaign was a just one, though, with a clear motivation. The liberation of Kuwait was of paramount importance; the unjust invasion of that country by dictator Saddam Hussein was something the UK had firmly got behind (in fact they'd committed the largest contingent of any European nation, the second largest contributor to the coalition force fighting Iraq). Operation Granby, it had been named. A matter of principle, defending the weak against the strong.

Hadn't that been one of the reasons he'd originally signed up to the army in the first place? Prepared for just such an occurrence. In spite of what people thought in the outside world, this wasn't just about oil. Innocent people were dying...

And so were *his* people: friends and comrades. He'd seen it close-up and personal, especially now... Henry looked across for signs of other survivors, but saw nothing. He shouted, but again he felt the stab of pain in his leg. He hadn't looked down at it yet, hadn't dared to... but now he did. It was twisted in an awkward way, the bone definitely broken, and shrapnel was sticking out of a wound at the thigh.

"Fuck..." Not only was he probably going to die himself from that, unless he was incredibly lucky, he couldn't even get up to see if anyone else needed medical attention. But the more Henry looked across at that devastation, the more bodies he saw there covered in blood – inside the flaming vehicles of the small convoy – and the more he realised that if anyone was still that close to ground zero they'd be beyond medical help. The fact that nobody had answered his call spoke volumes. Christ, the waste of those lives... he could hardly take it in. Men whose families would never see them again. Henry felt tears welling in his eyes, but he didn't have time to sit here and mourn for the lost. The smoke rising in the air was going to give away the hit, and more enemy fire would soon rain down to make sure they were out of commission for good.

Henry had to retreat, and fast. Removing his combat jacket and helmet to make himself lighter, he scrambled to get away, as much as it hurt him to do so. He crawled along on his belly, dragging his leg behind him. Sure enough another set of explosions came when he was only about twenty metres away; he ducked, lying still as the Earth beneath him shook. Sand rose all around and fell, both beside and on top of him. He knew that soon they'd come on foot to look around. He didn't have much time left...

Using every ounce of strength he had left, he made it to a set of rocks within crawling distance of the ambush. There he waited, and it wasn't long before enemy soldiers emerged to examine the wreckage. He heard that foreign tongue so familiar to him after two months posted here, and tried to shut out the faces of soldiers like Jimmy Handley, Max Clemens and Frank Oldham. Tried to block out the images of children's faces on photos posted up on lockers back at camp, of wives and girlfriends. With every fibre of his being he wanted revenge on those bastards just out of sight. But you should always be careful what you wish for.

While some of them picked over the remains, others fanned out to search the desert for any potential troopers who'd made it out alive. For all they knew, there could be at least a dozen marching their way back to report all this, to call down an air strike on the region. It's what Henry would do if he could walk. If he had access to a radio, he'd call them up anyway and just get them to do it right here and now. Bomb them all to crap and be done with it; wasn't as if he had any family to speak of, his mother and father dead, and Catherine...

The voices were growing closer. Henry moved back around the rock, shifting position. He risked a look, seeing two Iraqi foot soldiers heading in his direction, before forking off – only one coming over to check where he was hiding. Henry swallowed dryly. He had only a knife to hand as a weapon, so he drew it, then waited for the man to round the corner. When he did, the look of shock and surprise on the soldier's face was comical. He looked like he was about to raise his rifle and shoot, so Henry rammed the knife into his gut. There hadn't been time to register his age as Henry did this, only time to react. But, as he fell, Henry saw that the soldier couldn't have been more than fifteen, perhaps even younger. That gave him pause for thought – could it be that this lad was forced to join Saddam's forces like so many others? The threat of death hanging over his own family? If Henry had been able-bodied, maybe he could have used his hand-to-hand skills (as he was well versed in many forms of martial arts) to take the kid down without having to kill him.

As it was...

Bullets raked the rocks where Henry was, and he grabbed the discarded rifle – returning fire between the cracks in the boulders. He was outgunned and outnumbered: there must have been about fifteen Iraqis out there. Henry fired again, certain that at any moment his ammo would run out.

Then there was silence. Henry looked out over the rock, his leg throbbing in agony. There was no sign of the enemy troops who'd been firing in his direction. It was as if they'd simply vanished. He had theories, of course: they'd fled because they thought that air strike was already on its way (the coalition did control the skies, after all), or perhaps they thought there was more than just one survivor out there. Or maybe there had been other forces on hand that day. Whatever the case, Henry didn't question it back then... He was just grateful that they'd buggered off.

And his journey to find help could begin.

He tried again to walk, and failed; without a stick as a crutch it was absolutely hopeless on that injured leg. The shrapnel had also moved during the fight, loosening so much he had no option but to remove it. Sadly, that had been the only thing stopping him from bleeding out, and now he had another problem. Henry tried to stem the bleeding with a bandage, ripped material from his combats, but it was soaked in seconds.

Sighing, he began to crawl again. If he'd made it to the rocks, then he could make it to some kind of aid – or would die in the process.

The more he crawled in the heat, wearing just his vest and trousers, the more he began to think it would be the latter option. He was going to die out here, in the heat, blood pumping from his leg.

He began to feel woozy as he crested a hill, losing sight of the original skirmish. Henry rolled down the sand, tumbling over and over until he reached the bottom of the dune. It took great effort, but he looked up over the horizon – seeing nothing but ochre in the distance.

His mouth was dry, lips cracking as he attempted to crawl on. Henry clawed at the sand, pulling himself further and further along, a millimetre at a time. Until he had absolutely no more strength.

It was as he lay there that he became frightened. As the certainty that he was going to die really took hold. And it was then that he thought back to all those Sunday school lessons he'd been taught, his parents so staunchly religious it had made him hate every single syllable of the Bible.

He recalled the story about Jesus being tested in the desert and wondered if this was *his* test? And what he might get if he passed it. What he'd have to do in return for more life?

It was then, after years of turning his back on religion, that he finally prayed. Henry asked that God heard him, that he might spare him... and in return, he'd be a better man. He wouldn't swear, he wouldn't (kill young boys anymore; wouldn't leave fallen comrades to their certain death)... wouldn't do anything that the Lord didn't want him to do.

Henry was very surprised to hear an answer.

To hear the words of God, so sharp the Almighty could have been standing next to him and speaking in his ear. He told Henry that yes, he would be saved. But in return one day he would be called upon. There would be a battle at some point, and Henry must stand as *His* representative on Earth against the forces of darkness. One of God's warriors. Would he agree?

"Ye-yess..." mouthed Henry, spluttering grains of sand.

He was shown then a vision of what he would be up against. Marching over the sand, heading in his direction were men... At first, through his half-closed eyes, he thought they were Iraqis. But as they drew closer he saw they were all wearing strange kind of robes. They were all hooded, the cowls that same maroon colour, swinging some kind of swords as they came. Henry shivered, in spite of the heat.

He knew who these forces belonged to. If he was now believing in God again, then it stood to reason that he had to believe in the other side... His vision was fading, loss of blood and exhaustion finally catching up with him. If the army was real, then he could do nothing about it now – couldn't move, let alone fight.

But as he slipped into unconsciousness again, he heard the voice in his ear tell him that he'd also be called on one day to do something that would go against everything he believed in. That he would know what this was when the time came... And that it might just save the world.

Then there was silence.

The next voice Henry heard was a female one: "Lieutenant Tate? Lieutenant Tate... Can you hear me? Are you still with us..." The woman laughed faintly when he opened his eyes. "Oh, thank God...You've lost a lot of blood, so just try to relax. Let the morphine do its job."

He was in a field hospital back at the camp – eventually to be transferred out of the war zone altogether because of his injuries. He'd been spotted by the aircraft investigating the loss of contact with his convoy (the logical part of his mind said that maybe those Iraqi troops had caught wind of this and that's why they'd scarpered). He'd been evac-ed to safety and was safe now... or as safe as it got around here.

When he returned home, they operated on his leg several times and although they did the best they could, they told him he'd always need a stick and would walk with a limp for the rest of his days. Determined, though, he'd pushed that leg to its limits: exercising, getting stuck back into his martial arts – and he actually found that the more adrenaline that pumped through him (say, in a fight situation) the less his leg hurt. The more he actually *could* use it.

He only remembered flashes of what had happened to him before they found him, but Henry Tate did remember making some kind of deal. It didn't strictly involve him becoming a Reverend after he was honourably discharged from the army, but all those months recuperating had left him with lots of free time to read: to brush up on those Bible stories he'd once hated. And what fascinating reading they made... What a great deal of sense, especially in these troubling times. Not to mention those to come.

As he prayed now, Tate remembered seeing the hooded men from his... what, hallucination? This time for real, after Robert had come to New Hope asking for his help against them.

Reverend Tate knew the dangerous times that voice – the one he knew belonged to the Lord his God – had told him about were almost upon them.

He had been and would continue to be the warrior priest.

And he would wait, patiently, for the sign that told him it was time to save the world.

He was running through the forest, but not on human legs.

And the further he ran, the stronger those legs became. He looked down and saw they were a browny colour with white specks. Rain still fell from the leaves and he skidded to a standstill, watching one droplet land in a puddle nearby. Trotting over, he waited for the ripples to subside, for the surface to reflect his features. He was a young fawn, slightly older than Bambi from the Disney movie (Jack would have been proud at that filmic reference). Not yet fully grown, but not really a baby either.

He could live with that – and so he ran again, enjoying the freedom this form gave him. That and the freedom of the forest. He passed through more unfamiliar territory yet to be shown to him in the real world, but which he recognised instinctively here. His trek brought him to the huge lake near Rufford; where, once again, he could trot to the edge and look at his reflection in the water.

This time, however, he noted the stumps on his head – the beginnings of what would soon be antlers. Then, in the water, as if to show him what he *would* look like eventually, he saw another reflection. That of a fully grown stag. It was upside down, though, and it was also quite a distance away – yet he could see it perfectly. Perhaps it had skated over the vast expanse of the lake, perhaps it was just a trick of this place: being able to see everything from every angle simultaneously. If so, then it was another skill he needed to master.

For now, he was content to look at the reflection – tracing it upwards to the thing itself. The stag standing on the other side of the lake: staring at him. It opened its mouth, crying out a warning. But it should have been the other way around, should have been him calling out to the older stag... because there was a figure stepping out of the trees behind it.

Initially it looked like the man – dressed all in red – was holding a blade in his hand. But the closer he looked (zooming in, if that was possible in this place) the more he saw that the curving thing was a replacement 'hand'. And as the man approached, he held it out in front of him, readying to use it on the stag – who was so focussed on its younger counterpart it hadn't noticed its attacker.

But the same could be said for his own perception, because it was only now that he noticed the great shadow falling across the lake. Someone was behind *him* as well – was this some kind of mirror, events of the future? Or were they being attacked at the same time, by two different people?

That wouldn't be revealed today, because he snapped out of his dream at that point, waking in a cold sweat and seeing the skin of the lean-to above him. Mark shook his head, rubbing his eyes. He was still getting used to the intensity of these dreams, especially when they were in Sherwood.

As he emerged from the make-shift tent, he saw Robert doing the same on the other side of the clearing. It was dawn, and they would be eating breakfast soon: a meal the forest had provided, even though *they'd* hunted the small animals that would provide them with sustenance.

Neither of them spoke much over breakfast, but each could tell the other had spent time in that dreamscape – and were trying to work out the significance of the warnings.

Those signs and portents.

So it was with a mixture of relief and frustration that Mark helped Robert pack up their stuff, following him out, back up to the visitor's centre in Sherwood where they'd tethered the horses. Relief that the dreams wouldn't be so vivid that night, sleeping in his own bed back at the castle (even if they did now carry a part of Sherwood with them at all times).

But frustration because he hadn't had a chance to see what happened next, to try and work out what it all meant. They'd be back here soon enough, though, and he'd see more of it then he was sure...

In the meantime, he'd ride with the Hooded man.

Content that in the fullness of time, all would be revealed to them...

A CHRONOLOGY OF
AFTERBLIGHT BRITAIN

1. *School's Out* by Scott Andrews
2. 'The Man Who Would Not Be King' by Scott Andrews (short story included with *Broken Arrow* by Paul Kane)
3. *Operation Motherland* by Scott Andrews
4. *Arrowhead* by Paul Kane
5. *The Culled* by Simon Spurrier (takes place simultaneously with *Children's Crusade*)
6. *Children's Crusade* by Scott Andrews (takes place simultaneously with *The Culled*)
7. *Broken Arrow* by Paul Kane
8. 'Signs and Portents' by Paul Kane (short story included in *Children's Crusdade*)
9. *Arrowland* by Paul Kane, coming this Autumn/Fall

For information on these, and other titles,
visit www.abaddonbooks.com

THE AFTERBLIGHT CHRONICLES

SCHOOL'S OUT

Scott Andrews

Visit www.abaddonbooks.com for information on our titles,
interviews, news and exclusive content.

ISBN 978-1-905437-40-5
UK £6.99   US $7.99

Abaddon
Books

THE AFTERBLIGHT CHRONICLES

OPERATION MOTHERLAND

SCOTT ANDREWS

Visit www.abaddonbooks.com for information on our titles,
interviews, news and exclusive content.

ISBN: 978-1-906735-04-3
UK £6.99   US $7.99

Abaddon
Books

Follow us on twitter: www.twitter.com/abaddonbooks

THE AFTERBLIGHT CHRONICLES

BROKEN ARROW

PAUL KANE

Visit www.abaddonbooks.com for information on our titles,
interviews, news and exclusive content.

ISBN 978-1-906735-27-2
UK £.6.99   US $7.99

Abaddon
Books

Follow us on twitter: www.twitter.com/abaddonbooks